A FAERIE'S CURSE

Also by Rachel Morgan

THE CREEPY HOLLOW SERIES

The Faerie Guardian

The Faerie Prince

The Faerie War

A Faerie's Secret

A Faerie's Revenge

A Faerie's Curse

CREEPY HOLLOW
COMPANION STORIES

Scarlett

Raven

A FAERIE'S CURSE

CREEPY HOLLOW, BOOK SIX

RACHEL MORGAN

This is a work of fiction. Names, places, characters, and incidents are either the product of the author's imagination or, if real, used fictitiously.

ISBN 978-0-9946953-4-5

RACHEL MORGAN

PART I

CHAPTER ONE

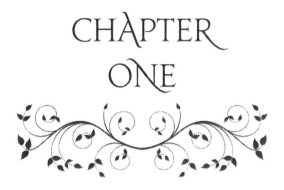

GLITTERING BEACH SAND CRUNCHES BENEATH MY BOOTS AS I walk hand in hand with a five-year-old faerie girl toward the palm grove that conceals her father's home. It's late in the evening, and a million scattered stars illuminate our path up the beach and away from the waves. The pain shooting through my right ankle—the result of skidding across a wet deck while being chased by a band of pirates—causes me to limp, and the gash below my ear is no doubt oozing blood into my golden hair. Not the best way to present myself to faerie nobility, but all in all, I'd say it was a successful rescue mission.

Unfortunately, it isn't the rescue mission I wish it was. Chase—the man who was once Lord Draven; the man I've found myself falling for despite the things he's done—is still chained in a secret dungeon beneath the Seelie Palace. His own mother made a deal with the Guild, trading his life for her freedom. It's been a week—an entire torturous week—since he was taken, and we're no closer to breaking into the Seelie Palace. Tonight's mission, however, will change that.

Elsie tugs my hand and says, "This is where you throw the gem."

I smile down at her. "Thanks for the reminder." From my jacket pocket, I remove the red gemstone I was given earlier. I throw it between the trees ahead of us as we continue walking. Layers of glamour magic begin to peel themselves away. The palm trees vanish, sand filters into the ground as lush grass and tiny flowers take its place, and a ruby-studded stone path appears beneath our feet. At the end of the path rises the grandiose home of Baron Westhold. Elsie reaches down and plucks a star-shaped yellow flower from the ground. She twirls it between her fingers as we head toward the house.

Now that this part of the mission is over, distracting thoughts circle my mind: Chase disappearing into the night sky in a Seelie Palace carriage, Mom's trial ending tonight, the horrible vision of a spell that will tear through the veil separating our world from the human world. That vision is the reason Mom ran away from the Guild years ago. It's the reason she's been on trial. *From the magic of the depths to the magic of the heights, with blood from one side and blood from the other. Together with the greatest power nature can harness, we shall tear this veil asunder.*

I shake away the memory of those disturbing words and point my thoughts firmly in a different direction. Tonight's mission isn't yet complete, and I can't afford distractions.

The two security guards at the entrance to the baron's home pull themselves a little straighter as Elsie and I walk beneath the pillared archway and toward the front door. Their blank expressions never faltered earlier today as they took me to see the baron, but now, as their eyes fall on the girl at my side, they can't hide their relief. The younger guard opens the door and steps back as we enter the house. "This way," Elsie says, tugging me past the mermaid statue and along a wide marble passageway, unaware that I already know where to go.

We've barely taken five steps when I hear a commotion up ahead. Something falling, hurried footsteps, and then a voice shouting, "Elsie?"

From around the corner at the end of the passage, his clothes rumpled and hair disheveled, Baron Westhold appears. A groan of relief escapes him before he runs the final distance toward his daughter and scoops her into his arms. He hugs her tightly to his chest while she pats the top of his head and says, "I'm fine, Father. I was with your friend, the captain. He said you wanted me to make gold for him."

"Dear Seelie Queen," Baron Westhold murmurs. "Elsie, that man was not my friend."

An older girl runs around the corner, almost skidding in her purple unicorn slippers, but stops short of throwing her arms around her father and sister. Instead she clasps her hands together and tucks them beneath her chin as her brow puckers. "I'm so sorry, Elsie. I'm so sorry. I only looked away for a moment, and then—"

"That's enough, Brynn," the baron says. He lowers Elsie to the floor and straightens. He blinks and clears his throat before turning to his older daughter. "Take Elsie upstairs."

"I'm so sorry, Father. You know I never meant for this—"

"We'll talk later."

I take a few discreet steps backward, distancing myself from the family drama. As Brynn attempts to plead her case, I reach down, wrap my hand around my ankle, and release additional magic into the area, hoping to aid the healing process. My mind reaches automatically for Chase, to update him on what's going on, before I remember I'm not wearing the telepathy ring. Gaius took it from me before the mission began.

"Please don't ground me," Brynn begs. "Elsie's safe now, and I promise I'll never lose her again."

"Brynn," the baron says, slow and precise, her name a warning on his lips. "We will talk later."

Brynn nods, her eyes downcast, and reaches for Elsie's hand. The little girl looks toward me and says, "Thank you." She stretches her hand out to me, so I step forward and take it. The flower she's still clutching tickles my skin, then seems to become … heavier. She pulls her hand back—and a solid gold flower sits on my palm.

Gold. *Real gold.* That isn't normal magic. My mind races to fill in the missing gaps from the brief I was given this morning. By the time I tear my eyes from my palm, Elsie is skipping ahead of her sister as they disappear around the corner. I look at Baron Westhold and find him staring at the gold flower. He sucks in a shaky breath, turns around, and says, "Follow me."

I place the flower carefully into the hidden pocket on the inside of my jacket and hurry after the baron, my limp almost gone now. We turn out of the passageway, cross an atrium with a fountain at its center, and head down another passage toward the office I met the baron in this morning. It's richly furnished with paintings in gold frames, a maroon and gold carpet, and dark wooden shelves lined with leather-bound books. A tall glass vase filled with liquid that glitters gold and maroon stands in one corner. Flames flicker and crackle in a fireplace, warming the chilly ocean air entering through the balcony doorway. The sheer curtains lift gently in the nighttime breeze, giving me a glimpse of waves tumbling onto the shore.

The baron walks to his desk and unlocks the top drawer with a stylus. He removes a slim rectangular case made of wood. "This payment doesn't come close to expressing my gratitude," he says as he hands me the case. "My guards told me it would be impossible to retrieve my daughter from that vile pirate's clutches. I didn't know if I'd ever see her again."

I remember the baron's words to me this morning—*How old are you anyway? Are you sure you can get this done?*—and manage to keep my response polite as I take the case. "We specialize in the impossible. That's why you hired us."

"Yes." He pauses a moment, watching me carefully, then adds, "And for complete confidentiality."

"Of course."

"If the Guild finds out what my daughter can do—"

"They won't. Not from us. We understand the need for secrecy, especially when it comes to Griffin Abilities."

The baron flinches at my use of those two simple words. Words he left out of his instructions this morning. Words he's probably been trying to deny ever since he discovered what his daughter can do. He must have been in possession of one of the griffin discs when his daughter was conceived. Except … there were no griffin discs five years ago. They lost their magic after Draven used them to unlock the chest Tharros's power was kept in. So how …

I push my confusion to one side and clear my throat. *No distractions,* I remind myself. "Besides," I add, "if we couldn't be trusted, no one would ever hire us. We rely on word of mouth, which means we need happy clients. Trust me, Baron Westhold. We don't want to make you unhappy."

The baron considers me for another moment. "I suppose not."

I slide the wooden case into the pocket with the gold flower. "If that's all …"

"Yes, thank you, that will be all."

"I can show myself out then."

"Good."

I nod politely, then turn and leave. With quick strides, I make my way back to the entrance hall. The guards need to see me leave, just in case the baron asks them, so I pull the heavy wooden door open. Instead of walking out, though, I release my control on the imaginary fortress around my mind and let my Griffin Ability free. I picture myself walking out into the night, and that's exactly what I see. The imaginary version of me continues along the path, and the guards watch her go. "How the hell did she get past all of Captain Nuvareed's men on that ship?" one murmurs to the other.

The other shakes his head as he moves to close the door. "Wish I'd been there to see it."

I smile to myself as the door slides shut with a heavy thud. I close my eyes and picture my imaginary self still moving along the path. When I've imagined her going far enough into the night that the guards can barely see her, I let go of that illusion and wrap a different one around myself. The illusion of invisibility. Then I turn back to face the mermaid statue and focus on the real reason I was given this mission: a party invitation.

When Gaius, one of Chase's team members, was called here late last night, he witnessed a conversation between the baron and his teenage daughter. Brynn was distraught, barely able to speak through her tears as she explained how Elsie had disappeared. Furious that Brynn had let her little sister out of her sight, the baron yelled, "You are grounded for the rest of the year. For the rest of your *life*."

With her tears shocked to a halt, Brynn was able to speak more easily. "What? But the party. I have to go. This isn't the kind of invitation you say no to."

"You won't be going near the Seelie Palace—or anywhere else for that matter—if we don't get your sister back."

And that was the moment at which Gaius became a lot more interested in the whole matter. With Chase confined beneath the Seelie Palace for a week now, and the rest of his team no closer to finding out how to get there, this invitation was the best lead so far. Despite the fact that it was extraordinarily unprofessional, Gaius asked, "What party is that?"

The baron ignored him—most likely because the question had no relevance to the current situation—and sent Brynn to her room. He then discussed the rescue mission details with

Gaius, who promised he would select the best member of his team for the job, and there'd been no further mention of the Seelie Palace.

Given the ease with which I can sneak around without being seen, Gaius chose me for this task. *No pressure*, I think as I remind myself that this is our one chance to get inside the Seelie Palace. *No pressure at all.* Wrapped securely in invisibility, I begin my search for Brynn's bedroom. I look into several unoccupied rooms upstairs before finding the right one. The door is ajar and I hear sniffling from within. I imagine myself as Baron Westhold, then knock on the door and push it open—and have to stop myself from blinking in surprise at the purple glitter covering almost every surface. *Focus!* I command myself.

Brynn, who was lying on her stomach with her face buried in her arms when I walked in, looks up with hopeful eyes. "Father?"

"I've decided you won't be going," I tell her in a voice that sounds just like her father's.

Her face falls as she pushes herself up into a sitting position. "But it's rude to decline the invitation."

"Don't tell me you care about politeness. I know you only want to go because of that boy." I have no idea if that's true, of course, but I imagine it's something an angry father might say.

"What—what boy?" Brynn asks, but her twisting hands and the way she looks down instead of holding my gaze tell a different story.

"Where is the invitation?" I ask.

She looks up, her eyes narrowing in confusion. "The

invitation to the party?"

"Yes, of course. What other invitation would I be talking about? I won't have you sneaking out on your own to attend this event."

Her frown deepens. "But you know I can't get there on my own. And don't you still have the invitation? It was addressed to you, not me. I don't even know what it looks like."

Shoot. I had hoped this would be as easy as taking the invitation from Brynn and leaving. How am I supposed to get the baron to give it to me? I focus hard on keeping the image of the baron covering me as completely as a second skin. I allow my folded arms to fall to my sides as I say, "I'm still not happy with you, Brynn, but it's late now, so we'll speak tomorrow."

"Okay, but please just think about—"

"Tomorrow, Brynn." I leave the room and pull the door closed. I release the image of Baron Westhold and switch back to invisibility as I hurry downstairs to his office, hoping he hasn't gone to bed yet. Reaching his office doorway, I see him standing at a gap in the curtains with his back to me, staring out at the night. I step away from the door and press myself against the wall beside it, giving myself a moment to clear my mind. I need to take more care with deceiving the baron than I did with his distraught teenage daughter.

I focus hard on picturing Brynn, on seeing her in my place. I don't move until I look down and see her slippers instead of my boots. Then I tell myself that I *am* Brynn, and I walk into her father's office. "Father?" I say, relieved that the voice I hear sounds more like hers than mine.

He turns and frowns at me. "You should be in bed, Brynn."

"I know, but I just wanted to ask if you've changed your mind about … about the party."

"We don't need to discuss it now," he says, returning to his desk and sinking into the leather chair.

"But … didn't we say we would attend? If you've changed your mind, then we need to let the palace know."

"Fine. I will inform the palace tomorrow."

I allow myself to look appropriately devastated. "Please, please don't do that. I've been looking forward to it for so long. This was just one mistake, and it will *never* happen again."

The baron folds one hand over the other and leans forward. "You allowed your sister to be kidnapped by a pirate. It wasn't just a *mistake*, Brynn. Can you even begin to imagine how devastated your mother would be if she were still alive? No, my decision is final. We will not be attending that party."

I wobble my lower jaw before pressing my lips tightly together. I imagine tears forming in Brynn's eyes. "Can I at least have the invitation as a memento?"

"You don't need a memento of an event you won't be attending."

I bite my lip, clench my fists, and prepare myself for a teenage tantrum. "You know what? I hate you. I *hate* you for ruining my life like this! I'm going to find that invitation when you're not around, and I'm going to that party without you. I don't care that I can't find the palace on my own. I'll find someone who knows how to get there."

Baron Westhold looks thunderstruck. I turn and flounce from the room before he can respond. I stop just outside.

Picturing myself as empty space instead of as Brynn, I look into the office once more. The baron slowly shakes his head, clearly shocked at Brynn's outburst. He leans back in his chair with a weary sigh, covering his brow with one hand. I start to consider what illusion I can use to get him to leave the room, but then he opens one of his drawers and removes a rosebud the color of champagne. He places it on the desk and the petals slowly open. Gold words appear in the air above the rose. I tiptoe into the room to get a closer look, but the baron brushes his hand against the petals, causing the words to vanish and the petals to curl closed once more. He stands, carries the rosebud to the fireplace, and—

No! My hand stretches out automatically, but I'm on the other side of the room, and the rose is already in the fire. *No, no, no!* I need a distraction—something—a noise—

The first sound that comes to mind is a child's scream. I go with it, clinging desperately to my invisibility as the shriek pierces the still night. The baron's head whips around. "Elsie?" He dashes from the room as I lunge for the fireplace. I drop to my knees, shove my hand into the flames, and grasp the flower. I breathe in sharply against the sudden, burning pain, scramble to my feet, and plunge my hand into the tall vase. I search the room with desperate, darting eyes for my escape. I need a way out, I need to think, and the vase's contents isn't providing nearly enough relief for my burning hand. I squeeze my eyes shut and hold in the groan of pain I would *really* like to release.

At the sound of running footsteps, my eyelids snap open. I pull my arm from the vase and rush onto the balcony, trailing drops of water behind me as my hand BURNS LIKE A

FREAKING INFERNO. Below, the white sand gleams in the starlight. It isn't too great a distance to the ground, so I should be fine if I jump. I don't want to crush the rosebud, though, so I form a bubble of shield magic around it. Breathing heavily against the pain, I coax the bubble into the air and watch it drift down toward the sand. Then—

"... didn't imagine it," a voice says from somewhere inside the house. Distant, but quickly growing louder. "If neither of my daughters screamed, it means someone else did. Search everywhere."

I climb hastily over the balcony railing. I look over my shoulder, and as the curtains flutter and a dark shape enters the room, I jump. I hit the ground a second later and roll to a halt. Sand shifts around me as I climb to my feet, making me slower and clumsier than I should be. Fortunately, my twisted ankle is almost fully healed. I imagine myself as invisible and shoot a glance behind me, hoping I don't find someone looking down from the balcony. I don't. In fact, I don't see any balcony at all. The glamour is once again hiding the enormous home, and all I can see are several palm trees and clumps of coarse grass here and there amongst the sand. Which means someone could be watching me, and I wouldn't know. Best to keep myself concealed.

Gritting my teeth against the pain that threatens to distract me from my illusion, I look around for a surface to write on. My eyes land on the nearest palm tree. I hold the bubble in my non-burned hand and run as quickly as the sand will allow. I've almost reached the tree when something strikes the back of my right boot. I stumble to the side and look behind me. A spark of magic shoots toward me, narrowly missing my arm as I dodge out of its path.

My footprints, I realize. Someone must have noticed the shifting sand as I ran for the tree. More magic flies in my direction, and then suddenly—shouts greet my ears and three figures appear almost exactly where I landed just now.

"Crap." Keeping myself concealed, I rush for the palm tree. Sand flies up around me as sparks strike the ground. I swing myself around the side of the tree and retrieve my stylus with my burning hand. I instruct myself—uselessly—to ignore the pain and the panic as I write a doorway spell onto the tree trunk. The rough surface melts away, revealing a dark space just wide enough for me to fit through. Holding the thought of Chase's lakeside house in my mind, I hurtle into the faerie paths.

CHAPTER TWO

SECONDS LATER, I RUSH THROUGH THE LAKE HOUSE LIVING room to the faerie door, pulling the key from one of my pockets. DAMN, MY HAND IS BURNING. Then I'm in another dark space, and then through a door into the foyer, and finally I'm back at Gaius's mountain home. *My* mountain home, seeing as nowhere else is safe for me anymore. I fled the Guild after they discovered my Griffin Ability, and they've been watching the homes of my family and friends ever since.

I hurry upstairs to Gaius's study—burning, burning, *burning* hand—and find him bent over a spider-like contraption that appears to be shooting sparkling dust from one spindly leg and ink splatters from another. "Mission number one complete," I announce, marching across the room and managing to feel immensely pleased with myself despite the horrendous pain scorching across my hand. "Here's the payment for the job." I remove the wooden case and the gold flower from my pocket. "Plus a bit of gold, because little Elsie felt like making it on the spot for me. And—" I lower the translucent shield bubble onto a pile of books and allow it to pop, revealing the rosebud "—the all-important invitation."

"You got it!" Gaius exclaims, standing so quickly his chair falls over behind him.

Despite my pain, a laugh escapes my lips. "I got it."

"And gold? You said she *made* it? And—your hand. That looks terrible."

"It's fine, I'll treat it in a moment. Open the invitation so we can see—"

"You haven't opened it yet?" Gaius asks as he rummages through one of his drawers and pulls out an emergency kit.

"No, I had to get out of there without getting caught. I didn't want to ruin the good reputation you and Chase have worked so hard to build among certain circles of fae."

"Ah, yes, probably a good idea." Gaius removes a small tub of burn healing gel and hands it to me. "Here you go. Fix your hand up while I open this thing."

As Gaius clears a space on his desk for the rosebud, I scoop some gel from the tub and smear it across my hand. The relief is instant as the gel's magic diminishes the burning to little more than a whisper of pain. With my attention fully on the invitation now, I lean over the desk and watch closely. Gaius touches a petal with one finger that shakes ever so slightly. The petals begin to unfurl. "This is it," he breathes. "Our ticket inside the Seelie Palace."

"Well, if we can find out how to actually *get* there," I remind him.

"Details," Gaius says with a wave of his hand. "We'll figure that part out." He squints at the gold letters that appear in the air above the flower. "Cordially invited … blah, blah, blah," he reads. "Princess Audra's birthday … masked ball … on the fourteenth day of … oh, goodness, that's—"

"Nine days away," I say, my heart sinking. "Nine whole days. How is Chase supposed to last that long?"

Gaius stares at the invitation, chewing on his bottom lip. "Well, this is our only option, unless you know how to get us in and out of the palace on a regular day without being caught."

"My ability—"

"Might not be enough. This is the most well-guarded place in our world. There will be magical protection everywhere. The easiest way in is during an event like this. Security will still be high, of course, but not impossible for us to get past."

I grip the edge of the desk. "Fine. But if … if there's even a hint of something happening to Chase before this party, then we have to go immediately."

"Of course. Which means we need to hurry up and find someone who knows how to get there."

"Yes." And that's something that someone else on the team will have to figure out, because my one and only potential contact is someone who never seems to leave the Seelie Court. I hold my rapidly healing hand out. "May I have the ring back? We need to update Chase." And I need to hear his voice. I've gone a whole day without hearing it, and it feels as though a piece of myself has been missing.

"Yes, of course." Gaius removes a book from one of his shelves and opens it. From a carved space in the center of the pages, he removes the telepathy ring I've been using to communicate with Chase since he was imprisoned. A ring imbued with a Griffin Ability someone didn't want. Fortunately, Chase was wearing the corresponding ring when he was captured. "I'm sorry I took it, but I didn't want you distracted by anything today."

"I understand, but I wish you'd trusted me to simply leave the ring in my bedroom. You didn't need to hide it from me."

"It isn't that I didn't *trust* you, Calla. I just wanted to be certain you wouldn't take it with you."

I raise an eyebrow as Gaius places the ring, a simple silver band with a green stone, on my palm. "So you didn't trust me."

He ruffles his already mussed up hair. "Fine. I'm sorry. It was your first mission for us and … well, it was very important."

"I'm fully aware of that, Gaius. I want to get Chase out of the Seelie Queen's clutches just as much as you do."

"Of course, I know, I'm sorry. I promise I'll trust you next time. Oh, you probably want your amber back too."

"You hid my amber as well?" I demand, curling my hand around the ring.

"It was a potential distraction."

"It's old and oversized and the only person I can contact is Ryn, so I definitely wasn't planning on taking it with me. You know that."

"Just taking precautions," Gaius says, handing me the antique piece of amber with a guilty smile. "Which I understand now were unnecessary. Won't happen again."

I shake my head in frustration as I tap the amber's surface. Gold writing fades into view. I tell myself I'll look at it properly just now, after I've spoken to Chase, but I see the words 'mom' and 'trial just finished' and I can't stop reading. A chill rushes across my skin. I feel faint, as if the blood has been drained all at once from my head. "The trial's over," I whisper, pulling my eyes from my brother's message and looking up at Gaius. "They—they're sending my mother to prison."

* * *

Chase, are you there?

I call his name once more as I sneak into the Guild just before midnight. I've been trying to get hold of him since I left the mountain, but all I can hear are my own thoughts. I tell myself not to worry. He's sleeping, that's all. He's fine. Well, he isn't *fine*. He's imprisoned in a dark, dirty cell with magic-blocking chains attached to his arms and legs. But he isn't dead. He can't be. The Seelie Queen wouldn't keep him alive for a week only to suddenly finish him off with no fanfare. No, she's keeping him alive for a reason, which means he's just sleeping. *You're just sleeping, right?* I whisper in my mind.

I swallow, trying to rid myself of the nausea in my stomach, and walk confidently across the Guild's great foyer. Moving around under the illusion of invisibility has become second nature to me. Still, it's a risk to come here so late at night when no one else is around and a surveillance device—which isn't a living being and can't be influenced by my projections—could so easily spot me. I casually pull my hood further over my head. I may look suspicious to anyone watching me on a recording orb right now, but no one would ever suspect me of being Calla Larkenwood, the runaway Gifted faerie who supposedly killed one of her classmates before making half the Guild sick with a disease-causing Griffin Ability.

I climb the stairs to Ryn's office, but I walk straight past his closed door. I stop near the end of the corridor and lean against the wall. I lift my hand, as if examining my nails while waiting for someone or something. In reality, I'm scouring the corridor with my eyes for any sign of a surveillance bug. I flinch when the door beside me opens, but my projection is intact, and the guardian who walks out does nothing more than lock her office and leave with a bag slung over her shoulder.

I examine the corridor for another few minutes. When I see no movement and hear no buzzing, I push away from the wall and walk back to Ryn's door. I open it, slip inside, and shut the door. "They're sending her to *prison*?" I say as I drop into the empty chair beside Dad and across from Ryn. "That's absurd. She was only a child when she broke her contract and fled the Guild. What happened to them fining her and leaving it at that?"

Dad, who looks sicker than I feel, shakes his head and covers his face with both hands.

I turn to Ryn instead. "She did receive a fine," he says. "For manufacturing high-strength potions without a permit. For breaking her Seer contract, the Guild has taken into account the seriousness of the vision she chose not to tell them about. They also seem to want to make an example of her so that other Seers don't make light of their contracts, which is why she ended up with six months in prison instead of a second fine."

"Six months? Your message said two years."

"The rest is for the other charge: keeping your Griffin Ability secret. Considering the mess at the Guild recently—the murder and the dragon disease and the big display you put on when you fled—they're taking failure to register Gifted persons very seriously. Apparently we're supposed to be *grateful* they only gave her a year and a half for that one."

"But—that's—" I struggle to put my thoughts together into a coherent sentence. "The mess at the Guild was my doing, not hers. She had no control over what I might use my ability for. And Dad didn't register me either, but they're not throwing him into prison."

"They've opened an investigation on me," Dad says quietly. "And it isn't just about failing to register you. It's … well, they want to know how we kept it quiet for so long. Given the stories surrounding the departure of every school you've been at, they find it hard to believe that no one else knew about you."

Icy apprehension fills my veins. If Dad is under investigation, there's no way he can continue to hide what he's done. "They're going to find out, aren't they," I whisper. "They're going to find out about the bribes."

Dad pulls back slightly as confusion creases his brow. "How do you know about that?"

"I overheard you and Ryn speaking." I leave out the fact that this eavesdropping took place during an accidental trip into the past while I was wearing a time-traveling bangle.

Dad watches me for several moments before saying, "Do you understand how serious this is?"

"Yes. What are you going to do?"

Dad takes a deep breath. "Well, as your mother said earlier, it's time to face the consequences for what we've done."

My throat tightens as I try to hold back tears. "That's what she said?"

"Yes. And she's right. We've broken the law. *I*, especially, have broken the law. Your mother doesn't even know the lengths I went to in order to keep your name off the list."

"Dad, I'm so sorry I—"

"I broke the law, Calla," he says firmly. "*I* did that. If I have to face the consequences, then I will."

"But—"

"We don't even know yet what will happen to me. Right now, our concern should be for your mother. She's the one being carted off to Barton Prison tomorrow."

"Tomorrow?" I gasp. "Where is she now? Can I see her?"

"No, of course you can't see her!" he says, his voice rising. "She's in the detainment area downstairs. Is your ability going to get you past all those guards? Probably not. And then you'll end up in the cell next to hers when you're caught."

Dad's lack of faith in my ability stings, but now isn't the time to argue. Not when he's clearly close to cracking from the pressure of Mom's trial and the devastating news of her sentence.

"I … I need some space," Dad says, standing. "I'll be outside in the forest." He places a hand on my shoulder and adds, "You've found yourself in enough life-threatening situations recently. I just want you to stay safe now."

The door closes behind Dad and I pull my feet up onto the chair. I wrap my arms around my legs and press my face against my knees as the weight of what I've done to my parents becomes almost too much to bear. "This is all my fault."

"Calla …"

"You know it is." I raise my head and look at Ryn. "Dad would never have had to break the law if not for me. And Mom … well, the Guild might still have punished her for running away in the middle of her training, but it wouldn't be this bad. It's because of me that they're doing this to her. I'm on the loose instead of in custody for supposedly murdering Saskia, and they're taking out their frustration at their own failure on Mom. They can't make me pay, so they're making her pay."

Ryn rubs his face. He closes his eyes and slowly shakes his head. "I don't know, Cal. You're probably right, but there's nothing we can do about it."

"What if …" My feet slip to the floor and I sit up a little straighter. "What if I turn myself in? Do you think that would make a difference?"

"What?" Ryn's eyelids spring open. "No! Are you crazy? Of course that wouldn't make a difference. You'd end up in prison along with your mother. You can't make this situation any better."

I flop back into the chair. "So we're supposed to just let this happen? Let her go to prison for the next few years?"

Ryn shrugs helplessly. "What's the alternative? Help her escape so she can be on the run for the rest of her life? Barton Prison isn't all that bad. Not like Velazar. Maybe it's better if she just does the time. Maybe … I don't know." He rubs both hands over his face this time. "I don't have all the answers, Calla."

I peer more closely at him. He seems more tired than I've seen him in a long time. "Are you okay?"

He sighs. "Yes. I just … have a lot on my mind. I took the rest of last week off after Victoria was born, so yesterday was my first day back. So many things to do. My team began looking into this so-called guardian hater group straight after Zed tried to take Victoria. I told them to question the owner of Club Deviant, like you suggested."

"Oh yeah? Did they discover anything?"

"They did, actually. One of my team recognized him as someone who escaped from the scene of a previous crime. They arrested him and searched his club. They found illegal potions that link him to another group we've been trying to take down for a while. Perhaps they're all part of this larger guardian hater group. Anyway, none of this proves he had anything to do with the dragon disease or the plan to hurt Victoria, and of course he says he knows nothing of a faerie named Zed. But we've requested permission to use a truth potion, so if that request goes through, we'll soon know more." Ryn stifles a yawn before adding, "Oh, and we've had a spike in disappearances in Creepy Hollow recently. That's not my department, of course, but I know Vi can help with her Griffin Ability. So I've been trying to discreetly get my hands on some of the belongings of those who've disappeared so Vi can attempt to find them. Amidst all my own work, of course." He leans one elbow on the desk and blinks at me, as though trying to wake himself up. "How's, um, Chase?"

"Oh." I automatically swivel the ring around my finger. "The situation's still the same," I say carefully. I told Ryn about the telepathy rings and that we know where Chase is being held prisoner, but I haven't told him what we're doing about it. I think it's probably best he doesn't know we're attempting to break into the Seelie Palace. He might feel obligated to try and stop us.

"I still haven't heard a thing about him," Ryn says. "Not even a whisper. I assumed there must be someone on the Council—the Head Councilor, at the very least—who knew about Draven's capture, but maybe I was wrong. Maybe Angelica negotiated directly with the Seelie Queen for her freedom."

"She mentioned the Guild, though." I continue twisting the telepathy ring, frowning at the desk as I remember that moment beside the Wishbone Rivers when I realized exactly what Angelica had done—traded her own son for her freedom.

"Do you love him?"

My hands freeze and blood rushes to light a fire across my skin. "What?"

"After he was taken," Ryn says, "you told me you care a great deal about him. I didn't question it at the time because you were so upset, but … well, you mentioned previously that I had nothing to worry about when it came to your feelings for him, but something's obviously changed since then." He leans forward and watches me closely.

"Don't do that," I say, pointing at him. "Don't feel what I'm feeling."

"Hey." He holds his hands up. "You know I have no control over that. Besides, the only thing I can feel is your complete mortification. It's impossible to sense anything beyond that."

"Good. You can keep feeling mortified then."

"So … do you really feel that strongly for him?"

I sit back in the chair and cross my arms. "Are you asking because you have a legitimate interest in knowing, or because you'd like to remind me that you think he's too old for me?"

"Well … he is."

I roll my eyes toward the ceiling before returning them to my brother. "Would you feel better if he were a hundred-year-old vampire? Because the rest of society seems to be okay with that."

Ryn cocks his head. "What are you talking about?"

I lift one shoulder. "Haven't a clue. Chase told me to say that if you brought up the age difference again."

"Right …"

"Anyway, back to Angelica."

He sighs. "If you insist."

"I don't understand why the Seelie Queen agreed to this bargain in the first place. I can't see her wanting her traitorous daughter set loose into the world."

Ryn leans his elbows on the desk. "Presumably she agreed because she sees Draven as a far bigger threat. She must have decided the swap was worth it. I just wish the Council wasn't keeping us all in the dark about it. It makes me wonder what other secrets they're hiding."

I frown. "Such as?

He gives a slight shake of his head. "I'm not sure. I thought I'd discover more after being invited onto the Council, but it seems there are secrets even within the Council. Secrets like Draven, and … whatever's happening downstairs."

"Downstairs?" My mind flits over the various levels below ground at the Guild. "The detainment area?"

"No. Some of the laboratories further down. I was following up on an assignment one day—a potion sample that needed to be tested—and I realized I don't have access to some of the rooms down there. When I questioned it, I was given vague answers that don't make sense to me. I've tried to find out more since then, but I haven't been able to."

"So you think they're hiding something in those labs?"

"It's possible." He breathes out a long sigh. "You know, there's a big part of me that wants to leave the Guild. I mean, they do a lot of good here, but not everything seems to be entirely aboveboard. I don't know if I want to be part of it."

His words remind me of Zed's accusations against the Guild. *It's a noble idea, but there's so much wrong with the system.* He obviously shouldn't have gone on to plant a deadly dragon disease spell that almost brought the Guild to its knees. And he shouldn't have tried to kill Ryn and Vi's baby to punish them for leaving him and dozens of other Gifted fae locked in Prince Marzell's dungeon years ago. But perhaps he was right about certain things.

"Anyway," Ryn says, standing and massaging one shoulder with his hand. "It's late. You should get back to wherever it is you're staying now. There's no way you can see your mother tonight—or tomorrow—but you might be able to sneak into Barton Prison once she's there. If you keep yourself invisible the entire time. Even then, it would be dangerous. Anyone watching surveillance recordings might see you."

"I'll take the risk. I can't go two whole years without seeing her. I haven't even said goodbye." Ryn nods, but his reply is lost in a yawn. "You should go home too," I tell him. "You look terrible."

He gives me a half-smile. "You don't look so great yourself."

I shrug. "I've been busy."

He raises both eyebrows. "I should probably ask what you're up to these days, but I think it's better if I don't know."

"It's definitely better if you don't know." He walks around the desk and lifts his jacket from the back of the chair Dad was sitting on as I add, "Hey, um, will you let me know if you hear any talk of a dangerous prisoner being held by the Seelie Court?"

"Of course."

"Thanks." I turn to leave, but he catches my shoulder before I open the door.

"Don't do it," he says.

"Do what?"

"Whatever you're planning to do now about your mother. Sneaking downstairs to see her, or trying to get her out. It isn't worth you getting caught."

"I'm tired, Ryn. I barely have enough energy left to focus on the invisibility required to get me out of the Guild let alone past all the security between here and Mom's detainment cell. And I'm not going to try and get her out. If she told Dad she's ready to face the consequences of her actions, then … I guess I have to respect that."

Ryn's eyes narrow. "You're not lying to me, are you?"

I look him straight in the eye and say, "No. I am not going down there tonight."

CHAPTER THREE

I WASN'T LYING TO RYN. NOT REALLY. HE TOLD ME NOT TO do anything risky *last night*, and I promised him I wouldn't. But this morning is entirely different. I wake early, after only a few hours of sleep, and return to the Guild. I *need* to see Mom before they take her away. I need her to know how sorry I am, because no matter what reasons the Guild might have given everyone, I know the length of her sentence is entirely my fault.

I head straight for the corridor that leads to the detainment area. I stop just outside it and peer in, watching the men guarding the gate halfway along. Invisibility won't work here, since I have to get through the gate. I need to project an illusion of someone else. Dad would be the best option, since he has the most reason to be here, and if somebody mentions it to him later, he'll realize what I've done and play along. Anyone else—any guardian or councilor—would deny it, and that would raise suspicion, which would lead to people taking a closer look at surveillance recordings.

I imagine myself as Dad and walk confidently along the corridor toward the guards and the gate. One guard looks uncertainly at the other, but before either of them can say anything, I open my mouth—imagining Dad's voice—and say, "I'm here to see my wife."

"Of course, Mr. Larkenwood, it's just that—"

"Linden?"

I manage to keep from flinching as someone behind me calls Dad's name. I look around and find one of the Guild Council members approaching me with a frown creasing his brow. "You're a little early, aren't you? We're supposed to meet in half an hour."

Meet in … what? Alarm bells shriek inside my head, but I force myself to remain still instead of pushing past this man and running as fast as I can. *Don't panic. Maintain the illusion. SAY SOMETHING, DAMMIT!* "Uh, well, can you blame me?"

The councilor gives me an odd look, and I wonder if Dad's voice sounded as strange to him as it did to me. "I suppose not," he says eventually. "This whole situation must be very … difficult for you. I feel for you, Linden. But rules are rules, so you'll need to wait up here until we're ready for the transfer. I'll send for you then."

If I really were Dad, I'd probably be furious at the prospect of being *sent for* like some trainee, but in this moment, I want nothing more than to get out of here in case my father really does show up early. I give the man a brief nod, then turn and stride along the corridor, fighting the urge to run with every step I take. Once in the foyer, I head for the grand stairway and duck behind it before switching back to an invisibility projection. I slump against the wall beside the elevator, keeping my head down and allowing my heart rate to return to normal. I have no hope now of seeing Mom before she's moved to Barton Prison. I didn't realize it was happening so early. I should have woken up sooner and—

Miss Goldilocks?

I tense at the unexpected voice in my head. Then I sag against the wall once more as relief floods me with warmth. *You're still there*, I say to Chase.

Yeah. Chained inside a dungeon cell, remember? I'm not going anywhere.

You know what I mean. I look past the stairway toward the entrance room on the other side of the foyer. Two guardians walk out, followed seconds later by another one. I decide to stay put for now. With everyone starting to arrive for work, it would be too easy for someone to accidentally walk into me in that small room. *I tried to speak to you last night and this morning but you didn't reply. I got a little worried.*

I'm sorry. I think I slept for longer than usual. I must be getting used to these charming surroundings.

Sleep is good. I try not to think of the very non-charming surroundings Chase has told me about. I'm amazed he ever falls asleep at all.

I assume you wanted to talk last night so you could tell me how spectacularly well your first mission went, Chase says as I walk around the stairway to where the steps lead down instead of up.

How do you know it went well? Several trainees walk past the stairway and toward the elevator—toward *me*. Although I know they can't see me, it makes me too nervous to stand right next to them as they wait for the elevator. I push away from the wall and stop at the top of the stairs that lead down.

You're one highly determined individual, Chase says. *I can't imagine you leaving the baron's house without that invitation.*

My hand tightens on the banister as I peer down the stairs. *Yes, well, it might have been a successful mission, but in case I was having any doubts about the universe sucking, I was once again proven wrong last night.*

What happened? Chase's question flashes into my head after barely a second's pause.

You have to survive another nine days *until the party, and the Guild is sending my mother to prison for two years.*

His thoughts grow silent, but I sense his sinking spirits. Eventually he says, *I'm so sorry about your mother.*

I'm sorry about you. I breathe out a frustrated puff of air. I can't keep still, so I begin descending the stairs. *Every day that goes by takes us closer to whatever fate the Seelie Queen has planned for you. We have no idea when she'll act. It could be tonight, it could be tomorrow, it …* I stop myself before the claws of despair can get too tight a grip around my heart. *I'm sorry. This isn't helpful. It's just … nine days seems like an eternity when your life is hanging in the balance.*

Everything will be fine, Calla.

Will it? I continue down the stairs, my fingers tracing

lightly across the banister's carved patterns. I haven't really thought about where I'm going, but Ryn's suspicions nudge at the back of my mind, stirring up my curiosity about whatever's going on behind locked doors down here.

Yes. I believe it will. Clearly your optimistic spirit has rubbed off on me.

I want to laugh at that because my optimism seems to have all but vanished these days. And as confident as Chase sounds, I know it's only a front. I can sense him distancing himself emotionally, trying to keep from communicating what he's truly feeling. I hesitate on the stairs as the quiet thought enters my mind, as it always does at some point during our mental discussions: *What are they doing to you there?*

Nothing I can't handle.

You always say that.

It's always true.

I shake my head as I continue downward. *Will you ever tell me?*

Perhaps, but not now. I don't want to drown in the details of this dark and hopeless hell. I'd rather imagine your surroundings instead. Are you at the mountain?

Uh, no. I pass the level that houses the labs I had potions classes in while I was a trainee and keep going, my boots silent on the emerald green carpet covering the stairs.

You sound guilty, Chase says. *What are you doing?*

Just … some private investigation. I stop at the next level down and look around.

On what?

I'm not entirely sure, actually. I'm at the Guild. I came early in the hopes of seeing Mom so I could apologize for being the World's Worst Daughter—

Not true.

—but I didn't get here in time. And I'm sure there aren't many daughters in the world who've caused their mothers to receive jail time, so I definitely qualify for that label. Anyway, now I'm sneaking around the lower levels of the Guild trying to find out what's happening behind locked doors.

What locked doors?

I don't know. I head along the corridor, eyeing the clean, plain doors. So much of the Guild is intricately patterned and lavishly decorated that it's odd to find a section of it so stark. Some of the doors don't even have handles. *Ryn said he came across rooms he doesn't have access to, which made him suspicious. Since he's on the Council, he thought he should know about everything that goes on here, but apparently not.*

Be careful, Chase warns. *You don't want to end up trapped somewhere.*

I know, I know. I hold my breath as a guardian with a clipboard in her hand and a stylus tucked behind her ear walks out of a room up ahead and comes toward me. As she walks past, I relax—and then her footsteps stop. Terrified I'll find her staring at me, I slowly look over my shoulder. But she's facing a door—one of the doors without a handle—and frowning at her clipboard. After nodding to herself several times, she takes her stylus and waves it across the door. With a brief flash of light, the door vanishes. She walks forward. Without stopping to think, I turn and rush through the doorway after her into a room illuminated by dim blue light. I look behind me as a second flash registers at the edge of my vision. The door has reappeared.

What's happening? Chase asks. No doubt he felt the burst of panic that flooded my chest at the sight of that closed door.

So … I'm inside a room I can't get out of, I tell him, *but it's fine. I'm not trapped. I'll just wait here until someone leaves or comes in.* Then I take my first proper look around the room—and genuine panic tightens my chest. Four rectangular glass boxes are suspended in the air at eye level, and inside each one is a person. They're motionless, their eyes closed, and the glass is so close—*so close*—to their faces, it's almost touching them. I press my hand against my mouth and shut my eyes and remind myself that *I'm not the one inside the box.* And I'm not inside a cage. I'm free. It will be easy to walk out of this room.

The lake. Think of the lake. The quiet lapping of water and the warm, gentle breeze and the soft, lush grass between your fingers. The memory of Lumethon's soothing voice takes my panic down to a manageable level within seconds. I open my eyes to the blue-lit room once more and remember how to breathe.

Calla? Chase calls. *Are you okay?*

Yes. Sorry. I was just … battling a bad memory. I tiptoe toward the nearest glass box, describing everything I see as I go. The woman inside is a faerie, judging by her two-toned hair. Her marking-free wrists tell me she isn't a guardian. On the lower edge of the box, a small plaque tells me her name is N. Thornbough.

"Alrighty," the clipboard lady murmurs to no one in particular. She's on the other side of the room, standing at a counter that's bare except for a tray of small spheres that glow faintly. "Let's try this again." She runs a finger down her clipboard, then selects a sphere from the tray. She approaches the other side of N. Thornbough's box. After waving her hand near the side of the glass, a hole materializes, similar to the way faerie paths doorways melt into existence. She puts the sphere inside the box, where it floats without moving as she seals up the hole. With another wave of her hand, the sphere drops and smashes beside the woman's arm. Nothing else seems to happen.

The woman sighs and returns to her clipboard. She makes a note before selecting another sphere. As she returns to N. Thornbough's box, I step quietly around it and read the name on the next box. J. Monkswood. Also not a member of the Guild, and—

I tense at the sound of pounding on the door. "I'm coming in," a voice shouts. A second later, the door vanishes and Councilor Merrydale rushes into the room, looking around. "Where is she? The hooded figure."

I freeze beside J. Monkswood's box as Clipboard Lady closes the second hole she just opened. "What hooded figure?"

"The guards in the surveillance room saw a hooded figure follow you in here just minutes ago. A woman."

She shakes her head. "I haven't seen anyone. Are you sure you've got the right room?"

"Of course. We both know you're the only one working on this at the moment, so it had to have been you she followed."

Crap, crap, crap. I take a careful step around the box as Councilor Merrydale moves further into the room, searching the floor, the walls, the ceiling with his eyes.

What's wrong? Chase asks. I don't answer.

"She's still here," Councilor Merrydale murmurs. "Only a handful of us have access to this room, so she couldn't have got out unless you let her out." He spreads his arms and moves closer, magic zapping at the tips of his fingers as he feels the air. "Close the door," he says to Clipboard Lady.

CRAP! I skip around him, pressing myself briefly against the counter's edge—the spheres wobble audibly in their tray—and dart toward the door. As Councilor Merrydale lunges for the counter, and Clipboard Lady dashes to the door, I just, *just* slip out in time.

And then I run. No point in wandering around casually if people in the surveillance room are already watching this passage.

Calla, please tell me what's happening.

Just making a hasty exit, that's all.

Up, up, up the stairs. I'm still invisible, so no one in the foyer bats an eye as I streak past them. Whoever's watching on the other end of a surveillance bug will be too late to catch me. I dodge to the side to keep from running into the trainee who just walked out of the entrance room. As I hurry into the room and write on the wall with my stylus, the image I project onto the guard is one of a blank wall. Seconds later, I'm inside the safety of the faerie paths, long before any guardian can come chasing after me.

Made it, I tell Chase.

Feeling immensely relieved, I walk out of the darkness into Chase's lakeside home in the human realm. I take only two steps across the open-plan kitchen and living area before noticing the figure standing by the wide kitchen window. I throw both hands up, automatically raising a shield of magic—but then I see the purple streaks of hair and the bundle of blankets in the woman's arms as she turns to face me.

"Vi? What are you—"

"I need help," she says, hugging her child more tightly to her chest. "Something isn't right with Victoria."

CHAPTER FOUR

"WHAT'S WRONG?" I ASK IMMEDIATELY, HURRYING TO Violet's side and laying a careful hand on Victoria's back. "Is she sick? Do we need to get her to a healing institute?"

"No, it isn't like that. It's not something immediately life-threatening. It's … I can't really explain it. She just seems different since … you know."

I lower my hand slowly to my side. "Since Zed took her." *Can we talk later?* I add silently to Chase.

Sure. Not going anywhere, remember?

"I'm probably just imagining things," Vi says in a low voice, probably so as not to wake Victoria. "That's what Ryn thinks. He says we didn't know her long enough before the Zed incident to tell if there's actually a difference now. And the healers checked her out within hours of Zed taking her, and they said she was fine."

"But?" I prompt.

"I don't know. I think something's different. Nothing visible, although I do think her birthmark is lighter than it was before." Vi leans against the kitchen counter. "It's more … her personality? She seems fussier. She cries a lot more. I can't … I can't make her happy. I talk to her and sing to her and hold her close, but it only makes things worse."

I quirk an eyebrow. "You sing?"

She narrows her eyes at me. "Not the point."

"Sorry, sorry." I give her an encouraging smile. "Aren't babies supposed to cry a lot? That's normal, isn't it?"

"Yes, but is it normal that I can't comfort her? She seemed to respond to me before, but now she doesn't. I finally got her to sleep, but I think it was more to do with complete exhaustion from all her crying than any comfort I provided."

"Well … I don't know. Is there anything I can do to help?"

"Yes. That's why I searched for you." She glances around the house. "This isn't where you live now, is it? I thought you were staying somewhere hidden from me, but I kept thinking of you this morning, and suddenly this place flashed into view."

Keeping the details vague so she won't be able to give anything away if the Guild questions her, I say, "No, I'm not staying here. This house is sort of … on the way."

"I see. Well, the friend you're staying with—the one who can take away Griffin Abilities—is a botanist, correct? I think you mentioned that?"

"Yes."

"Farah told me about a type of berry that's used to counteract harmful spells. She said it used to be an ingredient in many healing potions, but healers thought it had become ineffective over the centuries, so they stopped using it. But she believes it can still help against certain spells, and it has no negative side effects, so I thought I should try it." Victoria squirms in her sleep, and Vi gently strokes her back. "Farah doesn't know where to get any seeing as it isn't commonly used anymore, but I thought your friend might."

I watch the odd facial expressions Victoria is pulling in her fitful sleep. "He might. His greenhouse is overflowing with hundreds of different plants."

"Can you ask him if he has fire tongue?"

I look up. "You want to give a baby something called fire tongue?"

"Apparently the leaves burn your mouth if you eat them, but Farah says the berries aren't as bad."

"Hopefully she's right about that. Well, uh, if you don't want to know anything about where I'm going, you'll need to wait outside."

"Right, of course." She looks around. "Do you have a key for the front door, or … never mind." She opens a faerie paths doorway with a stylus and appears on the porch a moment later.

I head back to the mountain through the faerie door. I run upstairs, and then up again to the level with the enchanted greenhouse. Gaius is already there, digging through the dirt in the far corner to plant something new. He nods when I ask him about the fire tongue and adds that he still uses it occasionally in his own potions. He points me in the direction of the right bush. I gather a handful of berries, then stop at the rusted metal shelves near the entrance and select an empty glass jar from the collection. I drop the berries inside and return to the lake house.

I find Vi sitting on the porch step outside bathed in the twilight mix of orange and lavender light. I still don't know where in the human world this house is, but it's a number of hours ahead of both Creepy Hollow and the mountain. "What will you do with the berries?" I ask as I hand her the jar.

"I'm not sure. I think Farah will make some kind of juice from them."

She moves as if to stand and I quickly ask, "Can I hold her before you go? Just for a little bit."

"Oh, yes, of course. I have to wait another hour before I can meet with Farah anyway."

I sit beside Vi on the step and she places the sleeping Victoria into my arms. One tiny, clenched fist has broken free of the blanket that swaddles her. I run my finger gently over it, then across her fine, dark hair. "Have you had any clue as to what color she'll settle with?"

Vi leans her elbows on her knees and her chin on her hands as she watches her daughter sleeping. "Not yet. Her eyes are too dark to make out their color most of the time, and her hair … it seems to switch from light brown to dark, but I've seen no other color in the past few days, which is also what's been worrying me."

"It happened quickly with you, didn't it?"

"Yes. My parents weren't certain about my hair color, but

my eyes were a very deep blue-purple from the beginning."

I nod. "What birthmark did you mention just now?"

"Oh, it's this dark pink shape on her left shoulder." Vi lifts Victoria and holds her against her chest. She carefully pulls aside the blanket and clothing at the back of her neck. "See, it looks just like a flower. It's almost a perfect shape."

"That is so sweet."

"I know. It's grown lighter in the past few days, and I'm sad that it might fade away completely."

"I guess it doesn't matter what marks she does or doesn't end up having, as long as she's healthy."

Vi nods and kisses Victoria's head. "I just want her to have a safe, normal life. I can completely understand now why your mother never wanted you to join the Guild," she adds with an apologetic smile. "It's terrifying imagining my own child in the kinds of dangerous situations we've faced."

"Yeah, I guess." Looking at Victoria, I feel the same way. "Well at least she won't have to worry about keeping a Griffin Ability secret. It isn't possible for—" I cut myself off as that scrap of information I pushed to the back of my mind while at the baron's house rushes suddenly to the forefront of my thoughts. "Unless … hmm." I sit up straighter. "Unless it is possible. Unless our understanding of Griffin Abilities has never been complete."

Instead of looking surprised, Vi nods. "That's the question, isn't it."

"You've considered this?"

"I have. We've always been told that the Gifted were born to those who used a griffin disc. The increased power those people possessed while using a disc was somehow transferred to their children. But those discs lost their magic after they unlocked Tharros' power from the chest it was trapped inside, and that was over a decade ago."

"Right," I say. "But what if that's not the only way? What if … maybe … two Gifted can produce a child who's also Gifted."

"Exactly. I've wondered about this ever since I discovered I was pregnant, but there's no record of it on the Griffin List. If there are other Gifted couples out there who've had children in the past decade, they've kept their abilities hidden, just as we have." She looks out at the lake, becoming darker and darker as night draws near. "Without proof, we can only speculate whether this is possible or not."

"I think I've seen proof."

Her gaze snaps back to me. "You have?"

"Last night I rescued a Gifted faerie child whose touch could turn objects into gold. That isn't normal magic, and her father didn't deny that it was a Griffin Ability. She was only five years old."

Vi's eyes widen. She hugs Victoria closer as she murmurs, "So it must be possible then."

"Look, we don't know nearly enough about this to know if Victoria is Gifted. And even if she does turn out like us, is that such a bad thing? I mean, we've all managed to deal with our abilities."

Vi closes her eyes and groans. "This motherhood thing has given me so many more things to worry about. I don't—Oh." She hands Victoria back to me so she can remove her pinging amber from her pocket. A tiny fist smacks my jaw as Victoria continues to wriggle and make nonsense sounds in her sleep.

"She really doesn't enjoy sleeping, does she," I mutter as Vi reads a message on her amber.

"Oh, finally," she exclaims, her face breaking into a grin. "My dad's visiting on Friday."

As her words sink into my brain, I have to hold back a gasp of excitement. Vi's dad—the only person I know who works at the Seelie Palace—will be in Creepy Hollow on Friday night. Reminding myself to continue acting normally, I ask, "Hasn't he met Victoria yet?"

"He has. He was given a grand total of about twenty minutes off work the day she was born. But now he'll be able to spend the whole evening with us."

"That's wonderful." *For more reasons than one.* I don't know how I'm going to do it, but I *have* to get the location of the Seelie Court out of Vi's dad, and this will likely be my only chance.

Victoria's sleepy protest noises grow louder and her eyes are half open now. "Here we go again," Vi grumbles. "I should probably go before she starts screaming her little lungs out."

I look over my shoulder and check the time on the clock inside. "I have to go too, actually. I have a meeting."

"A meeting?" Vi asks as she takes Victoria from me and stands. "You know I'm curious, but I won't ask."

"Probably best." I'd rather she not know that we're about to discuss plans for breaking into the Seelie Palace.

CHAPTER FIVE

I DASH INTO THE MEETING ROOM ON ONE OF THE LOWER levels of the mountain and drop into a chair, noting that I'm the last person to arrive. The other five members of Chase's team are already seated. *Meeting time*, I tell Chase. *In case you want to add anything.*

"Late again," the elf girl with the spiked hair mutters from across the table. "You know some of us have actual jobs to be at in, like, ten minutes, right?"

I open my mouth to ask when last I was late, but Gaius gets in first. "Oh, did you find a new job, Ana? How wonderful."

She absently twists one of the piercings in her left ear. "Yeah, well, we might be busy cooking up the biggest mission of our lives, but I've still got bills to pay."

"You know you're welcome to stay here if you—"

"Thanks, but no," Ana interrupts. "I like my own space. Besides, Chase taught me well, so it wasn't too hard to find work."

"Oh, you're also a tattoo artist?" I ask, working hard to keep my tone polite.

"Of course I'm a tattoo artist. Did you think I was just the receptionist?"

Darius, the blue-eyed faerie slouching in the chair beside Ana, snorts. "Receptionist," he grunts in amusement. She flicks his arm with a tattooed finger.

"Perhaps we should begin," Lumethon suggests, focusing her gaze on Gaius. With her perfectly white hair and colorless eyes a stark contrast against her dark skin, she might be a faerie with particularly exotic coloring or some other being entirely. I thought it too rude to ask.

Beside me, the drakoni man named Kobe who never says very much, nods in agreement.

"Right," Gaius says. "Quick updates."

I told you Ana doesn't like me, I say to Chase as I fold my arms and focus on Gaius.

Give her time. She takes a while to warm up to new people.

The spider-like contraption I noticed on Gaius's desk last night climbs onto the table. Lumethon snatches her hand out of the way as the device made of cogs, wheels, various pieces of metal, magic, and needle-thin sticks for legs moves past her toward Gaius. One spindly leg holds a scroll and another holds a quill. "Excellent, very good," Gaius mutters with a smile.

Ana shakes her head and whispers, "Ridiculous."

The spider raises the scroll and allows it to unroll, the

bottom edge of the paper hitting the table and unfurling another few inches. Gaius leans forward to read whatever notes are on the scroll. "All other projects have come to an end, so we're now focusing solely on Chase, the Seelie Court, and this terrible veil-splitting vision that Amon and Angelica are so interested in." He looks around the table. "You'll be pleased to know I've found some information on the prison beneath the palace. Most people don't even know it exists, but it turns out an old friend of mine had a brother locked up there at some point, and he was allowed to visit before they, uh, carried out the sentence. And before you ask," Gaius adds quickly, "he does not know how to get there. He was both stunned and blind-folded."

"Seems excessive," Darius comments.

"Indeed. Anyway, this friend of mine has agreed to put together some drawings of everything he remembers. We can examine the drawings in depth once I've got them.

"Next ..." Gaius examines the scroll again. "Darius and Kobe met with the mer king last night and confirmed that the monument involved in the veil spell is under heavy guard. The king is still refusing to have it moved, though, and destroying it isn't just out of the question, it's apparently impossible as well."

"I wish he'd at least let us *try*," Darius says. "That would be fun."

Kobe frowns, his reptile-like eyes narrowing at Darius. I see a flick of his forked tongue as he says, "Do you have no respect?"

"You know I have no—"

"What's so magical about this trident monument anyway?" Ana asks. "I know the witch in the vision said something about magic of the heights and magic of the depths. And we all know the full moon can have a powerful influence on spells, so that's the height part. Obviously the mer statue is for the depths part, but what's so special about it?"

"As the name suggests," Gaius says, "it's been around since the time of the very first mer king. That was … oh, centuries and centuries ago. Every king and queen since then has added their magic to the monument in some way. That makes it a very powerful statue. Probably the most powerful object beneath the ocean's surface."

"Okay." Ana sits back. "I guess that makes sense."

"Right then," Gaius says. "Lastly, we now have an invitation to Princess Audra's birthday party at the Seelie Palace, so that's our way in. It's nine days away, including today, which means we still have time to find out how to actually get there. Ana and Lumethon, any luck with that?"

"Nothing yet," Lumethon says as Ana shakes her head. "As we're all aware, it's a well-kept secret."

"I think I can help there," I say tentatively. Everyone's attention focuses on me. "I know someone who works for the Seelie Queen."

Ana's hand slaps down on the table as her mouth drops open. "You didn't think to mention this before?"

Patience, I remind myself. She's a friend of Chase's and I need to make an effort with her. "I did think of it," I explain to the group, "but I decided there was no point in mentioning it since he hardly ever leaves the Seelie Court. It's been months since I last saw him and we don't have that kind of time where Chase is concerned. But I just found out that he'll be visiting my brother and sister-in-law on Friday evening, so we have until then to come up with a way to get the Seelie Court location out of him."

"Can't you just ask him?" Darius says.

I try to keep my frustration in. "He's a close advisor to the Seelie Queen. I am one hundred percent certain he won't approve of a group of outlaws breaking into the palace to rescue the man who enslaved our world a decade ago."

"I wasn't suggesting you tell him *that*," Darius says. "Just, you know, say that you're curious."

I raise an eyebrow. "Curious?"

"Okay, you have a point," Darius concedes. "He's definitely not going to just tell you."

"I wonder if it might be possible to follow him," Lumethon says. "You can keep yourself invisible so he doesn't know."

"I could, but what about the faerie paths? I assume they'd be involved for at least part of the journey, so I'd have to touch him in order to wind up at the same destination on the other side. How will I get away with that without him noticing?"

Lumethon looks at Gaius. "There are ways to follow him without being in physical contact."

Gaius nods, and I remember Ryn telling me something similar once. "Yes, there is magic that will allow you to follow him through the paths without touching him. One of those unstable spells that relies on precise enunciation of every word—and if I remember correctly, there are many words involved. It can easily go wrong, which is why it isn't taught in schools. I'll have to look it up." He nods at his contraption, which lifts the quill in one spindly leg and makes a note on the scroll.

"Does Chase have anything he might want to add to this meeting?" Ana asks, looking across the table at me. "Is his situation still the same? Would you even tell us if something changed?"

"Of course I would tell you. Why wouldn't I?"

"You seem to be mighty possessive of that ring that doesn't even belong to you. I just hope you're not hiding anything from us."

Breathing in deeply, I manage to refrain from crawling across the table and punching Ana. Instead, I tug the ring off and send it spinning across the table. She slaps her hand down over it, glares at me for another moment, then picks it up and swivels her chair around to face the wall.

I look at Gaius and mouth, *What did I do wrong?*

He shrugs. "Well, that's all for now. Some of you have work commitments, and Lumethon and Calla have a training session. I'll see you all tomorrow morning, unless something comes up before then."

Everyone except Ana stands and moves toward the door. Darius complains about his boring day job and Kobe tells him to get over his laziness. Then they agree to meet later for a training session in the gym room next door. Lumethon greets me at the door, but before she can say anything further, Ana pushes her hand between us, the ring sitting on her open palm. "He says you shouldn't wear it during training," she tells me as I take the ring from her. "He doesn't want to distract you."

Without waiting for a reply, she slips past me and out of the room.

"I know she can be … difficult," Lumethon says, "but give her a chance. She's had a tough life so far, and she doesn't trust easily."

I push the ring into my back pocket. "What happened, or shouldn't I ask?"

"Well, it isn't a secret," Lumethon says as we leave the meeting room. "She lost her whole family a year or two before The Destruction in an accidental fire. She lived with friends for a while, but … well, I won't go into details, but it wasn't a healthy situation. A few years after Draven's defeat, at the age of eleven, she ran away. She survived on her own for three years, becoming particularly skilled at stealing and even more skilled at evading guardians. When someone eventually caught her, Chase rescued her and gave her a choice: join his team or face the Guild."

"And she chose you guys, of course."

"Yes. She lived with me for a few years, then announced on her seventeenth birthday last year that she wanted a place of her own." We head upstairs toward the mountain's entrance hall. "I was a little worried in the beginning that she would simply run away," Lumethon continues, "but she's been fiercely loyal to us since the moment Chase took her in. And a valuable addition to the team. Exceptionally stealthy. The places she's snuck into would blow your mind."

Right, and here I am using invisibility to sneak into places. No wonder Ana looks at me with such disdain. "So she would have done a great job with last night's mission."

"Yes, she probably would have done that one if you hadn't joined us, but since last night's mission involved stealing from one of our own clients, we needed to be absolutely certain that whoever we sent wouldn't be caught. Anyway, enough about that," she says as we cross the entrance hall and stop by the faerie door. "It's desensitization time."

I shudder inwardly at the thought of the systematic desensitization I've been forced to endure every day since I admitted to the rest of my team that I have a phobia of confined spaces. "Yeah, I know. Let's get it over with. Where are we going this time?"

"Back to Rosenhill Manor Art Gallery."

"Oh, I love it there."

Lumethon smiles. "That's why we're going back."

I follow her through the faerie door to the lake house, where I place my hand on her shoulder as she writes a doorway spell on the wall. Moments later, we walk into the exquisite gardens of Rosenhill Estate. Green lawns, rose bushes and weatherworn statues surround us as we walk uphill toward the old manor house that was once the home of a Seelie Court lord. Now it houses room after room of magnificent art.

Luna, the old elf lady who saved Chase from his own misery and despair in the months after he ceased to be Draven, knew about this place. She never had the opportunity to visit the manor house herself, but she'd heard tales of the breathtaking artwork contained within and told Chase all about it. After she died and Chase found himself with her artistic ability, he came here for inspiration.

Lumethon and I walk through the grand entrance of the

manor house and pay for a ticket each. Wooden floorboards creak beneath our feet as we walk toward the first room. A kaleidoscope of color drips from every inch of all four walls, the pattern continuously changing as the enchanted paint shifts again and again into a seemingly endless series of designs. It's mesmerizing, but not exactly relaxing. This isn't the room we came here for.

We pass through a room with sculptures that move fluidly from one form into another, and then a room filled with floating glass spheres that each contain miniature scenes constructed entirely from pieces of scrap metal. Another room seems sure to burn up at any moment as flames lick their way across every canvas. It's an enchantment of the paint, though—paint I've been lucky enough to use once—so the canvases remain intact.

We end up in the water-themed room—my favorite and the most suitable for our purposes. A stream of glittering, silvery water flows diagonally across the floor from one corner of the room to the other where it disappears into the wall. Flat round stones floating above its surface allow visitors to jump across from one side to the other. The canvases on the walls depict scenes of lakes, waterfalls and oceans with enchanted water paint twinkling, twisting and rushing but never leaving any canvas. Lumethon and I use the rocks to get to the other side of the stream where a tree trunk resting on its side serves as a seat. "Are you ready to begin?" she asks as I sit.

"Yes." I try to clear my mind of all worries and distracting thoughts as I close my eyes.

"Breathe in through your nose," Lumethon instructs. "Feel

the air rushing into your body, feel it filling your lungs and expanding your chest. Now exhale, slowly, through your mouth, releasing all tension as you do so. And again, listening to the gentle movement of the water, slowly inhale. Focus on the air entering your body, filling you anew. Now release your breath and picture your lake, the place of relaxation you've chosen."

I reach my imaginary peaceful setting quickly now that I've done this several times. It's a version of the lake outside Chase's home in the human realm. A wide expanse of water stretches out before me, gentle waves lap at the shore of the lake, a carpet of lush grass is wonderfully soft beneath me, and a clear blue sky finishes the picture.

"Now that you've reached a relaxed state," Lumethon says, "think of your list. We're moving on to a scenario that produces a medium level of anxiety. Imagine yourself in that situation for as long as you can."

Doing my best to hold onto my sense of calm, I imagine myself standing and walking away from the lake. The scene melts away to reveal the lowest level within Gaius's mountain home. The level where gargoyles and other creatures are kept. It begins with a small room with rough stone walls and a narrow slit of space in one corner. A tunnel so narrow I've never been brave enough to go through. I take in another slow breath as I picture myself approaching that horribly narrow tunnel. My heart rate kicks up a notch, but I focus on the soothingly repetitive water sounds as I keep moving forward. *Breathe*, I remind myself. *In through the nose, out through the mouth.* I walk closer. I place my hands on the wall on either side of the dark space and stare into it. The tunnel is narrow enough that it might touch my shoulders if I were to enter it, and so dark that I have no way of seeing the other side. But despite the fact that my heart is jumping faster than normal, I don't feel overcome by panic. I take one step into the tunnel, then another. The darkness grows around me, pressing in, and that's when I shake my head, shudder, and open my eyes.

"I can't go into the tunnel yet," I tell Lumethon, looking around and finding her leaning against the wall between two paintings. "I was almost there. I *planned* to go inside and the thought didn't freak me out, but I couldn't actually do it."

"I know. You were projecting again. I saw everything."

"Not again," I say with a groan. "I told you this would be a problem. I can't keep control of my ability because I'm *too* relaxed."

"That's fine, Calla. The point here is to get over your anxiety. Once you reach that point, you'll be able to face these kinds of situations while retaining control of your projections. And you've already shown improvement," she adds with a smile. "When we did this two days ago, you didn't want to even approach the tunnel."

I nod. "True. It is getting a bit easier."

"Good. Now close your eyes, re-establish a relaxed state of mind, and go through the process again, imagining the same situation."

"Okay, but you'll watch the door, right? I mean, in case I project again, which I probably will."

"I've had a shield across the door the entire time. You needn't worry about anyone walking in."

I repeat the exercise, approaching the tunnel quicker this time, my anxiety only spiking once I'm actually inside the dark, tight space. I try to push myself further, to remain in the tunnel for more than two or three seconds, but the fear of something pressing in around me—touching me, suffocating me—becomes unbearable far too quickly.

"Well done," Lumethon says when I open my eyes and wriggle my shoulders as if to shake the fear away. "You're definitely getting there. Now, how do you feel about doing a real life test?"

"Real life?"

"The log you're sitting on is hollow. Do you think you can crawl through it from one side to the other?"

I stand up, walk to the end of the tree trunk, and peer down. Turns out it is hollow. Could I crawl through it? It's a ridiculously simple task, one that just about anybody else could easily perform, and yet … "I'm not quite sure about that."

"Why not try?" Lumethon suggests, pushing away from the wall. "We're in a non-threatening situation. The log is wide enough that it won't touch your back while you're crawling through, and you can see the other side."

I nod. Being able to see the other side and knowing how quickly it will be over definitely helps. I lower myself onto my hands and knees and look through. Lumethon crouches down on the other side and beckons with her hand. I eye the rough interior of the tree and let out a nervous laugh. "It'll be quite a tight fit. Even though it won't touch my head or my back, I'll know it's right there."

"Don't think of it. Look at me and think of wide open

space. Tell yourself you're crawling on the grass beside your lake and there's nothing above you but miles of fresh air."

I picture it—the blue sky and endless space—and slowly, carefully start crawling. Rough bark scratches my palms and Lumethon smiles encouragingly up ahead. I think of space all around me. Space, space, space and … the inside of the tree all around me. Closing me in. I suck in a breath and crawl faster. Faster, faster until I finally emerge at the other end. I grab Lumethon's hand and let her pull me to my feet. "Phew. Okay, that wasn't *too* bad. But, like you said, this is a non-threatening situation, so I had time to get myself into a relaxed state of mind first. That's not always the case."

"True, but we'll keep practicing until the relaxed state of mind is automatic and you no longer see confined space as a cause for anxiety. You're making good progress, Calla."

"I know, I just … I feel so ridiculous celebrating something this simple. It's such a silly fear. I know it is, and yet, when the panic takes over, all rational thought flees from my mind."

"Phobias aren't rational." Lumethon moves to sit on the log. "And you have an entirely legitimate reason for developing this particular phobia."

"Yeah," I mutter, thinking of the hanging cage I was locked in as a child in the Unseelie Prince's dungeon. The black water and the wailing prisoners and the stink of sweat and terror. I shiver. That scenario is definitely at the top of my anxiety hierarchy. I'm leaving that one for last.

"I've got about twenty minutes left until I need to get to work," Lumethon says, "so let's move on to illusion training."

"More training. Right." I push my hands through my hair. "Yes, okay. Let's do this."

Lumethon's eyebrows rise. "Is something wrong? Have you had enough of our training sessions?"

"No, no. I'm very grateful for all the time you've spent helping me, and I know this is important. It's just … Don't you ever feel so overcome by impatience that you want to tear your hair out?" I tug at my hair again, as if she might need an illustration. "I mean, we train every day, and everyone goes to work like they normally would, and every night we go to bed, and all the while Chase is *locked in a dungeon where someone could kill him at any moment.* I know we're doing everything we can, but it still feels like *nothing.*"

"I understand your frustration," an unexpected voice says, and I look across the room to find Gaius standing in the doorway. "I feel as if we should be actively searching for the Seelie Court at this very moment, not sparing a second for sleep or rest. I have to continually remind myself that we'd never find it that way, and even if we did, we'd never get in." He steps into the room, admiring the painting of water falling upward, crashing into quiet foam and the top of the canvas instead of the bottom. "Lovely art gallery, by the way. I've never been here." He leaps onto one of the floating stones and jumps to our side of the stream where he takes a seat on the tree trunk beside Lumethon. "So. Ready to trick my mind with your latest illusion?"

"You're here for my training? I thought Lumethon was doing that."

"We both are," she says to me. "Today we're attempting the one thing you keep telling me is impossible."

Wonderful. I tilt my head back with a groan and mutter, "Simultaneous illusions."

CHAPTER SIX

PERRY LETS OUT A GIANT GUFFAW WHEN I EXIT THE FAERIE paths at the old Guild ruins late that afternoon. "What is that on your head?"

"Um … hair?" I say, feigning confusion.

"It's blue! And short!"

"I like it," Gemma says, leaning back on her hands and examining my sleek blue bob. "It isn't real, is it?"

"No, it's a wig. I found it at the m—um, where I'm staying now." Turns out Chase's team has an entire costume closet of items to disguise one's appearance, since most magical beings are immune to glamours. Gaius pointed the closet out to me this morning after my unsuccessful attempt at projecting multiple simultaneous illusions. "I thought it might be a good idea to hide my telltale golden hair," I tell them, "since I almost got caught at the Guild this morning."

"You what?" Gemma says with a small gasp, covering her mouth with her hand.

"I was invisible to everyone around me, of course, but a surveillance bug must have flown past, so someone watching the orbs in that department saw me. I had to run."

Gemma drops her hand into her lap. "That was close. You shouldn't do that again."

"Yeah, probably not. I was sneaking around the lower levels."

"Sounds like fun," Perry says, rubbing his hands together. "What were you looking for?"

"Wouldn't you like to know," I say with a sly smile. I sit beside him and Gemma in the shade of a cracked and vine-entangled marble alcove that was once part of the old Creepy Hollow Guild. The Guild Chase destroyed when he was possessed with power that wasn't his. The thought of his past doesn't twist my insides into nausea as it once did. Chase is nothing like the person he was when he ruled as Lord Draven. I focus on the papers and textbooks spread on the ground around Perry. "You're acting unusually studious," I tell him. "Is that homework?"

"Nope. Something way more interesting. I'll tell you about my rule-breaking if you tell me about yours."

I roll my eyes, but I already know I'm going to tell them what I saw in that blue-lit room. They know of so much already, like my Griffin Ability and the fact that it was Zed who killed Saskia, spread the dragon disease, and framed me for both. I haven't told them who Chase once was, though, and they don't know anything about my relationship with him or that he's been captured. They *do* know about the prophecy that details the tearing down of the veil between our world and the human one. With Mom's trial taking place over the past few days, I figured they might hear whispers of the prophecy anyway. Best to give them the real story instead of letting them believe rumors.

I cross my legs and lean back on my hands as I tell them everything I saw in that horrible room with the glass boxes this morning. "I have no idea what it was about, but I doubt it's legal if they have to do it behind a locked door that only a handful of people are allowed through."

"Ugh, that sounds so creepy," Gemma says, pulling a face. "But you said it was Councilor Merrydale who came into the room? He wouldn't be involved in anything illegal, would he?"

"Okay, maybe not *illegal*, but … you know. Something that wouldn't be approved of if everyone knew about it. And that makes me wonder if maybe … it's something to do with Griffin Abilities."

"You think those were Gifted fae in the boxes?" Perry asks.

"I don't know." I pull one of his scrolls closer and write down the names N. Thornbough and J. Monkswood. "These are the two names I'm saw. I'm wary of going back inside the Guild if I don't have to. Could you search the Griffin List and see if these names are on it?"

Perry nods and takes the scroll from me, putting far more distance between himself and Gemma than necessary as he leans around her. He tucks the scroll into his bag. "This is messed up," he adds. "We're supposed to be the good guys, aren't we? Not the guys who put people into boxes and experiment on them."

"Well it isn't *all* of us," Gemma says, looking at me instead of Perry, despite the fact that he's the one she's talking to. "Only a handful of guardians."

"You know what I meant," he mutters, turning back to the books spread in front of him, one of which looks like a Guild manual with the words Security Spells on the front and someone else's name on a sticker. "Anyway, I think I'm getting closer to figuring this thing out."

"The detection spell?" I ask, referring to the magic placed on the homes of everyone close to me after I escaped the Guild. Perry told me he was sure there must be a way around it.

"Yeah, so this manual—that was conveniently left on a bench in the Guild dining room by a guard I was most definitely *not* distracting at the time—explains how to remove the spell. Unfortunately, it has to be done by the guardians who cast the detection spell in the first place, so that won't work. But I think I can put something on you to kind of … shield you from being detected."

"If that works, it'll be amazing."

"Mm, so I'm just figuring out … if …" He taps his stylus against the side of his head as he turns a page. "Where was that section about a—"

At the sound of footsteps moving through the overgrown weeds, my head snaps up. I quickly imagine myself invisible as someone walks around the crumbling piece of wall the alcove is attached to. "Oh, it's just you," Gemma says to Ned, placing a relieved hand on her chest.

I'm about to release my hold on the invisibility illusion when Ned frowns at Gemma, looks around, and says, "She's here, isn't she."

"Hey, Ned." I reappear and give him a friendly wave.

Instead of returning the greeting, Ned frowns as his eyes travel over my blue hair. He lowers his voice and says to Gemma, "I told you we shouldn't do this."

"Do what?" I ask, but I'm already remembering what Gemma said to me the day we painted the spare room with paint balloons. Ned didn't want to see me for some reason, and she told me he simply needed time to warm up to me. But perhaps it was more than that. Perhaps the real reason was that the Guild had already suspended me at that point.

In a flat voice, Ned says, "I just don't feel comfortable hanging out with criminals."

Well. From someone who doesn't usually say more than five words in an entire conversation, I wasn't expecting such blunt honesty. "I—I'm not a criminal, Ned. I haven't done anything wrong."

He meets my eyes for a second before looking away. "You're required by law to add your name to the Griffin List. If you didn't do that, then you broke the law."

"Ned …" Perry says.

Ned shakes his head and turns away. "I'm not doing this," he says, walking back the way he came.

"Ned, come on," Gemma calls.

"I'll go after him," Perry says, jumping to his feet and hurrying after Ned.

I comb my fingers through the blue wig, wondering if I

need to get out of here immediately. "Do you think … would he go back to the Guild and tell someone that I'm here right now?"

Gemma shakes her head. "I don't think so. He's a stickler for the rules, but I don't think he'd go that far. But we probably shouldn't let him know the next time we meet up with you."

I pull my knees up and wrap my arms around them. "I don't want you to have to lie to one of your friends because of me."

"Then I guess we'll just … omit information instead of directly lying."

"Isn't that kind of the same thing?"

"Not really. And you know how I feel about the Griffin List, so the only law you've broken is one that shouldn't exist."

"Yeah." I look around at the dappled afternoon light shifting across the overgrown ruins before returning my gaze to Gemma. "So, what's going on between you and Perry? You're acting really weird around each other."

"What?" Gemma laughs awkwardly. "No we're not."

"Gemma."

She blinks at me, then groans and covers her face. "Fine." She lowers her hands and plucks a leaf from the nearest vine. She twirls it between her fingers as her face, growing steadily pinker, remains firmly pointed toward her lap. "Remember when I got sick? From the dragon disease?"

"Yeah?"

"Well … Perry kind of … toldmehelovesme."

"Oh, finally!" I clap my hands together as Gemma's head flies up.

"You knew?" she demands.

"Of course I knew. No one who's spent any time around the two of you could possibly have missed it."

"I'm such an idiot." She drops the leaf and smacks both hands against her forehead.

"So what did you say to him?"

"I was kind of dying at the moment he said it," she mumbles, "so, uh, I didn't respond."

"Okay, and after you recovered?"

"Um … I still haven't said anything."

"Ah. Well, no wonder things are awkward."

"I know! But what was I supposed to say? I mean, it just came out of nowhere, and I have a crush on someone else, and Perry is … he's *Perry*. My friend. The guy who teases me, not the guy who tears down a magically locked door to give me a cure while telling me I can't die because he loves me."

I rest my chin on my knees. "That's quite heroic and romantic, actually." Thoughts of Chase crowd my mind along with a desperate longing to feel his arms around me, a desire so strong that I have no doubt he'd feel it if I were wearing the ring right now. Fortunately, I'm not. Some feelings probably shouldn't be shared yet. Feelings I haven't had time to properly examine.

"It is heroic and romantic," Gemma admits, "but I still don't really know how I feel about him. That's why I haven't said anything. I'm just … confused. And there are so many other important things to focus on. Assignments, and all the stuff you've been telling us about—the dragon disease and guardian hater groups and a terrifying prophecy that some ex-spy of Draven's wants to put into action. And now guardians are doing weird tests on unconscious fae. Next to all that, figuring out my love life seems completely trivial."

"I know," I say with a sigh. "I understand." I'm trying to sort out all the same problems while at the back of my mind the memory of that kiss in the golden river teases me, tempting me to look away from everything important I'm supposed to be focusing on. "But maybe you should say *something* to Perry. Just to let him know you're thinking things through rather than leaving him hanging after his declaration of undying love for you."

"Ugh, I know. You're right. It's all just so—" She cuts her words off as a faerie paths doorway opens nearby and Perry steps out. "And, um, then Olive was like, 'Are you kidding me? You can't even do a triple flip? Who the hell let you into fifth year?' And Lily started crying right there. You can imagine how impressed Olive was with *that*."

I shake my head, smiling in amusement at Gemma's abrupt change of subject. I wonder if the story's even true or if she made it up in desperation on the spot. Looking past her, I ask, "Did you talk to Ned?"

Perry nods as he resumes his spot on the ground on the other side of Gemma. "He says he understands that you're not a bad person but that rules exist for a reason and we're supposed to follow them, whether we agree with them or not." He spreads out a blank scroll and picks up a quill. "Anyway, it's impossible to argue with him, so after making sure he wasn't about to report your whereabouts to the Guild at this very moment, I left it at that."

"Are you sure he won't say anything?"

"He knows you're not the one responsible for Saskia's death and the disease spell, so he won't say anything because he obviously doesn't want you locked up for that. He does think your name should be on the Griffin List, though."

"Well, now that the entire Guild knows I'm Gifted," I say, a hint of bitterness creeping into my voice, "I'm certain my name has been added to the list."

"That's what I said. He still thinks you should have been the one to own up to it instead of waiting to be found out, but … whatever." Perry moves two open books next to each other and pulls the scroll closer. "Okay. Let's see if we can rustle up a shield charm specifically directed against this detection spell. There's a charm here for a full-body shield—" he leans forward and runs one finger down the page of the first textbook before moving to the one beside it "—and this manual details the exact words for the detection spell. So I think if we take the words from one and insert them into the other spell, we could make this work. I'm just not entirely sure *where* to put them in. And isn't there something else that's supposed to be added when you mix spells?"

I nudge Gemma's shoulder. "You're really good at charms, aren't you? You and Perry should be working on this together." She looks at me with wide eyes, probably trying to communicate that moving closer to Perry is the last thing she wants to do. I roll my eyes and mouth, *He won't bite.*

After sending a glare my way, Gemma shifts across the vines and twigs and picks up the security spell manual. "Okay, you don't need to include this whole spell. Just take this bit here—" she lowers the manual and points to something "—and put it in the shield charm over here, between these two words. And you're right. There's that extra incantation that needs to be woven in when you're blending two spells." She pulls another textbook closer.

I straighten my legs out and lean back as I pick through my memory of the bazillion spells I studied before the Guild allowed me to register as a fifth-year trainee. "Is this the one you're thinking of?" I ask Gemma before reciting the words that have come to mind.

"Yeah, that's the one," Gemma says, flipping through pages. "But we should probably check to make sure we—ah, here it is."

She and Perry finish writing out the words to their new spell within minutes. "Cool, let's test it," Perry says, quickly packing all his books and papers away.

"Now?" I ask.

"Do you have a better time in mind?" He stands and lifts his heavy bag into the air with a wave of his hand. It floats beside him.

"I guess not. Where do you want to test it?" Gemma and I climb to our feet, brushing leaves and dirt off our clothes.

"My house?" Perry suggests.

"What if it doesn't work? You'll have guardians rushing into your home to look for me."

"Then you'll just make yourself invisible and leave through

the faerie paths."

"And you'll be in trouble with the Guild."

"Why? I'll just say I had no idea you were coming to visit me. Actually, no. I'll tell them their silly detection spell is malfunctioning because if you're not there, then who set it off?"

Raising my eyebrows, I say, "You really will wind up in trouble if you tell Guild security guards that their spells are silly."

"Look, the spell's gonna work, so I don't know why we're discussing this. Gemma and I make a great team, so there's no way this shield charm is wrong." A flush appears in Gemma's cheeks once more, and Perry hastens to add, "A great *work* team. Obviously."

"Okay, let's try it."

"Brilliant. Come over here." Perry holds the scroll out in front of him and raises one hand just above my head. As he reads the words, I sense something moving in the air above me. I look up and find a cloud of glowing dust swirling around Perry's hand. As he reads the final word, the dust descends quickly upon me, coating every inch of my body. With a final flash, the glowing dust vanishes.

"Is it supposed to do that?" I ask.

"Don't know," Perry says with a shrug as he folds the paper and pushes it into a pocket. "Let's find out if it worked." He leans into the alcove and writes a doorway spell onto the cracked marble. "After you, ladies," he says as a dark space materializes. Gemma takes my hand and walks forward. I follow her, reaching back for Perry's hand. It doesn't escape my notice that Gemma put me between the two of them. I can't help but sigh as I walk into the darkness and try to empty my mind so I don't interfere with the destination Gemma's thinking of.

Light forms up ahead. The nothingness beneath my feet turns into solid ground as I walk into a tidy kitchen. I tense and drop Gemma's hand, looking around as if guardians might appear at any second. "Is an alarm supposed to go off?" I whisper.

"Not here," Gemma says. "That manual Perry stole said an alarm will go off in the security department at the Guild if the detection spell is breached."

"I should hide," I say immediately. "Just in case guardians are on their way here."

"I didn't *steal* the manual," Perry mutters. "Someone left it behind and I happened to pick it up. And what's the point in hiding now? They'll still have to bang on the door and wait for me to open it before they flash their permission scroll and barge in here."

I press my fingers to my temples. "Ugh, your parents are going to be so mad if guardians come trampling through here.

"My parents are often mad at me," Perry says, waving his floating bag toward the kitchen table. "It's like their default setting whenever I'm around."

"That's because *your* default setting is to push boundaries, break rules and annoy your mom," Gemma points out.

In the past, Perry probably would have laughed at a comment like that, but now he mutters something beneath his breath and walks out of the room.

Gemma looks at me with pleading eyes. "Help me!" she whispers. "I suck at this stuff. I just want everything to be normal again between us. I'd even take his constant teasing over this awkwardness."

"You could go after him right now and talk it out," I suggest. "I'll stay in here and get ready to vanish at the first sign of guardians."

Gemma looks terrified at the thought. "Maybe not right now," she squeaks.

"You guys coming?" Perry calls, as if his exit from the room was entirely normal and we were supposed to follow him. "Bring a snack."

"See?" Gemma says to me as she opens a cupboard and looks inside. "Now isn't a good time. I'll … talk to him later in the week."

"Right," I say, my voice filled with skepticism. Judging by the fact that she's never told Rick the Seer trainee that she has a gigantic crush on him, I don't expect this conversation with Perry to happen any time soon.

Gemma removes a bag of fizzing rainbow candies from the cupboard. I follow her into the next room where Perry is lounging in an armchair while tapping on an amber tablet. "No guardians yet," he says, placing the tablet on the arm of the chair and catching the rainbow candy Gemma tosses his way. "Told you the spell would work."

"Of course," I say as I take a seat on the couch opposite Perry. "Because the two of you are so great at making magic together."

Gemma looks utterly mortified at my words and Perry

chokes on the candy he just put in his mouth. As he leans forward, coughing and smacking his chest, I hide my smile behind my hand and give Gemma a wide-eyed look of innocence. She takes another rainbow candy out of the bag and throws it at me before seating herself in the chair furthest away from Perry.

After another half hour or so of idle conversation and no guardians showing up, Perry says, "Well, I think we can call this a success, Calla. Someone would *definitely* have shown up by now if they thought a dangerous Griffin Gifted murderer was hiding out here."

"Yeah. Wow, this is amazing," I say as the new reality of my situation hits me. "I could actually go home now if I wanted to." It's a strange thought. I've become used to Gaius's mountain home so quickly. "I mean, I probably won't in case it's the kind of charm that wears off quickly, and I wouldn't want to get my dad into any more trouble than he's already in. But at least I can visit my family now." I look at Gemma, then back at Perry. "Thank you. I'm so grateful to both of you."

Perry shrugs. "It was nothing." Despite his indifferent tone, though, he looks pretty pleased with himself.

"I should go before your parents get home," I say as I stand. "Wouldn't want to freak them out."

"You could just leave your wig on," Perry says. "I doubt they'd recognize you. They only know what the Guild told them when they sent guardians to put the spell on our house."

"I need to go too," Gemma says. "I'm supposed to be making dinner tonight."

Perry stands and fishes in his pocket for the folded up scroll.

"Here's the spell, Calla. Feel free to visit whenever you'd like to."

"Thanks." I take the paper from him. "Will I be able to perform the charm on myself?"

"I think so. There's nothing about this particular shield charm that says someone else has to cast it. Oh, one other thing," he adds. "I'm pretty sure the Guild is still monitoring our ambers, so I made another plan." He heads to the sideboard and opens a drawer. "These mirrors are brand new, so they should be safe." He removes two small circular mirrors, pushes the drawer shut with his hip, and hands one to me.

"Cool, thank you."

"Hey, how have you been staying in contact with your family? The Guild must be keeping an extra close watch on all their devices."

"We've been careful. You know those really old ambers? The ones that come in pairs and can only communicate with each other?"

"The ones that don't belong anywhere outside a museum?"

"Yes. My brother and I have been using those."

Perry nods. "Retro. Whatever works, hey."

"Yeah. Anyway, thanks for this." I slip the mirror and the spell into my jacket pocket. With a sigh, I add, "It's ridiculous how badly the Guild still wants to find me."

"Well, you know, you're supposedly a murderer and all that."

I shake my head. "I'll figure out a way for them to uncover the truth one day." One day when I'm not focused on rescuing Chase and stopping that veil-splitting vision from coming true.

"We can make that our next mission," Perry says. "Or," he corrects when he sees I'm about to protest, "you can wait until we graduate at the end of the year and get jobs as real guardians, and then I'll obtain official permission to re-open this case. Then you can't complain that I'll wind up in trouble for poking my nose where it doesn't belong."

I smile. "Sounds like a plan."

CHAPTER SEVEN

I'M CONFUSED TO SEE ANA IN THE KITCHEN WHEN I GET back to the mountain. "What?" she asks when I stop in the doorway with a puzzled expression.

"Nothing." I pull the blue wig off and watch her stirring something in a pot on the stove. "Weren't you telling us this morning how much you like your own space?"

"Yeah, so? I do like my own space. Doesn't mean I can't have dinner here when Gaius extends the invitation."

"Does he do that often?" I ask as I walk into the kitchen and lean against the long table.

Ana shrugs, keeping her back turned to me. "I guess."

"I suppose you guys are kind of like his family."

"Yeah. Kind of. Or we were until a stranger pushed her way

in," she adds under her breath, just loud enough for me to hear.

I decide that this animosity thing has gone far enough. I grip the back of a chair and ask, "Why don't you like me, Ana?"

She looks over her shoulder at me with a scowl. "What?"

"It's painfully clear that you don't like me. I'm just wondering why."

She does nothing but turn back to the pot and continue stirring.

"Is it something I did? Is it about Chase?" Crap, maybe she has feelings for him and she sees me as the one who butted in and ruined everything for her. Except … she's been unpleasant since the moment I first walked into Chase's tattoo shop.

"No, it's not about Chase," she mutters without looking around.

"Then what? Please just tell me what the problem is so I can do something about it. I'm not going anywhere, so you and I may as well sort this out."

"Fine." She bangs the lid of the pot down and swings around. "This team is all I've got, okay? They're not just Gaius's family, they're *my* family. I'm very protective of them, and I don't like outsiders. It's just been us for years now, and I thought it was going to be like that until … I don't know. Forever, I guess. And then you just barged in like you belonged here, and Chase didn't make a big deal of it at all, like he had no clue that maybe the rest of us might want a say in the matter. So … yeah. I didn't exactly feel warmly toward you."

"Okaaay," I say slowly. I guess I can see how that might

upset her. "But that doesn't explain why you didn't like me the first time we met. You didn't know me at all when I first walked into Wickedly Inked. I could have been a potential client, and you were downright rude."

She places her hands on her hips. "Yeah, well, I've never liked pretty girls."

That's the last thing I was expecting. "What?"

"The prettiest girls are usually the meanest." She runs her fingers delicately through her spiked hair. "I've been picked on by more than my fair share of beautiful girls, and these days I just don't have time for them."

I find myself slowly shaking my head. "I … don't … even know how to respond to that logic."

"It's fine," she says with a dismissive wave of her hand, moving further along the counter to where a pile of chopped vegetables sits beside an empty dish. "I've decided you're not that pretty after all. It was just the gold hair and eyes. Kinda dazzling and overwhelming at first."

"So … does that mean you've decided I'm not that *mean* after all?"

She flicks her hand and the vegetables jump into the dish. "Yeah."

"But you still don't like me."

She shrugs, performs another twirl in the air with her hand, and watches the dish of vegetables put itself into the oven. "I'm getting over that part."

"Really?" I sit down at the table and cross my arms. "It does *not* feel like it, I can tell you that."

"Jeez, just give me a bit of time, okay?"

"Fine. But for now, it would be great if you could keep your snide comments to yourself. I don't want to be the only one making an effort to be friendly."

She turns around, leans against the counter, and considers me. "I guess I could try that."

"Thanks," I say, eyeing her warily. I didn't expect her to agree to that. She continues watching me. After several uncomfortable moments, I ask, "Now what? Are you holding back all the comments you'd really like to fire my way?"

She tilts her head. "You completed your first mission last night, right?"

"Yeah," I say uncertainly. "The baron's daughter and the invitation."

She nods slowly. "Did anyone tell you about the tattoo tradition?"

"Tattoo tradition?"

"We each got a tattoo to commemorate our first completed mission after joining the team."

"Gaius has a tattoo? And Lumethon?"

The corner of her mouth curls up into what could almost pass for a smile. "Theirs are in more discreet locations. So, what do you say?" She walks to the table and wraps her inked fingers around the back of a chair. "Ready for that first tattoo? You're not properly one of the team until you do it."

"So … you're offering to tattoo me?"

"Uh huh," she says, nodding slowly as if I'm stupid.

I had thought my first tattoo would come from Chase. The phoenix he drew. But if this is a team tradition, I don't want to turn my nose up at it, and I can save the phoenix for Chase.

Unless … unless this is a trick and Ana's planning to tattoo some horrible, permanent image onto my body, like an ogre's skull. "Um …" I would ask Chase, but I don't have the ring on at the moment, and Ana will know exactly what I'm doing if I put it on right now. She'll know I don't trust her, and I can kiss goodbye to this fragile first step toward friendship she's offering me—if that's what this is.

"Well?" she asks. "I don't have all evening. Dinner will be ready in forty minutes."

"Okay," I say to her, deciding on a part of my body I can keep an eye on while she works.

"Awesome. What do you want?"

* * *

Later that night, with the lingering pain of my newly inked tattoos distracting me from sleep, I try to forget the worries plaguing my mind and instead calm myself with relaxation breathing techniques and the image of my peaceful lake.

It doesn't work. When I drift eventually into unconsciousness, my dreams are filled with smoke and black eyes and pointed teeth dripping blood over eerie, grinning lips. I'm locked in a cage again. A hand reaches through the bars and sharp fingernails scrape across my skin as I try to get away. The bars vanish. I'm on my back, my body incapacitated as smoke drifts closer. I use every ounce of strength trying to get my arms and legs to move, but an invisible force pins me down. The witch leans over me, her blonde hair falling in her black eyes and her ancient, blood-chilling laugh shattering the dream into a thousand pieces of glass that pierce my chest with sudden, sharp—

I gasp and cough as I wake and roll onto my side, pressing my hand against the pain in my chest. As the ache subsides and my heart approaches a normal pace, I push myself up. *Chase?* I call silently inside my head, because that's generally the first thing I do when I wake up, no matter what time it is. He doesn't answer.

I look across the room toward my enchanted windows. After unpacking most of my belongings and moving in here properly, I asked Gaius if I could paint my bedroom walls. It may be fun to live inside a mountain, but I missed not being able to see outside. In between training and trying to figure out how to rescue Chase, I spent hours reading parts of my art textbooks, teaching myself how to paint windows with landscapes that would reflect the time of day and the weather outside. Eventually, I succeeded. Now, as I look at the windows and wish I could open them to allow a refreshing breeze inside, I see stars twinkling like jewels in a dark blue sky. Morning has yet to arrive.

I kick the bedcovers away from me and climb out of bed. It isn't enough right now to simply see outside. I need to breathe in fresh air. After pulling a blanket off the bed and wrapping it around myself, I step into my boots and open my bedroom door. My boots lace themselves up as I head downstairs. An odd outfit, I'm sure, but I don't plan for anyone to see me at this early hour. I unlock the faerie door in the entrance hall and walk through it to the lake house. I'm confused for a moment by the light that greets me when I step into the living room, but of course; it's already morning here. The pattering of rain greets me as I move further into the house. I locate the front door key and walk outside onto the porch. I breathe in a long gulp of air, savoring the smell of wet earth and damp leaves. I sit with my back against the door, pull the blanket tighter around my shoulders, and run through every thought that was so determined to keep me awake.

Amon's still locked up at Velazar Prison. Angelica's on the loose and her whereabouts are unknown. Same for Zed, who disappeared after attempting to kill Victoria. I don't know if we should still be concerned about him and his group of guardian haters. Will Ryn's team manage to bring them down before they try something else against the Guild? And then there's the veil-tearing prophecy. That horrible vision my mother Saw so many years ago of witches spilling blood over a trident monument beneath a full moon and using a great bolt of lightning to tear the veil. The full moon is close—only two days after the Seelie Palace party—but the Monument to the First Mer King is still safe, and if we can rescue Chase during the party, then no one can force him to produce that lightning bolt of power. We'll be safe for another month while we try to find Angelica.

I lift my hands and look at the black patterns that now mark the tops of my fingers. They finished healing while I was sleeping. Only one is permanent—the flower I chose for the fourth finger on my right hand; a symbol of my first assignment—while the rest of the marks are temporary. I quite like them, though. Simple patterns formed from lines and dots. Perhaps I'll have them done permanently one—

Miss Goldilocks?

I smile to myself as Chase's voice fills me with warmth. *Hey.*

Still don't have much sense of time down here in this dark cell. Is it morning there?

I tilt my head back against the door. *Yes and no. It's not morning yet at the mountain, but it is at the lake house. Bad dreams woke me up. I'm sitting on the porch watching the rain now.*

What were you dreaming about?

Witches. Smoke. Blood.

The usual pleasant stuff, huh?

I laugh quietly. *Yeah.* I watch the heavy grey sky and the thousands of raindrops smacking the surface of the lake, and I begin to imagine a different scene. I start up high where the clouds are, using an imaginary brush to paint streaks of blue across the sky. Letting go of the fortress around my mind, I see the paint taking form, overlaying the real-world scene in front of my eyes. I finish the sky with varying shades of blue. I paint the lake with sparkling silver. I fill the ground with dabs of emerald green for the grass and magenta and saffron for the flowers. As my creation comes together, I remember when life was as simple as making art instead of worrying about villains and the possible end of our world. While I don't wish to have that life again, I miss the simplicity.

The Seelie Queen came to me tonight, Chase says, interrupting my work of art. In a blink, it's gone.

What?

The Seelie Queen. My grandmother. I've never seen her before. She was gone by the time I took over this court when I was

Draven. You know, I've lived in the magical world for over ten years now, but I still find it strange to associate the word 'grandmother' with someone who doesn't look any older than I am.

Did she speak to you? Did she … hurt you?

She didn't come close. She watched me for a long time. Eventually she said, 'Look at how powerless you are now.' Then she left.

How does she know you aren't some random halfling Angelica decided to bargain with? If she never met Draven face to face, then she doesn't know what he looked like.

There are others who've confirmed it for her. Some of her guards who were captured and marked during my reign. They were there when we were ambushed beside the mer monument. The night they took me. I suppose the queen wanted to confirm she was really getting the one and only Lord Draven before agreeing to free her traitorous daughter.

At least you still have the ring.

Yes. If she saw it, she thought nothing of it.

I wonder why she came to you now. I wonder if she's … Visions of all the terrible things the queen might have in store for Chase race through my mind. I try to stop my thoughts before he can hear them, but they're at the surface already. *What if we're too late? What if she's planning to do something to you now before the party, and we—Stop. No. I'm sorry.* I shake my head and press my hands against my forehead. *I'm sorry. I should be filling your head with positive thoughts, not negative ones. We'll make this work. We'll get you out of there. There is no alternative because you mean far too much to me and I can't consider a future without you.* I take a deep breath and force my thoughts to STOP before they can run any further. Before I can overwhelm Chase with just how much I feel for him. We can talk about all that once he's safely back home. We can speak about those final moments in the golden river. Those moments when I bared my heart to him beneath a shower of magic-infused droplets before a whirlpool plunged us into a cold reality where everything went wrong.

How? Chase asks after several moments of silence. *How did you manage to look past every horrific thing I've ever done and see the person I wish I could be?*

Or we could talk about it now instead. My heart squeezes and jumps a little faster, preparing to share its innermost thoughts. *Because you are that person now*, I tell him. *It isn't just a wish. Your past has made you what you are, and my heart chose that person. My heart chose all of you.*

Miss Goldilocks … His voice is a whisper in my mind. *My dreams should be filled with the horror of this place. The perpetual darkness, the echoing screams, the metallic scrape of chains on stone. But instead I dream of kissing you.*

A shiver runs down my arms, and I wish so badly to have him next to me that it hurts. I feel my face scrunch up as I force the ache away and choose positive thoughts instead. *I have to say, that sounds like the more pleasant option, as far as dreams go.*

It is, he says. *I keep reminding myself that they won't have to be dreams for much longer.*

Warmth spreads up my neck toward my face. *I like the sound of that.*

I sleepily restart my painting, making the sky orange this

time, before Chase says, *Has Gaius done anything more with regards to keeping the prophecy from taking place?*

The orange drifts away, mingling with the rain before disappearing. *Not much. Our focus is on getting you out of the Seelie Palace at the moment.*

While I'm grateful for that, you should probably be putting more energy into finding out what Angelica is up to. She won't be wasting her time now that she's free.

Probably not. A chill breeze lifts my hair. I huddle further down into the blanket. *I keep coming back to* why, *though. Why does she want the veil to come down? What would be the point in having no barrier between the magic and non-magic worlds? I still can't even imagine what that looks like. I know there are several places in the world where there are … openings of some kind. Where fae can cross over from our realm into theirs and back again. But this is different, right? If the veil is gone … will we be left with only one realm?*

I don't know what will happen, Chase says, *but I think I understand Angelica's motivation. Ignored since the day she was born, the youngest child of a queen with no time for anyone but her heir, Angelica has always wanted power and attention. She was told she was a waste of royal blood, and she's been trying to prove everyone wrong ever since. She began hunting down griffin discs while she was still a guardian trainee. She was the one who eventually found the chest containing Tharros Mizreth's power. I consumed that power in the end, and she pretended to be satisfied when I ruled over everything, but she wasn't. She would rather it have been her in the position of power than her son. Now, with her mother back on the Seelie throne, she has the opportunity to tear through to another world and rule that one instead. I believe that's her plan.*

I lean my head back against the door. *And Amon? Why would he want this to happen? He seemed so quiet and unassuming. If he had ambitions of power, why did he spend so many years as a librarian?*

Amon … That's a more difficult one to answer. I'm not sure I've figured it out yet. I started gathering notes on him after I realized what kind of visitors he was receiving at Velazar. That information is all at the mountain now, if you'd like to read through it. Look in my room in one of the desk drawers. You'll find a stack of papers tied together. My notes on both Amon and Angelica.

Thanks, I'll definitely—My thoughts screech to a halt as I feel the thud of footsteps moving through the house. I straighten.

Calla? Chase asks.

Hang on. I imagine myself as empty space as I climb quickly to my feet and move to one of the windows. Peeking through, I see a figure by the faerie door. A figure turning slightly, reaching into his pocket … I breathe a sigh of relief as I recognize him. *It's just Kobe*, I tell Chase as I let go of my illusion and open the door. "Kobe?"

He tenses as he spins around. "Oh, it's you, Calla." His shoulders relax.

"What are you doing here so early? Is something wrong?"

"Yes," he says gravely. "I just heard from our mer contact. The Monument to the First Mer King is gone."

CHAPTER EIGHT

"HOW THE HELL DID SOMEBODY STEAL THAT THING?" Darius asks. "It was protected by both magic and merpeople."

"No doubt it was stolen with magic too," Gaius mutters as he paces the living room. It's early Thursday morning and the rest of the team—several of whom appear to be half-asleep still—is now present after being alerted to the situation by Kobe.

"Angelica's obviously behind this," I say, crossing the room to the fireplace and holding my hands toward its warmth. "She's probably aiming for the next full moon."

"Which is a week and a half away," Gaius says, "giving us little time after rescuing Chase to stop her."

"We need to inform the Guild," Lumethon says. "An anonymous message. I can send it now."

"The Guild already knows," Kobe says. "My contact mentioned that several of their guardians were involved in protecting the statue."

"That makes sense," I say. "The Guild knows all about the prophecy now because of my mother. They also know that the reason she was abducted was because someone wanted to find out exactly what she Saw. She told them she believed it to be Amon, since he was the one who witnessed my mother and the other two Seer trainees when the visions struck them all those years ago. I don't know if they believe her about that, but at least they know that *someone* is trying to tear through the veil."

"Do we even need to do anything about this then?" Ana asks through another yawn. "There are hundreds, if not thousands, of guardians who can hunt down the person doing this—Angelica, obviously—and stop her. They don't need us to get involved. In fact, we probably shouldn't. We're criminals in the eyes of the Guild."

Darius points a skeptical look in her direction. "Do you really think those guardians are smart enough to figure out where Angelica has taken this statue?"

"Hey, guardians are not useless," I tell him. "Most of them are actually very good at what they do."

"Uh huh. Is that why we end up dumping law-breaking fae on their doorstep? Because *they're* the ones doing their job?"

"Don't exaggerate," Lumethon says. "We hardly ever need to do that."

"Our priority is still to rescue Chase," Gaius says, "given that the party is happening before the full moon. As Ana pointed out, we may not even need to get involved in this prophecy thing. We can reevaluate once we've got Chase back."

"Which will leave us only two days before the full moon," Kobe reminds him.

"Yes, but we've prepared for missions in far less time than that. It'll be fine."

"So … can we have breakfast now?" Ana asks. "Or do I need to return home to get some food before I go to work?"

"No, no, there's plenty of food here," Gaius says, waving everyone toward the door. "Let's cook something up."

As the rest of the team traipses out of the living room, Gaius motions for me to stay behind. "Next time you sneak into the Guild," he says, "or perhaps tomorrow night when you're at your brother's home, see if you can find out what the Guild knows about the monument. If they manage to locate its whereabouts, that would be useful for us to know, just in case we need to act."

"Yeah, sure."

"Oh, and I almost forgot," he adds brightly. "I found that faerie paths spell."

* * *

The spell that will allow me to follow Vi's father Kale through the faerie paths without touching him is a tongue twister of note. I understand now why they don't teach it in schools, since getting it wrong means potentially wandering the darkness of the faerie paths for days, weeks or even more. People have come out crazy on the other side, Gaius tells me, while others have never come out at all.

Wonderful. And now I have less than two days to perfect it.

After trying for almost three hours to memorize the spell perfectly, I decide it's time for a break. Remembering what Chase told me about his notes on Amon, I leave my room and walk to Chase's to find the stack of papers. After retrieving them from a drawer, I climb the stairs up to the greenhouse on the next level. It's raining at the lake house, so this giant room with its enchanted sunlight filtering through the enchanted glass ceiling is the next best option.

I find a rusted old chair and table on the far side of the greenhouse and transform one of the dirty, flat cushions Gaius likes to kneel on into something cleaner and puffier. Then I sit, raise my legs onto the table, and lean back to read about the guy who seems so intent on somehow joining our world with the human one.

According to Chase's notes—which I spend a few moments running my fingers across, memorizing his handwriting before reading the actual words—Amon grew up in the Mitallahn Desert. He was studious, enjoyed reading and learning, and his family was very wealthy. His father owned vast amounts of desert land and kept—*human* slaves? I bring the page closer to my face to make sure I'm deciphering Chase's handwriting properly. Yes, that definitely says 'human slaves.' Wow, I thought many centuries had passed since anyone did that. Amon lived an easy, comfortable life with his family in the desert until his abrupt, unplanned departure some time in his twenties. Beside this note, Chase has written 'WHY' followed by numerous question marks. I lower the page as I think.

Perhaps Amon was opposed to the idea of enslaving humans, which is why he ended up working at a Guild, an institution that protects them. But why did he then become a spy for Zell, an Unseelie Prince who didn't care about humans in the least?

I continue reading. The next few pages are filled with Amon's travels and activities before he began working at a Guild—before he ran out of money, essentially. He started out as a library assistant and advanced to the position of Head Librarian after three years. Chase mentions the unexplained death of the previous Head Librarian with the note, 'Suspicious.' Clearly no one in Creepy Hollow suspected Amon, though, since they promoted him and even sent him to other Guilds on occasion to share his knowledge and skills. One such work transfer took place at the Estra Guild. I check the date, count back to the year Mom must have been a first-year Seer trainee, and find that the years match. That must have been where Amon witnessed Mom Seeing her horrible vision.

The next pages contain answers based on Elizabeth's questioning of several Unseelie Court faeries. Presumably Chase didn't question them because they would have recognized him. They were able to tell Elizabeth the approximate year Amon began working for Prince Zell, and the kinds of information Amon passed on to him. Turns out Amon had some kind of helper spy within the Guild. A creeping vine of magical intelligence named Nigel. I squint at the page. "Seriously?" I murmur. "He named a *vine*?"

I move to the last page about Amon, where Chase's final note reads, 'Happy to follow others. Never shown much inclination for power. Why now?' Why now, indeed. Perhaps Amon simply got tired of never being at the top.

The next page begins Chase's notes on Angelica. I've just begun skimming through the details, most of which I know already, when Gaius enters the greenhouse. He walks over and hands me a piece of paper with the words to a short spell written on it. "Do me a favor, would you? Write these words somewhere on your body—anywhere, it doesn't matter—and let me know if you can hear me speaking while I'm in another room."

"Uh, sure." I find my stylus amongst the pages on the table and write the words on my arm. Gaius then takes his own stylus and adds a small mark next to the last word. "What's that for?" I ask.

"That tells the spell to listen for my voice as opposed to anyone else's." He writes the same spell the back of his hand, then asks me to add a mark at the end with my own stylus.

"Perfect." He hurries away. I stand and stretch my arms above my head, then lean down to touch my toes. I need to make use of the gym room downstairs. With my illusion training and phobia desensitization, I've been spending less time on physical training than I—

"Calla, can you hear me?"

I startle at the sound of Gaius's words in my ears. I was expecting to hear him in the same way I hear Chase—silent thoughts inside my own mind—but his words are somehow audible. "Yes, I can," I say out loud. "Can you hear me?"

"Yes. Wonderful. Okay, experiment over." He hurries back into the greenhouse and shows me how to remove the spell from my arm. "You can get back to work now."

I read the remaining notes—which detail just how ambitious Angelica's always been in her search for power—before returning my efforts to memorizing the faerie paths spell. I repeat it over and over as I walk in and out of the various parts of the mountain. The kitchen and the living room, the storage room full of old furniture, broken weapons and other bits and pieces, the meeting room downstairs, Gaius's laboratory upstairs.

After another few hours, as afternoon draws to a close, I walk into Gaius's study, hold the book behind my back, and recite it for him. "Very good," he says when I'm done. "Almost perfect. There was some hesitation here and there, which you should try to avoid, and a few words that you didn't pronounce correctly." He takes the book from me and points out the words I mispronounced. He enunciates them slowly, making me repeat each one until I've got them right.

"Have you used the spell before?" I ask.

"A handful of times, long ago. That's how I know the pronunciation."

"Did you ever get stuck inside the paths?"

"Fortunately not. And you won't either." He gives me an encouraging smile.

"Why do I have to memorize it? Since I'll be invisible, can't I simply read it quietly as I follow Vi's dad into the paths?"

"Hmm." Gaius looks thoughtful, as though he hadn't considered this before. "Yes, I suppose you could just read it. But if you're invisible, won't the book be invisible too? And if you're ever in a situation where you don't have the words with you, then it would, of course, be helpful if you've already memorized them."

"I suppose so."

"Either way," he says as he returns his attention to the scroll he was writing on when I entered, "it will be good for your young brain to practice a memory exercise."

I raise an eyebrow. "My young brain?"

He looks up again. "Sorry, that sounded a little patronizing, didn't it?"

"Just a little bit. But I guess my brain is a lot younger than yours. And most of the time you treat me like an adult, so … thanks for that. My parents and brother still think of me as a child most of the time, so it's refreshing to be treated differently."

Gaius raises both eyebrows. "Like a child? But your parents and brother know better than anyone the things you've been through since you were taken by Prince Marzell. And the burden of your Griffin Ability and having to start over again after every … what did you say your mother called them? Incidents?" I nod. "Given all that," Gaius continues, "I would have thought your family would understand that … well, you probably stopped being a child a long time ago."

I nod slowly. "Yeah. It has always felt a bit like that." But since there's no point in dwelling on the fact that I missed out on a normal childhood, I push my momentary sadness aside and get back to practicing the words of the spell.

Ana joins us for dinner again, and after we've eaten, Gaius reminds me that I've done no illusion training today. We work on distance first, pushing the limits of how far I can send out a projection. When Gaius and I tried it the first time, I was able to stand in the living room and project all the way up to the greenhouse and down to the gargoyle cave. Since then, I've managed to push a little further each time.

We leave the mountain and go to the lake house. The rain has ceased, but it's utterly dark now, with clouds blotting out the starlight. Gaius and Ana walk around the lake, using magic to light their way. Once they become tiny dots in the distance, I force my thoughts out toward them. Images of snowflakes falling and ice-skating humans twirling upon a frozen lake.

When I begin to feel drained, we head home. I assume I'm done for the night, but Gaius suggests I try simultaneous illusions again. I sit in the living room and try with every particle of my concentration to direct one imaginary picture at Gaius and another at Ana, but it's like splitting my mind in half. I just *can't* imagine two separate scenes at the same time. Either Gaius and Ana end up seeing the same thing, or they see something different, but the images are so unclear that neither of them can figure out what I'm trying to show them.

After an hour or so, I flop back against the armchair cushions as exhaustion consumes me. "Please can we stop now," I say, sounding a little breathless despite the fact that I haven't been moving around. I press one hand against my throbbing head.

"Yes, of course," Gaius says. "I apologize. I didn't realize this was sapping so much of your energy." I wave his words away, trying to tell him it's fine without the effort of using actual words. "You're doing well, though," he adds. "It's the first time you've managed to project two different images, even if they were fuzzy and unformed."

"Not sure it counts," I mumble with my eyes closed. Extensive use of my Griffin Ability normally leaves me feeling tired, but this is worse than usual. Probably because I spent so much brain power on complex spell memorization today.

"It counts," Gaius assures me. "And you'll continue to get better as you practice."

The thought of practicing more makes my head want to explode, so I say goodnight to Gaius and Ana. As I drag myself upstairs, I realize I haven't actually asked Ryn if I can visit tomorrow night. I drop onto my bed and pick up my ancient amber and stylus. I untidily scribble the words, *Can I join you guys tomorrow night when Vi's dad visits? Perry found a way to shield me from the detection spell the Guild placed on your home.*

My eyes slide shut and I'm almost asleep when the amber tingles in my hand. I open one eye and read Ryn's response: *Are you sure it's safe?*

We tested it at Perry's house. No guardians arrived.

That's great. Yeah, you can come. Stay over if you want.

I don't answer that last message. If everything goes according to plan, I'll be following Kale back to the Seelie Court instead of sleeping over at Ryn's house.

CHAPTER NINE

I REPEAT THE FAERIE PATHS SPELL ONCE MORE BEFORE LIFTING the knocker on Ryn's tree and tapping it a few times. A doorway melts into existence with Ryn standing on the other side. His gaze moves past me, examine the forest before returning to me. "Are you sure it's safe for you to cross this threshold?"

"I wouldn't risk getting you and your family into trouble, so yes. I am certain." I stood in front of a mirror back at the mountain just minutes ago, watching the cloud of glowing dust swirl above my head and then descend over my body.

Ryn steps back. "Come on in then."

I step inside and pause for a second, just in case I did something wrong with the shield charm. But if I have set the alarm off, we won't know until a guardian knocks on the door here, so I may as well relax for now. I lower my hood and walk through the hallway to the living room.

"What's that on your fingers?" Ryn asks as he follows me.

"Hmm? Oh. Tattoos." I almost add that it's a tradition—that these marks signify my first successfully completed mission—but Ryn's not supposed to know anything about what Chase's team gets up to. "I'm now friendly with more than one tattoo artist, so I decided it was time for some ink," I say instead. I raise my hands and display my fingers. "Do you like them?"

"I do, actually. They're pretty cool. Look at you, my badass, tattooed little sister." He swings his arm around my shoulders and gives me a sideways hug as we walk further into the living room where Vi is slowly pacing with a sleeping Victoria pressed against her chest.

"How's she doing?" I ask as Vi places Victoria in my arms and heads for the kitchen.

"Better, I think," she calls back to me through the open door. "She's barely cried at all since Farah gave her that berry concoction. Don't know if I should be worried about the *absence* of crying now …"

I look at Ryn and he shrugs and shakes his head. "She worries about everything now," he whispers.

"What do you want to drink?" Vi asks. "We've got honey apple and sparkling mirror berry."

"Honey apple, please." Ryn checks his amber as I sit on the couch and rest my arm on an overstuffed cushion. Filigree flies to the couch as an owl and shifts into squirrel form before crawling across my shoulders, jumping down beside me, and nestling against my side. "Hey, Fili," I whisper to him. "Are you not getting enough attention these days?" I scratch his furry head before returning my gaze to Victoria. I watch her frowning in her sleep, her forehead wrinkling as she unknowingly pulls the strangest expressions.

"Here you go," Vi says, returning to the room and placing a glass of layered green and gold juice on the low table before seating herself beside me. "I probably didn't need to give you a choice. You always pick honey apple."

"Hey, maybe one day I'll surprise you," I say with a smile.

"I'm so sorry," Ryn says, pocketing his amber. "I have to go back to work for a bit."

"What?" Vi sits forward. "But my dad will be here soon. I thought you made sure to get this evening off."

"I did, but this wasn't planned. Hopefully it'll be quick. It's …" He glances at me, then back at Vi. "I'll tell you about it when I get back." He leaves through a doorway, and Vi leans back against the couch, watching Victoria with a tired smile.

"So you really think she's getting better?" I ask.

"Well, she's a lot calmer now." She hesitates. "Very calm in fact."

Something in her tone makes me ask, "Too calm?"

Vi groans. "I don't know. It's like she's now limp and lethargic instead of squirmy and unhappy. I keep telling myself that at some point I have to stop worrying so much. It's just … I never thought I'd love anyone as much as I love Ryn—and it's not as though that's diminished. It's more like my heart has expanded and my priorities have shifted and now *everything* revolves around her." She nudges Victoria's little feet through her blanket. "Nothing has ever meant more to me. She's the focus, and I'm still trying to figure out how to slot all the other pieces of my life in around her."

"Well, at least you're not a workaholic anymore," I joke.

"Yeah, instant cure," she says with a laugh. Her expression slowly turns serious once more. "I still wonder about her color, though. We haven't seen any change in days. But then, some faeries have brown as their secondary color. It's rare, but perhaps it will be that way for her."

"Maybe," I say, thinking of Gemma's ebony and brunette locks. "And the birthmark?"

"Fading a little more every day." On the table beside my drink, her amber buzzes. She leans forward and reads the message. "Oh, brilliant," she groans, resting her head in her hands. "This evening just gets better and better."

"What's wrong?"

"My dad's not coming anymore."

My heart plummets as our precarious Seelie Court plan crumbles. "Why not?"

"Whatever he's been so busy with lately was supposed to come to an end today, but apparently it's taking longer than expected. He said he might be able to get here tomorrow morning."

"Oh, okay." So I may still get my chance. Good thing Ryn said I could stay over if I want to.

"Anyway, now we've got this wonderful dinner and only the two of us here to eat it." She picks up her stylus from the table, sits back against the cushions, and writes across the ambers surface. "May as well invite some other people."

Twenty minutes later, Vi's friends Flint and Raven arrive with their son Dash. "That was fast," Vi says as she lets them in.

"You mentioned food," Flint says, "so I didn't waste time."

Raven rolls her eyes. "You'd swear I never feed him. Oh, hey, Calla." She crosses the room and joins me on the couch with Dash, who must be nearing five months by now. "I thought you weren't able to come inside this house without setting off some kind of alarm at the Guild. Have they removed that spell now?"

"No, but a friend of mine came up with a counter spell. So here I am continuing to break the law."

"Oh, wonderful. Not the law-breaking, of course. Wonderful that you can visit your family while the Guild hopefully figures out who really caused that dragon disease mess."

"Yeah. Anyway, what does Dash think of Victoria?" I ask.

"Uh, he's smacked her in the face a few times," Raven says with a guilty look in Vi's direction. "But it was accidental, I promise. He just wanted to get a bit closer to her."

"I know," Vi says with a grin, watching both babies.

"Accidental, my ass," Flint comments as he walks across the room with an oversized baby bag trailing through the air behind him. "You know how boys are. Always teasing the girls they like."

Raven throws her head back and laughs. "A little bit early for that, isn't it?"

"Just a little," Vi says. "Give them a few more years before you start playing matchmaker, Flint."

"He's definitely fascinated by her, though," Raven says, allowing the little boy to bob up and down on her lap as he giggles and reaches for her face. "She was squirming in her sleep the other day and Dash stared at her for ages."

"That's because my little princess is so pretty," Vi says, chuckling as she leans down to take Victoria from me. "The boys can't help but stare at her."

"That must be it," Raven says.

Vi moves toward the stairs. "I'm going to put her to bed now. She's doing remarkably well staying asleep despite all our chatter, so hopefully she keeps sleeping while we have dinner."

"I need to get this little one down too," Raven says, standing and following Vi. "Could be a challenge. Can I put him in the study down here? I don't want him waking Victoria if he starts crying."

"Yes, that's fine," Vi says.

"Good luck," I call after Raven as she leaves the room with the baby bag floating behind her.

Flint and I move to the dining room and get the table ready for dinner. Filigree shifts into cat form and follows me around, rubbing himself against my legs every time I stand still. "I feel like I must be putting you in a difficult position," I say to Flint. "Being a guard at the Guild, you're probably fighting the urge to arrest me."

"Criminals are the only fae I get the urge to arrest, and you don't fit into that category." He places the last fork on the table and stands back. "I've never agreed with the Griffin List, so I fully understand why you didn't add your name to it, and I know you didn't kill your classmate and spread a deadly disease throughout the Guild."

I smile at him. "Thanks."

Vi comes back downstairs. When Raven eventually joins us, we begin dinner. We're about halfway through the meal when Ryn returns home. He sits at the table without fetching himself any food from the kitchen, shaking his head when Vi asks if she can dish up for him. "Bad news," he says. He focuses on me and adds, "Very bad news."

I lower my fork as my insides squirm with apprehension. "What? What's wrong?"

"Dad's … been arrested."

"What? The Guild only started their investigation two days ago."

Raven covers her mouth and Flint swears beneath his breath. "They uncovered the bribes," Ryn says. "They arrested him immediately while continuing the investigation. You know how strict they are about anything Griffin List-related. Too strict, in my opinion, but … that's the law."

I push my plate away and press the heels of my hands over my eyes. I shake my head. "This is all—"

"Stop," Ryn says. "Just … Yes, we know he did it for you, but it was still his choice. You never asked him to do anything."

"No, but I still have to live with knowing he's in prison because of me." I lower my hands. "I've sent my own father to prison."

No one responds—probably because they all know it's true. I stare at my plate, feeling sick at the thought of trying to finish the food sitting on it.

"He'll be held in the Guild's detainment area for now," Ryn says quietly.

"If the news gets out about why he was arrested, there could be anti-Griffin List protests again," Vi says. "Just like the last few times."

"Maybe," Ryn says. "Or maybe not. If everyone believes that the Gifted person Dad was protecting is the one responsible for the dragon disease that threatened so many lives, those fighting the list will probably be quiet."

I push my chair back, startling Filigree, who must have been sitting by my legs beneath the table. He becomes a sparrow and flits out of the room as I stand and begin pacing. My throat tightens as I push tears back. *Dad's in prison,* I say to Chase. *Mom's in prison. You're in prison—well, worse; more like a torture chamber. I know I'm supposed to be the positive one, but it is getting* really *hard.*

No answer comes. I assume he must be sleeping, but then I hear his voice. *None of this will last forever.*

I guess not, but that doesn't make me feel any better.

I know. Doesn't make me feel any better either.

I reach the edge of the room and turn again. I ball my fists and release a groan. *Why does everything have to go wrong at the same time?*

"Cal, please sit," Ryn says quietly. "Your pacing isn't helping."

The remainder of dinner is accompanied by stilted conversation, and when Dash starts crying, Raven says it's probably best if they head home. Once they're gone, I drop onto the couch and close my eyes. I try to believe that everything will eventually be okay. Ryn sinks against the cushions beside me and wraps one arm around my shoulders. "I won't try to convince you that life doesn't suck right now because I know it does. For multiple reasons. Do you want to stay here tonight?"

I lean my head against his shoulder and nod. "Yes. Thank you." I need to focus on the faerie paths spell and the fact that I may get the chance to use it tomorrow morning. I might not be able to help Mom and Dad, but I will damn well make sure I can help Chase.

That's the spirit, Chase says quietly in my mind.

A half-smile finds its way onto my lips. *Are my thoughts slipping out again?*

You're tired, he says. *You're always less guarded when you're tired.*

Vi calls Ryn to help her with something. He heads upstairs as I fetch blankets and pillows from the hallway cupboard. I used to sleep in the spare room upstairs when I stayed over here, but that room is Victoria's nursery now. After using the bathing room, I snuggle on the couch beneath the blankets and run through my plan for tomorrow. If Kale comes to visit—and he *has* to, since we have no other way to get to the Seelie Court—I'll hang around until he leaves. I don't know how long the journey to the palace will be, but I'll follow him the entire way. Once that's done, I'll consider whether to risk visiting Dad or not. Last week I wouldn't have hesitated, but I'm far more wary now that I've been spotted on a surveillance device.

I fall asleep with a string of images of the Guild and Dad and a palace I've only ever imagined running through my head.

* * *

At an undefined time of night, a heart-rending scream tears through the air. I wake with a jolt, my heart thrashing in my chest. The scream goes on and on, curdling my blood like nothing I've heard before. I throw myself off the couch and hurtle upstairs as icy terror closes its fist around my heart.

CHAPTER TEN

SHE DIED IN HER SLEEP. THE HEALERS SAY SHE DIDN'T FEEL any pain, but how can they know that if they don't even know what caused her death? I know, though … In the back of my mind, the truth of what happened to Victoria is there, crouched and lurking like a hideous, foul beast waiting for me to face it, to acknowledge it.

I refuse to look.

Hours after it happened, in the pale light of morning as family members and close friends begin to arrive, I'm still huddled behind the kitchen door, out of sight and trying to keep the horror at bay. I can still hear Violet's scream. It's a sound I'll never forget, not until the day I die. It raises the hair on my arms every time I think of it. The horrible scene keeps playing over and over in my head: Violet kneeling on the floor of the nursery, Ryn's terrified shouts—*Get help! Get help now!*—me rushing into their bedroom and searching for the nearest mirror, placing an emergency call and not caring who saw my face. Then stumbling downstairs into the kitchen and cloaking myself in the illusion of invisibility as healers rushed into the house. Ryn yelling at them in broken-hearted fury to get out once it became clear they could do nothing for Victoria.

Again, the scene plays through from beginning to end. Again and again and again.

Vi's been silent since the moment she stopped screaming. I've been biting down on my fists, allowing my tears to fall in silence, waiting for the sounds of mourning. Wailing, moaning, crying, *something*. But I've heard nothing.

The silence is worse.

The first voice I hear belongs to Zinnia, Ryn's mother. I hear Ryn as well, then, and the heart-shattering sound of his sobs. I bite down harder on my fists, relishing the pain as my teeth break the skin. Ryn goes quiet when Flint and Raven arrive. It's Raven's turn to cry. Then I hear Jamon, another close friend of Vi and Ryn's, and lastly Kale, Vi's dad. I'm supposed to … I should be … But I can't even contemplate trying to follow him through the faerie paths when he leaves. Not when all I can think of is that tiny, lifeless body upstairs.

No one else arrives. My father should be here too, of course, if the Guild hadn't arrested him last night. Stupid, hateful people. Don't they know what's happened? *Don't they care?* But perhaps it's better that he isn't here. He and Kale can barely stand to be in the same room these days, and the situation is probably tense enough with both Zinnia and Kale here already. Ryn's mother and Vi's father. They were together for a while after The Destruction—something I was too young to notice at the time—but it didn't last. And now three people who were friends for years, who were all grandparents to Victoria and should be helping each other through this time, can barely stand one another's presence.

The voices grow louder. Discussions of what could have happened to her and what to do now. I start to wish for the silence again because this—all this chatter—seems irreverent somehow. Clearly I'm not the only one who feels this way, because eventually I hear Ryn's voice, raised but as brittle as if it's about to crack. "Everybody. Get. Out."

The voices quiet, and Zinnia softly says, "Ryn …"

"Get out!" he yells. "I can't do this now!"

I hear murmurs and the shuffling of feet, and things are almost quiet once more when a voice I don't recognize says, "Uh, good morning, Mr. Larkenwood. I'm sorry to do this to you, but we've received word that your sister, a Guild fugitive, was seen here—"

"GET THE HELL OUT OF MY HOUSE!"

My body jerks in fright as something crashes against a wall. Something that splinters and rains onto the floor in a thousand tinkling pieces.

Then silence.

More silence.

Eventually I let go of the breath I didn't know I was holding. I force myself to continue breathing as I slowly push myself to my feet. My body aches from sitting in the same position for so long. I quietly step around the kitchen door and look into the living room. Ryn is sitting on the arm of a couch, staring at the floor.

"Ryn?" I say carefully as I take a few steps into the room.

Silence.

I keep walking, as if approaching a dangerous animal. When I reach his side, he continues staring at the floor and says, "I asked everyone to leave, Calla. That includes you."

"I know … I just …"

His hands clench suddenly into fists on his knees as he grinds out his next words. "I am trying *really* hard not to remember your part in all this."

"M-My part?" The beast circles closer. My chest constricts. I don't think I've ever felt this sick.

"We all know who did this, and we all know he'd still be behind bars if you hadn't let him go free."

His words are the final crushing blow that force me onto my knees in front of the beast. I'm staring head-on into its fathomless black eyes filled with nothing but the dark, horrible truth of what I've done. "Ryn, I'm—I'm so—" My words catch on the tears I'm trying to hold back. "I'm so, so—"

"GO!" he shouts. "I don't want to feel your guilt! I don't want to feel *anything*!"

I end up in the forest, crashing blindly through leaves and vines and over roots and fallen branches, as if I could possibly outrun the monster in my head. But it's there every step of the way, a shadow I'll never be rid of, a reminder for the rest of my days of the unspeakable grief I've caused.

PART II

CHAPTER ELEVEN

AN HOUR OR SO LATER, I'M CURLED IN A DARK CORNER OF the lake house living room, tears continuing to wet my cheeks like a tap that can't be turned off. I haven't been back into the mountain. I can't face explaining what's happened and having to tell everyone that our one chance of finding a way to the Seelie Court has slipped away. But Chase … it's easier to explain to him because I don't have to say a word. So as he wakes up in his dark cell and calls my name, I shrink further into my dark corner and let every agonizing thought pour out of my mind and into his.

I wish I could be there for you, he says when I'm done. *I wish I could hold you and kiss your hair and tell you that I understand the kind of pain you're in.*

I shake my head because as much as I wish for it too, I

know I don't deserve any comfort. *My brother has always done everything he can for me—even risked his life for me—and how have I repaid him? By getting his daughter killed. He will never, ever forgive me for this.*

He will. It might not be for a while, but one day he—

He won't. And he shouldn't. This isn't something I should ever be forgiven for.

Don't say that. You're not the one who did this.

I may as well have been!

Stop it. You can't hate yourself forever. That only leads to—

YOU STOP IT! I tug the ring off and fling it across the room, which makes me hate myself more. Chase is only trying to help, and now I've probably hurt him too. I wipe my tears away, stand up, and fetch the ring from the other side of the room. It sits on my palm for another few moments as I wrestle the beast that stinks of guilt into a cage in the furthest recesses of my mind. Then I return the ring to my pocket.

I stare blindly at the floorboards, my hands balled into fists at my sides as my brain begins to work again. Whether I should hate myself or not is debatable, but there's someone else I can definitely hate: Zed. He fooled me into thinking he'd done nothing to Victoria. *She's fine, I swear*, is what he said. But he was lying. He did something, performed some kind of spell or gave her a potion or cursed her. Something that slowly weakened her and caused her death. He must have had help, though. Zed hasn't done anything recently without the help of someone more powerful. First he went to Amon, because he knew that Draven's former right-hand man and spy would hate the Guild just as much as he does. But Amon was locked behind bars and couldn't help Zed directly, so he must have sent Zed to the witches. I know they were the ones who gave Zed the dragon disease spell, which means they probably helped him with whatever spell caused Victoria's slow death.

Zed is gone and I have no idea how to find him, but the witches … the witches did this magic, and I know exactly where they are. I might not be able to make Zed pay for what he's done, but I will make sure those witches regret the day they decided to help him.

* * *

I slip into the mountain and arm myself with various weapons before heading Underground. It's dangerous in these tunnels for a faerie who looks anything like a guardian, but I couldn't care less. In fact, I welcome the possible danger. *Try something*, I whisper in my mind to the pair of reptiscillan men who narrow their eyes at me as I pass. To the man in the hood with the glaring red eyes. *Just try something. I* dare *you to.* But I make it to the area of the tunnels where Wickedly Inked once was, where the witches now have their store, without incident. I walk boldly up to the entrance—

And find a dark, empty room.

My cry of frustration is almost a snarl. Clearly this isn't going to be as easy as I'd hoped, but I refuse to be put off. Someone must know where those two witches went. Someone must have seen or heard something. I begin my search of the wide, winding tunnels, walking into every bar, every shop, every area that doesn't look like it's a private residence. I discover nothing, and in several places I end up fighting my way out with the assistance of an illusion. In my current frame of mind, though, I don't particularly mind. Punching and kicking seem like excellent outlets for my pent-up pain.

Eventually I reach Club Deviant, the place owned by the drakoni man Ryn's team recently arrested. The drakoni man who knows Zed. He may not be around for me to question, but perhaps whoever's managing this place now has information I can use. The club is almost empty, given the fact that it's about midday. A smoky haze still hangs in the air, though. I doubt it ever lifts. I walk to the bar area and take a seat. The elf slouching against the counter behind the bar opens one sleepy eye and looks at me. "Mm?" he grunts.

"I'm here to see whoever's in charge."

"I doubt he wants to see you," the elf says, making an effort to open both eyes so he can trail them down over my body and back up. "Or perhaps he does. Come back tonight and you'll find out."

"I'm not coming back tonight. I'm looking for information about a guy named Zed, and I want it now."

The elf leans forward across the counter, close enough that I can see the glitter sparkling in his sleek black hair. "You want it now? Oh, well if you *want* it, then of course you can have it. That's the way the world works, right?"

"I don't have time for your sarcasm."

With lightning speed, his hand flashes forward and grabs my arm. "And I don't have time for your faerie entitlement. Think you can walk in here and demand whatever the hell you want? Think again, sweetheart. Nobody—and I mean *absolutely nobody*—in this club is going to be giving you *any* information about anything. And before I kick you out of here on your ass, I'll be teaching you a—"

"What's going on here?" a sultry voice asks. A feminine hand snakes around the elf's forearm. His grip on me loosens immediately. He sucks in a breath and tries to move backward, but the woman beside me—the woman I now recognize—yanks him closer. As he leans partway across the bar, gasping for breath, she whispers, "You don't want any trouble, do you, Lucimar?"

"No, no, of … of course not." He shakes his head and she releases him. He falls back, clutching at his throat and almost knocking over a row of brightly colored bottles on the back counter.

"You don't want to be here," the woman who is part siren tells him.

"I … I don't want to be here." He pushes himself away from the counter and staggers down a passage to the back rooms of the club.

The woman swivels on her seat to face me and crosses one leg over the other. Wearing a form-fitting dress, a long coat and heels, she's as glamorous today as every other time I've seen her. "Looking for trouble, Calla?"

"Elizabeth," I say evenly. "Or is it Scarlett? I never did ask which name I'm supposed to use."

She lifts one shoulder. "Doesn't matter. I answer to both these days."

"Well, Elizabeth." I stand. "Yes, I am looking for trouble, and so far I haven't been able to find it. So while I appreciate you interfering in a situation I was in complete control of, I need to keep searching."

She laughs as I turn away. "What an amusing way to pass the time. Perhaps I can join your search for trouble. Chase probably doesn't like the idea of you hunting for it on your own."

Chase doesn't know, I admit silently. "Not unless you can help me find a faerie named Zed or the witches who vanished from Underground sometime in the past week." And if she hasn't stopped by the mountain yet to offer her assistance with the plan to rescue Chase, then I doubt she'll want to help me. *I don't play well with others*, she once said to Chase.

"Witches?" Elizabeth repeats, pulling a glove onto her bare hand. "Since when are there witches around here? They know they're not welcome in this part of the world."

"I don't know," I say as I walk away. "I just need to find them."

"Hey," she calls after me. "Do you know their names?"

I stop and look back at her. "No."

She slides off her stool and sashays toward me. "Luckily for you and your trouble hunting, I might still be able to help you." I follow her out of the club to the dim tunnel where she asks me to tell her where I last saw the witches. When I mention that they had a store down here where they sold their wares, she looks pleased. "If they occupied that space for more than a few hours, they'll definitely have left traces of their magic." She tells me to meet her there in half an hour. She vanishes into the faerie paths, and I turn around to wander my way back through the tunnels. I could go straight to the shop through the paths, of course, but then I'd have to wait for Elizabeth. And waiting means I'd have to occupy my mind with something—something that would no doubt be swallowed up by the guilt-beast straining at the cage my mind has locked it in.

I focus intently on everything I see and everyone I pass as I stride along the tunnels. Anything to keep me from giving in to the guilt that wants to consume me. In the end, I arrive at the empty Underground room only a minute or two before Elizabeth. I've just finished casting an orb of light when I hear her footsteps outside. I send the light floating up to the ceiling as she stops in the doorway with a book tucked beneath her arm and looks around. "So empty," she murmurs. "I knew Chase moved out of here after you discovered his true identity. He mentioned a brief and unpleasant encounter with the new occupant of this space, but he forgot to mention it was a *witch.*"

"It was rather an unpleasant surprise to find those women here," I say, remembering the day I came to look for Chase.

Elizabeth steps into the room and walks around the edge, running her hand along the stone walls. Near the back of the room, beside a door that leads to a second, smaller room, she pauses, running her fingers through faint grooves I can barely see. "Yes," she whispers. "They definitely left traces of themselves here."

She turns back and moves to the center of the room, steps out of her high-heeled shoes, and sits on the floor. Despite her figure-hugging dress, she manages to appear graceful and elegant as she tucks her legs beneath her body. She places the book on the ground in front of her, removes a bejeweled ring from a compartment carved into the back pages, and turns to a specific page. Then she removes a mirror from her coat pocket.

"Should I sit?" I ask as she slowly enlarges the mirror, coaxing it to a size large enough to show one's head and shoulders.

"Yes. Sit there," she says, waving to the space on the other side of the book. She places the mirror beside it, removes one of her gloves, and puts the ring on. As I sit with my legs crossed beneath me, she begins reading from the book. The words don't sound like any faerie magic I've heard before. They sound … harsher somehow. As she speaks, she waves her arms in sweeping motions toward the walls. Something that looks like dust separates itself from the walls and floats on invisible currents. Streams of this dust curl and dance through the air before arcing down and plunging into the mirror. The mirror itself begins to cloud over. When Elizabeth finishes her spell, a billowing mistiness fills the glass surface.

"If the witches are anywhere near a mirror, they'll sense that they're being called," she says, pushing herself to her feet. "As curious as I am to know why you're so desperate to speak with them, I'll give you some privacy." She slips her shoes back on and walks out to the tunnel.

I pick up the mirror and balance it on my crossed legs. The misty surface slowly begins to clear, revealing moving shapes. One shape in particular—the shape of a person—grows larger and becomes still. The background comes into focus first. Endless sand dunes, and in the distance, a structure that looks like a pyramid with a second smaller pyramid sitting atop its apex. When eventually a woman appears, it isn't the one I expected. Not dark eyes and pointed teeth, but silver hair and a smile I want to tear off with my bare hands.

Angelica.

CHAPTER TWELVE

"OH, LOOK WHO'S CALLING," ANGELICA SAYS. "WE WONDERED if we might be hearing from you soon. Allow me to express my deepest condolences for your loss. Or hasn't that happened yet?"

She knows. She knows exactly what the witches did to Victoria. "I will tear you apart," I say between gritted teeth.

"Ah, so it has happened. And I believe you tried the tearing apart thing once already," she adds with amusement, "and gave up to run after my son instead. How did that work out for you?"

I hate her so much I can taste it. "Did I mention what a despicable waste of magic and breath you are?"

"I believe you might have."

"Whose life do you plan to trade next? You used your own

son to get yourself out of prison, so who will it be for Amon? Who are you going to exchange for him?"

"Amon can stay right where he is."

I shake my head. "You backstabbing bitch. He orchestrated this whole plan, and now that you're free, you're going to leave him to rot in prison?"

She cocks her head. "You should be glad. One less enemy running around for you to worry about."

"Remind me to thank you when I'm finished stabbing needles beneath my fingernails."

She laughs. "Oh, it is fun playing around with people again. One of the many advantages of being free."

"Not for long," I mutter.

She raises an eyebrow. "Do you plan to put me back in my cage … Calla?" She says my name as if it's a taunt. "I'd like to see you try."

"Come out of hiding and we can arrange that."

"I don't think so." She steps away, out of view, and it's a fair head that takes her place.

"You called?" the witch says, a lazy smile spreading across her lips. She's the younger of the witches I met Underground. The only one I've had any dealings with.

"What did you do?" I demand, my fingers shaking as I grip the mirror. "What spell did you give Zed? How could you *kill an innocent child like that*?"

"Zed?" she asks innocently.

"You know," I say, sarcasm dripping from my voice, "the one you gave the dragon disease spell to. The one who must have been *very* angry when he discovered you sold a cure to me."

She waves her hand. "We sorted that one out. He came to understand why I sold you that cure. Just business, of course."

"And then you helped him murder a child!" I yell. "You disgusting piece of filth! What spell did you give him to—"

"Don't shout at me about things you don't understand," the witch snaps. "You shouldn't be worrying about a child who's dead. Oh no, dear golden haired girl." Her voice turns low and threatening. "You should be worrying about yourself now."

"You can threaten me as much as you want, but it won't stop me from making you pay for what you've done."

That lazy smile creeps onto her face once more. "You're the only one who's going to be paying."

"What?"

"A little silver bird told me all about your special magic. Your *Griffin Ability*, as the Guild has named it."

A chill creeps up my spine. "So? You can keep dreaming if you think you're going to get your hands on my power."

She chuckles. "I don't need to dream. Not when I've already cast the spell that will let me take your power for myself."

A shudder runs through me. "You can't do that."

"Oh, but I can, and I have. The curse has already been performed."

I hate the quiver in my voice as I ask, "What—what do you mean?"

"It was quite complex. I'm rather proud of myself for

having completed it." She preens. "The effect is simple, though: the more you use your special ability, the weaker you'll become."

I shake my head. "That's ridiculous. All magic replenishes itself after use."

"Not anymore," she whispers, stepping closer to the mirror. "You and I are linked now, and I feel it every time you use that special power. Your core magic will grow weaker and weaker over time, and in that moment when the life finally vanishes forever from your body, the only magic that remains, the only magic I care about—your *Griffin Ability*—will flow out of your body and into mine."

I'm still shaking my head. "That isn't possible. You can't do that."

"You know nothing about what I can and cannot do with witch magic."

"I know that you can try to scare me with lies—which is what you're no doubt doing right now."

A predatory smile sits upon her lips. "You know I speak the truth. You've felt it already. You felt it the moment the curse was laid upon you."

An image of my nightmare flashes across my mind. Her black eyes, her scraping fingernails. "H-how?"

She tilts her head. "Don't you remember the blood you gave me?"

"But—but the vial broke. You can't have used my blood."

She laughs. "Oh, you silly girl. You think spilled blood can't be retrieved? I don't need it to be *clean*, if that's what you're thinking. The splinters of glass made no difference. On the contrary. They'll probably add a nice spike of pain to the effects of the curse, a needling headache whenever you use your magic."

I swallow. My hands are shaking properly now. How did this happen? How did this confrontation slip so quickly out of my control? It was supposed to be about Victoria—about finding out what the witch did to her and coming up with a way to *make everyone involved pay*—and now it's about … a curse placed on me?

With a wordless yell, I fling the mirror across the room. It shatters into hundreds of shards, sparkling in the enchanted light. Fear and hatred war within me. I choose the hate. I hate, hate, hate that witch more than I ever believed possible.

Elizabeth rushes into the room, looking around. "What happened? Why did you break my mirror?"

I ignore her as I push myself to my feet. I shout again, tilting my head back and baring my teeth at the ceiling. My orb of light cracks apart, sending flashes of light around the room before vanishing. In the ensuing darkness, I grit my teeth and speak. "I decided long ago that I never want to kill anyone, but … that witch … I want to kill her. *I want to kill her!* I will search every desert in the world if I have to, and then I'll make her *suffer* the way my family is suffering."

Elizabeth takes another step into the room and folds her arms over her chest. "That's … quite extreme."

"Someone is dead because of her magic."

"Oh, well of course you should kill her then." She waves her hand at the mess of shattered glass, causing it to sweep itself up into a neat little pile. "I'm sure it will make you feel much better, and you won't wind up regretting it in the least."

"Don't patronize me with your sarcasm," I spit. "You have no idea what I'm going through."

"No, but I know what Chase went through. I know what kind of person he turned into because he was bent on revenge, and I wouldn't recommend that path to anyone."

"This is different," I mutter.

With a snap of her fingers, the glass shards and empty frame vanish. "You want to hurt someone who first hurt you. It isn't different at all."

It is, I tell myself. I'm not trying to bring the whole world to its knees just to punish someone who hurt me. I simply want anyone who's caused me and my family any pain to pay for their crimes and to suffer as much as we've suffered. "Just … don't," I say to Elizabeth, pushing past her as I head for the door. "I don't want to hear what you have to say. Your opinion doesn't matter to me. Perhaps it would if you cared a little more about Chase than you pretend to, but your words are meaningless if—"

"Don't you dare question how much I care about him."

"You have a funny way of showing it," I say with a humorless laugh, looking over my shoulder at her. "You haven't even offered to help with the rescue plan."

Her eyes narrow. "What rescue plan?"

* * *

Elizabeth sweeps into Gaius's study where he's leaning over a drawing with Ana. "How could you not tell me?"

He looks up, startled. "Elizabeth—hi. And Calla! You're back!" He's about to address me further when Elizabeth smacks a fist down on his desk.

"Chase is in the clutches of the Seelie Court, and you didn't *tell me*?" she demands.

Gauis's eyes flick from me back to Elizabeth. He raises his hands in a placating gesture. "Look, you're not the easiest person to get hold of, and we've been preoccupied with the rescue plans. You've never wanted to be part of the team anyway, so what good would it have done to inform you?"

"This is *Chase* we're talking about! Of course I want to be part of any rescue plans you're putting together!"

Ana places her hands on her hips. "You can't just barge in here and—"

"I am part of this rescue mission. Don't you dare leave me out of anything."

"Well then," Gaius says. "I suppose that's settled. Now, Calla, I've been dying to know whether you were able to—"

"I didn't. I … couldn't. Something … Victoria …" I breathe deeply to hide the sob that rises up and shudders through my being. I push it down. Down, down, down into that hard core of hatred and guilt. "She died. During the night."

Silence. Elizabeth looks at the floor. Ana's face turns sympathetic. Then Gaius hurries around the desk, saying, "Oh, my dear, I am so sorry." He hugs me and rubs my back, and I wish he wouldn't because that makes it even harder not to cry. "Your poor brother," he murmurs. "And his wife. I can't … I just can't imagine."

They hate me. They'll never forgive me. "Can we … just … focus on getting Chase back?" My voice is weirdly high-pitched and shaky. I clear my throat.

"Yes, of course." Gaius pats my back one last time before returning to his desk. "Right then. We need a new plan for getting to the Seelie Court." He picks up a screwdriver and taps it against the drawing he was examining when we walked in here. "How about we find someone else who has an invitation to the princess's party, and Calla can follow him or her on the night of the event, then come back for the rest of us once she knows where she's going. Although …" He taps the screwdriver against his chin. "If it's a lengthy journey, there won't be time for that."

"We need to know the location before then," Ana says. "That would be cutting it way too close."

I move to the edge of the room, trying to breathe, trying to forget, trying to focus on anything other than Victoria and Ryn and Vi.

"You must know someone, Gaius," Elizabeth says as she sits in a chair in front of the desk and crosses one leg over the other. "You know everyone, don't you?"

"I'm flattered you think I'm so well connected, Elizabeth, but no. I do not know every royal, noble and high society fae invited to this event."

"Oh, what about Trian Hared, the musician?" Ana says. "Remember we got his dragon back for him when someone stole it? 'Cause he had no permit so he couldn't get the Guild involved? He definitely counts as a celebrity, so he might have been invited."

Gaius points the screwdriver at Ana. "He might have been." Then he frowns. "Now that I think about it, how would the Seelie Queen ever keep her palace's location such a secret if she holds events that so many fae who don't live there are invited to. I wonder if perhaps none of these people actually know where they're going. Perhaps guards are sent to guests' homes to accompany them to the palace."

"In which case guards are the only ones who know where it is," Elizabeth says. "That would make more sense in terms of security."

"Well, I'm going to speak to Trian anyway," Ana says, walking to the door. "Hopefully he remembers me."

"In the meantime," Gaius continues, "we now have a drawing of what my friend remembers of the dungeons beneath the Seelie Palace. I just need to ask Chase if he can see anything from his cell so we can attempt to figure out exactly where he's being kept." He looks at me.

"Oh, right." I feel in my back pocket for the telepathy ring and hand it to Gaius. I think of the way I shouted—silently—at Chase earlier, and the ache in my chest throbs more painfully. After a moment, Gaius removes the ring and leaves it on his desk. "No reply. Must be sleeping. I'll try again later. Calla, if you need to be with your family right now, I completely understand. There's nothing else for you to do here at the moment."

I nod and leave the room, but I don't head back to Creepy Hollow. I can't face Ryn, and I know I'm the last person he wants to see. I walk downstairs, intending to go to the gym to take out my feelings on a punching bag, but I find myself continuing further down. A punching bag won't help. A workout won't help. No exercise can distract my mind from the ache in my chest and the guilt-beast stalking my thoughts. The only true distraction is the one thing I never want to face: my phobia.

CHAPTER THIRTEEN

I FORGET ABOUT VICTORIA. I FORGET ABOUT THE SUPPOSED curse. I forget about the three very firm goals I now have: rescue Chase, stop Angelica from tearing down the veil, and make sure Zed and the witches pay for what they've done.

I stand in the stone room at the very bottom of the mountain's stairs and peer into the narrow slice of space in the corner. I see nothing but darkness. I step back, shake my arms, and jump up and down a few times as I prepare myself for this. I force myself to breathe in slowly as I close my eyes. Immediately, everything I've tried to block out threatens to come rushing back. I visualize myself rolling every worry and thought into a great big boulder. A boulder I then push to the edge of my thoughts where I can no longer focus on it.

Then I picture my lake. My calm and peaceful place. The

water nudges at grassy banks and a refreshing breeze skims across my skin. I breathe out slowly. I open my eyes and face the crevice in the wall. I step toward it, take another breath, embrace the rising panic, and run into the darkness. The tunnel is endless. In the utter darkness, I have to put my hands up to feel the walls—the walls that are pressing ever closer—so I don't trip. A squeal rises at the back of my throat, escaping in a rush of breath when I finally see light up ahead. I push myself faster … faster … and then I'm free.

I slow to a halt and look around in shock as I remember how to breathe. I'm standing in a cavernous space more vast than anything I ever imagined when I pictured this area. Like a wildlife park, it's divided into different sections. Part of it is a jungle, part of it is nothing more than rocks, and at intervals along the walls are openings to smaller caves. In the distance, I see a sandy desert patch, and off to one side, a collection of weatherworn towers and turrets. Movement fills the space. Gargoyles and dragons and—is that a nascryl? As my eyes dart around, I note the most important feature: not a single fence or enclosure in sight.

"Oooookay," I breathe, stepping back and flattening myself against the wall. At the sound of a snarling roar, I whip my head to the side. A dragon has noticed me. A dragon covered in glistening green and purple scales, and with jaws wide enough to encompass my entire body. The dragon takes one step toward me, its giant, clawed foot sending a shudder through the rocky ground. Silence descends upon the cave. Every creature looks my way. For a single heartbeat, nothing moves.

Then the dragon dives toward me, along with at least twenty other creatures.

I fling myself into the tunnel, which feels like safety now instead of a threat, and hurtle along it, expecting to feel claws ripping into me at any second. I reach the other side and catch myself against the stairway banister. I scramble up the first few stairs before turning around to watch the tunnel, waiting with heaving breaths for something to claw its way through.

Nothing happens. After several long moments, my shaky legs lower me onto the step. I swallow and close my eyes as adrenaline slowly works its way out of my system. Running into that cave without knowing what to expect probably wasn't the most sensible thing I've ever done, but it definitely tore my thoughts firmly away from the heartache of the past day.

Heartache that's slowly returning.

I drag myself back upstairs. I find that in the brief absence of my pain, I'm actually hungry. It's nearing dinner time, but I don't want to sit at a table with other people and have to make conversation. I rummage through the available food and find something small to eat, which I consume as I slowly walk upstairs to Gaius's greenhouse. I pluck some leaves from a herb I've seen my mother incorporate in many of her sleeping potions. Back in my room, I rub them across my pillow before climbing into bed. The scent alone won't be nearly as effective as taking a potion, but it's hopefully strong enough to send me into oblivion for a few hours. If I'm lucky, I'll be too drugged to have to confront my nightmares.

* * *

The herb's scent is gone by morning, but I don't remember my dreams, so it must have done its job. Leaning over to pick up the ancient piece of amber next to my bed, I'm filled with both dread and relief when I see a message on the amber's rough surface. Even if Ryn hates me, at least he hasn't stopped communicating. I rub my eyes and read the message—and find that it isn't from him.

The ceremony for Victoria will be held this evening beside the Infinity Falls. Zinnia

Great. Ryn definitely doesn't want to hear from me if he's given the amber to his mother. I roll out of bed and automatically call Chase's name before remembering I don't have the ring on. Silence permeates the upper levels of the mountain, so presumably Gaius is still in bed. I walk into his study and retrieve the ring from his desk. I speak Chase's name over and over as I use the bathing room and get dressed, but he must be sleeping.

As the hours of the day pass by and Victoria's ceremony grows closer, my mind is continually met by silence. "I still can't get hold of him," I tell Gaius, fighting the panic trying to wrap itself around my chest and squeeze all the air out of me. "What if … what if he's …"

"Leave the ring with me," Gaius says gently, patting my arm. "It's time for you to go, and you shouldn't be worrying about this while you're with your family."

"You know I'll worry about it any—"

"Don't." He takes my hand and pulls the ring off. "Put it

from your mind now. You can speak with Chase for as long as you want when you get back later."

If he's still alive, I add silently.

I swallow the terrifying thought as I walk downstairs. In less than a minute, I'm through the lake house, through the faerie paths, and walking into the late afternoon sun near the Neverending River. I squint up at the sky, wondering how the sun could dare show her face at a time as sad as this. It should be raining. All of nature should be pouring out its tears, mourning this tragedy.

I move closer to the group of fae gathered on the banks of the river but remain out of sight amongst the trees. I don't want to catch the attention of any of the Guild members who are here. I could use my Griffin Ability to hide myself and get closer to the proceedings, but the witch's words ring clearly in my mind: *The more you use your special ability, the weaker you'll become.* I don't know how much strength I'll need for the Seelie Palace mission when the time comes to rescue Chase, but I don't want to spend any of that strength if I don't have to. I tell myself that this is one of my reasons for not approaching Ryn—along with the possibility of accidentally revealing myself and getting him into trouble—but I know the only real reason is fear. I'm terrified of what he might say to me. Terrified that his words might confirm just how much he blames me for his child's death.

I can't see his or Violet's faces as they place the fully wrapped bundle into a small canoe. All I hear are sobs and sniffles from the gathered fae as they place the canoe in the water and watch it float magically upstream toward the Infinity

Falls. Natesa, Vi's reptiscillan friend, clings to her husband and whispers how unfair it is that something so awful could happen to such wonderful people. Nearby, Zinnia murmurs to someone else that by the time she got to the house yesterday, the baby didn't even look like Victoria anymore. That there was something grotesque and unnatural about the little body left behind in the wake of whatever magic took her. I move further away into the trees, my mind conjuring up horrifying images that will plague my nightmares later.

No one hangs around too long after the ceremony is over. They're all heading to Zinnia's house, based on the murmurs I've heard. I could go there too. I could keep myself concealed until it's safe to speak to Ryn and Vi. But I know I'll be too afraid to say a single word to them.

I flinch as a light pressure touches my shoulder, but, twisting my head to the side, I find nothing more threatening than a small, furry shape sitting there. "Hey, Filigree," I whisper. "What are you doing here?" I lift his little mouse form off my shoulder and place him on the nearest tree branch. "I'm going home now—my home, not yours—so you need to get back to Vi." He shakes his furry little head and takes a flying leap back onto my shoulder. "What's wrong? Is it …" I swallow. "Is it too sad there?" He nestles against my neck. "Look, I don't know what to say. I can't take you back with me. You don't belong to me, you—Ow!" His little paws dig into my earlobe. "So … you want to come with me? Is that it?" He doesn't move. "Okay, fine. I—I'll just have to send Ryn a message to tell him where you are." Filigree, of course, says nothing to that.

I arrive back at the mountain with renewed determination to find the witches. Or Zed. Perhaps I can risk an illusion strong enough and terrifying enough to force his location out of someone working at Club Deviant. Or I can go to Elizabeth and ask if she knows of a spell that can locate the witches. I don't care that it's dangerous to go after them. If it's something that might make up, even in some small part, for what I've done to my brother, I'll risk it.

With Filigree still on my shoulder, I look into Gaius's study. It's empty, though, and I don't see the telepathy ring on his desk. I walk down the passage. As I pass my bedroom, a low hum reaches my ears. I turn back and look around the door with a frown. It can't be the amber. It's so old it doesn't even—Oh, the mirror. Of course.

I hurry into my room and grab the small mirror Perry gave me a few days ago. Filigree leaps off my shoulder and onto the bed as I touch the mirror's surface and watch Perry's grinning face swim into focus. He waggles his eyebrows and says, "Want to know what the secret inner circle of the Guild Council is up to? Get your butt over to the Guild right now, and you can see for yourself."

CHAPTER FOURTEEN

I'M NOT THRILLED ABOUT SNEAKING INTO THE GUILD, BUT Perry's discovery sounds too important to miss. I grab a shoulder-length wig of black and pink hair from the costume closet and make my way to the Guild's library as quickly as I can, aware of every second of Griffin Ability use. I release my illusion the moment I reach the back corner of the library where Perry is waiting.

"I'm so sorry" are the first whispered words out of his mouth. "I am so, so sorry. I didn't know about your niece until just now when Gemma told me. I shouldn't have called you. If you need to be with family right now or—"

"No. I …" I might need my family, but they certainly don't want me around at the moment. "It's fine. I don't … I don't really want to think about it, so the distraction will be good."

"Are you sure?"

"Yes. So what was the urgency all about? What do you want me to see?"

"Oh, right. Come on." He motions for me to follow him to a door I've never noticed at the back of the library. "I got stuck with storeroom reorganization duty on Friday afternoon because of some homework I didn't finish." He opens the door and ushers me into a dark room, pulling the door shut before I can get a good look at what's inside. He snaps his fingers and raises a single flame above his palm. In the flickering light, I see desks and tables piled neatly on top of each other and shelf after shelf filled with boxes of cards.

"You organized all this?" I ask.

"Yeah. And I wasn't allowed to use magic. Oh, and don't make a noise on the floor, okay? Tiptoe." He leads me between the desks toward the back of the room. "Anyway," he continues in a whisper. "I was looking for my sound drops this afternoon and couldn't find them. I last used them while I was tidying in here, so I came to look for them, and …" He crouches down. "Do you hear that?"

I lower myself to the floor and listen. "Voices? From beneath us?"

"Yes," he whispers. "And if you look behind you and to the right, you'll see none other than a hole that leads straight into the room below."

I twist around and see a beam of light shining up from a roughly circular hole. I crawl toward it and lower my face until it's almost touching the floor. "No way," I whisper, looking down at the group of guardians gathered in a small but comfortably furnished room below. I count ten sitting in a circle around a coffee table, but I recognize only three of them: Head Councilor Bouchard from the French Guild, Councilor Merrydale, and Olive, my ex-mentor. The other seven guardians—assuming they're guardians; some of them have covered their wrists so I can't see if they have guardian markings—must be from other Guilds.

"... get it up and running, we won't have to worry about incidents like this again," Councilor Merrydale says to the group.

"I should hope not," Head Councilor Bouchard says in that precise, accented tone I remember from when I was unfortunate enough to meet him on my first official day here. "It is distressing to think you may have an invisible Gifted fae running around this Guild unseen. Who knows what such a person could get up to."

Crap, they're talking about me.

"You said you didn't see this person's face?" asks a woman with hair shaved so close to her scalp I can barely make out the two different colors.

"Unfortunately not. I reviewed the recording after I failed to find the intruder. The person was definitely female, but I was unable to see her face."

"What if it wasn't an intruder?" the woman suggests. "It may be that one of your guardians here is an unregistered Gifted person."

"That's also a possibility," Councilor Merrydale says. "In

fact, we probably have more than one unregistered Gifted faerie working here, as do the rest of you at your various Guilds."

"It's disgraceful to think of," someone else says, shaking his head. "Guardians working for the law while breaking it every day. You'd think they wouldn't be able to live with themselves while lying to us like that."

"Well, they do," Olive says with a bored sigh. "Hence the work that's going on downstairs." She leans back in her armchair and crosses one leg over the other. "Can we move on to the next item, Head Councilor?"

Her disrespect stuns me, but Head Councilor Bouchard doesn't seem to notice. He consults a scroll in his hand. "Hmm. Well, there is, of course, the Lord Draven matter, but as was the case with our last few meetings, the Seelie Queen has shared no new information."

A jolt of surprise shoots through me. These must be the Guild members Angelica negotiated with.

"Probably a good thing," the shaved woman mutters with a shiver. "As far as I'm concerned, he can stay imprisoned beneath the palace floors for the rest of his days."

Nods of agreement come from the rest of the group, and a man who hasn't spoken yet says, "I still can't believe he—"

"It's probably best not to dwell on that item," Olive interrupts, "given that we have nothing new to discuss."

"Yes, probably best," Councilor Bouchard agrees. "Then the final item, as always, is this week's surplus Seer visions."

"I've collected them all," Councilor Merrydale says, leaning forward and picking up a large stack of papers. "Including the ones Meira forgot to bring last week." Across the table, the woman with the shaved head nods.

"Have they been checked?" Councilor Bouchard asks. "Anything still to come?"

"No, they've all expired. I checked each one."

"Well, you know what to do with them," Councilor Bouchard says with a dismissive wave of his hand.

Councilor Merrydale stands and moves to the fireplace, and I watch in horror as he tosses the dozens of Seer visions into the flames. As Head Councilor Bouchard calls the meeting to an end, I pull my head away from the peephole. "I've seen enough," I whisper to Perry. We tiptoe our way out of the storeroom and back into the library.

"Did he *burn* those visions?" Perry asks me immediately. "I know there was a fireplace in there, but I don't want to assume—"

"Yeah. He did. Did you, um, hear everything?" *Did you hear about Lord Draven*, is what I really want to ask.

"Bits here and there," he says, "but not everything. I heard that last bit about the 'surplus Seer visions.'" He makes quotes in the air with his fingers. "Can you believe that? They actually throw visions away. Was that the stack of papers on the table?" I nod and he lets out a low whistle. "That's a lot. I can't believe they know about that many things going wrong that they just don't bother to fix."

"Yeah." I bite my lip and look around, keeping my eyes peeled for surveillance bugs. "If Zed knew about this, then I can see why he might not be so enamored with the Guild system."

"Zed's the guy responsible for the dragon disease?"

"Yes. He was trying to tell to me that the Guild system is messed up and that they don't help nearly as many people as they could. He wanted to know how they decide who's worth saving and who isn't."

"It's probably random," Perry says in disgust. "I doubt they put any more thought into it than that."

"Look, I agree that this is wrong, but it in no way excuses the things Zed did. He is a despicable, worthless—"

"What? No, of course not. I'm not excusing anything." Perry looks horrified. "Killing every guardian is *not* the way to go about this. The Guild should be training *more* guardians. Let non-faeries in. Or send all those extra visions to the Reptiscillan Protectors Institute. Don't ignore and then *burn* them."

I nod, staring at the floor as my mind ticks through possible solutions. "I wonder where they keep those surplus visions before bringing them to their secret meeting each week."

"Why? What are you thinking?"

"It's not a long-term solution to the Guild's problem, but … well, I have a friend—a group of friends—who could make sure those visions are seen to instead of wasted. We'd have to find the visions first and copy them."

"I'll see what I can find out. I might even have to talk to … ugh. Pretty boy what's-his-name."

"I assume you're referring to Rick," I say. The Seer trainee Gemma has a crush on, which Perry is all too aware of.

"Mm hmm," Perry says, looking as if he has a bad taste in his mouth.

"Well, I should go before I get caught. Thank you so much for showing me that. I'm not sure I would have believed it if I hadn't seen it for myself."

"I know. Oh, wait. I have to tell you some other stuff."

I peer around the bookshelf, then pull my head back and shuffle further into the shadows. "What is it?"

"Those two names you gave me to look up are both on the Griffin List. So whatever they're doing downstairs with those people in boxes is related to Griffin Abilities."

I nod. "The conversation I just overheard confirmed that. I think they're trying to come up with a way to test for Griffin Abilities. I assume it would be mandatory for everyone to be tested."

"That would suck big time."

"Now that I think about it," I say, "I wonder why they didn't come up with a test ages ago. They know they can't trust everyone to be honest enough to register themselves or their children."

"They've probably been trying for a long time and just haven't succeeded yet."

"Probably." I look around the bookshelf again. "Okay, so I need to—"

"Wait, just one more thing." He grasps my shoulders as if to keep me from running away. "I know you told me to stop snooping around Olive's things after you found out who really framed you for killing Saskia, and I did—sort of—but then I came across something yesterday. Remember I told you we found scrolls with non-Guild seals in Olive's office?" Without waiting for my answer, he rushes on. "I found out who the seal belongs to. None other than—" he smacks my shoulders as if beating out a drum roll "—the Seelie Queen."

"The—what? Are you sure?"

"Yes. I saw the seal in a textbook the other day."

"Olive? My bad-tempered ex-mentor is receiving correspondence directly from the Seelie Queen?"

"Looks like it."

"Maybe she was delivering the scrolls to someone else. Someone like Head Councilor Bouchard."

"Why would these scrolls need to go through Olive then? Why not directly to Councilor Bouchard?"

"That's … a good question." I place my hands on my hips as I consider it.

"And another thing that's weird about Olive is that she periodically disappears for half a day or so at a time."

"How do you know this?"

"My mentor's office is nearby. I notice stuff."

"Okay, but that might have absolutely nothing to do with the scrolls from the Seelie Queen." On the other hand, I add silently to myself, it might have *everything* to do with those scrolls. I don't want to get too excited yet, but it's definitely worth following Olive around for a day or two to see if maybe, just *maybe*, the place she disappears to is the Seelie Court.

* * *

Invisibility gets me safely out of the Guild without incident. I closely examine my level of fatigue when I arrive back at the mountain, but I don't feel any more tired than usual. Could it be possible the witch was lying about her curse? I can't forget that dream, though. The dream that ended with very real pain stabbing into my chest when I woke up. Perhaps I just didn't use my Griffin Ability enough tonight to feel the curse's effects.

Warm light illuminates the living room doorway along with the flickering shadows of a dancing fire. I walk into the room and find Gaius in an armchair. "Hey," I say. "I might possibly have a way to get to the Seelie Court. I'm not certain, but I'll investigate further tomorrow."

He looks up at me. "Oh, that's good. Excellent. Well done." Though he smiles, his tone lacks its usual enthusiasm.

"What's wrong? Is everything … Have you spoken to Chase yet?" I walk toward him and hold my hand out for the ring. It's been far, *far* too long since I heard his voice.

"Calla," Gaius says slowly, removing the ring from his pinkie finger and placing it on my palm. "I haven't been able to get hold of him. It's been over a day now and he hasn't responded. We don't know what that means, and we can't assume the worst, but we need to be prepared for … well, for anything."

A chill settles in my bones as I allow myself a glimpse of a dark future in which there is no Victoria, no brother who loves me unconditionally, and now no Chase. I shy away from the image with a shudder as I wrap my arms tightly around my chest and press my lips together. I don't think I can speak, so I simply nod as Gaius reaches up and squeezes my arm. Trying to comfort me, no doubt, but when I look into his eyes, all I see is the same hopelessness I feel.

CHAPTER FIFTEEN

YOU'RE NOT DEAD, I WHISPER SILENTLY THE NEXT MORNING as I get dressed. *You're not dead, you're not dead, and I* will *find you.* Despite the fact that I get no response, I tell myself that somehow Chase can hear me.

The witch's warning echoes at the back of my mind as I walk into the Guild under the cover of invisibility. I know it will weaken me to conceal myself, but this is too important an opportunity to pass up. With the Seelie Palace party only four days away now, this could be our last chance to find a way there. Wearing a brunette and orange wig and a tan jacket borrowed from Lumethon in place of the black one I always wear, I climb the stairs to Olive's office. Filigree's small shape is a comforting warmth in my pocket. I considered telling him to go back to my room when I found him hiding in the jacket earlier, but facing a full day of camping out in enemy territory felt easier with an accomplice at my side—even an accomplice as small as mouse-shaped Filigree.

Olive's office is near the end of a corridor where a group of chairs and a table form a small waiting area. I walk past her door, pick up a random textbook from the table, and settle into one of the chairs. As I lift the textbook to conceal my face, I pull my illusion back. My imagination is once again hidden behind a mental fortress, and I'm completely visible now. My heart pounds at the thought of my vulnerability. *Anyone* can see me sitting here! But I have to conserve my strength. I need all of it for the Seelie Court mission, and I have no idea when the witch's curse will begin to take a toll on me.

I hear footsteps and Olive's voice. I swallow and tighten my fingers around the open textbook. She probably won't notice me sitting here, but if she happens to see my face, she'll recognize me. I watch her feet beneath the bottom edge of the textbook. She continues past her office, moving toward me, but turns into another office before reaching the end of the corridor. I force myself to breathe out and relax my grip on the book. I'm not going to get caught, I tell myself. And even if I am caught, I can fight my way out of here. I've done it once before, so surely I can do it again.

For the next hour or so, I observe Olive coming and going from her office. For one terrifying moment, I'm certain I'm about to be discovered when a mentor I only vaguely recognize stops in front of me and asks why I've been sitting here for so long. I try to imagine Gemma's face instead of my own before lowering my book and saying that my mentor tasked me with memorizing two full chapters before she quizzes me about them. Fortunately, the mentor standing in front of me seems to accept this. After wishing me luck, she continues on her way. Before raising my book once more, I see Olive closing her office door and walking away with a trainee at her side. This is my chance.

I make sure no one is watching before imagining myself as invisible once again. I walk to Olive's door, test the handle, and find it unlocked. Glancing around to make sure I'm truly alone, I open the door and slip inside. Without wasting a second, I move to the desk. Olive might be doing training now, but who knows when she'll lose her temper, give up on her trainee, and come back upstairs. I search across the desk's untidy surface, looking for these supposed scrolls with the Seelie Queen's seal. Finding nothing, I move to the drawers. I open and close them, riffling through the jumbled contents. Nothing. Next, I move to the filing cabinet. I've just slid the top drawer closed when the door handle turns.

I rush to conceal myself, holding my breath as Olive pushes her door open and enters the office. She walks to her desk, frowns as she looks down at it, then grabs the stylus sticking out of a dirty mug before turning away. As the door bangs shut, I slowly release my breath.

I search the rest of Olive's office—with Filigree's assistance, though I'm not sure he understands me when I tell him what I'm looking for—and find nothing. I wonder if Perry left signs of his search here. Signs that would raise Olive's suspicion and cause her to hide the scrolls elsewhere.

I return to the waiting area, picking a different chair and a different textbook this time, and keep watch for Olive. By the end of the day, the only remotely interesting thing she's done is stand in the corridor and shout at Ling—her supposedly perfect fifth-year trainee—for failing to place in the top five for the knife throwing competition that I gather, based on her words, was held on Saturday. She adds that both she and Ling will be spending all night in the training center perfecting her technique and that she couldn't care less about the fact that Ling's parents will have to eat dinner without her.

I'm guessing this means Olive's not going anywhere exciting tonight, so as other mentors lock up their offices and head downstairs, I join the stream of people leaving the Guild. My restlessness rises a level as I think of my complete waste of a day. A day I could have spent searching for Zed or the witches. A day I could have spent sneaking into the French Guild, tying up Head Councilor Bouchard, and forcing a truth potion down his throat so he'll tell me everything he knows about the Seelie Court.

Gaius looks thoroughly alarmed at my suggestion when I lay it out for him that night. "No," he says. "Absolutely not. Capturing the Head Councilor is out of the question."

"We're running out of time, Gaius! If anyone at the Guild knows anything about the Seelie Court, it would be him, right? He could be our only option."

Gaius cautiously pats my arm as if soothing a wild creature. "Following your old mentor seems far more sensible, Calla. Give it one more day, okay? Then we'll reassess."

So I give it one more day.

I can't hang out in the waiting area any longer without

raising attention, and I don't want to project an illusion for hours at a time, so I slip into Olive's office while she's busy speaking with a mentor in the corridor and hide beneath her desk. I stay there for the remainder of the day, observing her. I conceal myself when I have to, but mostly I rely on the solid, old desk to hide me. I was worried she might kick me when sitting at the desk, but she piles so many things on her chair throughout the day, that she doesn't actually sit on it all that often.

As the afternoon draws to a close and my body begins to ache from being crouched in the same position for so long, I start to consider the Head Councilor plan again. I'll need to steal a truth potion from somewhere. It's the kind of potion that would be kept in a locked room or cabinet along with other dangerous substances, but as long as I'm not seen by a surveillance device, I can probably get hold of one.

I wait for Olive to leave again before crawling out from beneath her desk. I'm about to stand when her door opens and she strides back in. My projection of invisibility snaps over me immediately, but her attention is on the amber in her hand so I doubt she'd have noticed if I'd been a little slow to conceal myself. With a grumble under her breath, she slips the amber into her pocket. She turns back to the doorway and stops just outside it, leaning into the office next to hers. "Something's come up," she says. "I can't work tonight, and I'll only be back midmorning tomorrow."

"Seriously?" comes the response from Olive's neighbor. "Another one of your random emergencies? I can't cover for you every time you have to go off on another trip."

Another trip? A trip to the Seelie Court, hopefully. I tiptoe out the door as Olive says, "I'll make it up to you." She walks back into her office, retrieves her jacket and a small pouch from her top drawer, and locks her office door. Anticipation pounds through me as I follow her downstairs, practicing the words of the faerie paths spell in my mind. Thank goodness Gaius made me memorize them. They're scribbled onto a piece of paper stuffed into one of my pockets, but it would be too much of a distraction from my invisibility illusion to have to take the note out and read it. I've managed to repeat the tongue-twisting words twice by the time we reach the little room off the side of the foyer where Olive will leave through the faerie paths. I realize that I never asked Gaius if the spell will work if the words aren't uttered out loud, but fortunately it's noisy in here with two guards chatting to a flirtatious trainee. I wait for Olive to raise her stylus to the wall. The moment she begins writing the words to open a doorway, I start whispering the words. The doorway opens. As she walks into the darkness, I hurry after her, continuing with the spell as quietly as possible.

I say the final word. Darkness surrounds me, and I have no idea if it's worked. No idea if I'm trapped here. Then, up ahead, light appears with Olive's silhouette framed against it. I almost laugh in relief as I hurry after her. I find myself on the bank of a wide river filled with the clearest water I've ever seen. The riverbed is covered in sand so white it seems to reflect the silver glow of the moon. Luminous fish-like creatures zip here and there through the water. The moon itself hangs low in the sky, but I can't tell if it's rising or sinking. I'll figure it out soon enough, then we'll know what time of day we have to leave the mountain on Thursday.

I remind myself to remain concealed as I pay careful attention to my surroundings. The slim, elegant trees, and those bushes of luminous purple flowers and blue leaves. I'll think of that when we need to return here on Thursday. I return my attention to the river as a white boat with a seahorse's head rising from the bow slips silently toward the bank. It must have magically appeared while I wasn't watching, and since no one is inside, I assume magic is what steers it. It stops moving when it reaches the bank and bobs gently in the water. I watch Olive carefully and make sure to climb inside the boat at the same time she does. She chooses one of the parallel benches, and I pick the bench furthest away from her.

As the rocking of the boat subsides, it begins to glide away from the bank. With her usual expression of boredom, Olive examines messages on her amber. I, however, keep my eyes peeled, taking note of the overhanging branches, the lush vegetation on both banks, the pattern of stars sprinkled above us. I need to remember everything, just in case.

Before long, the boat comes to a stop against the other bank. I move at the same time Olive moves, being careful not to make any noise on the bank as I step onto it. My boots form indentations in the grass. I could extend my illusion to hide the footprints as well, but Olive's attention is pointed the other way. I follow her gaze and see a closed carriage pulled by four white pegasi.

"Hey," she says to the guard who steps out of the carriage. They exchange greetings in a familiar way that suggests they know each other. They both climb into the carriage as I consider how best to follow them. The carriage door shuts.

Shoot. Well, sitting inside the carriage with them for a journey that could last hours probably wouldn't have been a good idea anyway. I hurry over to the carriage and hoist myself onto the back. I probably shouldn't try to cling here the entire way, so that leaves … the top? If I were brave enough, I'd consider sitting on one of the pegasi, but I don't want to upset any of them, and I don't want to have to remain invisible for the rest of the journey. I'm already feeling the ache of weariness at the edge of my mind.

Keeping as quiet as possible, I climb onto the top of the carriage. As it rolls forward with a jerk, I remove my belt and quickly lengthen it. I tie one end of the belt to the decorative wooden carvings on the left side of the carriage top, loop it around my waist, then tie the other end to the right side. I lie down on my stomach and direct a stream of magic toward one end of the belt to tighten it further. Then, as the rumbling beneath the wheels vanishes and the carriage begins to tilt backward, I hang on for dear life and try to convince myself that this isn't the worst idea I've ever had.

CHAPTER SIXTEEN

I'M FLYING. THE WIND TEARS AT MY WIG AND THE TREES shrink as we speed across the sky toward the stars. Good thing my phobia has nothing to do with heights. As my eyes water and air is dashed away before I can even attempt to breathe it, I raise my hands and fashion a shield in front of my face. An invisible layer starting at the edge of the carriage roof in front of me, rising up over my head, and ending at the back of my neck. It's flexible, moving as I move, so I push myself up onto my elbows and take a good look below me. I memorize every landmark I can make out. A winding river; a hill over there and another one on this side; a lake flowing into a smaller lake, which flows into an even smaller lake, all three surfaces as smooth as glass.

As the moon climbs higher and time passes, I become aware

of a slow pounding at my temples. I'm too tired to hold myself up now, so I lower my head onto my crossed arms as I stare ahead. My headache worsens. I assume it's because of the curse and the fact that I projected more illusions today than I normally would, even if most of them were brief. A tight knot of fear takes form inside me, but I try not to focus on it. Now that I've solved the Seelie Court location problem, there's little else left to do before Thursday. I can rest all of tomorrow if I need to. And even if I can't regain any strength—*you'll grow weaker and weaker*, the witch said—I won't get any worse as long as I don't project anything. At least, I hope that's how it works.

The journey goes on and on. Hours pass, though I'm not sure how many. I'm tired and achy and cold when finally the carriage begins descending. I blink and look around for the palace. It must be somewhere below, but I see nothing. A glamour, probably, preventing it from being seen. As the carriage wheels hit the ground, I release my shield. A spark of magic from each hand severs both ends of my belt. I sit up slowly, leaving the belt tied around my waist, but shortening the ends so they're—

What the—

I gasp as the carriage roof vanishes from beneath me. I force a projection out instantly as I crash onto the carriage floor between the two seats. The guard, who was laughing a moment before, tenses and frowns at the floor.

"What was that?" Olive asks, leaning forward and squinting at the spot where I'm lying.

Shoot, shoot, shoot. Aware that I'm making a noise, I

scramble backwards on hands and heels until I hit the carriage door. I push myself up and jump. The guard leaps to his feet with magic crackling at his fingertips, but I'm already out of the carriage. My feet hit the ground and I stumble forward, managing to remain both upright and invisible.

"Stop!" the guard yells, and the pegasi come to an immediate halt.

I swing around to face him and freeze. Dammit, *dammit*! I can't get caught now. Not when we're so close to fixing this mess with Chase. I don't run because I know the guard will hear me. Despite the pounding in my head, I focus intently on making him see nothing except air. Stillness surrounds us as we stand beneath the stars on a tree-lined avenue. The only movement comes from the blossoms that float occasionally to the ground. Hands raised in front of him, the guard moves slowly in my general direction. Olive stands, and as a last resort, I imagine a cracking sound coming from the carriage floor. She startles and looks down. "How old is this thing?" she asks.

The guard lowers his arms and looks over his shoulder. "You think it was the carriage making that noise?"

Olive jumps up and down, and I close my eyes so I can properly imagine the sound of creaking, groaning wood. "Sounds like it. You should probably have this thing replaced at some point."

"Probably. I guess we won't be using this one on Thursday night. Wouldn't want guests falling out of the sky, would we." The guard swings himself back into the carriage—I add another cracking sound as he lands—and snaps his fingers.

"Fortunately," he adds as the pegasi begin trotting forward, "we have plenty more."

I don't release my illusion. I don't move. I barely even breathe as I watch them driving toward an archway with a sheet of water running down it. Olive raises a small dark shape above her head and shakes it. Something sparkles in the air before floating downward and disappearing. Moments later, the carriage and its two occupants drive beneath the archway, the water parting like a curtain to let them through.

I breathe more easily once they've disappeared, but despite my growing exhaustion and the throbbing ache in my head, I don't let go of my illusion. I'm standing in a driveway that leads directly to the Seelie Palace, so I won't fool myself into thinking there are no guards in these trees. There are probably dozens of them, hiding just out of sight. No way am I revealing myself to them.

Knowing how close I am to Chase, it's almost impossible to turn away from the palace. Only the knowledge that I wouldn't be able to get him out on my own makes me walk away. I move as carefully and quietly as I can, pushing my cold hands into the pockets of Lumethon's jacket to warm my fingers. At the touch of something warm and furry in the left pocket, I jerk my hand away in fright. But it's only Filigree, of course. He was so still the entire way here that I completely forgot about him. As I remove him from my pocket, he shifts into something larger. An ermine? I hug him to my chest as I continue walking away from the palace, my eyelids drooping and my legs feeling as though my boots have been filled with sand.

When I'm far enough away from the avenue of trees, I stop shuffling forward and allow myself to sit. I try to open a doorway to the faerie paths, but, as I suspected, the paths are inaccessible here. If it were possible to open a doorway, there would be no need for that long journey through the air. I lower my stylus and look out across my starlit surroundings. How long will I have to travel before reaching a place where the paths are accessible? All the way back to that river? Probably. The thought makes me want to cry, but I don't have to because fortunately I have something better to travel on than my feet.

"Filigree? What's the largest winged creature you can shift into?"

* * *

I stagger through the faerie door in the early hours of the morning and take a seat on the floor of the mountain's entrance hall. Did I really use my Griffin Ability that much during the past day? If I'm this weak after a few hours of simply concealing myself, how weak will I be after hours of complex illusions? I push the thought aside, too scared to consider it properly. I remain on the floor for a while, waiting to feel a little stronger before attempting the stairs, but my strength never seems to return and my head continues to ache. Eventually, when I feel I can manage it, I walk on shaky legs up the stairs, clutching the banister the whole way up.

I expect Gaius to be fast asleep, but I hear raised voices coming from the direction of his study as I reach the top of the stairs. He's either up exceptionally early or he hasn't been to bed yet.

"… everything about the layout of that dungeon, but we don't even know if he's *there* anymore."

"What else can we do, Elizabeth?" Gaius replies, sounding unusually frustrated. "We cannot contact him. We simply have to go ahead with the plan."

I arrive in the doorway in time to see her throw her hands up. "Right, this elaborate plan that relies on us getting to a place that *none* of us has ever—"

"I know how to get there," I announce, propping myself up against the door frame.

Gaius pauses with his hands halfway through tugging his hair. "You—you do?"

"I do. My former mentor has been in contact with the Seelie Queen for reasons I don't know. She was summoned there yesterday afternoon, so I followed her. The palace is inaccessible from the faerie paths for miles in every direction, so we had to travel out in the open to get there. It's … a long journey. I probably didn't need to go all the way to the end because …" I blink and force myself to remain upright. "Because, um, I think we just need to get ourselves to the beginning—to the river—and boats will appear. And after the river, there will be carriages with guards and pegasi to take us the rest of the way. But I … I know what most of the journey looks like, just in case."

"That's brilliant," Gaius says with a wide grin. "That's *wonderful.* You see, my dear Elizabeth? All is not lost. Now, Calla, you look like you could do with some sleep. Why don't you go and rest for a few hours, and I'll organize a final meeting for this evening. We need to make sure we have everything planned down to the most minute detail."

"Mm hmm. Night." I push myself away from the doorframe. I manage to make it to my bedroom without having to lean against the wall. I shut my door and shuffle toward the bed.

Without warning, the door opens. I turn—which takes far more effort than it should—and find Elizabeth in the doorway. "What's wrong with you?" she demands.

"What? I'm just … just tired." I reach for the bed post as my legs finally give way beneath me. I sag against the edge of the bed.

"Just tired?" she repeats as she shuts the door. "Gaius may be completely oblivious, but I'm not. Tell me the truth."

"Go … away," I mutter as I let go of the bedpost and drape the upper half of my body over the bed. It feels like far too much effort to get my legs up as well.

"Tell me," Elizabeth commands. "Are you sick? Is it something else? You're the one who has to get us in and out of the Seelie Palace, so if something's wrong with you, we need to know."

With a great effort, I manage to heave the rest of my body onto the bed. I crawl toward the pillows and collapse against them. Being horizontal, which my body has been craving for hours now, gives me the energy to open my eyes and focus on Elizabeth. Standing at the end of my bed with her arms crossed, she looks anything but concerned for my health. Which is what makes me decide to tell her the truth. "How … how do you break a witch's curse?"

She frowns, then comes around to the side of the bed and sits. "A witch cursed you?"

I nod. "The same witch who's been working with Amon and Angelica. The one you helped me contact. She knows of my Griffin Ability and wants it for herself. This curse … apparently I will weaken every time I use my ability. My core magic will slowly be depleted until there isn't enough left to keep me alive. When I die, the only magic left will be my Griffin Ability, and it will flow from my body into the witch's."

Elizabeth's frown deepens. "Well. That could potentially put a wrench in our plans to rescue Chase."

"Exactly. So how do I get rid of this curse?"

"Either the witch must lift it, or …" She hesitates, then sighs. "Or the witch must be killed."

"As if I need another reason to want to kill this woman," I mutter.

"Why haven't you told anyone about this?"

"You know why. Our plan hinges on me being able to create a strong enough illusion to get us in and out of the Seelie Palace without being caught. If Gaius knows about the curse and that it could weaken me to the point of … well, *death* … then he might want to come up with a different plan, and we don't have time for that."

"And you don't think *I* might want to come up with a different plan now that I know the current one might kill you?"

"No. I know you care about Chase far more than you care about me. You know this is the only way to get him back, so you're not about to change all our plans."

"True. But I know Chase might never forgive me if I let you die in the process of rescuing him. He'd never forgive himself either."

"He'd get over it eventually," I tell her. The thought hurts, but hopefully it's true.

"And what if you die in the middle of the mission? That will ruin everything."

I ignore her callous words and say, "I'm not going to die in the middle of the mission. I'm weak, but I'm not at death's doorstep—yet. So I just have to make sure I don't use my Griffin Ability at all between now and tomorrow night, and I should be strong enough to get through the whole event."

"Should be?"

"Will be. I *will* be strong enough."

Elizabeth shakes her head and sighs through her nose. She stands. "Give me ten minutes."

I fall asleep while she's gone, so I don't know how much time has passed when she returns with a collection of ingredients, a bowl, a flask, and an old book. "I can't lift the curse, but I know enough about witch magic to be able to alleviate the effects for a limited time." She places everything on the table. At my questioning look, she adds, "I couldn't very well mix up a tonic right there in Gaius's laboratory if you don't want anyone knowing what it's for. It may be the middle of the night, but he's still puttering around doing who knows what." She reaches for the book, which looks like it may be the same one she used when contacting the witches. Faded foreign lettering runs down the battered spine, reminding me of the large leather-bound book that was on display in the witches' Underground store.

"Is that a witch's spell book?" I ask.

"Yes." Elizabeth opens the book and scans through the contents, keeping her back to me.

"What kind of spells are in it?"

"A lot of elemental-based magic. A few witch classics—summoning and changeling magic—plus some darker spells. Chimaera creation, energy rituals, ancient curses. That sort of thing."

"How did you get it?"

Her piercing gaze lands on me as she looks over her shoulder. "Do you want me to answer questions all night or make this tonic?"

"Sorry," I murmur. My eyelids slide shut. I think I fall asleep again because the next thing I'm aware of is Elizabeth sitting on the edge of my bed with a spoon, a bottle of brownish liquid, and a glass of what appears to be water. She sets everything on the bedside table as I push myself into a sitting position. "Dilute a spoon of this in a glass of water whenever you've used your ability and are feeling depleted," she tells me, following her own instructions and adding a spoonful of brown liquid to the glass. "It will replenish some of your strength."

I take the glass from her and sip the contents, preparing myself for a horrible taste. It isn't that bad, though: sweet with a herbal scent. I gulp down the rest of the drink and, to my surprise, start to feel better within seconds. I stare at the empty glass in my hands. "I assume this won't work indefinitely."

"No. I don't know how long it will keep the curse's effects at bay. Days, weeks, I'm not sure. Just keep using it until it stops working."

Not the best plan, but I suppose I can't ask for much more at this point. "Thanks, Elizabeth."

"You're welcome." Then, as my eyes slide shut, she adds, "Now don't you dare screw up tomorrow night's mission."

CHAPTER SEVENTEEN

I WAKE UP SOME TIME IN THE AFTERNOON FEELING ALMOST normal, which is a great relief. I know I'm only postponing the inevitable effects of the curse, but I don't care at this point. I simply need to make it through tomorrow night without collapsing. If I survive, I'll worry about getting rid of the curse afterwards—hopefully by getting rid of that witch at the same time.

Late in the afternoon, the rest of the team—which now includes Elizabeth—gathers in the mountain's meeting room for our final run-through of the plan.

"Problem," Ana announces the moment she walks in. None of us are seated, and Lumethon hasn't even arrived yet. "I spoke to Trian Hared. He—"

"Who?" Darius asks.

"The musician. He—"

"Oh, that guy you got all swoony over?"

"Darius!" Ana punches his arm before continuing. "Trian wasn't invited to this party, but he's been to an event at the palace before. He said he doesn't remember where the journey began, but it was ridiculously long. Three or four hours at least, and not only was his invitation checked by someone at three different points during the journey, he was also supposed to have some special charm to get him through the entrance."

"What charm?" Gaius asks.

"There's a waterfall of some sort at the entrance to the palace. If you don't have this charm on you as you drive through it, the water becomes solid and knocks you backward out of your carriage. The guards almost arrested Trian, but then it turned out he hadn't opened his invitation properly. Apparently when the person or people the invitation is addressed to first open it, a charm is released that allows those people passage beneath this waterfall curtain."

"Oh dear," Gaius mutters, followed by a far more colorful curse from Elizabeth. "We don't have that charm."

"I know," Ana snaps. "The baron and his daughter would have received it." She drops into one of the chairs around the oval table and buries her face in her hands. "Whyyyyy does everything have to be so hard?"

"What's so hard?" Lumethon asks as she walks in, looking alarmed.

"We don't have the charm that will allow us to pass through the Seelie Palace entrance," Kobe tells her.

"Hang on," I say, holding my hands up as my last memory

of Olive springs to mind. "The person I followed to the palace last night sprinkled something over her herself before she drove beneath that waterfall. Something she kept in a pouch in her desk at the Guild. Maybe it's the same kind of thing. Something that allows her to pass through the water."

"And what if it's not?" Ana says as she looks at me between her splayed fingers. "What if it was something entirely unrelated?"

"Then why would she bother sprinkling it on herself just before entering the palace grounds?"

"Whatever it is, we have to try it," Gaius says, seating himself at the table. "Calla, can you get this pouch from her office?"

My eyes meet Elizabeth's across the table. We both know I shouldn't be projecting any illusions before tomorrow night, but this has to be done. "Of course. I'll go as soon as this meeting is over."

"Excellent. Let's run through everything then."

Those still standing take a seat at the table, and Gaius begins by telling everyone to be here at midday tomorrow. We'll get ready—masks, weapons, relevant spells and charms—and leave the mountain in the late afternoon, which means we should arrive at the palace in time for the party in the evening.

Two or three hours later, when we've been through our plan in detail and talked through every possible obstacle we might encounter, Gaius calls the meeting to an end. He invites everyone to stay for dinner, but I tell him I'll eat when I get back. I want to get that pouch out of Olive's desk before she locks her office for the night.

I'm tired of wigs—they itch my head—but I know they help me to blend in far more easily than if I'm wearing a hood. I use the shoulder-length black and pink one again and stick with my normal black jacket. Lumethon's tan-colored one spent far too many hours hanging around Olive's office yesterday.

I expect the Guild to be emptier, given that it's evening and training should be over. Anyone working through the night should be upstairs in an office or out in the field on an assignment, but instead I find a bustle of activity in the foyer. Councilor Merrydale is there, speaking with two other guardians while tapping his foot and glancing over his shoulder every so often. Olive is present, as are several other guardians I recognize. Relieved to be covered by invisibility, I walk confidently across the foyer and up the grand stairway.

Olive's office is unlocked, so I slip inside with no trouble. I hurry over to her desk and open the top drawer. The pouch, of course, isn't there. Because, as Ana pointed out, everything about this mission is hard. Grumbling beneath my breath, I yank the second drawer open—and there it is. "Okay, scratch that," I whisper to myself. Not everything is that difficult. I pick up the pouch and find a symbol—the Seelie Queen's insignia, I'm guessing—stamped onto the fabric. Pushing the drawer closed with my hip, I open the pouch and peek inside. The powdery contents glitter in the light of the glow-bugs attached to Olive's ceiling. "This had better work," I murmur as I pull the string to close the pouch. I open my jacket and drop the pouch into the inner pocket—just as I hear footsteps pounding along the corridor outside.

"… right now?"

I'm not here. Don't see me, don't see me.

"Yes. Not more than a minute ago. I saw her—"

The door swings open and Olive storms in with a thunderous expression. "Who's hiding in here?" she demands, her eyes darting around. She marches to the desk. I squeeze around the other side as she yanks her chair back and looks under the desk. "You didn't see her leave the office?" she asks the guard standing in the doorway.

"No, but I might have missed something while on the way here. We'd have to go back to security and ask if one of the other guards saw—"

"Was the woman wearing a hood?" Olive asks as I inch around the edge of the room.

"No. She was a faerie. Pink and black. Or dark brown. I couldn't quite tell from the—"

"Get inside here and close the door," Olive snaps.

No, no, no! I suck my stomach in and hold my breath as I side-step past the guard. "Yes, of course," he says, moving into the room and slamming the door.

But I'm out. I'm out and I'm running. Not the best idea because it will draw attention, but if guards are watching for me, they'll see me anyway, no matter what speed I'm moving at. And they'll send people after me. *Get out*, my instincts tell me. *Just get out as fast as possible.* Corridor, stairs, foyer. It's almost empty now, allowing me to run straight across without having to dodge anyone. Through the doorway into the entrance room, I see Councilor Merrydale. But he's chatting with the guards, so it'll be easy to open a way to the faerie paths under the cover of invisibility and get myself out of here. I dash into the room—

And something shocks me. I can't move. I'm stuck in the doorway. *What the …* I'm visible. I'm *glowing*. Councilor Merrydale steps back, raising a hand to his mouth in surprise as he stares *straight at me*. "Oh, it—it worked." In an instant, his surprise vanishes. "Seize her before she gets away," he shouts.

I wrench myself free of the magic constraining me to the doorway and stumble backward. The guard launches through the doorway and tackles me to the ground. I kick and squirm and elbow my way out of his grip. Scrambling away and aware of a least five guardians rushing toward me, I cast about for a suitable illusion. My desperate mind starts screaming—and screams are what I hear out loud. The blood-chilling screams that filled Ryn and Vi's house, magnified and echoing across the great foyer. The sound sends chills across my skin as my pursuers look around, searching for the source. Glittering weapons blaze into existence all around me. I jump to my feet and find that despite the deafening shrieks of despair, every guardian still runs for me.

Fire, as searingly hot as I can imagine it, tears across their path. They leap away from the flames, giving me time to run for the exit. I dive through the doorway—and I'm stuck again. "Argh!" I writhe and shout and try to imagine flames consuming the foyer behind me and—

A heavy force knocks me into the room. A person, strong and fierce and pinning my arms behind me. "Got you," a voice snarls in my ear as she rips the wig from my head.

Olive.

"Release her immediately!" my projection shrieks, and though I've never seen the Seelie Queen in real life, I think of her portrait in the library upstairs and picture her in the most opulent gown my imagination can come up with, along with an expression of fury and a commanding, pointing finger.

"Your—your majesty?"

I take advantage of Olive's momentary confusion and thrust my elbow back as hard as I can. She grunts in pain and her grip loosens. I repeat the action, knocking her further backwards. I scramble away, turn around, and force a pulse of magic straight at Olive's chest. With a cry, she flies backward and hits the wall.

"What is the meaning of this?" my imaginary queen yells as she moves toward the doorway. I jump to my feet, fumble for my stylus, and scribble across the wall.

"It isn't real!" someone shouts on the other side of the queen.

A doorway of dark space materializes in front of me. I take my first step—and Olive throws herself around my legs. I fall into the darkness of the faerie paths with the lower half of my body still sticking out. "Ugh, get off!" I yell, wriggling and shooting sparks of magic from my fingers.

"You're not getting away this—"

"Yes I am!" I sit up, lean forward, and swing my fist at her face. Surprise, more than anything, is probably what makes her let go. I give her a good kick and squirm my way into the darkness as my doorway closes up behind me. I stand up in the darkness and scramble awkwardly into the lake house on the other side of the paths. "*Flip*, that hurt," I mutter, clutching my aching hand. And now, in the quiet of the lake house as fatigue and a headache creep up on me once more, my mind finally has a moment to comprehend what just happened.

A spell. To detect Gifted. That's what that woman was testing downstairs. She must have put it on the entrance room doorway after I was already inside the Guild. That's why there were more people than usual in the foyer. They cast the spell and then everyone went home, probably never suspecting they'd get a chance to see it in action so soon. And the damn thing *works*, which means that every single Griffin Gifted fae who—

Ryn. Crap. I have to warn Ryn.

I'm about to rush straight to his house when I remember the other spell I'm supposed to be avoiding. Stupid Guild and their stupid detection spells. What were the words to that shield charm Gemma and Perry put together? It was so much simpler than the tongue twisting faerie paths spell but, darn it, I can't afford to get it wrong.

I unlock the faerie door and run through it. Then into the entrance hall, past the living room, and

"Oh, Calla, did you—"

"Yes, got it!" I shout as I run for the stairs. Gaius can examine the contents of the pouch later if he wants. I find the page with Perry's spell beside my bed. I rush into the bathing room, stand in front of the mirror as I hold one hand above my head, and read the spell. Looking into the mirror, I make sure the glowing dust forms and settles over me. "Done," I murmur to myself as I leave the page on the bed. I hurry back downstairs, and barely a minute later, I'm stepping out of the faerie paths into Ryn's living room.

Dark, quiet and musty, the room's only light comes from the open door leading to the kitchen. I take a careful step forward, and then another, afraid to disturb the stillness. The room is tidy, with everything in its place except for the open books on the coffee table and the bottle standing beside them. A bottle containing some kind of alcohol, judging by its shape. Human-made alcohol, I realize as I step closer. The kind that knocks faeries out after only a few sips. It's unopened, though, which provides me with some relief.

"What do you want?"

With a jolt, I realize Ryn is sitting on one of the couches. So still and silent, I hadn't noticed him there. I clasp my hands together as the pounding of my headache intensifies. "I—I know you probably don't want to see me, but I need to warn you about something. The Guild has set up a spell across their entrance that detects those with Griffin Abilities."

He says nothing, his eyes remaining trained on the floor.

"I know you might not be going back to work for a while, but when you do, you'll need to figure out how to get in without setting off their detector."

Still, he says nothing.

"Well, I'm not saying *you* have to figure it out," I add quickly. "I have a friend who can probably come up with a way around this. As soon as he does, I'll let you know."

Nothing.

"Ryn ..." I swallow. "I—I know I'm responsible for this.

I'm not denying that. But the magic—the spell that did this—came from a pair of witches. I know who they are, and I swear I'm going to find them. They … they must be stopped. They mustn't be allowed to do this to anyone else."

I expect some form of reaction from Ryn, but it's like speaking to an empty room. I can no longer stand the one-sided conversation, or the darkness or the stuffiness. The desperate desire to *make things right* grips me as I walk into the kitchen. I cast about for something to do. Something that will help. The center of the kitchen table is piled with envelopes and folded notes. That's the spot where mail materializes when it reaches this house, which means Ryn hasn't touched any of it. I gather everything and sort it as best I can into two piles, one for business mail and one for personal. The personal pile is much larger. Condolences, no doubt. I leave them on the counter where Ryn will see them when he next comes into the kitchen.

A few dirty dishes sit in the sink, so I get a spell going to clean them while I prepare a hot drink for Ryn. Despite the fact that it's his favorite, he probably won't drink it. He might throw it at me in an outburst of anger—which, now that I consider it, would be preferable to the deathly silence he's directed at me so far. I return to the living room and leave the mug on the coffee table within his reach, but still he doesn't move. If it weren't for the occasional blink and the slow rise and fall of his chest, he could pass for a statue.

Next, I go upstairs. Quietly, so I don't disturb Violet. The bedroom door is open. I expect to see her asleep on the bed, or perhaps staring at nothing, but the room is empty. After looking briefly into the other rooms upstairs, it becomes clear she isn't here. I tidy up wherever I can, but there isn't much mess to begin with, so it doesn't take long before I'm walking back downstairs.

Ryn hasn't moved. Steam curls lazily into the air from the mug on the coffee table. I wrap my arms around my chest and swallow. "Where's Vi?"

He doesn't say anything for so long that I assume he's still ignoring me, but then, in a hoarse voice he says, "She left."

"Okay. Um …" I cast about for something else to say. "When will she be back?"

The breath he breathes in is more of a gasp, and it shudders on the way out. "I don't know if she's ever coming back."

Somehow, the silence seems to intensify as I come to understand what he means by 'left.' "You mean … like …"

"Yes. Like she didn't just leave home, she left me too."

"Ryn …"

"Go," he says quietly.

I press my eyelids closed, and a tear drips down my cheek. When I've managed to swallow down the guilt and pain enough to speak, I whisper, "I love you and I'm sorry."

Then I turn to leave. My gaze lingers on the bottle of alcohol—should I take it with me?—and I notice again the books lying beside it. Books with pictures, one of them with Vi's handwriting scribbled in the margin. I pause, squinting down through the darkness, and this time I see something I recognize: a pyramid with a second, smaller pyramid on top of the first. My heart stills a moment before jumping into action. I lift the book, looking back at Ryn to see if he might be about to object. His staring gaze is pointed elsewhere, though, so I close the book and take it with me as I leave with renewed determination.

I finally know where the witches are.

CHAPTER EIGHTEEN

THE GUILT-BEAST CIRCLES MY THOUGHTS AS I ENTER THE mountain with Vi's book tucked beneath my arm. Food is the furthest thing from my mind, but Gaius comes out of the living room and points toward the kitchen. "I kept some dinner for you," he says with a smile. "You need to keep your strength up for tomorrow night."

My strength. His words remind me of the weariness tugging at my body and the ache pounding my head. I don't need food. I need some of that tonic sitting beside my bed. But Gaius is already taking my arm and leading me toward the kitchen, so I decide it's easier not to fight. "You said you managed to get that pouch from your old mentor's office?" he asks as I sit at the kitchen table.

"Hmm? Oh, yes." I remove the pouch from my pocket and

hand it to Gaius. After waving his hand briefly at the stove to heat up whatever's in the pot, he takes the pouch.

"Very interesting," he murmurs, looking inside.

"Gaius," I say, opening Vi's book to the page with the pyramids. I cover her handwriting with one hand as I point to the pictures. "Do you know this place?"

He turns his attention away from the contents of Olive's pouch. "Uh … Mitallahn Desert." He reads the name out slowly, as if unsure how to pronounce it correctly. "Yes, I've heard of it."

The name is familiar, but I can't remember why. "Do you know anything about it?"

"Yes, I remember Chase saying something about it several months back. It was … oh, yes, it came up in his research on Amon. That's where Amon grew up."

Of course. That's why the name is familiar. I read it in Chase's notes. I close the book and place it on my lap.

"More research on Amon?" Elizabeth asks from the doorway.

I look up to find her watching me closely. "Um, yeah. Oh, thanks, Gaius," I add as he places a plate of food in front of me. "I'm going to eat upstairs, okay?"

"Oh, all right. Yes, I suppose we should all get an early night."

"Yes, we should," Elizabeth says, still watching me. Her gaze remains upon me the whole way up the stairs.

I shut my bedroom door and sit on the bed. I push the plate to one side, place the book in front of me, and turn to the

Mitallahn Desert page. I lean forward for a closer look. I've definitely seen this pyramid construction before, in the background of the mirror when I spoke to the witch. Could she and the other witch and Angelica still be there now? Is that where they're staying? Possibly, if they're working for Amon and this is where Amon used to live. I guess he doesn't know yet that Angelica's decided to leave him in prison.

I turn the book sideways and read Vi's notes. *V spell placed by Z. Spells belongs to Z. Follow spell, find Z. Pyramids. BUT HE WASN'T THERE!*

I assume V is Victoria and Z is Zed. So Vi has obviously been looking for Zed. With her Griffin Ability that allows her to find anyone as long as she's touching something that belongs to that person, it shouldn't be too difficult—except that she doesn't have anything that belongs to Zed.

Oh. The spell. The magic that slowly killed Victoria. That's the only thing Vi would have access to that belonged to Zed. I cringe away from the image of Vi touching the lifeless body of her child in the hopes of finding the man who killed her.

BUT HE WASN'T THERE!

Her words glare up at me, screaming silently. Of course he wasn't there, I realize. Because the spell or curse or whatever it was that he placed on Victoria didn't belong to him. The witches made it. It would belong far more to them than it would to Zed. So when Vi touched Victoria and saw images of pyramids in a desert, she was seeing the location of the witches.

Which lines up with what I saw in Elizabeth's mirror.

I snap the book shut and head to my bathing room to fetch

a glass of water. After mixing a spoonful of Elizabeth's tonic into the water, I drink it slowly, listening to Gaius walking down the passage to his bedroom. *We should all get an early night.* Hopefully he's taking his own advice. I, however, am not.

I tie my hair back, strap weapons to my body, zip my jacket up, and listen at the door for a minute or so. When I hear no further sound, I slip out and head downstairs. The guilt-beast, that ever-present shadow of dark and terrible truth, follows me. Hopefully, when tonight is done, that foul, stinking creature will plague me no more.

I stop in front of the faerie door. As my hand reaches for the doorknob, I hear footsteps behind me. "Look at you," Elizabeth says in a sing-song voice, walking past me and placing herself between me and the faerie door, "making me go against my selfish nature in order to do the right thing."

My words are almost a growl. "Get out of my way."

"No. I know where you're going, Calla, which unfortunately means I'm the one who has to stop you."

"You don't know anything."

"Don't I? 'I'll search every desert in the world if I have to.' Isn't that what you said about the witch?"

My glare intensifies. "Bravo. So you know where I'm going. How clever of you."

"You're not going," she says.

"Look, if you're worried about the mission, don't be. I'll be back in time for that."

"I'm not worried about the mission. Well, I am a little bit, but mainly—believe it or not—I'm worried about you."

"Move," I tell her.

She shakes her head. "You know you're not going to do this."

"Elizabeth—"

"You won't. You might plan to. You might think you will. But in the end, you will not kill those witches. It isn't you."

"You don't know anything about who I am."

"Oh, but I do. Chase has told me plenty about you. And don't—don't be mad at him for that. He and I are ... kind of like family. We tell each other everything, and we've kept each other's secrets for years. So that's how I know that you're so much stronger than either of us ever was. We were both new to this world and didn't know what to do with the power we found ourselves with. I was weak and let others control me; Chase was scared and angry and broken, and that led him down a terrible path."

I ball my fist and press it against my chest. Emotion makes my voice quaver. "What if I'm scared and angry and broken too?"

"You might be, but you're also brave and honest and optimistic. You endured things no one should ever have to endure, and you came out on the right side at the end of it, unlike some of us."

I squeeze my eyes shut and shake my head. "Stop. I can't be any of those things right now. I don't *want* to be any of those things. I have to do this."

"Why?"

"Because my brother will never forgive me!"

Opening my eyes, I see confusion on her face for the first

time. "What do you mean?"

"I let this happen! And he … what if he never …" My throat constricts and I can barely breathe. All I can see is Ryn sitting alone in the dark, refusing to look at me, his heart turned forever cold toward me. "You don't understand how … how he's always been there for me … *always*. And now …"

Elizabeth touches my shoulder. "Whether your brother holds you responsible or not, do you really think killing the witches whose magic brought this about will make everything right?"

I can barely force a sound out as I whisper, "I just want to hate someone other than myself."

"Calla," she says gently, kinder than I've ever heard her. "If you do this, it will only make you hate yourself more."

I cover my eyes with my hands as tears fall. Perhaps she's right, but I can't do nothing. I can't leave Ryn sitting in perpetual darkness and do *nothing*. I sniff and wipe my tears away. "Fine," I say. "Fine. I won't kill them. But I'll capture them and leave them tied up outside the Guild. And I'll get them to tell me where Zed is so I can capture him too. I'll leave a note pinned to the witches explaining that they're the ones responsible for the dragon disease. The Guild will question them with truth potion, and they'll—"

"Calla," Elizabeth interrupts. "It isn't the right time for this. You know how important tomorrow night—"

"Of course I know," I snap. "But I can do *both*. I can surprise the witches, tie them up, and take them to the Guild. And then Ryn will know that the people responsible for Victoria's death will be properly punished."

"Calla! This is our one chance to rescue Chase. You need to sleep tonight instead of fighting witches, and you need to be ready to leave with the rest of us tomorrow afternoon. You can't risk not being here when we depart." She grasps both my hands and squeezes them. "I know you want to do this for your brother so he'll stop blaming you. And I know you want to rescue Chase. But you can't. Do. Both."

I can't do both. The realization leaves me feeling weak. "I can't do both," I whisper. At least, not tonight. And not tomorrow night. The night after that, the witches might be gone, but I'll search for them anyway. I'll search forever if I have to. One day I'll make them pay.

CHAPTER NINETEEN

ELIZABETH CLEARLY DOESN'T TRUST ME TO STAY IN MY bedroom all night, so she conjures up a magical, glowing string, ties our wrists together, and falls asleep beside me. When I wake in the morning, she's gone.

I spend the first part of the day with Gaius looking through the costume closet and choosing outfits for everyone. He and Ana will be posing as the baron and his daughter Brynn. If all goes according to plan, they're the only two who will be seen tonight. Lumethon and Elizabeth will be beneath the palace floors, searching for Chase and keeping out of sight. But if someone does happen to see any of them, they need to be dressed appropriately so they can pretend to be nosey partygoers who wanted to explore the palace and ended up getting lost. Kobe and Darius, who will also be searching for

Chase, will be dressed as palace guards. They can pretend to usher the tipsy ladies back upstairs if need be. Gaius and I alter two Guild uniforms—I don't ask where he got them from—by changing the color to midnight blue and adding the Seelie Queen's insignia to the top of each arm, using my projection of the guard I saw the other night as a reference.

I'm the only one who doesn't have to wear party clothes. I'll be hiding outside the ballroom, staying in constant contact with the team, manipulating illusions, and essentially playing the puppet-master. My clothing will be as dark and inconspicuous as the shadows I intend to hide in.

We lay out all the formal wear and masks on the meeting room table as the rest of the team begins to arrive. Lumethon, whom I cannot imagine in a dress, picks the least frivolous garment, lengthens it with a simple clothes casting spell, and passes Darius and Kobe their guard uniforms. Gaius, already dressed, makes adjustments to his mask.

"If that's what royals have to wear," Darius says, eying Gaius's outfit, "then I'm happy to be one of the common folk."

"Ha!" Ana says as she walks in. "You'd be common even if you were royal."

"It's traditional faerie formal wear," Gaius explains to Darius. "Haven't I ever sent you to a formal event for one of our missions?"

"Nope. You always make Kobe go to those things."

"I don't mind," Kobe says with a shrug.

"No way," Ana exclaims as Lumethon hands her a purple gown. "You want me to wear *this*?"

"Now who's the common one?" Darius whispers loudly into her ear before leaving the room with his uniform.

"Do I have to wear this ridiculous thing?" Ana moans. She turns to me. "Can't I wear something normal and then you just imagine this puffy dress on me?"

"I think we should leave her here," Elizabeth says. I glance over my shoulder and find her leaning against the wall fixing Ana with a less-than-impressed stare. Her glittering red dress is her own. Nothing out of the costume closet for her.

"I'm not going to spend the entire evening picturing your dress for you," I tell Ana. "You and Gaius are close enough in appearance to the baron and his daughter. Once you're inside and have your masks on, I'm not wasting any more energy disguising you."

"This is for Chase, remember?" Lumethon says quietly, patting Ana's arm as she walks past with her own dress.

With a sigh, Ana gathers up her dress and walks out to find another room to get changed in.

I look around at Gaius and Elizabeth. "Well, if you need me, I'll be upstairs getting ready."

"Don't forget a wig," Elizabeth adds. "You won't stay hidden for long with that gold hair flashing around."

"Is there an easy alternative?" I ask. "A hair dye spell or something? Those wigs are uncomfortable. I don't want to be thinking about my itchy head when I should be picturing an illusion."

Elizabeth looks at Gaius. "Do you have obsidian thorn?"

"The bush with the black berries? Yes, I believe I do."

With a sigh, Elizabeth pushes away from the wall. "Great.

I'll go crush some berries while you get dressed, Calla."

I return to my room and change my clothes. My attire is pretty much exactly what I would wear if I were a guardian on an assignment: black from head to toe, close-fitting and easy to move in. My boots are black too, except for the blue laces, and my everyday jacket is, of course, also black.

While waiting for Elizabeth, I dilute some of the tonic she made into a bottle of water small enough to fit into an inner pocket of my jacket. I make it a little stronger than she suggested, knowing I'll almost certainly need a boost at some point tonight. I screw the lid on tightly, slip it into the pocket, and zip my jacket up. The bottle isn't the only thing hidden within my clothing. I wrestled with a few clothes casting spells earlier until I was able to add several straps and extra pockets inside the jacket for a mirror, some throwing stars, and other useful items.

I'm about to turn away from the bed when I notice Filigree sitting in cat form between my pillows. He pads forward, stops at the edge of the bed, and stares up at me with wide, mournful eyes. "No," I say sternly. "This is one outing you can't come along for. I'm serious, Filigree. No sneaking into my pockets." He lies down, lowers his head onto his paws, and continues watching me with sad eyes.

Elizabeth knocks and walks in carrying a bowl of black liquid. "Ready?" she asks.

"Yes. Thank you. Sorry to make you do that. I hope you didn't get any juice on your dress."

"Oh, I didn't do the actual berry crushing. That's what magic is for."

"Right. That's true. So … do I need to lean over the pool?"

"Yes." She walks past me into the bathing room. "Well, you don't have to, but it might be cleaner that way."

I kneel down on the enchanted grass beside the pool and pull my mass of golden hair over the water. "Do I need to wet my hair?"

"It doesn't matter. Magic's involved, so you don't really need to do anything."

I feel cold liquid pouring onto my head, but I can see Elizabeth leaning against the wall, which means she's controlling everything from a distance. Her hand flicks to the side every now and then, moving my hair or the dye, but mostly she remains relaxed against the wall. A stream of water arcs up and rinses my hair without wetting the rest of me, and when I sit back, hot air blows through my hair and dries it within minutes. "You're actually quite good at this," I admit when she tells me to stand.

"I know," she says. "Remember when you and I first met? I told you I was Chase's hair stylist, and you didn't believe me."

"Of course I didn't."

"Well, now you know who helps him out with his two-toned faerie hair disguise so he doesn't look like a halfling."

I nod slowly as I walk to the mirror. My eyes widen at the sight of such dark hair atop my own head. "It looks pretty cool, actually. How long will it last?"

"Only until you wash your hair. I assumed you didn't want a permanent change, which is why I went for the berry juice option."

"Cool." I pull my hair back into a high ponytail, secure it

tightly, and say, "Okay, let's go."

"Makeup?" Elizabeth asks.

I pause. "What about it?"

"Are you going to put any on? Your face is as pale as a moon in a starless sky against all that black. You'll hardly blend into the shadows that way."

Well, as poetic as that sounded, it was hardly a compliment. I cross my arms. "What do you want me to do? Paint my whole face black?"

"Not your *whole* face, but we could put a ton of black makeup around your eyes, at the very least."

I raise an eyebrow. "A ton?"

By the time Elizabeth's done, it looks like some kind of ink-streaked black swan is painted across the top half of my face. It actually doesn't look too bad. Elizabeth nods approvingly. "Pretty badass. Definitely not my style, but badass nonetheless."

Badass. I like the sound of that. We head to the door, but I pause after opening it and look back at her. "I don't want to dwell on this, but it's possible I might actually … die tonight."

"Oh, don't be so dramatic," she says, stepping past me.

"I'm being realistic, Elizabeth." And I'm trying not to let the fear of death consume me. "This curse isn't a joke. If your tonic stops working and I use my Griffin Ability too much—which is highly likely, given everything we've planned—then tonight could be the night I become too weak to keep going. So if I don't get to see Chase again, will you—"

"Honestly, Calla, you need to stop worrying about this," she says, continuing along the passage, making me hurry to catch up to her. "Concentrate on not messing up tonight, and we can deal with the curse afterwards. If you were going to die any time soon, Luna wouldn't have Seen you in Chase's future."

My steps come to a halt. A shiver raises the hairs on my arms. "What?"

A few paces ahead of me, Elizabeth freezes. She doesn't look around at me, but I hear her curse beneath her breath. "I forgot he never mentioned that bit to you," she mutters.

I close the distance between us and take hold of her arm. "What are you talking about? What did Luna See?"

"I … I'm not completely sure. You'll have to ask Chase."

"You're lying. If you and Chase really do tell each other everything, then he would have told you about this."

"Look, Calla," she says, removing my hand from her arm. "It isn't my place to say anything, and I honestly don't remember any details beyond the words 'woman in gold.' The vision was about you and Chase, and if he decided not to tell you, he must have had a good reason. I should have kept my mouth shut, and I'm sorry." She walks away.

"So that's it?" I call after her. "I have to go into this mission now and completely forget about what you've just said?"

"That's exactly it."

With a great deal of effort, I force my questions to the back of my mind, telling myself that if all goes well tonight, it won't be long before I can ask Chase exactly what Luna Saw. I'll probably be so happy to have him back, though, that questions like this will hardly matter. I smile at the thought, my insides filling with warmth as I imagine finally being able to touch and see and hear him again. I give myself one last silent lecture as I follow Elizabeth: *I'm not going to die, it doesn't matter what Luna Saw, and every thought needs to be pointed toward our mission now.*

Downstairs, I find the rest of the team assembled in the entrance hall. "Everyone ready?" Gaius asks, at which I feel a twinge of nervousness. Everyone nods, so I nod too. I am ready, I tell myself. It's just the curse I'm a little concerned about. "Shall we do the communication spell then?" Gaius adds.

"Will it last long enough?" Lumethon asks.

"It generally lasts about half a day, I think. We won't have another chance to do it, though, so it has to be now." Gaius passes a scrap of paper around to remind us of the words. We each pull out a stylus and write on some part of our skin. Then, the tedious part: we each have to mark everyone else's skin so that we're all in contact with each other.

"There has to be an easier way than this," Darius mutters. "This is magic, right? Isn't magic supposed to make our lives easier?"

"Trust me," Elizabeth says. "This is easier than those little devices humans have to put in their ears."

"Right," Gaius says when we're done. "Calla, do you want to test out the illusion you'll be using most of the way there?"

I nod and step away from the group so I can visualize the scene properly. Gaius and Ana will be Baron Westhold and his daughter, and the rest of us won't be there. I close my eyes and picture it. The baron, Brynn, no one else.

"Wow, this is weird," Darius comments. "Looking down and not seeing myself."

I let go of the picture and pull the wall back up around my mind.

"Wonderful," Gaius says. "Let's go."

* * *

I pour my full concentration into the illusion from the moment we step out of the faerie paths and onto the bank beside the clear river. I'm aware that there are other fae dressed in gowns and masks standing in what could roughly pass for a line, and that more than one white boat is floating along the river, but I try not to pay attention to anything except my illusion.

Gaius and Ana join the back of the line, and the rest of us stand to the side, holding hands. It seems silly, but we can't see each other, so this way we at least know where everyone else is. Quiet chatter fills the area, but neither Gaius nor Ana joins in. Before we left the mountain, I instructed everyone to keep their mouths shut. "If I need the baron or his daughter to say something, I'll imagine it happening."

At the front of the queue, before climbing into a boat, each guest is required to present their invitation to the Seelie Court guard standing on the bank. When it's Gaius's turn to hand over his champagne-colored rosebud, the guard skims through the list of guests on his amber tablet and frowns. "Your reply indicated that you wouldn't be attending."

"Oh? I'm terribly sorry," I imagine Baron Westhold saying.

"I thought I had contacted the palace to change that."

"I'm afraid you did not."

"Well, we're here now," the baron says, with a chuckle that sounds as nervous as I feel. "Can we get into the boat?"

"Hold on." The guard lowers his amber tablet, and the image of a face rises above it. "Please remove your mask, Baron Westhold." I hold my breath and concentrate more fiercely as Gaius pulls his mask off. The guard looks back and forth between Gaius and the image of the baron's face. Satisfied, he nods. Then he turns to Ana and repeats the process, bringing up an image of the baron's daughter. He nods again and returns the rosebud invitation to Gaius. He holds his hand out toward the boat and says, "Thank you for your patience. Have a pleasant journey."

Gaius and Ana climb into the boat, and the rest of us hurry to do the same, causing a little too much sloshing. With five additional people that no one can see, our boat sits far lower in the water than any of the others. The guard is busy with the next invitation, though, and no one else seems to notice.

I breathe more easily once we're moving, but I don't dare let go of the illusion. I'm aware of a growing weariness at the edges of my mind, and it scares me to know how quickly the curse's effects are working now. Definitely faster than before. I pat the front of my jacket and feel the comforting edge of the bottle tucked into the inner pocket.

When the boat journey comes to an end, we climb out and find a row of carriages each pulled by pegasi. The guard who greets Gaius and Ana checks their invitation, but there's no confusion this time about whether they're supposed to be here or not. The message must have been passed on somehow. Gaius and Ana climb into the carriage, but when the guard moves as if to climb in after them, I imagine the baron turning around and holding his hand up. "I like my privacy. My daughter and I will sit alone."

The guard opens his mouth but hesitates, as if he wasn't prepared for this situation.

"Surely you have a seat at the front of the carriage?" Baron Westhold asks.

"Uh, yes, sir. I do. But the pegasi direct themselves, so … But it's fine, sir. I'll sit at the front. Have a pleasant journey." He bows and strides around to the front of the carriage.

As the rest of us climb inside, I realize what a tight fit it will be. I hadn't considered this part. Will the guard notice the extra effort it takes for the pegasi to get us off the ground? I bite my lip as the carriage jerks into motion, continuing to chew on it as we speed up. Fortunately, these pegasi seem to be far stronger than I gave them credit for. With little more than a heaving creak, we're in the air.

Finally, I let go of the illusion. I figure we're safe for the next few hours. Gaius and Lumethon whisper to each other, and Kobe watches the sunset through the carriage window. Ana and Darius fight over limited space, elbowing each other repeatedly until Lumethon asks them to stop. Elizabeth tilts her head back and closes her eyes. From the way she remains perfectly still, I can tell she isn't sleeping. I look toward the window and pretend Chase can still hear my thoughts. *We're coming*, I whisper silently. *We're almost there.*

* * *

Hours later, I'm roused from my half-asleep state when someone touches my knee. "We're descending," Gaius says. He holds up the pouch I stole from Olive. "Hopefully this will get us safely through the entrance." He passes it around the carriage, and we take turns sprinkling some of the powdery contents over our heads.

"I really hope this works," Ana mutters.

"It will work," Gaius says.

Moments later, the carriage wheels touch the ground. I remember the roof disappearing at around about this point last time, so I quickly picture the people who are supposed to be inside this carriage: the baron, Brynn, no one else. Seconds later, the carriage roof vanishes. Without looking too closely, I take in our surroundings. The trees that line either side of the avenue are strung with tiny lights, and the delicate scent of the blossoms drifting to the ground fills the air.

Up ahead, another carriage rumbles toward the archway. It reaches the waterfall, drives through, and disappears from sight as the water draws back over the space like a curtain. I tense as our carriage approaches the archway. My hands clasp tightly around one another and I prepare to be thrown backward by a wall of solid water. We're so close now. Almost there, almost there—

And then we're through. My sigh of relief isn't the only one. I strengthen my illusion once again as we enter a courtyard filled with the same pink- and orange-blossomed trees that lined the avenue. We circle around the edge before the pegasi come to a stop. Looking up and around, I see white pillars and towers, spiraling stairways and elegant balconies

No, stop, concentrate.

I can't afford to be distracted, no matter how beautiful my surroundings. Gaius and Ana—the baron and his daughter—climb out of the carriage. The rest of us follow just behind, reaching for each other's hands again once we're out of the carriage. The guard leads them to a second archway, where their invitation is checked for a third time and floating images of their faces are once again compared. "Walk around the fountain toward the wide open doorway on the other side of the courtyard," the guard says, pointing through the archway. "That's the ballroom. You can't miss it." Gaius and Ana walk below the archway, and ever so carefully, the rest of us slip through after them.

We've made it. We're inside the Seelie Palace.

CHAPTER TWENTY

THE OPEN DOORWAY ON THE OTHER SIDE OF THE FOUNTAIN gives us a glimpse into a ballroom filled with masked fae, twirling dancers, magnificent gowns, and floating platters of exotic delicacies. "Good luck, everyone," Gaius says, his voice as clear in my ear as if he were standing right beside me. "And remember, if anything goes wrong, get out of here. We can reassess on the outside and make another plan, but we're useless if we all get caught inside the palace." He and Ana pull their masks down over their faces and disappear into the crowded ballroom. I let go of the illusion disguising them, focusing now on keeping the rest of us invisible.

"We need to head inside," Lumethon says. "Find that passageway with the unicorn tapestry." The invisible person in front of me—Elizabeth, I assume, given that I'm holding a gloved hand—veers to the left toward another room leading off this courtyard. It's open and airy with twisting branch-like banisters on the stairway and scenes of magical creatures carved into the pillars on either side of the room. Looking out to the right, I see lawns and rosebushes, statues and fountains, and the side of the ballroom. No glass covers the tall windows, and sounds of laughter, music and chatter reach our ears. "We should probably head down that passageway first," Lumethon says. I don't know where she's looking, but there's only one passageway leading off this room, on the far side behind the stairway.

"I agree," Kobe says. "It's unlikely the entrance will be upstairs, considering the prison is below us."

I hang onto Elizabeth's hand and let her lead me through passages, around corners and across courtyards as I remain focused on the thought of empty space wherever we happen to be walking. When Gaius's friend was brought to the dungeons here, he was taken through an outside entrance some distance from the actual palace. But when it came time to leave, the guards accompanying him were in a hurry. They brought him out through a door within the palace itself. A door hidden behind a tapestry of a unicorn in a corridor with stars and moons painted onto the walls.

"Any luck yet?" Gaius asks. "My friend said he passed the ballroom on his way out, so I imagine you won't have to go too far."

"Nothing yet," Lumethon tells him. "Everything okay in the ballroom?"

"The Queen isn't here yet," Ana tells us, "but I saw Princess

Audra just now. She was dancing with someone, and at least six hundred guards were standing on tiptoe, trying to keep her in their sight."

"Exaggerations," Gaius mutters.

"Well, this is completely boring. I wish we were also searching for Chase."

"Everyone has their part to play tonight, Ana," Lumethon says, "and this is yours. So stop complaining and pay attention to whatever's happening in the ballroom."

"Shh, here it is," Elizabeth says. I look around as we walk out of a small sitting room and into a passageway painted midnight blue and sprinkled with stars and moons. The stars are specks of twinkling yellow light, and the moons glow silvery white, possibly painted with moonlight itself. The passage curves around, keeping us from seeing further than a few paces ahead.

"I'll go around the corner and look," Lumethon says. I hear and see nothing, but I assume she's walking away. A few moments later, she says, "I'm back. I saw the tapestry. A guard is stationed beside it, so we may need an illusion to distract him. Perhaps the fainting one we discussed."

"Let me try first," Elizabeth says. "If I can't persuade him to leave his post, then Calla can project something into his mind."

"Have you ever been unable to persuade someone?" Darius asks.

"Hmm." Elizabeth releases my hand. "Chase has been oblivious to my powers for years, but men in general don't have the mental strength required to resist my persuasion."

"Brilliant," Darius mutters. "I'll try to remember never to

piss you off."

"A wise move," she whispers, becoming visible as I adjust the picture I'm seeing in my head. She walks around the curve in the wall, swaying her hips and slowly pulling one glove off.

"Don't hurt him," Lumethon murmurs as Elizabeth disappears from our sight.

"Just a precaution," comes her answering whisper. Seconds of silence pass by. Then I hear her sultry voice as if she were right next to me, and a deeper, male voice, further away and hard to make out. She tells him how beautiful the gardens are tonight. She tells him he wants to find the nearest window and stare out of it until the sun rises tomorrow morning. Then she says, "All clear."

I glance around to make sure we're still alone before dropping the illusion so we're all visible once more. "You'll hide somewhere out here, Calla?" Lumethon says to me.

"Yes." I don't want to, of course. I want to go into the dungeons with them. I want desperately to be there for the moment they finally free Chase. But everyone agreed during the planning stages of this mission that I should hide somewhere on my own, keeping my mind clear of distractions and ready to force an illusion onto someone at a second's notice. "If you need me to imagine something, give me as much detail as possible." She nods. "And be careful, please. All of you."

Lumethon, Darius and Kobe hurry around the corner. I follow just far enough to see the tapestry and watch my fellow team members pull it aside and slip through the door behind it.

When the tapestry slides back into place, I lean against the star-studded wall and close my eyes. Exhaustion settles over me. Heavy limbs and sluggish thoughts. It's terrifying how quickly it's happening now. With shaking fingers, I reach inside my jacket for the bottle. I take a sip, give myself another minute or two, then push away from the wall. Though it hurts my head to picture it, I conceal myself once again as I head back toward the ballroom, my teammates' whispered commentary filling my ears.

"Oh, man, the stench is bad."

"Why aren't there more guards down here?"

"I don't think it's the kind of place you break free from. They probably don't need many guards."

"If you do come across a male guard," Gaius says, "Elizabeth must try to get information about Chase out of him."

"I know, Gaius. I was there for the planning meeting."

"Oh, hell, there's a guy coming toward me with his hand out," Ana says. "Calla, make him go away!"

"Seriously?" I ask, pausing in the room with the stairway.

"Yes! I can't—Uh … Hi, hello. No, no thank you. I … I don't dance."

Darius's snort of laughter fills my ears.

"Would you shut up?" Elizabeth whispers fiercely. "Can you see where we are right now? You should not be laughing."

As I cross the lawn toward the outer wall of the ballroom, Lumethon describes the dungeon in low whispers. Dark, cold and pieced together from uneven stone bricks. Thick metal gates and chains. The air thick with the stink of urine, blood and feces. Some cells are empty, while others contain bloodied, tortured fae, some moaning and crying, others silent and barely breathing. It's the kind of place I'd expect to find beneath Velazar Prison or perhaps the Unseelie Palace, not here beneath the blossoming flowers, bubbling fountains and merry chatter of the Seelie Court.

"No sign of Chase?" Gaius asks.

"Not yet," Lumethon says.

"The Queen still isn't here," Gaius adds. "Seems strange. Why would she miss her own daughter's birthday party?"

"You don't think she's down here, do you?" Darius says.

"If she likes witnessing torture, she very well might be," Elizabeth murmurs.

The team falls silent for a while. I seat myself within the shadow of a rosebush beneath one of the ballroom windows. With a sigh of relief, I let go of my invisibility. I wrap my arms around my knees and listen to the music and laughter. As a headache begins to throb near my temples, I consider taking another sip from my bottle. I should probably save it, though. If I'm this weak already, I'm going to need a major boost before we leave—

"Oh no," Gaius mutters. "Someone just recognized me. An old client of ours. She's coming this way. Calla, can you—Oh, hello, Madame Marlize." Gaius laughs nervously. "However did you recognize me beneath this sparkly monstrosity of a mask?" As Gaius pauses for Madame Marlize's response—which I obviously can't hear—I stand up and peek over the window ledge into the ballroom. My eyes dart over a waterfall gown, a rainbow floating above someone's head, a skirt covered entirely in red roses, and dozens of other outfits before I manage to spot Gaius. "Ah, yes, well, I've had some dealings with the Seelie Court, believe it or not," he says to the large woman in the yellow feather adorned dress standing in front of him. "All confidential, of course, but let's just say I managed to earn myself an invitation with my exceptional services." He adds in another awkward chuckle, growing quiet as he listens to Madame Marlize, now pointing somewhere behind her. "The princess?" Gaius says. "That's very kind of you to offer. I actually haven't been introduced to her yet. I fear I've been somewhat … *distracted* since I arrived here tonight."

Right. A distraction. That's what I'm here for. I ignore my pounding head as I concentrate on the feathers hanging from the bottom of Madame Marlize's dress. I imagine them catching fire, the flames spreading rapidly up the skirt. "Oh, goodness me," Gaius says, stepping hastily backward. Madame Marlize might be halfway across the noisy ballroom, but I have no trouble hearing her shriek the moment she notices the flames. She grabs a drink from the hand of the nearest guest and throws it at herself. I let go of the flame illusion and instead picture smoke rising from the feathers.

"Excuse me?" Ana says. "What do you mean? Of course I'm on the list. You're the one who let me in here."

Oh no. I search the crowd, but I can't see Ana.

"What's going on?" Gaius asks, swiveling around.

"Shh," I say. "Don't panic. I'll fix this."

"Go with you where?" Ana demands, and finally I find her.

She's standing near the back doorway in front of the guard who ushered us through the archway toward the ballroom.

"Don't panic," I say again. "I'm thinking, I'm thinking …" And my head is pounding and the only thing my body wants to do is lie down.

Focus! I yell at myself. "Okay, I've got it," I say.

It's dangerous, terribly dangerous, but I picture Princess Audra herself. She slips into the ballroom through the door behind the guard and grasps Ana's arm. "There you are!" she says. "I'm so glad you could make it. I feel like it's been forever since I last saw you."

The guard immediately straightens, his arms going rigid at his sides. He tilts forward in a quick bow, then says something to the imaginary princess. Something that I, of course, can't hear.

"She's quick, that's how," Ana says with a laugh, answering whatever question the guard must have directed at Princess Audra.

Another voice sounds in my ear—Lumethon, I think—but I'm too focused to pay attention to it. "I have to be," my imaginary princess says, "if I hope to greet everyone tonight. And we have so much to catch up on." She smiles at Ana, then sends a somewhat annoyed look in the guard's direction. "That will be all, thank you."

He bows again before marching hurriedly away. Instead of vanishing suddenly into nothing, I imagine the princess slipping back out the door before I let go of the illusion of her.

"That was awesome," Ana says. "I thought I was going to be whisked into a hidden room and never seen again."

"You're welcome," I mumble as I sink onto my knees in the shadows, my eyes sliding shut.

"Lumethon, is something wrong?" Gaius asks. "You called Calla's name just now."

Crap, have I managed to mess up already?

"It's fine, we made a plan."

"A guard saw all of us," Darius says, "but he's now locked in an intimate embrace with our half-siren accomplice. I think he—Ah, the intimate embrace has come to an end."

"Shut up," Kobe growls.

"Do you know what I heard?" Elizabeth purrs, presumably to the guard she just had to make out with. "I heard there was a very special prisoner being kept down here. A prisoner more important to the Queen than any other. Do you know who I'm talking about?" Silence fills my ears as I wait for Elizabeth's next words. "Yes, that's exactly who I mean. Would you perhaps consider telling me all about him? I'd love to hear everything you know."

The silence stretches on after that as we wait for Elizabeth to relay whatever the guard is telling her. I slouch against the wall, listening to the chatter and laughter, the swish of ballgowns, and the joyous lilt of the music. With my eyes closed and the irresistible pull of exhaustion tugging me toward sleep, I'm barely conscious by the time Elizabeth swears loudly in my ear. "Chase isn't here."

Her words shock me into sitting up. "What? Where is he?"

"This useless guard doesn't know. He said no one went near Chase for almost two weeks. Then a few days ago, the Queen … she …" Elizabeth's voice falters. "They began torturing him." Nausea overwhelms me. "He was moved either today or yesterday. The guard doesn't know because yesterday was his day off, and he only began his dungeon rounds this evening."

I breathe deeply past the nausea. "Do you think … are we too late?"

"He must be here somewhere," Lumethon says, her voice wobbling just a little bit. "We need to find the torture rooms.

"Keep looking," Gaius says. "We've still got time. This party will go on all night."

"I'm coming to help," I say, cloaking myself with another illusion before standing. "I can't—"

"No, Calla, we need you focused," Gaius says.

"I'm focused on rescuing Chase! We should *all* be underground looking for him. Why do we need you guys in the ballroom anyway? You're just—"

"Something's happening," Ana says, speaking just as the music changes. "I think the Queen's here."

I look back through the window. Sure enough, everyone stops dancing and turns to face the dais. It's a wide platform with several thrones upon it. The center throne is, of course, the largest, and it's this throne that the woman sweeping out of a side door heads toward. She stops in front of it and remains standing, looking around at the various royals who walk out of the crowd and seat themselves upon the smaller thrones. Then she faces the rest of the ballroom. A serene smile settles upon her face. Her dress—black lace over bottle green fabric—is exquisite, and her hair is twisted into an elegant knot. Her personal guard—men and women dressed in a dark plum-colored version of the Seelie guard uniform—line up in an arc behind her throne.

The Queen spreads her arms out toward her guests and speaks. "Welcome. It's an honor to have you gathered here tonight to celebrate my daughter's birthday." She looks to her right where Princess Audra sits upon one of the smaller thrones. "I have a gift for you, my darling daughter." Turning again to her guests, she continues. "There have been rumors in recent years, whispers of enchanted storms and a power that should have ended a decade ago. Tonight, I shall lay the rumors to rest." She pauses before delivering her final shocking statement. "Lord Draven did not die ten years ago." Gasps and whispers ripple across the gathering like waves. "But," the Queen adds, her voice ringing out above the murmurs, "I have him in my clutches, and my gift to you, dear daughter—" she holds her hand out toward the door she entered through "—is his head on a platter."

The world tilts. My legs weaken. I blink and grasp the window ledge to keep from falling. My team members' voices clash against my ears, but my brain makes no sense of their words as I struggle to figure out what this means. She didn't … she wouldn't … but we've heard nothing from him in days, so …

"Here, for all to see," the Queen shouts, "is the once-powerful Lord Draven."

I see him then, finally, not a head on a platter, but a whole person. Dirty, bloody and bound in chains, but alive nonetheless. My utter, all-consuming relief clashes with the horror of the state he's in, sending my head spinning once again. Guards drag him into the ballroom and dump him on the dais. Every royal except the Queen and Princess Audra bolts from the platform.

"Calla! CALLA! Can you hear me?" I finally become aware of Gaius's fierce whisper in my ear. "You have to do something. I don't know what, just *something*. Distract the Queen while we try to reach Chase. Bring a dragon flying through here if you have to, but—"

"You can see Chase?" Elizabeth asks.

"Calla!" Gaius repeats. "Can you—"

"I—I'm here," I whisper. "I'm thinking. I'm …"

"He will no longer threaten our rule," the Queen says. "He will be gone for good, and one day when the time comes, you, my daughter, will safely ascend the throne."

Think, I tell myself. *THINK!* But I'm so tired and shocked and—

"Not so fast, mother *dear*." I assume at first that it's Princess Audra's voice ringing out, but she's looking confused—looking up—and the guards are shouting—and a flash of silver is falling from the domed ceiling—dropping from a rope—landing on the throne—shrieking and swinging back a mighty sword and—

—a spray of blood—

—a scream of horror—

A moment of absolute silence.

The Seelie Queen's head strikes the marble floor. Her body crumples beside it. Her emerald-studded crown rolls off her head, comes to rest, and shrinks to the size of a bangle.

"Holy crap, Calla," Ana whispers. "That was some illusion."

"I—I—" I'm so horrified I can barely speak. "I—That wasn't me."

"What's happening?" Elizabeth demands.

A piercing scream issues from Princess Audra's mouth. The plum-clad guards, however, are frozen as still as statues. Princess Angelica leaps off the throne and spins around, her sword slicing cleanly through the air and then through her sister's neck, cutting off that chilling scream in an instant. A woman stalks up the right side of the dais, and another on the left. They seem almost to glide in their dresses that billow and curl about them like smoke. Even without being close enough to see their depthless black eyes, I know exactly who they are. As every remaining guard in the ballroom rushes toward the dais, the witches throw their hands out. Brilliant, blinding light fills the ballroom for a moment. When it subsides, a translucent layer, glowing faintly silver, surrounds the dais and those upon it.

Angelica bends and picks up the crown. At her touch, it expands to its original size. With magical strength, she stabs her sword into the platform and leaves it standing there. She raises the crown with both hands and places it on her head. "Behold," she shouts, "your new Queen."

The madness that follows is almost comical. The screams, the running, Gaius and just about every other member of my team shouting at me to *project something! Save Chase!*

But the fatigue is finally too much to bear. Perhaps that last illusion pushed me over the edge, or perhaps it's my close proximity to the witches, but it's all I can do to remain conscious. As my legs give in and I drop onto my side behind the rosebush, I fumble with the zip of my jacket. My shaking fingers find the bottle of Elizabeth's tonic. I screw the lid off as the world around me begins to blur and Angelica's wicked screech of a laugh echoes in my ears. I raise the bottle to my mouth, and I think I'm drinking the contents, but I can't quite tell because I'm falling, falling, falling into darkness ...

PART III

CHAPTER TWENTY-ONE

I'M PULLED SLOWLY TOWARD CONSCIOUSNESS BY THE growing ache in my neck. My eyelids peel back a fraction, revealing a mottled pattern of light and dark, before sliding shut again. I try to stretch out of the painful position I seem to be lying in, but a rustling prickliness obstructs my limbs. I become aware of the smell of soil and the texture of hard earth beneath my cheek, and that's when every horrifying detail of the Seelie Palace party slams into me.

The Queen is dead.

Princess Audra is dead.

Princess Angelica has claimed the crown.

And the last I saw of Chase, he was lying motionless upon the dais, his body battered, bloody and broken.

My head swims as I push myself up into a sitting position. I blink a few times before I can focus on anything. Through the rosebush leaves, I see the morning sun peeking out from behind streaks of lavender-peach clouds. I shift so I can see past the bush. The Seelie Palace gardens spread out before me, serene and still with the pink flush of morning light. Against this beauty, last night seems like nothing more than a nightmare.

As I climb to my feet, using the wall to help me up, I step on something hard. Looking down, I find the small bottle my shaking fingers were clutching as everything faded to black last night. It's empty. That, combined with the fact that I don't feel utterly drained and exhausted, must mean I managed to drink it all before passing out—and that it's still effective enough to keep the curse at bay.

I turn and look through the ballroom window. It's as still and quiet as the gardens, but frozen in disaster. Smashed glass and platters of food; scattered masks; feathers, sequins, and the odd shoe lying here and there. My eyes move to the dais, to the two bodies still lying there. The sight of them turns my stomach, so I look away and notice the guards frozen in place behind the throne. Are they dead? Is it a spell that keeps them in place? And where is everyone else? The other guards, the remaining royals, the rest of my team.

"Gaius?" I whisper. "Lumethon?" I peel back the sleeve of my jacket and find that the words I wrote there have vanished. The communication spell has faded.

I turn back to face the garden. With no idea where any of my team members are or if they're even still alive, there seems to be only one course of action left to me: complete the mission on my own.

I step around the rosebush and set off across the grass toward the open room with the decorative pillars. There are so many uncertainties, I don't know where to start with my search for Chase. If Angelica left the palace, would she have taken Chase with her? If not, would she have sent him back to the dungeon? Would she have … killed him? No. Not if she plans to use his power to bring down the veil. He can't be dead. I refuse to consider the possibility. I will search, and I *will* find him.

I start by returning to the passageway painted midnight blue and decorated with stars and moons. No guard stands beside the unicorn tapestry, and the door, I discover when I pull the tapestry aside, isn't locked. Stepping beyond the door is like entering another world: I leave behind delicate architecture, white marble finishes, and fresh-scented air, and walk into a world of cold stones, lamps flickering in darkness, and the smell—the *smell.* Darius mentioned it was bad, but I can barely breathe as I descend the stairs.

I find no guard at the bottom. I continue past cells of stone and metal. In those that are empty, chains trail across dark, dried stains. I start to call Chase's name. Prisoners look up at the sound of my voice. Some reach through the bars for me, but none of them are Chase. I pass torture rooms in between the sections of cells, pausing only long enough to ensure Chase isn't inside any of them before cringing away from the spikes, whips, tools, and more blood stains.

It's ridiculous how long it takes me to reach the other end of the dungeon. What does the Seelie Court need so many cells for? Don't most criminals end up in normal prisons rather than down here? And I can't do a quick scan of the area. I need to search every single space, just in case Chase is in the next one. When I eventually find myself at the end of the dungeon with nowhere else to go, I turn and run all the way back, aware that time is ticking by.

The sun has moved substantially when I get back up to the palace, indicating that I've been down in the dark for *hours*. Flip! How did that happen? A spell? Some form of magic making me wander the dungeons far longer than I thought? I continue my hunt with renewed fervor. As I search through endless empty lounges, bedrooms, bathing rooms and more, I start to lose my sense of direction along with my sense of time. Have I been this way already? That chaise longue beneath the painting of a faun looks awfully familiar.

I move up to the next level and keep going. Why does this palace have to be so big? *Why?* I find myself in an area with no windows to the outside, and no matter which way I turn or which passages I run down, I can't seem to get myself out. Panic rises along with the irrational certainty that the walls are closing in, trapping me, suffocating me.

Stop.

I force myself to stand still in the middle of a room and close my eyes. Breathing in shaky breaths, I imagine Lumethon's voice. I picture my lake. I know I'm wasting time with this silly exercise, but I'm of no use to anyone in a state of panic, so I remain still, breathing in and breathing out. When finally I've calmed myself, I open my eyes and continue on. Several minutes later, I reach a corridor where I can once again see outside. I note the afternoon light and instruct myself firmly not to freak out about how much time has passed. *It's fine*, I tell myself. *You'll find him. Just keep looking.*

I enter another bedroom—and I'm startled to see a dark-clad figure on the other side of the room. I freeze—and so does the figure. It takes another moment for me to realize I'm looking at a tall mirror and seeing my own reflection. I almost laugh. I'd forgotten about my mask-like black makeup, coal-black hair, and even the tattoos across my hands. Elizabeth was right. I do look totally badass—and nothing like myself.

I glance around the unoccupied room. I'm about to leave when I hear voices. Swinging around, I look toward the sound. An open doorway beside the mirror leads onto a balcony. I hurry to it, duck down, and creep outside. Peering out between the balusters, I see them: the two witches and Angelica. She walks tall with the crown upon her head, pausing to look up at the sky. I follow her gaze and see something that either wasn't there this morning, or was somehow less visible in the light of sunrise: A great silvery dome sitting over the palace and part of the grounds. Translucent, like the layer of magic that protected the dais last night, but not invisible like normal shield magic. Still, I'm almost certain it's a shield of some sort.

The witches stop to admire the shrubs clipped into shapes resembling winged creatures. One of them reaches out to touch the red petals of the little flowers hidden amongst the topiary creations. My hatred for these women burns anew. While they walk around, free and unconcerned, my brother sits at home in the dark, mourning the loss of a child who will never grow up to know the beauty of this world, and the wife who may never return to him. Did the witches consider this when they sold the spell that would kill a child? Did the thought even flit across their minds? I doubt it.

But despite my hatred for them, I can't kill them. The image of the decapitated former queen is too fresh in my mind. Too horrifying. I may have entertained the fantasy of the witches' deaths. I may have tried to embrace the dark part of my soul that craved revenge. But witnessing the violent end of a life was a shocking reminder that *I do not want to do that.* I'll happily blast them with stunner magic and dump them in the Guild's hands, though. Problem is, I can only stun one of them. I'd have no time to gather enough power to stun the second, and there's Angelica to worry about too. I could certainly injure the two I don't stun—I have a knife in each boot and several throwing stars secured inside my jacket—but with their magic, the two of them might still overpower me.

"How long can you hold it in place?" Angelica asks, still squinting against the midday sun as she looks up at the silver layer.

"A week," one witch says. "Perhaps longer."

"Without growing any weaker?"

"Yes. We prepared for this before leaving Creepy Hollow, remember? Together, we have the magical energy of at least fifty men."

Fifty men? What kind of magic could give them so much power?

"Wonderful. If you—" At that point, a guard hurries up to her. The first guard I've seen since last night, other than the guards still frozen in the ballroom. Any hope I might have had of this guard running toward Angelica to attack her, to take back the crown she stole, dies when I see him bow his head.

"You asked me to keep you updated, Your Majesty. Several guards have confirmed that your brother and nephew and the rest of the royal family got away in one of the carriages last night as the guests were fleeing."

Angelica clenches her fist and punches the air as she lets out an angry shout. One of the topiaries catches fire. "I should have slain them before they ran off the dais," she grumbles. "And *you* should have worked faster in getting the shield up." She directs her fury at the witches for a moment. After taking a breath, she turns back to the guard. "Well, there's no point in guarding the tunnel anymore." She crosses her arms. "Where is everyone else hiding?"

"The palace staff are in their quarters, Your Majesty."

"And the guards not loyal to me are still under control?"

"Yes, Your Majesty. Down in the kitchen. Once we've stunned them all, they'll be moved to the dungeon."

"Good." She breathes out a long sigh. "Now I suppose I'm going to have to hunt down the rest of my family."

"Leave it until after the full moon," a witch suggests.

"Yes, it can wait until then." Angelica dismisses the guard. To the witches, she says, "Do whatever you want around here to pass the time. I'll be busy for the next few hours."

I perk up at her words. If only the two witches are left out here, I can risk taking them on. Stun the one, and immobilize the other with illusions, magic and knives. If I have enough strength left, I can even get them into a dungeon cell. They can wait there for the Guild—which I assume is sending guardians back here as soon as possible—to find them.

As Angelica turns to walk away, I begin gathering magic above my palm. "Where will you be if we need you?" asks the older witch.

Not bothering to look back, Angelica says, "With my son."

Three simple words, and my plan evaporates.

Chase. He's alive and she's going to him now. I have to follow her. But … my eyes dart back to the witches, to the swirling magic forming above my palm, and then to Angelica once again, disappearing around a corner now.

Dammit!

I wrap myself in invisibility and leap over the balcony, landing as lightly and silently as a cat with the assistance of the magic I just gathered. I follow Angelica from a safe distance, treading lightly and remaining invisible in case another guard appears or she looks over her shoulder. As we walk on and on through the palace, I start to believe that it must be bigger on the inside than it appears from outside. Finally, after climbing another three floors, traversing a great hallway, and walking through a hollowed-out wall between two rooms, Angelica reaches the end of a passage. Stopping in the open doorway, she looks down. I move to the side so I can see past her. At her feet is a spiral stairway leading down to the bottom of a circular room. At the level of the door, a balcony rings the circumference of the room.

Angelica descends the stairs. As I move into the doorway, the room below comes into view: richly embroidered curtains hanging on either side of the window, a pedestal holding a bowl of fruit, and—

And Chase. Lying on the floor on his side, his wrists and ankles still cuffed to chains and his skin a crisscross pattern of gashes and cuts. Silent and unmoving.

CHAPTER TWENTY-TWO

I CLUTCH THE BALCONY RAILING TO KEEP MYSELF STEADY AS I look down at Chase. They tortured every part of him, but his back is definitely the worst. I have to look away from the torn mess of skin so I don't throw up. I inch along the balcony, barely breathing as Angelica reaches the base of the stairs. She nudges Chase's arm with her foot. He doesn't move. "The witches told me to leave someone guarding you," she says, "or to at least attach these chains to the wall. But I knew you weren't going anywhere. I left the bowl of fruit here to prove it to them. To show that even though you're starving and no doubt *desperate* for food, you're unable to move an inch. I'm glad to see I was right." She leans back against the balustrade, swinging something around and around her finger: a key on a string. "I haven't decided what to do with you yet. I wasn't counting on your dear, dead grandmother revealing your existence to everyone. I thought she'd torture you in private and then get rid of you rather than admitting to the world that her precious guardians failed to defeat the great Lord Draven a decade ago." She crouches down and grips his chin between her fingers, turning his face toward her.

Up on the balcony, I release my aching grip on the railing, turn my hands over, and begin gathering magic above my palms. *Patience*, I instruct myself. *Don't act too soon. You'll only get one chance.*

"The fae realm is probably in a flurry of panic right now," Angelica says. "The death of the Seelie Queen and the return of Lord Draven—all in one night! What next? Another Destruction? Another winter?" She pats his cheek and lets his head fall to the side again. "I suppose it might be like another Destruction when the veil comes down. Who knows? The only thing I do know is that chaos will reign as our two worlds merge into one, and I will be the one to take charge amidst that chaos." Chase doesn't respond. Angelica stands and crosses her arms. "You know, I look at the state you're in now and wonder if I should feel bad. You are my son, after all. Shouldn't I feel *something* for you? But then I remember that you've never really been my son, and I've never really been your mother, and then I don't feel bad at all."

She laughs—actually *laughs*. I grit my teeth, telling myself to wait just a little longer, gather just a little more magic.

"In fact," she adds, "given that you left me to spend my remaining centuries in Velazar Prison, I don't think it would have bothered me at all to witness your torture." She brings her foot down hard on his fingers, on his nails that are already split and bleeding. He jerks away—the first sign of life he's shown—groaning in pain.

My heart cries out at the sound, and I throw everything I've got at Angelica. My magic strikes her in the chest and throws her clear across the room. It isn't enough to stun her, but it's enough to leave her in a groaning heap on the floor. My illusion gone, I leap over the railing and land in a crouch, jumping up immediately as all the training I've ever had kicks in. Magic in the form of fire blazes across the room, but I lunge to the side, drawing Angelica away from Chase. My hand shoots out, a sizzle of sparks leaving my fingers and striking the wall just above Angelica's head. She shouts something as she rolls away and springs to her feet. I advance on her, imagining thick mist between us to blind her seconds before I throw myself at her. I slam her against the wall, but she retaliates with a hard punch of magic to my stomach. I stumble backward, gasping for breath, and knock into the pedestal. It wobbles and falls. The fruit bowl shatters, sending oranges and apples rolling across the floor. I dance around the fruit, dodging again as Angelica runs at me. Her magic transforms into hundreds of tiny sharp stones, but I fling them aside with a sweep of power. I spin around and kick. She falls backward against the wall, the quiet ping of a metal key hitting the floor accompanying her gasp. I drop down, grasp the pedestal, release magic to help me hoist it up, and throw it with all my might. It slams into her chest and throws her backward once more. The whack of her head against the wall is audible, and when she slumps to the floor this time, she doesn't move.

After scrambling to the window, I pull the tasseled gold tie-back from the curtain, sever it in half with a spark of magic, and use it to bind Angelica's wrists and ankles. Her magic can probably burn through these ropes in seconds, but if she wakes soon, those seconds might be all I need to fight her down again.

With Angelica bound, I can finally turn my attention to Chase. My eyes dart across the floor, searching for the key Angelica dropped. There! The rusted metal is dull against the shiny marble floor. I dash across the room, grab the key, and drop to my knees beside Chase. Bending over his arm, I examine the metal cuff around his wrist. This metal is the magic-blocking kind, but it isn't stuck to his skin the way the ring at Velazar Prison stuck to my finger. It's just loose enough to shift around and leave his skin raw—which hopefully means it requires only this key and not the special spell the Velazar guard used to remove the ring.

I push the key into the keyhole and twist it. It takes more force than I expected, but eventually the metal springs apart and falls away from Chase's wrist. I gently lift his arm and push the chains aside. Before allowing myself to look at him properly, I remove the other three manacles. I kick them away and scramble back to his side, tears already pricking behind my eyes. For two and a half weeks, I've longed to be close enough to touch him, but now that he's right beside me and I can see the damage done to his body, I'm afraid any touch will hurt him. My hands hover above his arms, his torso, his neck. So many wounds. So much dried blood. I don't know what to do or where to start, and it's so overwhelming that I can't help the tears that fill my eyes.

His eyelids flutter, and a low groan escapes him. "Chase?" I gently take his face between my hands, my thumbs rubbing across the rough stubble along his jaw. "Can you hear me?" His lips move but no sound comes out. His eyes swivel, blinking but not seeming to focus on anything. "It's me, Calla. Please … please say something." I bow my head and squeeze my eyelids together as tears wet my face. "Please, please, please," I murmur. Please everything. *Please remember me, please be okay, please tell me how to save you.*

A rasping whisper breaks the silence: "Goldilocks." My breath catches. "What did you do to your hair?"

I open my eyes, laughter mingling with my tears as relief crashes into me. "You—you're okay," I manage to say. He raises one arm as if to touch me, but his face contorts with pain. It's enough to force my brain back into action. "Um, okay. I removed the manacles. Your body should be able to heal itself now. But it could take a while. You … you're not in a good way."

"I know," he forces out between gritted teeth, closing his eyes and twisting slightly as if he can somehow move away from the pain.

"Don't roll onto your back. It's bad. I—I don't know if it needs to be treated in some way before your magic closes up the wounds. I don't have any potions with me, though."

"My magic will … be enough. I'm stronger than you know."

I look over my shoulder at Angelica. She hasn't moved yet, but she could wake at any moment. I turn back to Chase. I know his magic is strong—I've seen him gather stunner magic within seconds and conjure a blizzard into being in almost an instant—so I don't doubt that he can heal himself without assistance. My concern is for how long it will take. I consider transferring some of my own magic into his body—it's the only kind of healing I know how to do—but the effect would be minimal given the extent of his injuries. It would probably be a better use of my magic to move him up the stairs and out of Angelica's sight instead of trying to heal him down here.

"Chase?" I say. As he struggles to open his eyes again, I scramble away, grab two apples, and return to his side. "We have to get out of this room before Angelica wakes up. We can't escape the palace, but we can hide until help comes. I don't know what happened to Gaius and the rest of the team, but I know they won't just leave us here."

Chase swallows before speaking. "Tunnels," he says. "Emergency escape tunnels for the royal family. That's how Angelica got in."

"Escape tunnels?" That must be what Angelica was speaking to the guard about. "That's perfect. Do you know where they are?"

"Greenhouse. I think. A witch mentioned coming in that way."

"Okay. I don't know where that is, but we can find it."

"I know it. The rose one. I've … been here before."

"Okay. Great." I push one apple into my right pocket and the other into the left. "I'm going to use magic to levitate you up to the—"

"I can stand," Chase says, his face twisting again as he tries to push himself up. He slips back now, panting from the effort and the pain.

"Are you crazy? Just let me do this."

"Seriously," he says. "I can … stand. Just help me up. My arms … I don't know … They're hard to move. But my legs are fine. Bruised, not broken."

I shake my head, but reach for his shoulder anyway. Using a little magic to assist me, I manage to pull him to his feet. Once upright, he lurches forward, but I catch him before he falls. "Rethinking the levitation plan yet?"

"No. That would leave you … way too … exhausted."

I almost laugh. "My potential exhaustion really isn't a concern right now. You're the one I'm worried about. Besides, I'm using magic anyway to help keep you upright."

"Not nearly as much as levitation would require."

I glance over my shoulder at Angelica. One of her bound hands twitches, but her eyes are still closed. "Fine," I whisper to Chase, placing his arm carefully across my shoulders. "We'll do this your way. We're going to conquer the stairs, and we're going to do it quickly."

A huff of air he may have intended to be a laugh blows past my ear. "I've missed your optimism, Miss Goldilocks."

I smile to myself. Warmth expands across my chest, and the urge to pull him into my arms and tell him every single thing I've missed about him is almost overwhelming. *Later*, I promise myself. *Get the hell out of here first.*

Our journey up the stairs is painfully slow. I keep my arm around Chase's back but with a buffer of magic between us, both to stop me from brushing against his wounds and to help push him up the stairs. I look over the balcony as we reach the top. Angelica is beginning to stir.

"Hurry," I whisper, dragging Chase out of the room. He stumbles along beside me, far slower than I'd like. "Turn here." We take a corridor Angelica didn't walk through on her journey here. "I don't know if we should—" A roar of anger echoes from somewhere behind us. "Crap, she just woke up. She'll be out of those bonds in seconds. Where can—Oh, an elevator!" I steer Chase toward it, trying to ignore his groans of agony. I throw a glance over my shoulder as we wait for the door to vanish. The moment it does, we rush inside. As the door reappears, I turn to the semicircular dial. In place of numbers, there are symbols. "Mean anything to you?"

"No. Just go to the bottom."

I move the pointer to the far left of the dial and hope there's nothing mixed-up about this elevator. At first it moves up, but as I'm about to panic, it moves right, down, left and down again. It continues down, down, down until it comes to a gentle halt and the door vanishes. I peer out before we move anywhere and find an empty courtyard. "We're outside, so that helps." We move across the courtyard and look out at the gardens beyond. "Hey, there's a greenhouse right there." I point straight ahead of us to the glass structure, unable to believe our luck.

"No. Not the right one. We need the rose greenhouse."

Okay, I guess we're not that lucky after all. "Are you sure?"

"Yes. The witch was complaining about all the roses that had grown over the tunnel trapdoor. They scraped her when she climbed out." He looks past me. "Uh … just let me think … Yeah, it's that way." He motions to the right.

As we move in that direction, keeping close to the side of the palace, I take an apple from my pocket. "Here. You seem a little less breathless now, so hopefully you're able to eat without too much difficulty."

"Thanks. You don't happen to have a three-course dinner in your pocket, do you?"

"Unfortunately not. Your second course is another apple." We skirt around a hedge, and on the other side, as I look up to make sure we're still alone, I see a statue not too far away. A statue of a trident rising out of rough, stormy waves, mounted atop a cylindrical base.

"What's wrong?" Chase asks when I stop moving.

"The monument." I point ahead. "The monument required for the veil-tearing spell. It's *here*."

"She's going to do the spell here," Chase murmurs.

"What are we supposed to do? We can't take it with us. We're going through a tunnel. Besides, we have no idea what kind of magic is required to move it."

"We … we have to leave it here. At least now we know where Angelica will do the spell. We can come back." He nods past the statue. "And there. That's the right greenhouse."

As quickly as Chase can move, we hurry toward the small domed greenhouse pieced together from stained glass of different colors. The exquisite perfume of roses greets us as we enter. "So we're looking for a trapdoor?"

"Yes. I guess we'll have to look beneath all the bushes."

I let go of Chase—then jerk back as someone in a plum-colored uniform steps out of the bushes. I grasp for an illusion to conceal us, but it's too late. Then I see who it is that's standing in front of us in the uniform that marks her as a member of the Seelie Queen's personal guard, and I'm so shocked I probably would have dropped whatever illusion I came up with.

Olive.

CHAPTER TWENTY-THREE

"MISS LARKENWOOD," OLIVE SAYS. A GUARDIAN SWORD forms in one hand and a knife in the other as she shakes her head. "On the wrong side of the law once again, I see. However did you manage to find your way to the Seelie Court?"

"It was all thanks to you. You lead me right here."

She narrows her eyes. "Still a liar, I see."

"Since we're on the subject of liars," I say as I move slowly in front of Chase, "what are you doing wearing someone else's uniform?"

"This is mine," Olive snaps. "I've been part of the Seelie Queen's personal guard for over three decades."

"If that's true, why aren't you frozen on the platform with the rest of the guards who were supposed to be protecting the former queen last night?"

"Not that I'm required to answer to you, but I returned from my duty in Creepy Hollow late last night. It appears I missed the festivities."

"So you're … what? The Queen's spy? You keep an eye on everything going on at the Guild and then report back to her?"

"Yes. There is one at every Guild. Total waste of time having to deal with Guild business and useless trainees, but that's what the Queen wants. Well, *wanted*, given that she's no longer with us."

"Hey, at least you have one less useless trainee to waste your oh-so-precious time on now."

She points her sword at me as she inches closer. "You know, Calla, it's a pity you turned out to be Griffin Gifted and a murderer. You would have made an excellent guardian if not for those two rather large stains on your record."

"Of course I would have. All thanks to your *exceptional* training methods, I'm sure."

"What is your Griffin Ability anyway?" she asks. "I haven't quite worked it out yet."

"Don't fight me, and I'll consider telling you."

She remains silent, watching me. I return her gaze, waiting. I know it's about to begin. The question is, who will make the first move.

She flings her knife forward. Instantly, I raise my arms, a shield shimmering just beyond them. The knife hits my shield and vanishes. I push Chase sideways into the roses and run at Olive. I hear his cry as he falls, but I try not to feel bad. Rather a few scratches as he lands amongst thorns instead of a guardian knife to the head. Olive slashes her sword through the air, but I change direction at the last second and leap out of reach. She throws another guardian knife. I drop down, letting the knife fly over my head and—is that the corner of a metal trapdoor in the dirt?

I scramble away through the bushes, pulling a knife from my boot and shouting, "Why are you wasting time fighting me? You should be fighting Angelica."

"I'll get to her, don't worry. In the meantime, I need to stop Lord Draven and his murderous accomplice from getting away. Fortunately, the former lord is already close to death, and you—" the bushes ahead of me rustle in protest as Olive leaps in front of me "—are about to find yourself in a similar state."

"I don't think so." An imaginary version of Chase—whole and healthy and powerful—appears behind Olive. She swings around at the sound of his voice, and in her moment of confusion, I stab my knife into her foot and pull it back out.

Her scream of pain is cut off a second later as a ball of magic flies across the greenhouse and hits her abdomen. It knocks her into the air and over the bushes. She lands on the gravelly path running along the center of the greenhouse and doesn't get up. I stand, look around, and see Chase—the real Chase, barely recognizable beneath a mixture of blood and grime—panting slightly as he watches my fallen ex-mentor.

"You stunned her?" I demand.

"Yeah."

"But ..." Instead of reminding him that he's supposed to be healing himself and not wasting large amounts of magic, I hurry to his side to help him. "I think I saw the trapdoor while

I was crawling across the ground." I wipe my blade on my pants and push it back into the sheath in my boot. Ignoring the scratch of thorns, I move bushes aside until I find the metal square in the ground. "This must be it." I point magic at the ring on one side of the square and tug it back toward me. Nothing happens.

"Are you trying to open it?" Chase asks as he steps unsteadily away from me. "Only the royals can do that. The tunnel is for them, after all."

I slowly lower my hand to my side as his words sink into my brain. "What?"

He gets onto his knees with some difficulty. "The trapdoor can only be opened by someone from the royal bloodline."

I stare at him. "You tell me this *now*? How are we supposed to open it?"

He raises an eyebrow. A grimace that could pass for a smile pulls at his lips as he waits for me to arrive at the answer.

"Oh. Right." I press my hands to my face and groan. "I'm an idiot. Why do I keep forgetting you're actually a prince?"

"I don't mind," he says as I lower my hands. "At least I don't have to worry that you're only after me for my title." He's smiling fully now as he watches me. He wraps his hand around the metal ring and says, "Ready to pull?"

I extend my magic again and tug. This time, the trapdoor lifts. Chase lets go of the ring as I pull the trapdoor all the way, allowing it to drop onto an already partially flattened rosebush. I peer into the darkness and see stairs leading down. With a final glance over my shoulder at Olive's prone body, I step carefully down the stairs. I stop after several steps and reach back for Chase. He takes my hand, using it to keep himself steady as he moves down the stairs.

We reach the bottom together. I look up toward the trapdoor and send magic out to pull it closed. Complete darkness surrounds us. Then, without warning, light blazes into being, glowing from beneath the tunnel floor. "Did you do something?" I ask Chase.

"I used the wall to hold myself up. Do you think that counts?"

"Perhaps. Maybe it's your royal touch."

"Maybe." Chase pushes away from the wall. With all the dried blood smeared across his body, it's difficult to tell if his wounds are healing. But he isn't as stooped as he was when we first ran into the garden, and his expression is no longer tense with agony. He must be growing stronger. "Are you okay with being down here?" he asks. "It's a little narrower than the Underground tunnels we've traveled along in Creepy Hollow."

I look around, realizing I hadn't even noticed the closeness of the tunnel walls. Lumethon's desensitization exercises must have made more of a difference than I thought. "Yes, I'm fine, actually. Compared to the gargoyle tunnel, this is like being out in the open." I slip my arm around his back. "Can you run? If Angelica figures out we came this way, she'll be after us in no time."

"Almost. I'm still weak, but most of the pain is gone. You run. I'll try to keep up."

I walk at a brisk pace, holding on to Chase's hand and running a little every few steps. With his longer stride, Chase keeps up with me. "Did you know about the escape tunnels before you heard Angelica mention them?" I ask.

"Yes. At least, I'd heard stories of them. But this palace didn't interest me much when I was Lord Draven, so I never bothered to learn more. The tunnels didn't cross my mind again until I heard Angelica and her witch companions speak of them."

"I suppose it wouldn't have helped us if we'd known they existed. We wouldn't have known where the other side is, and we wouldn't have been able to open—" I stop as a pounding echo reaches us. "Did you hear that?" I whisper.

Chase pauses and listens as the echo comes again. "Perhaps Olive's woken already and is trying to get through the trapdoor."

"She's going to be trying for a long time if royals are the only ones who can open it. At least we know she won't tell Angelica, since she plans to go after her too." I look over at Chase as we continue moving along the twisting tunnel. "Why are some of the guards happy to serve Angelica? She spoke about the guards who are not loyal to her, which implies there are some who are."

"I don't know for sure. It may be that the guards who've been here for a long time, those who were around when Angelica was growing up, saw the way her mother treated her. They may have felt sorry for her, and perhaps some even wished she was the heir instead of her older sister."

"I suppose that could be it." As Chase moves faster beside me, I quicken my brisk walk to a jog. My brain struggles to comprehend how fast his body has managed to heal itself. If I looked anything like he did when I found him just now, my body would take days, not hours, to recover.

"Looks like … the end," Chase says, sounding a little breathless. He doubles over as we stop in front of another set of stairs.

"That was shorter than I expected." I look over my shoulder, more out of paranoia than anything else, then up at the trapdoor. I raise my hands and push against the air with magic. "I think you need to touch it," I say when the trapdoor doesn't budge. Chase climbs the stairs and lifts his hand to the square of metal above his head. I push again, and this time it moves.

Climbing out of the tunnel, we find ourselves in a forest bathed in the pale light of early evening. Though I wonder briefly how it took me the *whole day* to find Chase, I'm just glad we've made it out of the palace. The tall trees that reach elegantly for the sky and the faintly luminous colors surrounding us remind me of the river and the forest at the beginning of the Seelie Court journey. I look behind me. Through the trees, white walls and towers rise up in the distance, separated from us by a translucent layer of silver. The witches' shield. "Still feels like we're far too close to the palace," I say as I close the trapdoor. "Let's get as far away as possible."

"I won't argue with—Look out!" Chase throws his hand out toward me. A rush of air knocks me backward—out of the path of an arrow. I hit the ground on my back. Winded and struggling for breath, I force myself to sit up while looking wildly around.

A centaur gallops through the trees toward Chase, his bow raised. And another one over there—and another! I drop the mental wall around my mind in an instant. I picture the Seelie Queen—the former queen, Angelica's mother—rising from the ground as if she just climbed from the tunnel. I'm invisible; Chase is invisible; there's no one here but her. As I watch her raise her hands and bellow out a command, fatigue hits me, immediate and unyielding. I feel it drain my energy, faster than ever before. I can't stop, though. I need this illusion to get us out of here.

The centaurs, at least a dozen of them, some bearing the evidence of a recent fight, emerge from between the trees. Though some appear confused at our sudden disappearance, they all lower the front half of their bodies and bow their heads to the projection of the Queen. I climb shakily to my feet as something bumps into me, almost knocking me over again. It's Chase, grasping for my arm, my hand. We creep away slowly through the trees, hanging onto one another as I keep my gaze focused over my shoulder, watching the Queen instruct the centaurs to stand guard over the tunnel entrance while she escapes her enemies. "The enemies *you* allowed into this tunnel!" I add to her words. It's a guess, but I assume that's the reason these centaurs are here: to guard the tunnel entrance from a royal traitor just like Angelica.

The centaurs gather around the trapdoor as my projection of the Queen slips through the trees and Chase and I sneak further away. I stop imagining her, but I don't stop thinking of us as invisible. Even when we're far from the centaurs, and even though the effort is exhausting me, I don't let go of the illusion. Centaur eyesight is sharp, and I don't want either of us to wind up with an arrow in our backs.

We start running when I guess they can no longer hear us. Chase gasps beside me from the effort, and I'm breathless from the curse's effects, but still we keep running. Finally, as we reach the edge of the forested area where a formation of multiple rocks encircles a small pool, I let go of the illusion. We climb over a rock, around a few smaller ones, and collapse onto the ground. I lean back against the rough stone surface, breathing deeply and hoping my exhaustion passes. Chase shifts around to face me and rests his side against the rock. His eyes are closed as he pants, "I'm sorry, I'm just … a little lightheaded."

Though fatigue has settled over me like a heavy blanket I can't shed, breathing is at least easier now that I'm sitting. I reach for Chase's hand. Despite being stained with blood and dirt, his skin is smooth. Healed and whole. I slide my fingers between his. "We did it," I whisper. "We actually made it out alive."

CHAPTER TWENTY-FOUR

CHASE'S EYELIDS OPEN AND HIS WARM BROWN EYES SETTLE on me. For a long, silent moment, we simply watch each other. Then he raises his hand and rests it against my cheek. His thumb brushes beneath my lashes where dark makeup stains my skin. He moves his hand down my neck to my shoulder, where he rubs a strand of my charcoal-colored hair between his fingers. "My dark angel," he says. "That's what you looked like spinning around the tower room, fighting off a queen." His hand slides down my arm and closes around my fingers. "After they began the …" He swallows, choosing not to say it, to skip past the word *torture*. "I was afraid I'd never see you again. I was afraid I wouldn't … last until the ball."

Perhaps it's my curse-induced exhaustion. Perhaps it's the thought of what he suffered through, or the realization that I finally, *finally* have him back, or the ever-present ache surrounding Victoria's death and my parents' incarceration, or the knowledge that the full moon is only a day away and our fight is far from over. Perhaps it's everything. But suddenly I feel a dam's worth of tears rising up behind my eyes. They spill down my cheeks as my face crumples and a sob wrenches free from my chest.

Chase's arms encircle me, pulling me tightly against his chest. I worry that I'm going to hurt him, but I don't see any remaining lacerations through my falling tears. I sink against him, letting him rub my back as I cry myself empty. I feel terrible because I'm the one who should be comforting him, not the other way around, but I can't seem to stop.

When eventually I stop shuddering, I pull gently away. "I'm sorry," I mumble as I wipe my tears, my fingers coming away black from the smeared makeup.

"*I'm* sorry," he says.

I wipe my fingers on my pants. "For what?"

"The smell. And the blood and dirt. You can probably tell it's been a while since I showered."

I laugh through my remaining tears. "You don't honestly think I care about that, do you?"

He smiles and takes my right hand. Lifting it, he says, "I see you got a few tattoos."

I nod and sniff. "First mission. Ana said I wasn't properly part of the team until I got some ink. This is the only one that's permanent." I point to the rose on my fourth finger. It's the clearest shape; the other marks are fading already. "I, um, still want the phoenix on my back. And I want you to do it."

He raises my hand to his lips and kisses each finger before saying, "When all this is over, I'd be honored to do that for you." His fingers slip between mine as he lowers our hands. He looks down. "The last time we spoke with the rings—"

"I'm know, I'm so sorry. I shouldn't have shouted at—"

"No, stop." He shakes his head. "I'm not looking for an apology. I … I want to know how you are. How you're … dealing with what happened."

I pull my hand away from his and wrap my arms around my knees. "It's shameful to admit, but … I wanted to kill Zed. I wanted to kill the witches. I'm filled with so much guilt over what happened that I was desperate to somehow make it right. I'm *still* desperate to make things right, but now I've realized that … I can't. Nothing I do—*nothing*—will ever bring Victoria back or make Ryn and Vi hate me any less. And that leaves me feeling so … helpless."

Chase nods. "I know."

Of course he knows. He knows better than anyone what's it like to cause grief and pain and have no way to ever set things right. "What's left, then?" I whisper. "What can I do?"

"The only thing you can do: apologize. Sincerely and from the depths of your heart. After that, it's up to them whether they choose to forgive you or not."

"And what if they don't?"

"Then that's something both you and they have to live with."

I look away, nodding as more tears rise to the surface and keep me from being able to speak. Eventually, when I've blinked them away and got my emotions under control, I force a half-hearted smile onto my face and say, "I'm officially changing the subject now." I look him up and down. "It's remarkable how quickly you've healed."

He stretches his arms out in front of him, turning them over as he examines them. "It helps to have an unusually large amount of magic. Actually, it helps to have *any* magic. If I were human, I'd have to worry about infection, blood poisoning, scarring. But none of that's a concern." Eyeing the black vine of thorns twisting down his left arm, he adds, "Even my tattoo has returned to normal, which I find amazing."

"It is amazing. I thought the tattoo would be a mess once your skin healed. What about your back, though? That seemed to be the worst."

"Still feels tender," he says, twisting around so I can have a look. "That was from …" He shudders. "Well, I'd rather not speak about it. Are there any open wounds left?"

"No," I say with some surprise. "Your skin has healed over every single gash. They look more like pink, shiny burns at the moment. Well, from what I can see past all the dried blood."

He swivels back around. "I think it's time to get clean. If we have to spend the night out here, which I assume is what we're doing if we can't access the faerie paths, then I'd rather not subject you to the smell any longer."

"Well, we could start walking," I say as he pushes himself up, "but it would take us a long time to reach an area we can access the paths from. Gaius will have come back for us before then." And walking anywhere in my current state of fatigue does not seem appealing.

Chase extends a hand and pulls me to my feet. "Is there a

possibility the rest of the team is stuck inside the palace or on the grounds?"

"I don't think so. Our agreement was to run if anything went wrong and regroup somewhere far beyond the Seelie Queen's reach. If there was enough time for the guests to get away, then I assume our team got away too."

"Good." Chase climbs between the rocks. He pulls off the remaining shreds of his T-shirt, wincing as his barely healed skin stretches across his back. In the dim light, I take in the full canvas of crisscrossing stripes. I picture the whip cracking down—and look away, blinking and stopping my thoughts before they can make me sick. I look to the sky instead. The blue-purple of twilight and the first stars twinkling faintly. "Are you coming?" Chase calls as he lowers himself into the pool.

"Yeah," I say, covering a yawn as I follow him. If only sleep would help me, but it's Elizabeth's tonic that I need.

"Aren't you getting in?" Chase asks as I sit on a rock beside the pool and cross my legs.

I shake my head, feeling shy all of a sudden. "I'm not nearly as smelly as you are," I say instead of admitting my self-consciousness.

"That's true." He immerses himself fully in the water and rubs his face and hair before standing again. He pushes his wet hair back, then rubs his hands up and down his arms, removing the blood and layers of grime he collected while in that horrible dungeon. "Hey, did you mention a second apple earlier?" he asks.

"I did." I remove the apple from my pocket as he wades closer to fetch it.

"Do you want some?" he asks.

"No, I'm fine, thank you." I'm actually pretty hungry, but he needs food far more than I do. "Stand here and turn around," I tell him. "You eat, I'll clean." He devours the apple as I lean down and rub my hands gently along his shoulders and the top of his back, wiping his skin clean. My fingers move carefully over the pink twisted scars. They'll soon be gone, but they're probably still hurting as the flesh beneath them continues to knit itself back together. "I didn't know the former queen could be so cruel," I murmur.

Chase is silent as he tosses the apple core into the trees beyond the rocks. Another few moments pass as my fingers continue to move across his back. I can't reach further down from where I'm sitting, but I don't want to stop either. "I was a cruel lord," he says quietly. "She was probably just making sure I paid for that."

"It's too bad she waited so long." My hands come to rest on his shoulders. "The cruel lord she wanted to punish no longer exists."

He reaches for my right hand while leaning back so his shoulders press against my knees. As our fingers lace together, sparkles of light begin to dance around our hands. "In the human realm," he says quietly, "they talk about sparks flying when two people are attracted to one another. It was only after I got here, to this world of magic, that I realized sparks really do fly."

My heart thunders in my chest, leaving me almost breathless. I want to slide my arms around him and press kisses against his neck. I want to join him in the water and take up right where we left off when the golden river whirlpool sucked us down. But I also want an answer to an important question, and I may not ask that question if I let a distraction get in the way first. "Chase," I say as he turns his head to the side and kisses my hand. "What did Luna See about me?"

He stills. The sparkles float away. "Elizabeth told you."

"She accidentally said something. Not much. Just that I didn't need to worry about dying while rescuing you because Luna Saw me in your future."

"She … she did See you." He lets go of my hand and turns to face me. "Are you upset that I didn't say anything to you about it?"

"I … I don't think so. I don't know. Should I be? Is this one of the secrets you kept since the moment you first saw me?"

"No. I didn't even think of the vision when we first met. Luna told me about it so many years ago, her vision of a woman in gold—which I assumed meant someone *wearing* gold—that I filed it away in the back of my mind and barely thought of it in the years that followed. It wasn't until the day I first took you to the mountain and Gaius removed the time traveling ability from you that I remembered it. We had returned to Wickedly Inked. You were about to leave, and I wondered if I'd ever see you again, and that must have … sparked something in my memory, I suppose."

I try to remember the moment, but it's a little fuzzy, obscured by the attack that came straight afterward when Saber arrived in search of his time traveling bangle. But I think I remember Chase looking oddly at me. I think I asked him if something was wrong. And he said … he said … but I can't remember what he said. "So. What was in this vision?"

He hesitates. "Are you sure you want to know?"

"Is it something horrible?"

"No." He smiles. "At least, I don't think it's horrible. But futures aren't set in stone, and ours could easily change. Perhaps it's changed already. The reason I didn't say anything to you about it is because I didn't want you to feel as if you have no choice. As if you somehow had to make what she Saw come true."

I frown. "Now I'm not sure if I want to know what it was about. I mean … if it was a picture of you and me and twenty babies, I'm not sure I'm ready for that."

Chase laughs. Loudly and properly and for the first time since we escaped. "It's up to you," he says when he's recovered. "If you want to know what she Saw, I'll tell you. But if you want to live life certain you've made your own choices and were never influenced by anyone else's interpretation of a possible future, that's fine too."

I narrow my eyes at him. "Are you trying to convince me not to ask you?"

"No." His smile is genuine and honest. "I will tell you if you want to know."

"Hmm." I shift backward, swing my legs to the side, and untie my laces. "I think—" I pull my shoes off "—I will—" I tug my jacket off "—make my own choices." I slide into the water and look up at him. "I'm curious about what she Saw, but if you decided not tell me, then I can respect that. And like you said," I add, "our future's probably changed already anyway."

His hands slip around my waist and pull me closer. "Did I tell you I missed you?"

I push my fingers into his wet hair, then run them down his neck and over his chest, trailing dancing, flashing sparks across his skin. "Yes," I breathe.

His eyes close as his brow touches mine. "Did I tell you I dreamed of kissing you?"

My hands rise again and gently clasp his face. The air between us fills with specks of golden light as my thumb brushes over his lips. "Yes."

His head tilts to the side. I feel his apple-scented breath on my skin.

Then he freezes.

"What's wrong?" I ask, my eyes flying open.

Chase frowns as he focuses on something over my shoulder. "That had better not be a full moon."

I twist around and see the silvery orb hanging above the horizon. "No. Full moon is tomorrow night."

"*Tomorrow*—Are you serious?"

I turn back to him. "Uh, yes."

"We have to go back. Immediately. We have to stop her."

"Of course we have to stop her, but you and I can't do that on our own."

"Actually, we can," he says, moving past me to climb out of the water. "I don't generally like to bring this up, but I single-handedly destroyed large parts of the fae realm once upon a time. As long as there's no morioraith around, I can probably take out my mother and a pair of witches."

"I'm fully aware of the devastation you're capable of *on a normal day*," I say as he pulls me from the pool. "But several hours ago, you were close to death. Your wounds may have healed, but you're still weak. You haven't eaten in days—and no, the apples don't count. You need to *rest*!"

Chase stops on top of a rock and looks back at me as he drips water all around him. "So what do you propose? We find something to eat, rest here for the night, and take on Angelica some time tomorrow?"

"Yes. That sounds infinitely more sensible."

He nods. "You're right. I'm sorry. I'm going to blame the hunger for my illogical Plan A."

"Since we're no longer rushing back to the palace, would you like to add 'fix torn T-shirt' to Plan B?"

"Ah, yes." He looks down at himself as if just remembering that he shed the tatters of his T-shirt. "Unfortunately, I'm not very good at clothes casting."

"I'll do it quickly," I say, bending to retrieve the T-shirt from where he dropped it earlier. "It won't be neat or clean, but it'll at least be whole." When I've joined the torn pieces with my limited clothes casting knowledge, I hand it to him. "So what now?" I ask, rubbing my hands up and down my arms as I begin to shiver. "We scour the nearby trees for anything edible?"

"Yes." Chase climbs back down beside me, wavering a little on unsteady legs, and raises his hands. A blast of warm air spins around me, tangling my hair and drying my skin in seconds.

"Stop wasting your energy!" I tell him when he stops.

"Stop worrying. I've got all night to recover. Are you dry yet?"

I pat my pants. "Mostly. My clothes are still a bit damp."

The blast of hot hair comes again, wrapping around us both this time. It's almost impossible to breathe with the air being continually sucked away from me, so I'm breathless by the time he's done. "Okay, let's start looking. There must be something edible out here."

I push my arms into my jacket sleeves and pull my boots back on. "Not that it's important," I say as we climb over and around rocks toward the trees on the other side of the pool, "but what were you doing looking over my shoulder when you were supposed to be kissing me?"

"It's dangerous out here," he says. "I was just making sure we were still alone."

Hopefully that's the truth. Hopefully he wasn't bored before our kiss even began.

Not wanting to alert the centaurs to our presence, we search as far into the trees as we dare, finding nothing more than a clump of roots that Chase assures me are edible. He grasps the purple leaves and yanks the bulbous hairy root from the ground. "You're sure we can eat that?" I ask, my tone doubtful.

"Yes. Luna often cooked with this."

"We're not exactly equipped to boil stuff out here."

"That's what magic is for," Chase says.

We return to the rocks, which feel safer to hide amongst than the trees. I lean over the pool and clean the mottled roots, then lower my head further and splash water onto my face, doing my best to clean the remaining black makeup off. Chase holds the roots one at a time between his hands and heats them until their skin begins to split. Then we sit together in the darkness, our only light the luminescence glowing from the pink buds in the nearby trees, and eat our meager dinner.

"Hmm," Chase says. "They're pretty bland. And not quite the same as if they were boiled."

"But good enough to … fill an empty stomach." My jaw strains as I yawn widely in mid-sentence. I rub my tired eyes.

"You need to sleep, Miss Goldilocks. We need to be—" He straightens, his gaze pointed toward the sky. "Did you see that?"

I blink. "See what?"

"The shadow that passed across the moon for a moment. It looked a bit like … a flying creature."

I grip Chase's arm. "Like a dragon or a gargoyle? Do you think it could be Gaius or someone else we know?"

"I'm not sure. I'd rather not send up a signal, and then it turns out to be an acquaintance of our new Queen."

"That would suck."

Chase stands and looks around. "I'm going to send the signal over there," he says, pointing to a flat, open patch of ground beyond the trees. "We can remain hidden here, but we should be able to see who it is. And if the centaurs notice the signal, it won't bring them directly to us."

"Okay. What is this—" A second later, a skinny fork of lightning zigzags down and strikes the ground Chase was pointing at. "Right. That kind of signal."

We duck down and keep watch between the rocks. I count

the seconds. Nothing happens for almost two minutes, but then a large, winged shape swoops down and lands almost exactly where the lightning struck. "That's a dragon," Chase whispers. "It could be Gaius riding it. He's not a fan of the gargoyles."

"Is anyone a fan of the gargoyles?"

"Uh … not really."

A much smaller shape slides off the dragon and lands on the ground. It walks to the side, past the dragon, and I can now make out its silhouette. Tall, lanky, with a tuft of messy hair. "Yeah, that's Gaius," I say with a smile.

Chase raises his hands and forms a ball of light, dim as a dying candle, between his palms. It takes Gaius a few moments before he notices it. When he does, he ducks down immediately. "He doesn't know it's us," Chase murmurs. He rotates one hand, and the light begins to shift and change. Slowly, it transforms from a ball into a zigzag. A perfect miniature lightning bolt.

Gaius jumps up and hurries toward us. He pauses to flatten himself against a tree, looking around, before continuing. "Chase?" he whispers once he's almost at the rocks.

Chase allows his light to vanish as he stands. "Looking for me?" he asks.

CHAPTER TWENTY-FIVE

A SECOND DRAGON ARRIVES CARRYING ELIZABETH AND Lumethon, along with four gargoyles, one each for Darius, Kobe and Ana, plus a riderless gargoyle. Ana dashes through the trees, leaps over the rocks, and flings herself at Chase. "You're alive, you're alive, you're alive," she whispers as she hugs him tightly.

"Of course I'm alive," he says as he embraces her. "It takes a lot to finish me off." He meets my gaze over the top of her head. I look away as I try not to think of how close to death he was when I found him. How much longer would he have lasted without access to his magic?

Chase's reunion with the rest of his teammates is more contained but no less heartfelt. "You braved the gargoyle cave for me?" he says as he clasps Darius's hand. "Thanks, man. I'm impressed."

"Yeah, well, don't expect it to happen again. Damn thing nearly bit my arm off." A low growl comes from the gargoyles' direction.

"I think he heard you," Ana says with a low giggle.

"Well done, Calla," Gaius says as he pulls me into a brief hug. "We were all so worried after you suddenly stopped responding last night, but I told everyone you'd be fine. I told them you'd rescue Chase."

"Oh, yeah, you sound super confident *now*," Ana says, giving Gaius's arm a playful shove. "You were just as freaked out last night as the rest of us."

"Hey, can we all get down amongst the rocks?" I whisper. "Centaurs are guarding the forest, and if they weren't sure where we were earlier, they'll have no doubt now."

"Your illusion told them to guard the trapdoor," Chase says as we all crouch down and make our way back to the pool where the rocks form a natural barrier around us. "Hopefully they'll continue to obey that instruction."

Something soft touches my arm before a smooth, cold object is pressed into my hand. A little glass bottle. I look around and find Elizabeth just behind me. *Thanks*, I mouth to her as I wrap my fingers around the bottle. I know exactly what's in it.

It's a challenge to fit eight of us into the small space beside the pool, but somehow we manage it. As we shuffle around, I remove the lid from the bottle and tip the contents down my throat. By the time we're all settled, the empty bottle is somewhere behind me and I'm already beginning to feel better.

Lumethon faces away from the group and raises both hands. I sense a prickle of magic in the air above us. "You talk," she whispers to the rest of us. "I'll fortify the area." Kobe lifts one hand and adds his magic to hers.

"How long have you been searching for us?" Chase asks.

"Several hours," Gaius answers. "We started on the ground, which meant we couldn't cover much area, but we wanted to wait until nightfall before taking to the sky."

"We didn't know if you'd made it out of the palace, of course," Elizabeth says, "but since we can't get past that dome-like shield and back onto the palace grounds, we figured we'd just keep searching out here. Darius," she adds. "The backpack?"

"Oh, right, the food," Darius says. "And clothes."

"The statue is here," Chase informs the group. "The Monument to the First Mer King. Angelica's obviously going to try to tear through the veil right here at the Seelie Court."

"I saw it too," Gaius says, "from the carriage as we were flying away last night. That's why we came back prepared. Flying creatures, more weapons, unbreakable rope, food."

"Food," Chase repeats with a low groan as Darius unwraps several delicious smelling bundles. Cold meat, fruit, a mixture of nuts.

"Yeah, we figured we wouldn't be leaving here again without a fight," Ana says.

"And given the, uh, state you were in when we last saw you," Gaius adds, "we thought you might need some … sustenance."

"What happened to you after Angelica pulled her insane stunt?" Darius asks. "We were running out of the dungeons so we missed it, but Ana filled us in pretty quickly."

"I wasn't aware of much," Chase says as he passes me some food after pulling on a clean T-shirt. "I was taken to a room in one of the towers. I faded in and out of consciousness until Calla showed up some time this afternoon."

Everyone turns to me to fill in the rest. "I, uh, stopped responding because I kind of … passed out. I think it was from overuse of my Griffin Ability. It drained a lot of my energy." Which is the truth. No need to add that there's a curse involved. I quickly fill the team in on everything that happened after I woke up amongst the rose bushes this morning. I crunch on a handful of nuts and add, "What happened to all of you?"

"We got out of the dungeons fairly easily," Elizabeth says. "There was no guard by the tapestry. Plenty of screaming coming from the direction of the ballroom, though. We were completely visible as we ran back through the palace, but no one paid any attention to us. Once we saw the madness in the ballroom and the terrified guests flooding out, we realized why. Everyone fled to the carriages, so we joined them."

"I wanted to get Chase off the platform," Ana says. "I mean, he was *so close*. Right there in the same room as us. But Gaius said we wouldn't be able to get through the witches' shield and that we had to stick to the plan. Get out and regroup before attempt number two."

"Yes, and I still think that was the right thing to do," Gaius says.

"We did search for you, Calla," Lumethon adds, looking

over at me. "We didn't just abandon you. We called and called, we searched the crowd, we looked around the courtyard and the nearby rooms, but eventually we had to leave. We got one of the last carriages."

"I understand," I tell her. "That was the plan, so I'm glad you stuck to it. If not, you'd probably be trapped in the palace and we'd be out here waiting for you to come find us."

"Fine, I guess the plan was sensible," Ana admits. "Oh, and Gaius made us sleep in the carriage on the flight back. Can you imagine that? Trying to sleep after seeing the Queen beheaded and Chase looking like ... well ... you know."

"Considering we planned to remove our costumes and gather our things immediately upon getting home and come straight back here to fight our new Queen," Gaius says, "sleep seemed like a good idea."

"So what's our plan now?" Kobe asks, bringing the conversation back to the matter at hand. "How will we get through the dome of magic protecting the palace?"

"We don't have to," I say, since Chase's mouth is still occupied with his dinner. "We can get back in through the royal family's escape tunnel. Chase can open it for us since, you know, royal blood and all that."

"Wicked," Ana says with a grin.

"We'll just have to draw the centaurs away from the tunnel trapdoor."

"Easy enough," Darius says with a shrug. "Cool, so shall we go now?"

"Well, Chase ... hasn't yet regained his full strength," I say, trying to avoid offending him by using the word 'weak.' "We were planning to go back tomorrow. Early in the morning before it's light." And I'm trying to avoid using my Griffin Ability to conceal everyone.

Darius looks around the group with raised eyebrows. "Am I the only one feeling a sense of urgency here?"

"No, you are not," Lumethon says with a sigh. "But taking Angelica down is likely to be a whole lot easier if Chase is as strong as possible."

"Unless there's a morioraith hanging around," Chase says. "We'll need to be prepared for that."

"We are," Gaius says. "We brought bells. Not ideal, but I'm afraid I don't own any gongs, and attempting to create some would have taken time."

"Bells?" Chase repeats. "That old set of handbells from the storage room?"

"Yes, the ones my father owned. If you enlarge them before ringing them, they produce quite a deep, full reverberation. Should be enough to get a morioraith to back off."

I look at Gaius's backpack, which isn't all that big. "I assume you shrunk these bells before coming here?"

"Oh, yes, of course. They're tiny. We can each take one in a pocket. Just be ready to use an enlarging spell."

Chase nods. "Okay. Everything will be fine, then. Angelica can't begin the spell until the moon is high tomorrow night. We'll have stopped her by then."

"Wait, hang on," I say as my mind runs once again through the details I saw in the visions. "If Angelica doesn't have you—" I look at Chase "—how will she produce the massive amount of energy required to tear through the veil? You know, that lightning bolt from the visions."

"That energy doesn't have to come from me," Chase says. "In fact, in the original visions, I don't think it was ever meant to come from me."

"But … in the vision my mother had, there was a man—which would have been you if this had been carried out years ago—who climbed onto the monument. He held the trident and it started glowing as the witch began her spell. I assumed the glow and the bright flash at the end both resulted from your power."

"That was my first thought, but then what about the third vision? Remember all those people in the tower? The dozens and dozens who were killed?" I nod as I reach forward for another few strawberries. "The amount of magical energy released from that many people would be far more powerful than any lightning bolt I could produce."

I pause with a strawberry halfway toward my mouth. "You're saying the energy could come from … *people*?"

Beside me, Ana nods. "Elizabeth was explaining this on the way here. You know what happens to magical energy when someone dies, right?"

"Yes. It's released into nature. It can't be captured. Although," I add as my mind spins back through everything I've heard, "Tharros somehow did it, didn't he? He stored magic in those griffin discs."

"Possibly," Chase says, leaning back on his hands now that he's finished eating. "I've done a lot of reading on the subject, and the stories have become mixed up over time. Some say Tharros had those six discs long before he was killed and that he used witch magic to transfer his—and possibly other fae—magic into the discs. Others say the discs were created after his death in order to lock the chest, and during the magical locking process, some of his power was transferred into those discs. Others say that both stories are true: The discs were already in existence, and the reason they were used to lock the chest was because Tharros's magic was so powerful it could only be contained by equally powerful magic. In other words, his own."

"I think the Guild's official explanation is the second one," Gaius says. "They obviously don't like to make reference to any story that could include the capturing of a person's energy."

"So … is it possible then?" I ask.

"Yes." Elizabeth leans forward, resting her elbows on her knees. "The witches have rituals for capturing energy from other beings. Other fae have learned these rituals over time."

"So *that's* why Angelica and Amon are working with witches," I say. "Well, just Angelica now, since she's clearly going ahead without Amon." Now the words I overheard yesterday make sense. *We prepared for this before leaving Creepy Hollow. Together, we have the magical energy of at least fifty men.* I shudder at the thought. Did all those men come from Creepy Hollow?

"So that's why I think the power to rip through the veil was never meant to be *my* power," Chase says, "I assume that in the vision, I was the one who absorbed all the released energy from those people and channeled it into the trident. But I think anyone could do that part. Anyone who knows the witch rituals, at least."

"What do you think the Guild's doing about this?" Ana asks. "I bet they're feeling like total idiots for letting Angelica go free."

"Well, if the Queen—the previous Queen—told them to free Angelica," Gaius says, "they probably couldn't say no. And the Guild didn't know about the visions at that point, did they?" Gaius looks at me.

"No, my mother's interrogations began the day after that."

"The Guild is probably planning an attack as we speak," Chase says. "Who knows, we may even end up fighting beside them tomorrow morning."

"Ugh, what a nightmare," Ana says. "Let's make sure to stay out of their way."

"Perhaps we should rest," Kobe says, "seeing as we're not doing anything until dawn."

"Yes, good idea," Gaius says. "Chase and Calla can sleep, and the rest of us can take turns to keep watch."

"Oh, I'm fine," I say, not wanting any special treatment. "I can also keep watch."

Elizabeth stares me down. "You were fighting while we were resting. You need to sleep." I can hear the threat behind her words. The threat to tell everyone about the curse if I don't make sure I'm properly rested. I want to remind her that sleep doesn't do nearly as much for me as her tonic does, but that would require explaining myself to everyone. I almost decide to do it, to blurt everything out instead of keeping the curse a secret from Chase and the rest of the team, but I remind myself that we may very well need my Griffin Ability to help defeat

Angelica tomorrow. I can't have everyone babying me and telling me not to use it.

So I keep silent as everyone shifts around, removing jackets to use as pillows and trying to make their tiny space as comfortable as possible. We're all squished against each other, except for Lumethon and Gaius who agree to stay awake for the first part of the night. My exhausted body thanks me as I lower my head onto my rolled-up jacket. Chase, lying right beside me, reaches for my hand. My lips curl into a smile as my eyes slide shut, and I fall asleep with his hand wrapped around mine.

CHAPTER TWENTY-SIX

AN HOUR BEFORE DAWN THE FOLLOWING MORNING, WE'RE all ready to bring the threat of this veil-tearing vision to an end. Well, almost all of us. I had hoped to be more rested, but I'm nearly as tired as I was last night. Instead of dwelling on what this means about the curse and how far it's progressed, I focus on our plan: find Angelica and stun her. Find the witches and stun them. Immobilize all three women and wait until the Guild arrives before disappearing back through the tunnels.

Yeah. I'm almost certain it isn't going to be that easy.

Getting back into the tunnel goes smoothly enough, though. Darius and Kobe draw the centaurs away from the trapdoor, then circle back to join us in the tunnel. At the other end, we place the communication spell on ourselves before Chase carefully opens the trapdoor into the greenhouse. We thought guards might be stationed here, or even the witches. We considered magical beasts, or weapons rigged to fly through the air as soon as we climb out of the tunnel. But nothing moves to attack us as Chase pushes the trapdoor back. He stays on the stairs and throws a stone up through the opening. An alarm that sounds like voices screaming blares through the silence.

"Well, there goes the element of surprise," Ana says.

"Yeah, but we didn't think we'd have that for long." Gaius replies.

Elizabeth peers up the stairs. "So that's it? Just an alarm?"

Chase throws another stone, but nothing else happens. We ascend the stairs and push bushes aside as we step into the greenhouse—and that's when the real obstacle becomes apparent: A translucent layer of silver—a miniature version of the dome-like shield protecting the palace—covers the whole of the greenhouse.

"So she plans to trap us here," Chase says above the screeching alarm. "That's probably why it was so easy to draw the centaurs away from the tunnel. They *wanted* us to get inside. No doubt they've returned and will do everything in their power to keep that trapdoor from opening."

"Horrible woman," Ana says. "She's probably on her way here right now."

"Let's not waste any time then." Chase pushes his way through the bushes to the path running along the center of the greenhouse. "Now would probably be a good time for everyone to block their ears. And perhaps cover your eyes. Actually, use a bit of magic and cover yourself with a shield. I think I'm about to bring the greenhouse down."

I do as he says, pressing my fingers into my ears and covering myself with magic. Seconds later, bright light illuminates the world beyond my eyelids and a crack of thunder rips through the air. Glass shatters around me, glancing off the layer of magic that envelops my body. Silence reigns as the pattering of glass comes to an end. I guess Chase's magic shattered through the screaming alarm as well as through the glass. I peek through one half-open eyelid. "Did it work?"

"Not yet," Chase says. "I thought that would be strong enough, but … I'll try again."

"Are *you* strong enough?" Darius asks.

"Yes. I just wasn't expecting this much power from the witches."

The second flash of light is almost bright enough to burn through my eyelids. The crackle and *crash*, the shudder of earth, the shockwave rushing through the air—it's enough to leave me breathless. I open my eyes and slowly remove my fingers from my ears, which are ringing despite the fact that I blocked them. "I'm guessing that worked?"

"Yes. Come on, let's get moving. Spread out and begin searching," Chase instructs. "Gather stunner magic as you go. Don't hesitate if you see a witch or Angelica. If you can get them into the dungeon while they're stunned, even better. And keep verbal communication to a minimum; it can be distracting."

We step out of the greenhouse into the quiet, still gardens. Stars still sprinkle the sky above us, but along the horizon, a patch of purple-gray indicates the coming dawn. "Hang on." I point to an empty patch of the garden. "Isn't that where we saw the monument?"

"Damn, that thing must be easier to move than the merpeople let on," Darius says. "Was there anything in one of the visions that might indicate where the monument needs to be for the spell to happen?"

"There was a tower," I say, "although the actual spell didn't happen there, and I don't remember the tower in the vision looking like the towers here. So perhaps the spell can happen anywhere as long as Angelica has the mer statue and a full moon."

"Well, keep an eye out for the statue while you're searching," Chase tells everyone. "Let's go."

We separate into our smaller prearranged groups. Darius and Kobe remain outside to begin their search of the grounds. Ana, Lumethon and Gaius aim for the thick, twisting vines covering part of the walls on the left side of the palace. Vines they climb easily before hoisting themselves onto a balcony and slipping through an open door. Chase, Elizabeth and I hurry toward the right side of the palace, where we duck into the courtyard that leads to the elevator.

We choose a symbol at random on the dial—a tiny picture of a book—and the elevator carries us up, sideways, and up again before opening into a library far grander than any I've stepped foot in before. Endless shelves of gold-embossed spines rise from floor to ceiling. Does anyone ever read these books? Are they real, or simply empty pages displayed for show?

"I doubt Angelica's in here," Chase whispers, "but let's take a quick look anyway."

I remove my two knives from my boots and grip them tightly as we peer down rows of books and into the recesses each tall window is set into. Cushioned seats form comfortable reading nooks beneath each window, but each is as empty as the last. We tread silently on the carpet, and the only thing I hear are the occasional words whispered directly into my ear via the communication spell. As long as I don't hear urgency in anyone's voice, I ignore the murmurs from my teammates who are searching elsewhere in the palace.

As we reach the other end of the library, Chase stops and raises a finger to his lips. *Listen*, he mouths. I stand still, barely breathing as I listen intently. Seconds of silence pass before a faint echo reaches us. The echo of footsteps.

"How can there be footsteps," Elizabeth whispers, "if the library is carpeted?"

I look up to the second level of the library, a mezzanine filled with more towering shelves of books and ringed by an ornamental railing. "Perhaps there's no carpet up there." We head upstairs and find the same carpet covering the floor, but the footsteps are still audible, closer now than before. We follow the sound, but every time I dart around a shelf, convinced I'm about to see something, I find the space empty.

"Split up," Chase whispers. "Look out for doors along the edge of the room. There may be passages running through the library walls."

We move off in different directions. My solo search turns up no doors or hidden passages. At one point, I hear the footsteps above me, but then they sound to my left. I'm almost certain now that this is a spell of some sort, not genuine footsteps, but I continue left anyway. I peek around another shelf and narrow my eyes at the empty space on the other side, wondering if something invisible is waiting there, watching me. As I continue staring, I feel a presence behind me, a tingle of magic in the air. With my heart thumping in my chest, I whip around, slashing an X through the air with both knives—but there's nothing there.

"They're playing with us," I whisper, slowly turning on the spot and looking all around me.

"I know," Chase replies from wherever he is. "Taunting us. I'm getting tired of it. If they won't come out and face us, then let's—"

At that moment, the reverberating clang of a bell breaks through the silence. Over and over it rings, the sound bouncing across the library. "I'm by the stairs!" Elizabeth shouts into our ears.

I spin around and run as the clanging of the bell comes to a sudden stop. I'm out from between the shelves and racing alongside the balcony when I see her at the top of the stairs, her arms raised and magic flashing in the air above her. The bell lies discarded on the floor. Chase reaches her side before I do, but she's already got things under control. Within a spherical shield of magic, a black form rebounds in every direction off the inner surface of the shield, rapidly stretching apart and pulling together, and occasionally shifting into black smoke. A morioraith. "I got it," Elizabeth says breathlessly as I stop beside her.

Gaius's voice sounds in my ear: "Everyone okay?"

"Yes. I saw it coming. Got the bell out just in time." Her

arms move in response to the twisting, reforming sphere. "Can you get rid of this thing?" she asks Chase. "I'm kinda struggling to keep it contained."

He lifts his hands and adds his own magic to the sphere. "I've got it. You can let go." He moves toward the nearest window, so I run ahead of him and push it open. Outside, the edge of the sun has just broken across the horizon. I step aside. Chase stands at the window with the sphere floating just ahead of him and throws his arm forward. The trapped morioraith soars through the air. A second later, lightning zigzags down and strikes it. In the thundering boom that follows, I search the air and the garden, looking for black smoke or a dripping black creature. "I don't know if that worked," Chase says, "but I don't see it anywhere."

We head downstairs and out a different door. We've barely looked both ways down the corridor before laughter echoes toward us from the left. "More games?" I murmur.

"Probably trying to lead us somewhere," Chase says, "so I vote we turn right instead."

We turn right, walk to the end of the corridor, and enter a wider hallway. We continue, but not a minute passes before we hear the laughter again, up ahead of us. "Infuriating," Elizabeth mutters as we stop and look around. The laughter sounds again, more childlike this time. Chase clenches his hand into a fist. Thunder booms loudly and unexpectedly, rumbling and echoing off the walls. In response, the laughter increases in volume, coming at us from all directions. High-pitched, wild, overlapping in layer upon layer of sound.

"Just keep going," I say, wishing I wasn't holding knives so

I could instead cover my ears. "They're watching us from somewhere, but if we keep looking, we'll find them eventually." *I hope,* I add silently.

We move swiftly along the hallway and into smaller passages, looking in every room we pass. The wild laughter follows us. At the end of another corridor, we find ourselves in a room full of bathing pools. Steam rises from each one and petals float upon the water. White columns wrapped with ivy and glow bugs stand between the pools. I breathe in the rose-scented air and cast a longing gaze at the pools before turning away and leaving the room. If only I could soak in steaming water and forget every care and concern.

With a sigh, I follow Chase and Elizabeth back along the corridor and down the stairs we decided to ignore until after we'd checked the remainder of this floor. As the stairway curves away from the wall, I look out a window—and see a moving figure.

"Oh! A witch!" I blurt out. "Down there by the maze." As I say the words, laughter shrieks right beside me, causing me to flinch, and the woman far below in the garden turns and looks directly up at the palace. Up at *me.* It's so creepy that I shrink immediately away from the window.

Elizabeth climbs back up a step and looks out the window. "Are you sure? I don't see anyone there."

"It was definitely one of the witches. Long blonde hair, and those smoky dresses they seem to be so fond of."

"Smoky dresses?" Elizabeth repeats, looking at me as her eyebrows pull together.

"Yes, well, they look like they're made of smoke."

Elizabeth returns her gaze to the window, seemingly perplexed.

"Let's get down there," Chase says, already hurrying down the stairs two at a time. We reach the floor below and have to find another set of stairs before we can descend to ground level. I wonder if anyone who lives here ever knows where they are; I find it utterly confusing.

The rosy golden light of sunrise floods the garden by the time we make it outside. Beyond a small pavilion and a little bridge curving over a stream rise the outer hedges of the maze. Without pause, we run toward it. At the entrance, I hesitate, knowing this has to be some kind of trap. Elizabeth, who seems to be having similar thoughts, says, "Can't we burn it down? That seems safer than entering."

A flame burns above Chase's palm a moment later, but it refuses to ignite the hedge. "It's protected," he mutters. "Look, it may seem silly to enter the maze knowing a witch has lured us here, but we can handle whatever she throws at us. Besides, even if we could burn the maze to the ground, the witch would get away long before that and we'd have to hunt her down again."

"Then let's stop wasting time," I say, "and get in there."

As we take our first steps onto the grassy path of the maze, the light above us fades, as if a heavy cloud has been drawn across the sun. A chill crawls across my skin. We move as quickly as we can, paying attention to whether we've chosen to go left or right each time our path branches. Soon enough, we come to a dead end and have to go back. Memorizing our path—left, left, right, left, right—as well as the changes we have to make for every dead end, is a welcome distraction from thoughts of what may lie at the center of the maze. I tense before rounding every new corner, wondering what obstacle may greet us. But we see nothing, and the only sound is the rustle of grass beneath our feet.

When we walk around what feels like the millionth corner and find that we're suddenly in the center of the maze, I jolt to a stop, my grip tightening on my knives. Only a few paces away, on the back of a stone unicorn, sits the younger of the two witches. The older witch stands just behind her. "Ah, there you are," the younger one says, an ancient wickedness reverberating beneath her sweet, clear voice, "We were going to lead you on for a little longer, but you had to look out the window, and now the fun is over."

"The fun's actually just about to start," Chase says, bright white magic already crackling around his fingertips.

The witch, however, ignores Chase and focuses on me. "Not going to try and confuse us with an illusion?" she asks innocently. In the pause that follows, she starts laughing. "I didn't think so. Your magic is almost mine, sweet girl. I can *feel it.*"

Chase's gaze snaps to mine, confused and questioning, before flashing back to the witch. He raises one hand—but Elizabeth reaches out and stops him. "So it is you," she says, addressing the witches. "Tilda. Sorena. I was curious when I heard there were witches in Creepy Hollow, but I told myself it couldn't be either of you. Didn't I leave you to die in a volcano?"

The younger witch, Tilda I presume, jumps down from the

statue. "Scarlett?" she says, squinting into the dim light. "Little Scarlett?" She tilts her head back and laughs. Sorena remains silent, her black eyes glaring at Elizabeth. "Well, well. Look at you, dear Scarlett," Tilda says. "You could have been one of us by now. Powerful and dangerous and part of a great sisterhood of witches."

Wait, what? Elizabeth was almost a witch? I look over at Chase to see if he's as surprised as I am, but his expression hasn't changed. Of course he knows, I tell myself. Didn't Elizabeth say they've told each other all their secrets? At least I understand now how she came to be in possession of a witch's spell book.

"I'm powerful and dangerous as I am," Elizabeth says to Tilda. "And I can do without the sisterhood crap."

"Clearly," Tilda answers, her smile turning icy, "since you decided to kill one of my sisters."

"Self defense," Elizabeth says with a shrug.

"We should strike her down where she stands," Sorena growls through her pointed teeth. "Tell the ground to swallow her whole."

"Ah, Sorena," Elizabeth says. "Do you have a voice now, or are you still shrinking into the shadows of others?"

Sorena's words are a dangerously low whisper: "You will pay for what you did."

"You are the ones who should pay!" Elizabeth shouts. "How many men died to fuel the dome you've placed over this palace? How many innocents are you planning to kill tonight in order to bring down the veil?"

Tilda quirks her head. "Who said they're innocent?"

"Malena wasn't innocent, but that doesn't mean I should have killed her. Likewise, you shouldn't be killing anyone tonight."

Tilda's lips spread into a wide grin. "Come and stop me then."

The fork of lightning is almost instantaneous. I look away, squinting against the glare. When it's gone a second later, I turn back and see the statue shattered and the two witches on the ground. They're unharmed, though, scrambling to their feet as a silvery layer becomes apparent around them. Tilda laughs, but the sound is a shadow of her former glee. She's clearly shaken, despite her pretense at dignity. "You think we would stand before the former *Lord Draven* unprotected?" she asks in mocking tones. Beside her, Sorena holds up a black cylindrical shape. A candle.

"No!" Elizabeth shouts, lunging forward as Chase whips a tornado into existence. But the candle is inside the witches' shield, and it catches light the moment Sorena snaps her fingers. With a cry of rage, Chase brings down another bolt of lightning more blinding than the first. It shakes the ground at my feet and almost deafens me.

The witches, however, are gone.

"Dammit," Chase mutters. "That should have broken through their magic."

"It would have," Elizabeth says, "if they'd still been standing there. You were a split second too late, I think."

"But—how did they get away?" I ask. "The faerie paths—"

"They don't use faerie paths to travel," Elizabeth tells me. "They use candles. The black candle—"

Her words are cut off as the ground shudders once more. "Are you doing that?" I ask Chase as I struggle to keep my balance on the oddly undulating ground.

"No." Chase looks all around, his eyes coming to rest on the pieces of the unicorn statue. Slowly, the pieces sink into the ground as the grassy surface on which they sit turns to green liquid. The liquid begins to spread. "Run!" he yells.

CHAPTER TWENTY-SEVEN

My feet pound the grass as I struggle to remember the turns we took to get here. With the ground rolling beneath my feet, I trip and catch myself against the tall hedges numerous times. As I race around a corner and come to a dead end, I realize I've taken a wrong turn somewhere. Chase slams into me, and so does Elizabeth. I tumble forward against the hedge. Branches scratch across my palms as I grasp hold of them and keep myself upright. I swivel around with difficulty as Chase and Elizabeth remain pressed against me.

"Jump!" Chase yells, grabbing our hands. We bend and spring into the air, and an impossibly powerful tornado sweeps us up. My hair whips around, blinding me as I spin and tumble through the air. Seconds later, I land on the ground, breathless and dizzy. I push my hair out of my face and find that we're some distance away from the maze.

"What the hell was that?" Elizabeth gasps.

"'Tell the ground to swallow her whole,'" I say between my panting. "I think that's what it was."

"Damn witch magic," she mutters.

"They must have transported themselves to somewhere else on the grounds," Chase says, looking around after he stands. "Or perhaps outside the dome-shield. Presumably somewhere close enough for them to retain control of it."

"You're all okay, right?" Ana asks from wherever she is in the palace. "Don't want to distract you or anything, but we were biting our nails over here listening to you yelling about running and jumping and the witches getting away."

"We're fine," Chase says. "Anything to report on your end?"

"Not much. We've dodged a few guards and other randoms who must have come onto the grounds with Angelica. Unsavory-looking types."

"Guys!" Darius shouts, the first we've heard from him in a while. "Who's closest to the ballroom? Just spotted Angelica walking that way. I mean, she looks tiny from way up here, but I'm pretty sure it's her."

"I think we're closest," Chase says, spinning around and heading immediately back toward the palace. "Are you in a tower?"

"Yes. Can't see any of you, though. You must be on the other side. But we can see that courtyard with the fountain. The one leading into the ballroom. Angelica just crossed it."

"We're on our way," Chase says, launching into a run.

I race after him, pushing myself to keep up. *Just keep going a little longer*, I tell myself. *It's almost over. Then you can rest properly.* The gardens rush by, but I pay little attention, keeping my eyes focused on Chase. We run alongside the palace for a while, then across an open corridor, and there it is—the courtyard with the fountain.

"We're here," Chase says, panting a little. "We're about to go in."

"What do you want us to do?" Gaius asks.

"Come to the ballroom, but stay out of sight. Don't interfere unless you see I need help. If things go badly and we need to make a quick exit, we'll meet at the rose greenhouse. The dome-shield might be gone, but we can't get through that waterfall at the palace entrance. We'll have to take the tunnel and fight off the centaurs instead."

The rest of the team acknowledges Chase's instructions while the three of us cross the courtyard. We pause in the wide ballroom doorway, looking in. Angelica's on the other side, walking toward the throne on the dais. She moves slowly, swinging her skirt around her, clearly unaware that we're here. The bodies of Princess Audra and the former queen have been removed, as have the guards who were frozen behind the throne. But the masks, food, glasses and other party debris still remain.

We enter the ballroom, Chase moving slightly ahead. Dark, threatening clouds gather near the ceiling, and wind gusts through the ballroom. As Angelica's loose hair flutters around her and several masks go skidding across the floor, she spins around. She seems surprised for a moment, but recovers quickly. "My, my," she calls out to Chase. "You do look a lot better than the last time I saw you." When he keeps advancing and doesn't answer, she adds, "I thought my witchy accomplices would keep you busier for a little longer, but no matter. I'm fairly certain you're too late to stop it."

"We've stopped it already, Angelica," Chase tells her.

She laughs before replying. "Oh have you now?"

"Yes. You know you can't fight me. And the full moon is still hours away. You'll be in chains long before it rises."

"Will I?" Her words are answered by a zigzagging bolt of lightning that flashes down from the ceiling and out one of the windows. A boom of thunder follows instantly. Angelica clasps her hands together and shouts, "Ooh, I do love a good storm." The wind whips faster around her, swirling into a tightening vortex filled with masks, glitter, feathers and bits of glass. "Fortunately for me," she yells, "my witch friends left me with a little present." She raises her hand above her head, and in her grasp is a glowing object with ridged edges that reflect the light. A crystal of some sort. She throws it onto the ground—and it explodes.

The vortex scatters, and Angelica is thrown back toward the dais, her crown spinning across the floor and shrinking. Chase stumbles backward a few paces, but he wasn't close enough to the crystal to be forced off his feet. "Not so fortunate," he shouts, "when you throw *yourself* off your feet instead of your opponent." He races across the ballroom, colliding with her just as she gets to her feet. Elizabeth and I edge closer, but neither of us gets involved in the battle. The flash of magic, the swirl of mist, the hailstones flying about, and the spinning, dodging, kicking and punching.

Eventually, Chase wrestles Angelica to the floor. He pulls a piece of rope—unbreakable rope from the collection of items Gaius brought with him—out of his pocket. As Elizabeth and I hurry to help restrain Angelica, he lengthens the rope with magic. Her arm comes free, and she releases a pulse of magic at Elizabeth, sending her sliding across the floor. I reach for her flailing arm, but she slashes at me with sharp nails.

"Stop!" I yell, finally grabbing her elbow and pinning her arm back while Chase gets the rope around her wrists.

"Oh, don't the two of you work together *so* nicely," she taunts. "Perhaps you can work together for me in the new world I'll be ruling."

"You're delusional," Chase says, climbing off her and pulling her up onto her feet. He picks up the fallen crown, which enlarges at his touch, illustrating his royal lineage. "Now, you're going to walk with me to—"

He's interrupted by an odd crackling sound, followed by a shockwave that rushes through the air, punches into us, and knocks us to the floor. I'm dazed for several moments, but I sit up as soon as I can, looking around for the source of the shockwave. "What was that?"

"The dome-shield just went down," Darius answers. "Either the witches did it, or someone on the outside managed to break through."

Nearby, and still bound by unbreakable rope, Angelica laughs quietly. Whatever's going on, she's enjoying it. Chase and I climb to our feet, leaving her sitting on the floor. A short distance away, Elizabeth is already standing. "What's that noise?" she asks. I listen carefully as an odd sound reaches my ears.

"Holy freak," Ana says. "A bajillion guardians just arrived. Get down, Gaius! They'll see you."

Wonderful. The noise belongs to the running feet of hundreds of guardians. Guardians who are flooding into the courtyard at this moment. "Is that the Guild?" Angelica asks, looking toward the ballroom door. "Oh, how wonderful! Everyone's come out to play."

"Run," Chase says, waving a hand through the air and filling the ballroom with thick fog. I don't know which way Elizabeth goes, but I grab Chase's hand, since he's right beside me. I run with him, thinking he's heading for one of the side doors near the dais, but then we stumble over two or three stairs, and we're on the dais itself. By the time the mist starts clearing, we're crouching behind the enormous throne.

"Why are we still in this room?" I whisper.

"So we can watch and listen." Chase points to the base of the throne, which is constructed of a metal latticework. We can bend right down and look through it, getting a criss-cross view of the ballroom. "I want to make sure Angelica doesn't have some other ridiculous bargain up her sleeve. She needs to go straight back to prison."

I look through the latticework and watch the guardians rush into the ballroom. Leading them is none other than Head

Councilor Bouchard himself. "What's happened here?" he demands when he reaches Angelica's side. "Who bound you?"

"Would you believe me if I told you it was my darling son?"

It's a good thing she didn't see where we ran. I have no doubt she'd point us out in a heartbeat if she knew we were hiding here. "Take her," Councilor Bouchard tells several guardians. "Make sure you keep her restrained. There's a prison cell waiting with her name on it."

Angelica struggles against the guardians who hurry forward to lift her from her floor. "Don't you *dare* touch me!" she shouts. "I am your Queen! Royal blood runs through my veins, and what you are doing is treason!"

"And what you did was assassination," Councilor Bouchard says. "Which means you're going right back to prison."

Another guardian runs up to Councilor Bouchard with a mirror about the size of her hand. "Councilor," she says, "You need to—"

"I don't have time right now," he tells her.

"This is urgent."

"Is anything more urgent than dealing with the woman responsible for the Queen's assassination?"

"Yes." She holds the mirror toward him. "You need to speak to Councilor Threshmore. There's been a massive explosion at Velazar Prison. The protective layer over the island is gone, hundreds of prisoners have escaped, and most of the guards have disappeared."

"What? Give me that." Councilor Bouchard snatches the mirror and paces to the side of the ballroom, speaking in low tones. All I can hear now are the low murmurings of the guardians gathered in the hallway and Angelica's quiet laughter.

"Oh no." Chase grips my arm, leaning toward me with urgency in his gaze.

"What? What are you thinking?"

"The tower," he says. "The tower in the visions. The tower where all the people died."

"Yes?"

"It's at Velazar Prison."

Ice settles in my veins. "Velazar Prison. Where Amon is."

"Yes."

I find myself slowly shaking my head. "Angelica didn't leave Amon out of her plans. He *was* the plan. She's been distracting us."

Chase nods. "And by the time we get there, it could be too late."

By the time we get there, it could be too late. My heart becomes leaden and plummets down, down, down at the sound of his words. "What do we do?"

Chase shakes his head. "Access to the faerie paths is hours away. Then we still have to take boats to Velazar Island. Even if we arrive in time, with the witches so powerful and with all those escaped prisoners ready to fight for their freedom … I don't know if I can stop them. The Guild can send every guardian who isn't here. They'll arrive in time. But will there be enough of them to overpower the witches?"

My eyebrows knit together. "So …"

"So we can't do this alone." He moves to stand. "And neither can they."

"No, wait." I grasp his hand because I know what he's about to do and I know how insane it is. "Don't—"

"We have to," he tells me. "This is our world we're talking about." Still holding the crown, he rises fully. With hands raised in a non-threatening gesture, he walks out from behind the throne and faces the ballroom full of guardians.

CHAPTER TWENTY-EIGHT

HUNDREDS OF GLITTERING GUARDIAN WEAPONS POINT toward the man who was once Lord Draven—and at least half of them flash through the air a second later. Chase clenches one raised hand into a fist, and every weapon slams up against an invisible barrier before vanishing. The air ripples as Chase lets go of his shield magic, clearly unconcerned by the possibility of another attack coming his way. I remain hidden behind the throne, my hands clasped over my mouth and my heart pounding as I watch through the latticework of the throne's base.

"We have a problem," Chase says to everyone. "A new threat. And we're only likely to stop it if we work together."

"Oh, we have a problem, all right," Head Councilor Bouchard growls. "You're supposed to be *dead*."

"Yes. I'm aware of that. As you can see, however, I am very much alive and no longer under the influence of Tharros Mizreth. His power was destroyed a decade ago while I was wearing the Unseelie Queen's eternity necklace. That necklace prevented me from dying."

"So you've been in hiding all this time," Councilor Bouchard says, slowly shaking this head, "waiting for the chance to reclaim your power."

"No. I don't want power. I don't want a throne." Chase shakes the Seelie crown, and the emeralds glitter in the light of so many weapons. "My mother might have been after this crown, but she and I are not allies—as you very well know. After all, you chose to set her free in exchange for me." A wave of murmurs spreads across the crowd. "Something you may have chosen not to tell the rest of your Guild about, I see," Chase adds. "But that's irrelevant right now. What matters is this: You believed Princess Angelica planned to tear through the veil that separates our world from the non-magical world, which is one of the reasons you came here to apprehend her. This, however, has been a ruse. A distraction. There is a man in Velazar Prison who has been freed by the explosion you were just informed of. He is the one who will perform this spell tonight, and if we don't stop him, two worlds that should forever remain separate will begin to merge."

Councilor Bouchard draws himself up to his not-so-impressive full height as his face flushes pink like the streaks that run through his dark hair. "There is no *we*," he says. "How can you possibly think we would ever be naive enough to trust you?"

"Perhaps because you have no other choice? The witches assisting with tonight's spell are impossibly powerful. They've consumed the energy of dozens, perhaps hundreds, of fae. You could lose countless guardians in the fight against them—or you could let me help you."

The Head Councilor's jaw trembles as he struggles to contain his obvious rage. "How dare you? How *dare* you stand there and attempt to negotiate with us as if the atrocities you committed ten years ago meant nothing? You are filled with nothing but *evil.* You are responsible for more devastation than any other person in history, and we will *never* forget that."

Chase slowly bends and places the crown on the platform floor. His voice is quiet, strained as he straightens and responds. "I will never forget either. Never. So let me do this. Let me help you save our world. Please, before it's too late."

"The only thing you will help us do is—"

Before Councilor Bouchard can finish his sentence, light blazes behind him and a figure appears. A witch. Guardians everywhere react instantly, but Tilda doesn't waste a second. Her black candle is already burning, and she lunges for Angelica. In a second flash of light, Tilda, Angelica, and every guard restraining Angelica disappear from the ballroom.

Several moments of confusion pass as weapons fly across the empty space and guardians come to a halt, twisting around, their eyes searching. They fall still in the moment they acknowledge exactly what's happened: Princess Angelica, assassinator of the Queen and usurper of the Seelie throne, is gone.

Councilor Bouchard lets out a wordless cry of fury, turns

back to Chase, and races for him. Every guardian follows. Magic crackles, weapons fly, guardians shout—before a whirling blizzard blocks out all sound and sight. I jump to my feet as a hand wraps around my arm and pulls me away so fast my feet can barely keep up. I can't see a single thing through the freezing blizzard, and if I were on my own, I'd surely be swept away by the powerful wind. But Chase pulls me along as easily as if the wind means nothing to him—which I suppose it doesn't, since he's the one creating it.

We're somewhere outside with grass racing by beneath our feet when the snow clears enough for me to see where we're going and the wind subsides to the point where I can hear the yelling in my ear: "*What the flipping hell is happening?*"

"Run!" Chase yells back. "Get to the greenhouse!"

I let go of his hand so I can pump my arms faster. "Around the outside, right?" I pant. The greenhouse is all the way on the other side of the palace, but I'd rather take the longer route than have to navigate the passages and hallways of the palace.

"Yeah." Chase pulls ahead of me, leading the way. "Faster, Calla. Some guardians may know of the tunnel."

I push myself to the point where my chest starts burning. The blizzard vanishes and the gardens flash by. Statues, fountains, topiary bushes, hedges. We reach the end of this side of the palace and slow as we turn, then speed up again, Chase urging me on the whole time. I hate that I'm slowing him down, but I can't push myself any faster. More hedges and a pavilion and trees whipping by, and then we're around the next corner. I see it now, the jagged edge of the shattered greenhouse dome—and there, approaching from the other direction, are three figures I recognize.

I slow as we race through the greenhouse entrance, almost dropping to the ground in a gasping heap. Chase skids to a halt and pushes through the rosebushes, panting, "Everyone here?"

"Yeah."

"Open up."

"Dude, what the *hell* were you thinking in that ballroom?"

"Just get in the tunnel!"

Within seconds, we're all stumbling down the stairs and into the dark tunnel below. The trapdoor slams shut, and light appears a moment later after Chase touches the tunnel wall.

"Seriously," Darius says to Chase. "Are you *insane*?"

"Can we argue about my possible insanity later?" Chase says, already running.

I've barely gathered my breath, but I'm all too aware of the urgency, so I force my tired limbs to keep going. Moving as quickly as we can, we soon reach the other end of the tunnel.

"What's the easiest way past the centaurs?" Lumethon asks as we stop by the stairs.

"Probably an illusion," Gaius says, looking at me.

An illusion? My mind feels as weary as it did when I awoke this morning, but I can probably—

"No, I'll do it," Chase says as he climbs the stairs and raises his hand to the trapdoor. "Lightning should temporarily blind them, and I'll add a thick mist to bring visibility right down. But they may shoot arrows at random anyway, so keep a shield around you as we run."

"An illusion is simpler and safer," Gaius says. "Just let Calla do it."

"Yeah, I can do it," I say, stepping forward, my chest still heaving a little.

"No." Elizabeth places a hand on my arm. "Chase, go ahead. You're far stronger than the rest of us, so you may as well handle it."

"He just conjured an entire *blizzard*, Elizabeth," Ana says. "He's probably feeling a little tired at the moment."

"Can someone just get us out of here?" Darius asks.

"I'm perfectly fine," Chase announces, "and I'm opening the trapdoor now." He places both hands against the metal, then heaves. I shut my eyes as blinding light shines down into the tunnel, followed by the crack of thunder. "Run now!" Chase shouts.

I hasten up the stairs. Out in the forest, I focus on both the layer of protective magic over my body and the foggy shape of my closest teammate running in front of me through the mist. I don't know if Chase has any idea where he's leading us, but I simply keep following. As the mist begins to clear, and it becomes less likely to trip over obstacles or each other, we run faster. "Calla," Chase calls to me. "We're nearing the edge of the forest, but I don't see the rocks."

I look around as I slow. My memory of the area is almost nonexistent, considering I was concentrating on both an invisibility illusion and keeping Chase upright the last time we came this way. "Uh, I think we were further left last time. We didn't run straight when we came out of the tunnel, remember? That centaur arrow came out of nowhere from the right."

I'm worried I may be remembering incorrectly, but we veer

toward the left anyway, and after another few minutes, the rocks come into view. "Yes," I murmur to myself as sweet relief hits me.

We race onward, around the rocks, and toward the flat, open area. The gargoyles have moved into the shade of the nearest trees, and the dragon is curled up and sleeping in pretty much the exact spot it landed last night.

"Get on the dragon with Gaius," Chase tells me as we reach the creatures. "There's space in the harness for two of you." I don't complain. Climbing onto a dragon's back may be awkward and scary, but not as terrifying as being near the ridged horns, protruding fangs, and demon-like faces of the gargoyles. In no time at all, I'm clutching onto Gaius and dragon wings are beating the air, and then we're rising up, up, up, leaving the forest and the centaurs and every horror of the Seelie Court far behind us.

* * *

Once we're high in the air and Gaius has conjured up a curved layer of magic in front of us to keep the wind from tearing at our faces, I fish through all the inside straps and pockets of my jacket until I find my stylus and the little round mirror Perry gave me. With a few quick strokes across the mirror's surface, I've written the spell to call him.

He answers quickly, as if he wasn't far from his mirror. "Calla! I tried to call you last night."

"I'm sorry, I've had a lot going on."

"Did you know about the Seelie Queen's assassination? And Princess Angelica taking the crown? And flipping *Lord Draven*! We heard last night. I think the whole world is probably in a panic by now. The Guild totally freaked out. Dispatched at least half our guardians to the Seelie Court some time during the night, plus guardians from every other Guild. They're scared of that veil prophecy you told us about."

"I know," I say when I can get a word in. "They caught Angelica. And then she got away."

"Where are you?" Perry interrupts before I can get to my point. "Why are the clouds moving oddly behind—Wait, are you *flying*?"

"Yeah, I'm on a dragon. Long story. But I need to tell you something, Perry. I assume you're going to hear about it soon, but just in case Councilor Bouchard is idiotic enough to think it's all a trick and not take it seriously, I need someone at the Guild to know: There was an explosion at Velazar Prison, and a prisoner named Amon is going to perform the spell—the magic that tears through the veil—tonight with the assistance of two witches, and presumably Angelica, since she's free again."

"But … so … what about Draven?"

"That's not important. I don't have time to explain it now, but … he's not Draven anymore. This isn't about him. This is about stopping Angelica and Amon. It'll take the guardians here hours to reach a place the faerie paths can be accessed from. So every guardian who isn't here needs to get to Velazar immediately. Can you pass that message on, if Councilor

Bouchard hasn't already done so?"

"I—Yes. It's early here. I'm not at the Guild yet, but I can go now. Did you …" He shuts his eyes for a moment and gives a brief shake of his head. "You said 'here.' Are you … at the Seelie Court?"

"Uh … maybe."

"Whoa! How did you—Oh, did you follow Olive there? Is that where she disappears to periodically?"

"Yes. But, Perry, you have to get to the Guild *now*, okay?"

"Of course. I understand. I assume you'll head to Velazar as soon as you can access the paths? I'll see you there, then. We can kick the bad guys' butts together."

"What?" I grip the harness tighter as alarm floods me. "No, you mustn't go with."

Confusion lines Perry's face. "Why not?"

"Because … you're not a guardian yet. And it's going to be seriously dangerous."

He raises one eyebrow. "Are you going?"

"Well, yes, but that's different. The Guild has no control over what I do."

Perry's mouth quirks up in amusement. "You think the Guild has any control over what I do? Sure, it's against standard procedure for trainees to get involved in something like this, but I doubt anyone will notice. Everyone's too busy worrying about the return of Lord Draven right now."

"Lord Draven isn't a threat! Trust me. He's actually trying to help. And you need stay out of—"

"Help? Did you say he's trying to *help*? Okay, now you're smoking something."

"Perry!" I release a groan of frustration. "Just get to Guild, okay? And whatever you end up doing, just don't get yourself killed."

He smiles and reaches up to tap the mirror. "Same to you, Calla," he says before his face vanishes, leaving a reflection of the cloud-streaked sky in my little mirror. Before putting it away, I start the spell again, this time pointing my thoughts toward Ryn. I wouldn't previously have risked contacting him this way—the Guild is probably still monitoring every mirror and amber in his home, aside from the old one I gave him—but somehow I think the Guild has more important things to worry about now than catching me. Besides, with my amber being almost the size of a brick and too large to comfortably fit in any of my pockets, a mirror call is my only option right now.

Ryn doesn't answer, though. I didn't really expect him to, but I had to try anyway. I wish I could call Dad and tell him what's going on, but that's not an option. No mirrors or amber down in the Guild's detainment area. I return my mirror to the inside of my jacket, pull the jacket zip right up, and hang tightly onto the harness, aware of every second ticking by. I shift around as much as the harness will allow, but that doesn't keep my body from beginning to ache from sitting in the same position and tensing against the air that's a lot colder up here than on the ground. I could warm myself with magic, but the curse has left me tired enough as it is. Best to save my energy for the actual fight.

When the torturously long journey finally comes to an end and we land beside the river where our mission began two days ago, Chase wastes no time jumping off his gargoyle. "Everyone get your gargoyles—and dragon—into a line adjacent to one another so you can touch hands without dismounting." He opens a doorway to the faerie paths and pulls it wider, wider, and wider still, until eventually it's wide enough for us all to walk our creatures through together. "Ana, focus on that cliff above the beach near Velazar Island. The rest of you, keep your minds clear."

"Wait, where are you going?" Gaius asks.

"Back to the mountain to get the rest of the gargoyles. If the guardians fail us, we'll need all the help we can get with an island full of escaped convicts."

"Chase!" Ana protests loudly. "We can't—"

"Yes you can. I won't be long. I'll probably catch up to you on the way."

I undo my harness and slide to the ground. "I'm going with you. I need to contact Ryn, and that old amber is back at the mountain. Besides, you don't actually have a key to the faerie door."

Chase hesitates for a second, then nods. "True."

As the rest of the team grudgingly agrees to the change in plan and moves forward through the enormous faerie paths doorway, Chase opens a second doorway beside it. He takes my hand, and together we hurry into the darkness. Early morning light slants across the lake house living room as we walk to the faerie door. I retrieve my key from one of my hidden pockets and push it into the lock.

"Calla."

I freeze at the sound of that familiar voice. The voice I haven't heard since … since before she began screaming that terrible night. I twist around and see her moving out of the shadows. "Vi."

CHAPTER TWENTY-NINE

I WANT TO RUN TO HER AND THROW MY ARMS AROUND HER. I want to tell her how sorry I am. I want to hear her cry or shout or wail. Anything but the cold, dead expression in her eyes as she watches at me. "I didn't want to have to involve you," she says, "but I'm getting nowhere on my own. This man who was once your friend. This man who … who killed Victoria. Do you have anything that belonged to him?"

Something that belonged to him? "You mean … you're trying to find him?"

"Of course I'm trying to find him," she says, her voice still deathly quiet. "He murdered my child. Do you expect me to let him get away with that?"

My head spins at the reversal of roles. How do I talk her out of this when part of me still wants to go after Zed myself?

Should I talk her out of it? Yes. I should. If I've learned anything from Chase, it's that revenge helps no one. "I don't expect you to let him get away with it. I want him to pay. I tried to find him too, but someone talked me out of it." As gently as possible, I say, "This isn't going to change what happened. It won't—"

"DO YOU HAVE SOMETHING OF HIS?" she shouts, her carefully controlled emotion erupting without warning.

I take an involuntary step backward. "I—no. I don't."

"Don't you dare lie to me. You have almost as much to make up for as he has."

There it is. The horrible truth I keep wanting to flee. The horrible truth I have to deal with if I hope to have any chance of moving on. "I know. *I know!* And I am so, so sorry. From the very depths of my heart, I am sorry. So take your hurt out on *me*. I'm right here!"

"I don't want to take it out on you! You didn't know what would happen, but *he did*!"

I'm about to respond, but Chase takes my arm and gently pulls me back. He steps between the two of us. "Don't do this," he says to Vi. "It will consume you. It will destroy you."

"That was my CHILD! I can't just let this go!"

He grasps her shoulders. "You have to. You have to be stronger than I was. Please, *please* be stronger than I was. Fight for everything you still have and not for what you've lost."

With a furious cry, she wrenches her arms from his grip and storms away to the far side of the room. "Violet, please," he calls after her, but she's already opening a faerie paths doorway. "Please, just—" But she's gone, the edges of her doorway sealing up, leaving us standing in silence.

I press my hands over my eyes as the overwhelming urge to fall apart hits me. The fresh reminder that I'm responsible for so much pain is almost too much to bear. And I'm so tired. So, so tired. I want to curl into a ball on the floor and never get up. But Amon—the full moon—the spell—

I pull my hands away from my face and grip Chase's arm as urgency fills me. "No time. There's no time for this. We have to *move*."

My words snap him free of whatever memory he was lost in. "Yes. Go." He yanks the faerie door open and we run through the void to the door in the mountain's hallway. I rush to the stairs, but, looking back, I find that he's paused by the faerie door. "There were times I wondered if I'd ever see this place again," he murmurs. Then he shakes his head and crosses the hallway. "Message your brother. Then come to the gargoyle cave. Be quick."

The first thing I do upon entering my bedroom is run for the bottle beside my bed. Not much brownish liquid remains. I pour a spoonful into a glass of water and gulp the mixture down. Then I decant the rest of the undiluted tonic into the smaller bottle that fits into my pocket. I hate that I've kept the truth from Chase about this curse, but I don't regret it. Not if my Griffin Ability can still make a difference in some way. I know Chase is far more powerful than the rest of us, but he may have met his match with a pair of witches who can consume the energy of so many magical beings. In the end, a simple illusion could be the only thing that stops them—especially if they know how much the curse has already drained me and aren't expecting me to use my ability.

I grab the old piece of amber and place my stylus against its surface, hoping Ryn's mother gave the corresponding amber back to him after she passed on the message about Victoria's ceremony. I scribble a message to Ryn, my handwriting barely legible in my haste.

Veil spell. Tonight. Velazar Prison. We'll stop Amon, and I SWEAR I will not let the witches get away.

And then, though it terrifies me to think of the curse finally catching up to me, I add, *I love you.* Just in case everything goes wrong tonight and I never get to say it again. Then I toss the amber onto the bed and run for the door.

A loud chirp behind me makes me swing around in the doorway. Owl-formed Filigree launches himself off the top of my wardrobe and shifts into cat form before landing on the floor and running to me. "Filigree, I'm so sorry," I say as he paws at my leg. "I know I haven't been around." I crouch down and let him climb into my arms. He nuzzles against my neck. "You must be missing Vi. And Ryn. And I—I can't take you back to them now. I can't take you with me either. It's way too dangerous. You have to wait here a little longer." His claws press into my arm. "I know. You're not happy about that, but I seriously do *not* have time to argue right now. Please, *please* just stay here. I—I promise I'll come back." I stand and back out of the room, guilt welling up in my chest as Filigree sits and watches me with his mournful cat eyes.

In the corridor, I turn around and run. To the end and

down the stairs to the entrance hall. Then down again. Running, running, running until eventually my feet hit the bottom level—the level with the gargoyle cave. The narrow gap in the corner is dark and silent and ominous, but I have *no time* for fear. Less than no time. So I don't work myself up to it. I don't think of my lake, and I don't calm my thoughts. Instead, I aim straight for the source of my terror and *run*, letting my fear push me faster. I race blindly through the darkness, my hands skimming across the walls on either side and my breaths tearing their way in and out of my chest.

I skid to a halt just inside the cave and bend over, my hands on my knees. "Okay," I gasp. "I'm okay, I'm okay, I'm okay." Straightening, I look around. Last time, the creatures filling this cavernous space wandered freely and randomly. Now, dozens of gargoyles are gathered in a group in the distance near the crumbling wall of towers and turrets. I see Chase amongst them, so I take off in that direction, swatting at a cloud of tiny bugs I happen to run through.

At the sound of a ferocious roar behind me, I almost trip over my feet and wind up on the ground. I twist around as I stumble to a stop—and find myself facing a dragon. *Crap.* I'm not certain, but given the green and purple scales, I think it may be the dragon that chased me out of here last time. I back away as it approaches me with slow, earth-shuddering steps.

A piercing whistle tears the dragon's gaze away from me. "Hey! Samson!" Chase shouts. "Back off, man, she's with us."

A low growl ripples through the air before Samson lowers himself to the cave floor and lies there watching me. Wishing I didn't have to turn my back on him, I swing around and run the rest of the way toward Chase, throwing a number of glances over my shoulder to make sure Samson isn't coming after me. I catch Chase's arm as I come to a stop, breathing heavily and reminding myself that I don't have to be afraid of the horns, fangs and snarling expressions surrounding me. "I pity any intruder who finds his or her way into this cave."

Chase grins as he loops a rope around the nearest gargoyle's arm. "Samson does make an excellent guard dog. As do most of the other creatures down here."

"Do they all listen to you?"

"Mostly. The nascryls—" he looks up at the creatures with black leathery wings and oddly charred-looking clawed feet clinging to the cave ceiling "—often require a little magical reminder of who's actually in charge down here. There are only about four or five of them, and they're pretty wild. Found their own way in here one day and decided to stay."

"Are they all—" I pull my head back as several moths flutter past my face and up toward the ceiling. Clearly large creatures aren't the only creepy things that live down here. "Uh, are they all coming with us?"

"Only the gargoyles. It's more difficult to get the dragons through the faerie paths if they don't each have a rider, and the nascryls definitely aren't team players. The gargoyles, though …" He pats the gargoyle's shoulder before moving to the next one with the same rope. "They let me lead them."

"Why? How did they all end up here?"

"They were treated terribly at the Unseelie Court. Gaius, Kobe and I freed them all in one of our first missions together. I thought the gargoyles would make their own way in the world, but instead they followed me. We had to make a plan for them after that. Gaius already had two dragons down here, so we enlarged the cave, created a few different environments, and let everyone loose."

"And they all play nicely together?"

"For the most part. The other end of the cave—around that corner there; you can't see it from here—is open to the outside. They come and go as they please, hunting out there in the wild somewhere." He steps back from securing the end of the rope around the last gargoyle's arm. "Okay, we're ready. Let's get moving. You're riding one gargoyle, I'm riding another, and the rest are attached behind us so we can all make it through the paths together."

"Uh, okay." Pushing aside the unpleasant memory of the gargoyle ride that took place a few days after I met Chase, I follow him to the front of the group. I want to cringe away from the wrinkled leathery hide, but there's *no time* for freaking out about anything, so I climb awkwardly onto the back of the gargoyle that crouches down for me. At least there's a harness, unlike the last time I clung to a gargoyle. Chase wraps part of the harness around my back and secures it. As he steps away, my gargoyle rears up, causing me to let out a startled yelp. But the harness holds me in place. Chase climbs onto the gargoyle beside mine. I lean over to help him with his harness, but he's already secured it. "Time to move!" he shouts out.

My gargoyle drops down onto all fours. He rushes forward with the others while I bounce up and down in the harness. Then with a leap, he rises awkwardly and jerkily into the air, his wings creating an unpleasant smelling wind around me. We follow the cave around the corner and then shoot out into the fresh air above the lake. The lake I remember flying over the very first time Chase brought me to the mountain.

With sections of rope tugging between each gargoyle, our flight to the ground on the other side of the lake is bumpy and unpleasant. The moment we land, Chase climbs free of his harness and jumps down. He opens a doorway to the faerie paths, pulling it wider and wider. After returning to his gargoyle and climbing onto its back once more, he points and shouts, "Forward!"

And together, we move into the darkness.

CHAPTER THIRTY

THE DARKNESS OF THE FAERIE PATHS DISSIPATES AROUND US to reveal a cliff overlooking a rough sea. "Remove the ropes!" Chase shouts. I twist around and see every one of the gargoyles slashing at the ropes Chase tied around their arms. "And into the air!" he yells. The gargoyles begin running. Wings flap way too close to my body as the cliff edge races to meet us. And then, just as we're about to tumble over it, my gargoyle leaps, and then we're rising, rising, into the air.

As we gain height, I release my breath, and look past the flapping wings and out at the ocean. My hope almost shrivels into nothing when I notice the position of the sun on the horizon. "It's almost sunset," I shout to Chase, though I'm certain he's already noticed this. "I didn't realize it was so much later here."

"Yeah," he shouts back to me. "Which is why Angelica told us we'd be too late to stop Amon."

"Was she right?"

"No. She underestimated our speed." He urges his gargoyle to fly faster and yells, "FORWAAAAARD!"

My gargoyle's wings beat harder, and icy air bites into my skin. The sky grows darker as clouds gather above us. Over the sound of wings and wind, a rumble reaches my ears. I look up in time to see light zigzag across the growing cloud mass. Spots of rain wet my face. I lower my head and hunch my shoulders, looking down to where the growing gale whips the waves into white peaks far below us. I don't have to ask Chase if he's the one doing this. I already know the storm is his. I face forward again with a small smile on my lips. I defy even the strongest of fae to look up at us—an army of gruesome creatures propelled forth by typhoon winds amidst lightning, sea spray and thunderous dark clouds—and not be afraid.

It might all be for nothing if we're too late, though. Velazar Prison is built upon a floating island that moves around and is never in exactly the same place, so I'm concerned about how long it might take us to get there. But we haven't been flying long when a dark shape begins to take form on the horizon up ahead. With an enchanted wind at our backs, we race across the sky toward Velazar Island.

The dark shape grows larger. Larger and larger, until eventually it isn't just a shape, but a massive piece of earth floating some distance above the waves. Tiny dots in the water below turn out to be boats, and the grey squares squished together on top of the island take form as Velazar Prison itself.

Nervous anticipation races through me as we come close enough to see smoke rising from the building and tiny figures moving back and forth outside amidst bright weapons and flashes of magic. As we fly overhead, I capture a mental picture of the scene so I can orient myself once we've landed: the prison taking up most of the lower left side of the island; a small silvery dome-like layer near the top right; a monument within it, pointing straight toward the stormy sky. Further right, separating the silver dome from the right hand edge of the island, is a grove of trees. And there, top left of my mental map, is the tower. The tower where hundreds of people hopefully haven't yet been killed.

Seeing all the elements of the spell together in one place, the reality hits me: this could actually happen. We could fail, and our enemies could rip through to a world that should forever remain separate from ours.

As we circle over the island, I'm able to make out what's happening in more detail. The dome-shield protects the trident statue and several figures who look like Angelica, Amon, and the witches. Beyond that, in a roughly semi-circular formation, hundreds of figures in prison overalls fight the glittering weapons of black-clad guardians. What I didn't expect, though, is to see prisoners fighting with magic—which means someone removed the magic-blocking bands they would have been wearing when they were freed. I'm not certain, but I think I see some of our teammates amidst the action. I almost call out to them but then remember the communication spell has faded. I definitely make out two or three gargoyles, and Gaius's dragon is breathing streams of fire straight at the dome-shield.

Chase pulls his gargoyle alongside mine. "Do you see any of the prison guards?"

That's what's missing from the scene: figures in prison guard uniforms. The guardian who informed Councilor Bouchard of the explosion mentioned that most of the guards had disappeared. But where would they have—

"The tower," I shout. That must be where they are. People need to die in order for this spell to work, and Amon would far rather kill the guards than his fellow prisoners. And with prisoners far outnumbering guards, it probably wasn't that hard to overpower them and get them all into that tower.

Chase signals his gargoyle army to join the fight. They swoop down together in one movement, both thrilling and terrifying to watch. "Head for the tower," he shouts to me—or, more likely, to my gargoyle, since I have no idea how to direct it. Both our gargoyles tuck their wings back and dive toward the ground beside the tower. We land clumsily, but our harnesses keep us from falling off. I remove mine and jump off the gargoyle's back. Not too far away, the battle of prisoners, guardians, gargoyles and the rest of our teammates rages on.

"How do we get in?" I ask, rushing to the side of the tower and running my hand along the bricks as I walk around the outside. I think of what I saw in the vision—an empty interior, hundreds of writhing bodies at the bottom, and a great round boulder falling and crushing them all. "What is this even used for? Why would an empty tower be standing here?"

"I don't think it was empty," Chase says as he joins my

search around the outer wall of the tower. "It was a look-out tower. It probably wouldn't have taken too complex an architectural spell to remove the stairs spiraling from the bottom to the top."

"Ah, here's a door." I try the handle, but it's locked, of course. "I can't hear any sound from within. Maybe none of the guards or prisoners have been brought here yet."

Chase tries to ram the door open with force. When that doesn't work, he uses magical strength and unlocking spells, but still the door won't budge.

"Chase," I say quietly, nausea coalescing in the pit of my stomach. "Look at the bottom of the door. That's … that's blood seeping out."

A slow, mocking laugh pulls my attention away from the blood. I look around and see a prisoner on the ground nearby, wounded and probably flung all the way over here by someone's magic. "You're too late," he rasps. "The witches performed the ritual as soon as they got here earlier. If it makes you feel any better, there were prisoners in there too. Convicted criminals."

Dead. They're all dead. A tower full of people just … dead.

"The witches have even more power now," Chase murmurs. "They'll be even harder to defeat."

"Oh, it's our princess who has all the power," the prisoner says, then breaks off as he starts coughing. "Our Queen," he corrects when he's recovered. "Our Queen Angelica. The witches absorbed it all and then channeled it into her. They gave us power as well. They said there was so much, such an overwhelming abundance, that they were afraid it would be too much for the Queen. They gave her everything they could, and then strengthened as many of us as time allowed before the first guardians arrived."

My stomach heaves. I'm utterly horrified and sickened. "We have to stop them. We have to stop them." But I can't move. All I can see is the blood seeping out from under the door. All I can think of is the crushed bodies inside.

"Yes, we have to stop them!" Chase says, grabbing my arm and pulling me away from the tower. I shake the horror off as best I can. I know I'll be useless if I continue to focus on it.

We race around the edge of the fight, dodging sparks of magic. Reaching the edge of the witches' dome-shield, I look through the silvery layer and see how close we are to being too late: the two people who have to be sacrificed—the blood from one side of the veil and blood from the other—are already draped across either side of the statue. A man on the right and a woman on the left.

"Look away," Chase tells me. "I'm bringing it down."

I cast my eyes over my shoulder, squinting into the melee as light flashes behind me. When I look back, the dome is gone. I don't stop to think. With howling wind and the constant rumble of thunder as my battle cry, I run at Tilda, forcing both magic and an illusion out ahead of me. Sparks to sting and burn, and an illusion of screeching harpies. They dive at her, flapping and screaming and slashing with clawed feet, and my hope is that the witch will end up cowering, shielding her face from the attack and giving me a chance to take her down.

This doesn't happen. "Your illusions are *weak*!" she shouts, dancing out of reach. "You can't fool me." And with that she runs and tackles me. I wriggle and shout and kick as she pins me down, but I was tired before this fight even began, and she has the strength of many men. "Why aren't you dead yet?" she growls into my ear as she traces a finger around my wrists. Narrow black ropes appear. I try to kick her as she moves to my feet, but she sits on my legs and traces around my ankles with her pointed nails. "I've felt it coming on for days now, but you've been fighting it somehow."

Over her shoulder, I see Chase battling with Sorena and Angelica. The older witch raises a glowing crystal above her head, and I recognize it as the same kind of crystal Angelica threw in the ballroom. "No!" I shout as the crystal lands at Chase's feet. The resulting explosion throws him backward and toward the grove of trees, out of my sight.

I writhe against my bonds, but it makes no difference. "I've thought of a use for you," Tilda says. "You wanted to stop us from bringing the veil down? Well guess what. Now you're going to help us do it." She drags me across the ground and pushes the man off the right side of the statue. Then, using magic, she lifts me up—and I realize exactly what she meant. I know there are no words that will convince her, so my screams are wordless. On and on and on I scream and struggle. I don't want to die like this, helping perform some terrible spell, not knowing if Chase survived the crystal's explosion.

"It's almost time," Tilda says. "We can't see the moon beyond this spectacular storm, but we know it's there. We know it's rising."

"Please just *stop*!" I shout. "Why are you even involved in this? Do you plan to rule a mixed-up, half magical world alongside Angelica?"

"Rule?" she repeats with amusement. "Of course not. We're not interested in that kind of power." She looks out at the crowd where the Velazar prisoners with their increased magical strength are still managing to hold back the guardians and gargoyles. "Feel the energy," she says. "Taste it on the air. That's the kind of power we seek."

Her words send a chill through my bones. "You're twisted and sick," I tell her.

She ignores me, her gaze moving to the other side of the statue where Sorena stands with an axe in her hands. Amon, the man who sat quietly in prison waiting for his big moment while the rest of us chased Angelica around, stands beside her. On top of the monument, grasping a spear in one hand and holding onto the trident part of the statue with the other, is Angelica. "Ready?" Tilda asks.

"Yes," Angelica answers. "I'm ready." She nods to Sorena. Sorena raises her axe, but instead of bringing it down on the woman lying across the other side of the statue, she swings it around with all her might—straight at Amon.

I see a spray of blood and hear the crumpling thud of his body hitting the ground. I'm so shocked I stop squirming. "What … what did you …"

Angelica looks down at me. "You didn't think I was planning to *share*, did you? Especially not with someone like *him*. No ambition. Always hanging onto someone else's success. First his father, then Zell, then Draven. No. He rallied the prisoners for me while I was gone, and he set everything up after the explosion, but his use has now come to an end." Her gaze moves to Sorena. "Now," she says, "we are ready to begin."

As Sorena brings her axe down toward the unconscious human woman, I start screaming again. Screaming and wriggling and tearing at the bonds. Tilda holds me down with magical strength as Sorena moves toward me, raising her bloodied axe.

Then, behind her, a glittering weapon flashes though the air. Sorena is thrown aside as a guardian spins around and kicks. Tilda lunges for him, but he slashes at her with two knives and kicks again, sending her flying behind the statue. Then he lifts me. Ryn, my brother—*what is he doing here?*—lifts me from the statue. How did he get past all the fighting? He runs a short distance away and places me on the ground near the trees, then slices through my bonds with one of his golden, sparkling knives. Knives that can cut through almost anything. A moth, one of those creepy moths from the gargoyle cave, flits past his head. Then his hands are on either side of my face, searching my eyes. "Are you okay? You have to be okay. Please, I can't—"

Taloned fingers wrap around his arms and yank him away with magical strength. He goes flying through the air and lands at the base of the statue, his head whacking the ground with a sickening thud. Tilda runs after him. *Get up, Ryn, get up*, I plead silently as I push myself shakily up onto my knees and press my hand against my neck. But it's all Ryn can do to roll weakly onto his side.

"You want to interfere with our magic?" Tilda demands.

"Fine. I'll show you what happens to people who interfere." A flick of her hand flips him into the air and onto the statue. "It'll be better for me if the girl dies naturally anyway."

"No," I gasp, the word too quiet for anyone to hear. I force myself up onto my feet. Tilda looks about for Sorena. She's on the left side of the statue, being helped to her feet by Angelica. But the axe is lying on the ground where it fell when Ryn attacked Sorena. Tilda bends and picks it up. "No!" I shriek. "Stop!" I run toward her, but something grey rushes past me. A gargoyle. It leaps at Tilda with claws outstretched and pulls her to the ground.

I expect her to stay down longer, but she fights back immediately. Her blast of magic throws the gargoyle aside. It whimpers as it slides across the ground and comes to a stop, its form rippling and—changing? "Filigree?" I whisper as the gargoyle shifts into a cat and limps toward me. But I tear my eyes away from him as Tilda crawls across the ground and reaches for the axe. I rush toward her, but I'm too late, because Angelica's spear is already flying through the air and—

—and piercing straight through Ryn's abdomen.

Time seems to stop. I know I'm screaming, but I can't hear anything. Then suddenly everything moves again, and my scream is so loud it almost deafens me. And when finally I run out of breath, the scream goes on—but it isn't mine. I twist around, searching the ever-present, ever-advancing crowd desperately. I don't see her, but she must be here somewhere. She's the only other person who would scream like that for Ryn.

I turn back and stumble toward my brother—just as Angelica, standing atop the monument once more, her spear discarded and both hands wrapped around the trident, goes rigid. Light shoots from the top of the trident. Blazing and blinding, lighting up the stormy sky. A horrendous ripping, shredding sound tears past my ears. And there in the sky, an opening appears, as if a gargantuan claw ripped right through it. And on the other side—a field on the outskirts of a town. Early evening, with a sprinkle of glowing lights in the distance.

She did it. Angelica actually did it.

Behind me, everything goes still. The shouting, snarling, and clanging of weapons—it all comes to a halt. All attention is fixed on that tear in the sky. Not just a tear, but a widening gap. And in the field beyond, sparks sizzle in the grass, turning it to ash. A car stops on the road beside the field and people tumble out, staring, pointing, shouting, and I should be trying to *stop all of this*. But my attention is tugged back to Ryn. To his motionless body and that spear sticking up, and the blood running down the side of the statue.

Is he dead?

My heart splits open at the thought, and I run for him—just as a figure slams into Tilda and knocks her to the ground. Chase. My relief that he's okay clashes with my terror that Ryn is already dead. As Chase forces both Tilda and Sorena away from the statue and Angelica stares in rapture at the growing tear in the sky, I rush to Ryn's side. I grab hold of the spear and tug it free. It falls from my hands to the ground. I'm about to move him when something soft touches my legs. Filigree, cat-shaped a moment ago, starts shifting into a bear. He scoops Ryn up. I run beside him as he lumbers away from the statue into the nearby trees. I drop to my knees as Filigree places Ryn on the ground. I push his shirt and jacket up and press my hands against his stomach, looking away from the wound and the gushing blood and squeezing tears from my eyes. I release magic into his body. I don't care that I have little left. I'll happily give him everything if it'll save him.

"Come on, come on, come on," I murmur as Filigree becomes a mouse and hides beside Ryn's neck, below his ear. "You have magic. You can heal from this." But he was thrown against the ground with such force just minutes before he was stabbed. And the sound of his head hitting the ground … I shudder remembering it.

I glance up as shouts and the sizzle of magic break through the silence. The guardians surge forward once more and the prisoners fight back. Though gifted with extra power from the witches, the prisoners are weakening, and the guardians, far more skilled in combat, are pressing ever closer to the monument. I'm about to turn my eyes back to Ryn when finally I see her.

Violet. A whirling fury. Blades flashing and purple hair whipping around as she kicks, dodges and slashes her way through the army of prisoners. She breaks through the battle and races toward me, falling onto her knees on Ryn's other side. "No no no no no," she gasps, tears streaking her face as her hands join mine. She lowers her head and presses her forehead against his chest, whispering words I can't hear.

Lightning flashes and cracks of thunder draw my attention back to where Chase and the two witches are battling within the spinning winds of a mini tornado. And not too far away—

finally—the first few guardians make it past the prisoners.

"Tilda!" Angelica shrieks. "Stop the guardians!" But I doubt Tilda even hears her.

Angelica leaps off the monument, runs past Chase and the witches, and throws her hands into the air. I blink against the flash of light. When I can see again, a translucent layer, the same kind of shield the witches are able to produce, stands between us and the guardians. Not a dome this time, but a wall. A wall of magic stretching right across the island and as high up into the sky as I can see. With the guardians stopped for now, Angelica turns her attention to the tornado. She bends and picks up her spear.

With a shout, I push myself up and run. With whatever strength I have left, I force a pulse of magic from my hands. It's horribly weak, but enough to force Angelica to stumble forward a few paces. I drop the mental wall around my mind, but I've barely thought of an illusion when she cries out in anger and sweeps her hand in a wide arc through the air. I'm knocked off my feet, spinning and tumbling through the air, and—

Whack.

Every part of my body screams at me as I hit the ground. I cough and gasp for air as I struggle to raise my head. Chase is beside me, groaning and pushing himself up. We're amidst the trees, even further from the monument than Vi and Ryn. And the witches … they're nearby, moaning on the ground, probably knocked here with the same rush of energy we were. "Are you okay?" Chase asks as he helps me to sit.

Before I can answer, Tilda shouts, "What was that for?"

"You were in the way," Angelica shouts back. "Help me strengthen this shield. The guardians are almost through, and we still need time before the tear reaches the ground here."

I look past Chase and see the silvery shield struggling and stretching against the magical assault of hundreds of guardians. Amidst the crowd, I make out Olive, and Councilor Bouchard. "They're here. Everyone who was at the Seelie Court."

"It's time to end this," Chase says.

"They're so much stronger," I say, still breathless, still barely able to hold myself upright. "We keep fighting and they keep forcing us back."

"They won't be strong for much longer. I've been waiting, holding back, allowing them to deplete their energy. And look at them, pouring everything into that shield. They're growing weaker by the second. All three of them." He looks down and holds his hand out to me. "It's time, Calla. We can end this now."

"Okay." I try to stand, but my legs seem to be too weak to hold me, so I end up collapsing back onto the ground.

"What's wrong?" Chase asks immediately, crouching down, examining my legs. "Are you injured?"

"I'm fine, I'm fine. Just … a bit weak."

"Are you sure it's not—"

"I'll be fine. Besides, it's not like you need my help, Mr. I-single-handedly-destroyed-large-parts-of-the-fae-realm." I smile at him. "You've got this."

His face twists in concern. "Calla …"

"Go," I tell him, taking his hand and squeezing it. "Do your hero thing. Save the world, and everyone watching will finally know what I know: you're fighting for the right side now."

His expression turns to one of amazement, a quiet laugh upon his lips. "That was it," he murmurs. Then he grasps my shoulders and presses a kiss to my lips. He pulls back and stares into my eyes. "I love you. Fiercely and desperately and with everything inside me. I love you."

My heart leaps into my throat, but he's up and running before I can say a word. *I love you too*, I whisper silently.

As the edges of my vision grow darker, and everything becomes oddly quiet, I see the whole scene as if from a distance. Vi bent over Ryn; the guardians pressing against the shield; Angelica, Tilda and Sorena with their hands raised toward the silvery layer, and Chase racing toward them with lightning crackling around him. I know as I watch them that they no longer stand a chance against him.

Blinding light flashes again and again, and thunder deafens me as I reach with shaking fingers for the zip of my jacket. Wind scurries down from the sky and blasts across the ground, pushing me down with its strength. Through the hair whipping around my face, I see Chase standing outside a spinning vortex of air and dust, the three women trapped inside and the wind so powerful they can't get past it. As I fumble with my zip and manage to pull it halfway down, light zigzags down from the sky and straight into the center of the whirlwind. The deafening crack that follows sends a shudder through the ground.

Everything becomes still. The wind quietens, the silver shield vanishes, and Chase looks down at the three women lying on the ground. Electrocuted, probably. Or stunned, perhaps. Not dead. Not when magic runs through their bodies and can heal them. Not when Chase is the one standing over them. Chase, the man who will fight and protect and save, but who won't kill. And I don't want him to, even if the witches' deaths would mean an easy escape from my curse. Killing isn't something I've ever wanted anyone to do for me. Angelica, Tilda and Sorena are incapacitated, and that's good enough for now. The Guild can deal with them, and we'll figure out another way around the curse.

Chase looks around—and suddenly, with a collective roar, the guardians rush forward. "Chase!" I scream, but I can barely hear my own voice. They're upon him within seconds, magic sparking and weapons glittering. Mist, snow, hail, lightning—I can't see a thing through the violent mix of stormy elements. I push myself up, fighting the lightheadedness. My fingers finally free the bottle from my pocket. A crack runs down the side, and the outer surface of the bottle is wet, but it's still more than half full of undiluted, full-strength tonic.

The storm settles. Someone shouts, "Move back!" The crowd of guardians obeys, moving out of the way to reveal Chase kneeling in front of the monument, restrained by several guardians and their glittering ropes. And I realize suddenly that this will never end. No matter how much good he does, they'll never forget the devastation of the past. Even if he escapes them now, they'll never stop hunting him, and this will go on and on until eventually, one day, they catch up to him.

Unless I do something.

I remove the lid of the bottle and tip the contents down my throat. I'm aware of familiar voices calling my name, but my every sense is focused on the herbal-sweet burn rushing down my throat. As energy shoots through my body, shocking me back to life, I know there's only one way for me to end this.

violet

CHAPTER THIRTY-ONE

I KNEEL BESIDE MY DYING HUSBAND AS THE WORLD FALLS apart around me. Violent wind, shuddering thunder, sea spray flying over the edge of the island, and a great rip in the sky—but I have eyes for none of it. "I'm sorry, I'm sorry, I'm sorry." They're the only words I can whisper, over and over again. My blood-covered hands move to either side of Ryn's face, pouring out as much magic as I can. I should never have left him. I should never have gone after that despicable murderer Zed. *Fight for everything you still have and not for what you've lost.* That's what Nate—Chase—said earlier. And he would know, wouldn't he? He watched his parents die. He let the desire for revenge consume him. Just as I was about to let it consume me. Even now, recognizing just how destructive a path it is, part of me still yearns for it. Part of me longs to turn off the pain and feel only the hate and the anger—especially now, faced with the horrifying possibility that I'm about to lose the only other person I love as much as I loved her.

Victoria.

Thinking her name brings fresh tears to my eyes. I bow my head and rest it against Ryn's chest once more. This is what I should have been doing these past few days: crying with my beloved. Letting our tears fall together. Not leaving him alone in his pain while I attempted to fulfill my own mission of revenge. "You won't die," I whisper to Ryn. "You have plenty of magic, and you're strong. You can survive this. I know she's—she's gone, and we'll never get her back, and my heart keeps breaking over and over, but please … please don't leave me. You promised you'd never leave me." As my tears soak his shirt, I imagine that I can feel the slow beat of his heart through his chest.

"I … know," he replies.

I pull back with a jolt. I look into the brilliant blue eyes I love so much, at his face smeared with blood and twisted with pain, and I can't speak past the tears that stream down my cheeks. I lean over him, burying my face against his neck, and hug him as tightly as I dare. My body shudders as sobs rip through me. I don't understand how I can be heartbroken and happy at the same time, but I'm overwhelmed by both.

A tiny soft figure wriggles between my shoulder and my neck and settles below my chin. Filigree. My dear, sweet Filigree. I have no idea how he ended up here, but his presence is as much a comfort to me as it's always been.

Ryn strokes my hair and mumbles, "I don't think I'm …

gonna be … sitting up for a while."

I pull gently away from him—just as the tumult of the storm dies down and silence descends upon us. I look up and find the whirlwind over. Angelica and the two witches lie motionless on the ground with Chase standing over them. The shield that separated us from the rest of the battle—the faeries, prisoners, gargoyles, and even a dragon—is gone. Chase turns to face the silent crowd of guardians.

They surge forward and attack.

"No," I gasp, too shocked to move. He fights back, but the guardians number in the hundreds, and they restrain him in under a minute. As they force him onto his knees, my eyes are drawn to the ever-growing hole in the sky and the field in the world beyond. The lower edge of the hole has reached the grass on the other side of the trident monument. Slowly, inch by inch, the grass on our side and the grass in the field seem to be … merging. Sparking, turning to ash, and disappearing. As if our two worlds are colliding and … destroying one another. "Oh no," I murmur. "I'm guessing that that is *not* what Angelica was hoping for."

"What?" Ryn asks. "What's happening."

"There's a giant rip in the sky. I can see the human realm on the other side. But … both worlds are slowly being consumed by each other. We're going to have nothing left if we don't stop it. And Chase …" I turn my attention back to him. He's struggling uselessly against the guardians, but then, as if digging deep within himself and calling upon his reserves of power, he flings his attackers back into the crowd. Instantly, another shield shimmers into view, translucent silver, like the one the witches had up earlier. But if it's a witch shield, that must mean …

Just as I think it, one of the witches climbs to her feet. Chase swings toward her and throws her down again, but her blast of magic hits him directly in the face. He drops to the ground and doesn't get up.

Afraid to leave Ryn, but desperate to help Chase, I climb to my feet. As the witch scrambles up and crawls toward Chase, I look around for Calla. She must have disappeared into the trees, though, because I don't see her anywhere. "What's happening?" Ryn asks again, groaning as he tries to sit up.

"Hey, don't you dare move." I push him back down, and by the time I look up again, the witch's hands are hovering above Chase's body, moving in odd circular motions. Her lips twitch, but I'm too far away to hear her words. "Hey!" I yell, hoping to distract her. She ignores me, and a second later, bright green flames ignite upon Chase's chest. They race across his body without pause.

I cry out and race toward him. Without bothering to look up, the witch retaliates, her magic flashing out and punching me. I stumble backward, doubling over and gasping for breath. I drop onto my knees, coughing and sucking in air that doesn't seem to be there while Ryn calls out to me, asking if I'm okay.

By the time I can breathe again, Chase's body is consumed by an inferno. An enchanted fire so scorchingly hot I can feel the heat from where I'm kneeling, a considerable distance away. A grating howl rises on the air, followed by another and another. A chilling cacophony of gargoyle misery. Ryn shouts again, demanding to know what's going on, but I can't speak.

The horror of it—Chase's *burning body*—sickens me to my core. I look around again for Calla, but she's still nowhere to be seen. Fear entangles itself with the nausea in my stomach. Where is she? What's happened to her?

My gaze snaps back to the blazing green flames and the witch standing nearby. She sways. Then, as if she's finally spent the last of her energy, she collapses back onto the ground beside the other two unconscious women. As the shield vanishes, I run toward the fire. I get as close as I can without searing my skin, but I'm far, far too late to help Chase. These flames burn hotter and faster than any I've seen, and his clothes, his flesh—I look away as my stomach turns. There's barely anything left of him.

Movement catches my attention at the edge of my vision. The guardians behind me, I assume, moving closer to examine the fallen Lord Draven now that the shield is gone. But no. As I turn slightly, I see someone else. The witch—the one who fell to the ground barely a minute ago, swings her axe back and—

A snarling gargoyle slams into her, throwing her flat onto the ground. It rears back and roars. Then its form seems to ripple. It shifts and changes and grows into scales, clawed feet, wings, a forked tongue, and talons the size of my forearms. Dragon-formed Filigree roars again. His head swings down and his jaw clamps around the witch—around the entire woman. He shakes her broken body back and forth with dizzying speed before tossing her into the crowd.

Shocked and trembling—I've never seen Filigree shift into a form so enormous—I stumble away from the fire. Filigree breathes a stream of flames toward the sky before beginning to shrink. I turn and run back to Ryn's side. "Oh, thank goodness," he gasps as I drop to my knees beside him. He's on his side now, as if he was trying to move, to sit up. "I thought … I thought you were …"

"I'm fine. But Chase …" I shake my head and wrap my shaking fingers around Ryn's hands. "He's … did you see? I couldn't …" Tears sting my eyes again as Filigree scampers toward us in squirrel form. "I couldn't do anything. The fire was too quick. I was too late, and I don't know where Calla is, and that tear in the sky …"

I look up at the gaping wound between the worlds and the guardians gathered below it. They've moved between us and the enchanted fire now, and I can barely make out the flickering tops of the flames consuming Chase's body. High above us, the heavy clouds of Chase's storm have scattered and vanished, revealing a star-studded sky and a full, silver-yellow orb.

Someone steps forward and climbs onto the monument. I recognize him as Head Councilor Bouchard when he turns to face everyone. "Two days ago," he calls out, his voice magically magnified, "it was revealed to us that Lord Draven has not been dead for the past ten years, as we were led to believe. Our world went into a flurry of panic, imagining a second Destruction. But tonight—" he shakes his fist in the air "—Draven has been vanquished forever. He will never again threaten our way of life." Applause and cries of victory rise from the crowd.

I press my eyelids closed and shake my head, sickened to hear them rejoicing for this horrifying death. "They're celebrating the wrong thing," I whisper.

"There is, however, another threat that needs to be addressed." Councilor Bouchard pauses, looking out at the crowd, waiting for complete silence. "I wasn't planning to do this for another several weeks, but I couldn't waste this opportunity when it presented itself. This moment in which almost every guardian in our world would be assembled in one place." He raises his hand and holds something high in the air. Something spherical and glowing. He lets go. In the silence, I hear the splintering smash of glass. A ripple of magic rushes through the air like a breeze gently lifting my hair. And then—my body begins to glow. The glow spreads across Ryn, wrapping us both in faint light.

"What the hell is this?" he murmurs.

"I don't know." My gaze flies up again as apprehension pounds through my veins. In the crowd of guardians, I pick out glowing forms here and there.

Councilor Bouchard raises his voice and speaks again. "Griffin Gifted," he booms, "you have been revealed."

violet

CHAPTER THIRTY-TWO

IN THE SHOCKED SILENCE THAT FOLLOWS COUNCILOR Bouchard's revelation, I meet Ryn's gaze. Every thought racing through my mind is reflected in his eyes. As if we haven't been through enough in the past week, our world has once again shifted suddenly and irreversibly. The secret each of us has kept our entire lives is now evident for everyone to see.

Griffin Gifted. Feared. Not trusted. Not permitted to work for any Guild.

Councilor Bouchard scans the murmuring crowd, his eyes settling on every glowing form, memorizing the men and women who've broken the law by failing to register themselves and working illegally as guardians. His eyes narrow as they focus on me. I know he recognizes me from the dealings we've had in the past. My support of the reptiscilla petitions. My request to remain a guardian in service of the Guild while working at the Reptiscillan Protectors Institute. "They called you 'Guild traitor,' did they not?" he shouts to me. "Seems they were right. You've been lying all along. You and all the other Gifted hiding among us." He looks out at the glowing fae with disdain as the murmurs rise and the crowd shifts and moves apart, leaving rings of space around the 'traitors' who've managed to keep their abilities secret until this moment. "We'll soon get you all on that list where you—"

"Hey!" I yell, jumping to my feet, unable to endure for one more second just how *wrong* this all is. Celebrating death, revealing innocent Gifted, and all the while our world is slowly sizzling into nothingness right behind our foolish Head Councilor. "Have you seen what's happening behind you? Have you seen the tear growing larger and the two worlds slowly eating each other up? Stop turning us against each other and DO SOMETHING!"

Shouts of agreement and cries of concern tell me I'm not the only one worried about the growing hole. Councilor Bouchard stares at me for a moment, stunned, before swinging around and finally paying attention to the most important reason everyone assembled here tonight: to prevent a tear in the veil. A task we have utterly failed at. Councilor Bouchard must have known the hole was there; he couldn't possibly have missed it as he pulled himself onto the statue to do his big Griffin Gifted revelation. But perhaps he didn't notice it was growing bigger. Perhaps he didn't realize until now that this island and everyone on it will soon be consumed.

The edges of the gap slowly eat away at the sky as the hole

grows large, moves closer. On the other side, in the human world, the field is almost gone. In the road just beyond, a car stands abandoned with doors flung open. Another car comes to a halt behind it, reverses, turns, and speeds away. On our side, the grass just beyond the monument sizzles and vanishes.

Councilor Bouchard leaps off the statue and backs away along with the rest of the crowd. Shouts rise up, questions of what to do or where to run. Some guardians raise their hands toward the tear, clearly trying to stop it with magic, but it inches ever closer.

Think, think, think, I tell myself, but I have no answer for this. Nothing I've ever learned, read or heard has prepared me for a tear in the very fabric of our world. I bend over Ryn to check his wound as my mind continues racing. The skin's starting to knit together, but I'm sure there's still plenty of damage underneath.

"We can't stop it," Ryn says. "We have to get away. Find out how to stop it and come back. Where's—" He struggles to sit, but I push him down before he hurts himself further. "Where's Calla?"

"I don't know." I look wildly around, as if she might suddenly materialize.

"She must be here … somewhere. She wouldn't have …" He pauses to take in a few heavy breaths. "She wouldn't have left Chase."

"I know, but I don't see her. Filigree, help me lift Ryn," I add as I stand. We have to get down to the boats somehow. The one that brought me here wouldn't rise into the bottom of the island the way the boats normally do when they get here, perhaps because the canal that receives the boats was already full. My magic propelled me up, but it's going to be a lot more challenging getting back down with Ryn.

"We can't leave without Calla," Ryn says, groaning as Filigree, bear-shaped now, lifts him from the ground. "I only came here to make sure she—aah, sharp claws, Fili—to make sure she didn't get herself killed going after those witches."

"The only place she could have gone is further into the trees. Filigree can carry you, and I'll start looking—" Louder shouts from the guardians make me turn back as Filigree lowers Ryn's feet to the ground so he'll stop complaining. At least half the guardians are running now, clearly having given up on trying to seal the tear. As for the tear itself … "Oh crap. It's reached the monument." Which means it isn't far from reaching the edge of the grove of trees. And if Calla's in there … Fear throbs at my temples as the base of the statue collides with what remains of the grassy field. I need to *move*, to find her, but I'm frozen in place, both wanting and not wanting to see a monument that's stood for centuries, the powerful guarding force of the mer kingdom, crumble as it meets the edge of the veil.

It doesn't.

I suck in a breath and hold it. Waiting, counting, hoping. Still, the veil's edge moves no further. Looking out to either side, it doesn't seem to be stretching any wider. "It's stopped," I whisper. "Is that … possible? All we needed to do was place a powerful enough obstacle in its way?"

"You say that as if it's a simple solution," Ryn says, his arm around Filigree's neck as Filigree holds him upright. "How many objects containing several centuries' worth of magic do you see lying around?"

"I suppose it makes sense," I say, answering myself. "The monument is powerful enough to create an opening in the veil, so it should be powerful enough to ... close it? Do you think we can—"

"Stop them! Don't let them get away!" My gaze swings away from the trident statue and toward Councilor Bouchard. Following his line of sight, I see two glowing figures racing away past the side of the prison. "Don't let *any* of those lying traitors get away!"

Madness follows as guardians tackle the Gifted faeries in their midst. Some detach themselves from the crowd and run toward us.

"Dammit," I mutter, backing away as Filigree lifts Ryn. There's nothing behind us but trees and the edge of the island, but if we have to jump into the water far below, that's what we'll do. I don't want to be interrogated or have my guardian markings deactivated. I don't want to be tagged so the Guild knows my exact whereabouts for the rest of my life, and Ryn feels the same way. "Filigree, we have to—"

A whooping cry sounds from the sky, and a gargoyle and its rider come swooping down. A young man falls off the gargoyle's back as it lands clumsily. I don't know who he is, this tall faerie with green in his hair, but he stations himself between us and the guardians racing to catch us. With snarling growls, another three gargoyles land beside him and face our pursuers.

Someone touches my arm. With a yelp, I jump away, a

knife flashing into existence in my hand. "Hey, careful!" a woman says breathlessly. "I'm here to help! You probably don't remember me, but I'm Chase's friend." She tugs my arm—with a gloved hand—and suddenly I recognize her.

"Scarlett?"

"Yes! Come on."

I hesitate. After all, she tried to kill me once, and she used to work for the Unseelie Prince Marzell. But if Chase managed to change his ways, maybe Scarlett did too. Besides, Ryn and I don't exactly have many options right now.

"Go with her," Ryn says, struggling to look past Filigree at the guardians and gargoyles. "Now!"

We race into the grove as fast as Filigree's bear legs can move. Zigzagging between trees, dodging beneath branches, sparing a glance or two over my shoulder. It isn't long before we reach the other side. On the grass, right near the edge of the island, a group of fae are gathered in a huddle. As we come to a halt, they look around at us, concern written on each of their faces. Someone moves aside, and I see who's kneeling at the center of their circle.

I jolt backward in fright, my brain immediately rejecting what I'm seeing. He cheated death once before, but this time he had no eternity necklace. Nothing to save him from the blazing inferno. "You—you're—dead. I saw you die … in the fire …"

Chase looks up at me with pleading, desperate eyes. "That never happened. She made you see everything. And now we can't wake her up."

violet

CHAPTER THIRTY-THREE

AN ILLUSION. OF COURSE IT WAS AN ILLUSION. I SHOULD have realized when Calla didn't go racing to rescue Chase, and when he was overpowered so quickly by the witch. But it was all so real. Surely the flames that almost seared my skin with their intense heat were real. That can't have been an imaginary fire. But if the fire was real … then who was burning within it?

I push my questions to the back of my mind as we make our hasty escape from the island. Ryn and I—and Filigree, in mouse form in my pocket—take the dragon that swoops down to join the company moments after we arrive at the edge of the island. I'm told by everyone here that dragon riding is a far smoother experience than gargoyle riding, which means Ryn's wound is less likely to reopen. Everyone else takes a gargoyle. Chase rides with Calla, strapping the harness around both of them and holding tightly onto her unconscious form. I tell myself Calla's just exhausted from projecting such a detailed illusion, that's all. Nothing more sinister than that. It's impossible not to worry, though, especially with Chase looking so concerned.

It isn't long before we see the cliffs in the distance. As we speed through the air toward them, I keep my arms wrapped firmly around Ryn's chest, high enough above his middle that I'm nowhere near hurting him. I almost lost him tonight, and I don't plan on letting go of him any time soon. His hand settles over mine, and I rest my head against his back, remembering a journey from long ago that took place on a dragon named Arthur.

I don't know where we're headed now, but it doesn't matter. If it's somewhere that's safe for Chase and his friends, then it will be safe for us too. It's probably the same place Calla's been staying. The secret place she wouldn't tell us anything about in case Ryn or I were ever questioned by the Guild. The secret she no longer needs to keep from us, since it's unlikely we'll ever set foot inside a Guild ever again. The thought forms a hollow ache that adds itself to the well of pain residing deep within me.

I look away from the pain and focus on where we're going. Into a giant faerie paths doorway, side by side. The elf on the gargoyle beside us stretches her hand toward me. I lean down and take hold of it as darkness surrounds us. Then we're moving out of the paths and onto frost-covered ground devoid of life, except for the vast lake stretching out toward a snow-capped mountain. Next, we're flying again, speeding over the water toward the mountain. And finally, we soar through an opening in the side of the mountain and into a gigantic cavern.

Chase's gargoyle has barely touched the ground when he starts removing his harness. He climbs off the gargoyle and carefully takes Calla into his arms. Then he strides away with her, Scarlett following close behind him. No, not Scarlett. Elizabeth. That's what everyone seems to call her now.

As I help Ryn down off the dragon, the tall woman with startlingly white hair and pale eyes stops beside us. Lumethon, if I remember correctly from the hurried introductions that took place before we left the island. "I'll help you upstairs," she says. "We need to get through a narrow tunnel first, which might be a little difficult, but if he can walk—"

"I can walk," Ryn says, though how he knows this, I'm not sure. He hasn't taken a single step since that spear went through him.

"Then it will be easier," Lumethon says. "There are several unoccupied bedrooms upstairs, and you're welcome to rest in one of them. Also," she adds, "I have knowledge of certain healing magic. If you'll let me, I'm sure I can help."

"Thank you," Ryn says. "I'd be very grateful for that."

We move away from the dragon, and it turns out that Ryn can walk after all. But it causes him a considerable amount of pain, so in the end, once we're past the narrow tunnel, I ask Filigree to carry Ryn. He climbs out of my pocket, where he's been nestling since we left the island, and shifts into a bear once more.

As we follow Lumethon upstairs, I say, "Please explain to me what happened back on the island. With the illusion, I mean. What was real and what wasn't? It's … unsettling not knowing the difference."

"Of course," she says with a smile. "Let's see. When the battle with the prisoners was over, we took the gargoyles around the side of the island and landed in the trees. We reached Calla's side just as Chase was being restrained. We were ready to rush in and fight every guardian to get him out, but Calla stopped us. She said the Guild would never stop hunting him and that the world would live in fear of his return, and that the best way to end this would be with the world believing he had died.

"So while you were seeing whatever Calla wanted you to see, we forced every guardian holding onto Chase back into the crowd. They couldn't see us, so they weren't expecting to have to fight anyone off. Then three of us created a shield layer. I think Calla imagined it silver, so everyone would think it was from the witches. Darius and Kobe then brought the body of one of the dead prisoners. Elizabeth started the fire. It was the same as the fire Calla imagined. Powerful, enchanted witch flames that would consume a body quickly. Easy enough for Elizabeth to do, since she's familiar with witch magic. Then we all ran into the trees to hide, planning to get away as soon as we could. That's when Calla collapsed."

"From overuse of magic?"

Lumethon looks away as we reach a hallway and continue going up. "I don't know. Hopefully that's all it is."

"So when I ran at the witch to try and stop her from doing that fire spell and her magic threw me back … how did that happen if it was an illusion?"

"That was Gaius, actually," Lumethon says, her voice taking on an apologetic tone. "His magic threw you back. We couldn't risk you interfering."

"But … okay." I shake my head. "How did you pull this off if you were seeing the same illusion everyone else was seeing? That must have been tremendously confusing."

"We weren't seeing the same thing you were seeing. At least … Calla was trying not to show it to us. But she hasn't yet perfected that particular technique, so we saw a fuzzy, translucent version of what you saw. Which was actually quite helpful," she adds. "At least we knew what everyone else was seeing."

We finally reach the top of the stairs and head along a carpeted passageway. We pass a room with books and plants, and then a bedroom on the right—Calla's bedroom, judging from the fact that Chase and Elizabeth are standing by the bed. "Do you think …" I lean back as we pass the door, trying to see more of what's going on. My voice edged with fear, I say, "What if there's something else wrong with her?"

"Go and find out," Ryn says from Filigree's arms. "Please. I need to know if she's okay."

I reach for his hand as we turn into another bedroom. "I don't want to leave you."

"I'm fine," Ryn insists. "I'm a faerie. A hole in the stomach is nothing."

"It's definitely not nothing."

Lumethon lights the lamp hovering in the corner while Filigree lowers Ryn onto the bed. I don't let go of his hand. As he settles back against the pillows, relief passes over his features.

He squeezes my fingers. "Please. Please just go check on her. I'm not going anywhere. You can come straight back here and tell me what's going on." After a pause, I nod. I turn to leave, but he tightens his grip and says, "Wait." He pulls me down toward him and presses a kiss to my lips, and then his cheek against my cheek. "I love you," he whispers. "Thank you for coming back to me."

I can't speak all of a sudden, so I nod and swallow and finally manage to whisper, "I love you too."

The sound of raised voices reaches my ears as I turn back down the corridor toward Calla's room. I reach her doorway as Chase shouts, "You should have said something! You should have told the rest of the team."

"It was her choice not to say anything," Elizabeth replies.

"About what?" I ask as I walk in. "What's going on?"

Chase drops his hands to his sides and shakes his head. "Ask Elizabeth," he says, his tone hard.

As I walk to the side of the bed, toward the still, golden haired girl I love as much as if she were my own sister, Elizabeth speaks. She tells me of a witch's curse that would drain Calla of her power every time she used her Griffin Ability. She would grow steadily weaker until her core magic was depleted and life vanished from her body. Then her Griffin Ability would become the witch's.

I lower myself onto the edge of the bed, my hands pressed over my mouth.

"She didn't want to tell anyone," Elizabeth says. "She knew Gaius and the others would try to keep her from using her ability, and without her, we had no way into the Seelie Palace to rescue Chase. I made her a tonic to keep the curse's effects at bay, but there was no way of knowing how long it would work."

"Well now we know," Chase says quietly, stopping beside me and taking Calla's hand gently in his. "That last illusion tonight was too much."

"How do we heal her?" I ask. "Or is it too—" My voice breaks. "It is too late?"

"If the witch won't lift the curse, then she must be killed." Elizabeth turns her gaze to Chase. "And we know how you feel about killing."

A flicker of hope burns within me as I remember Filigree coming to my rescue in a form more ferocious than any I've ever seen him in. "One of the witches is dead."

Elizabeth's eye snap back to me. "How? Which one?"

I wonder how none of them saw this, but they must have been back in the trees by then, with their attention focused on Calla. "I don't know which one. Filigree—uh, my shape-shifting pet—transformed into a dragon when one of the witches tried to attack me. He … well, the witch ended up between his jaws. He flung her around and tossed her away. I didn't see her after that, but … his fangs punctured through her body, and her neck must surely have been broken from being shaken around like that. I don't believe she could possibly have survived."

Elizabeth's expression is grim. "You don't know what a witch can survive," she says as she stares at Calla.

"If it was the right witch," I say, "and she did die, then what does that mean for Calla?"

Elizabeth gives a slight shake of her head and lifts her shoulders. "Hopefully it means the curse ended just in time." She moves to the other side of the room and leans against the wall with her arms crossed.

I turn to Chase and quietly ask, "Will you stay with her?"

"I won't leave her side," he says, which is pretty much what I expected.

My heart is heavy as I walk back to the other bedroom. I don't want to tell Ryn what's happened. I don't want him to have to consider losing his sister so soon after losing … *Victoria*. And the way I last spoke to Calla … I shouted at her. Blamed her. But I didn't mean any of it, and I may never get to tell her that.

I breathe in a deep shaky breath as I enter the bedroom. Relief fills me when I see Ryn's closed eyes and his gently rising chest. "Is he asleep?" I ask Lumethon, who's quietly packing bottles back into a bag.

"Yes. I'm sorry. I gave him something for the pain, and drowsiness is a side effect. Since all his body's energy is going into healing him right now, it didn't take long before he fell asleep."

"That's fine. No need to apologize. I'm glad he's resting properly now."

She takes her bag and stops beside me on her way out, giving me a reassuring smile. "Gaius and I will be around if you need anything."

"Thank you."

She shuts the door.

Silence.

Before I let everything come crashing down, I remove my shoes. I take my jacket off. I gently move Filigree, sleeping in curled up cat form, to the bottom of the bed and climb beneath the covers. I get as close to Ryn as possible, placing my head beside his on his pillow and wrapping my arm around him. He mumbles, half-asleep, and reaches for my hand. His fingers wrap around mine before relaxing again.

I breathe out slowly as everything, *everything*, washes over me. Our baby is gone. Calla is cursed and possibly dying. Our names are on the Griffin List. We'll never again work for the Guild. We'll be on the run forever if we don't want to be tagged and tracked.

But I still have Ryn.

My tears soak the pillow as I drift gradually toward sleep, filled again with that odd combination of pain and peace.

calla

CHAPTER THIRTY-FOUR

I KNEW I'D REACHED THE END OF MY STRENGTH WITH that final illusion. I knelt on the ground, my fingers digging into the earth as I poured every bit of my remaining magic and focus into that illusion. And not only projecting the illusion itself as far across the island as possible, but trying to *keep* it from my team so they wouldn't be horribly confused. My body begged me to let go, but I refused until I felt hands on me, heard voices saying we'd done it. We saved Chase while everyone thought he was burning. Only then did I let go of the illusion and allow my teammates to become visible around me. Only then did I fall into the welcoming arms of darkness and rest.

* * *

Soft light caresses my eyelids. I open them and find the first hints of sunrise appearing in my enchanted painted windows. I rub my eyes and slowly push myself up, and for the first time in days, I feel rested. A single, simple thought comes to mind: *I'm not dead.* I smile as I let the thought sink in properly. I'm not dead, despite the fact that I was convinced the witch's curse was about to consume me. I'm not dead—but I am horribly thirsty. I reach for the glass of water beside my bed and down it. Then I notice the second glass. A glass filled with layers of green and gold. I don't remember telling anyone here at the mountain that I like honey apple, but I must have. I take a few sips before returning the glass to the table.

I push my hair away from my face, noticing that it's blonde and gold, no longer black. Someone must have bathed me. As awkward a thought as that is, it's probably a good thing considering how long ago my previous shower was. I look around—and find someone lying beside me. Chase. So quiet I wasn't aware of him there. A slight frown creases his brow despite the fact that he's asleep. His face is clean-shaven, and his hair is properly free of the blood and dirt that caked it when I first found him at the Seelie Palace. His hand is stretched out toward me, as if perhaps he was holding mine before he fell asleep.

I place my fingers over his. As his eyelids flutter and open, I push every worrying thought aside—the tear in the sky, Ryn's spear wound, Mom and Dad in prison; my ever-present guilt—and appreciate this moment: we're both alive, safe and together. His frown vanishes the moment he sees me. He sits up, moves closer, and pulls me into his arms. "I thought the curse had taken you," he murmurs.

My arms come up around his body. I press my head against his chest. "So did I," I whisper. "Why didn't it?"

"One of the witches was killed in the fight yesterday. Gaius confirmed it with someone from the Guild. But we had no way of knowing if it was the witch who cursed you. The fact that you weren't gone yet gave me hope, though. And now that you're awake … well, it must have been her."

"I'm so sorry. I'm sorry I didn't tell you. I just wanted to be able to help."

He kisses the top of my head. "I know."

I pull back suddenly. "Is Ryn—"

"He's fine."

"And the tear in the sky? It was getting bigger when—"

"It stopped when it met the monument."

My eyes slide shut and my shoulders droop beneath the relief. "Thank goodness."

"From what I've heard, guardians have been trying to seal the gap, but they've had no luck. It sounds like there's a group of them guarding it with a glamour, keeping humans away. Not a permanent solution, but it'll work for now. What's interesting is that Velazar Island has stopped moving."

"Oh. I suppose the monument and the tear are keeping it in place."

"Yes." Chase lifts his hand to my face, and his thumb caresses my cheek. "Do you remember everything else that happened?"

My smile returns. "I remember you telling me you love

me." As his lips stretch into a smile wider than mine, I add, "But you ran away before I could respond."

He tilts forward and kisses my nose. "What would you have responded with?"

I lean past him and whisper into his ear, "I love you too. Just as fiercely and desperately and with everything inside me."

His lips brush my jaw, but I push him gently back. "Wait. Tell me what you meant just before that. When you said, 'That was it.'"

His eyes crinkle at the edges as he grins. "I think you know."

"I think I know too. But tell me anyway."

Chase pulls me toward him. I shift around so that my back is pressed against his chest. He wraps his arms around me, and our fingers lace together. "This is what Luna said to me: 'I see you with a woman in gold. The background is filled with one of your storms. She doesn't say it, but I can see in her eyes that she loves you. She loves you so much that she doesn't want you to go. But because she has faith in you, she tells you to go. She tells you to go and save the world so that everyone will know what she knows: that you're fighting for the right side now.'"

"Amazing," I murmur. Amazing that someone could know almost exactly what I would say so many years ago.

"I didn't believe her," Chase says. "It wasn't the first vision she'd Seen of me, but mostly they were little things in the near future. Some never came to pass, and I dismissed this as one of those. How unlikely, I thought. How could anyone know all the things I've done and still love me?"

I lift our entwined hands and kiss his fingers. "Now you know how."

"Do you understand why I didn't mention it when I first remembered it? We barely knew each other then. What would you have thought if I told you that you were one day supposed to love me? And even after the golden river, after you kissed me and told me that what I'd done in the past didn't matter to you, I didn't want to say anything. If you grew to love me, I wanted it to come from *you*, not from a vision you might have felt you had to fulfill."

I nod. "I understand. I'm glad you didn't tell me, and I'm glad I didn't force it out of you." I twist around to face him again. "And I want you to know that these words come from *me*." I place both hands on either side of his face and look into his eyes. "I love you." I kiss one eyelid and then the other. "I love you." I kiss his nose. "I love you." And I want to move to his lips. I want to kiss him the way we kissed in the golden river. But in this exact moment, Gaius walks past my open bedroom door and realizes I'm awake. His joyful cry is loud, and in the next few minutes, all the members of our team, all the people I didn't realize were waiting anxiously for me to wake up, begin crowding into my bedroom.

* * *

Later in the day, I come out of the faerie paths inside the lake house. Chase gave the house to Vi and Ryn to use for a while. They can't go home unless they want to submit themselves to the Guild for questioning, tagging and deactivation of their guardian markings. They were welcome at the mountain, of course, but Chase felt they might need their own space. Their own time. Time to grieve and time to figure things out.

He moved the faerie door to Lumethon's home Underground so Vi and Ryn wouldn't have to deal with people traipsing through their living room in order to get to the mountain. Not so great for Lumethon, but apparently she offered.

I cross the open living area and look out the kitchen window. On the grass just beyond the porch steps is a blanket. Vi is curled up on her side, and Ryn sits next to her, writing in a notebook. The scene is so peaceful that I almost turn away and leave. But the longer I wait to speak to them, the harder it will be.

I open the front door and step outside. Terrified, my heart pounding painfully in my chest and the guilt-beast circling at the edge of my thoughts, I walk down the steps and stop on the grass. "Ryn?" He lowers his notebook and looks around as Vi pushes herself up. "I—I don't want to disturb you, but I just wanted to say that—"

He's up in a heartbeat, running toward me, his arms around me before I can move. A second later, Vi joins us, her arms encircling us both. "I'm so, so sorry," I sob, weak with relief and utterly overcome by the fact that they can still love me after the pain I've caused them. I hear Ryn crying in my ear. Vi's arms shudder around me. Their tears only make me cry harder, and it's a long time—a long, long time—before any of us is able to speak.

"You almost got killed trying to stop those witches," Ryn

says, his voice wobbling and his arms tightening around me as he speaks.

"*You* almost got killed trying to save me," I say with a sniff. "And I owe you so much already. Can you imagine if you'd … if you'd …" I shake my head against his shoulder. "I wouldn't have been able to live with that guilt added onto all the other guilt."

Ryn pulls back, widening our little circle. "You don't have to carry any of that guilt around."

"I do! If I hadn't—"

"I don't blame you," he says. "I was hurting—hurting so, so much—and all that hurt and anger spewed out on you, because you were there and because I could feel your immense guilt. But I don't blame you."

I shake my head as more tears wet my cheeks. "You should blame me. She … she wouldn't have died if I hadn't let Zed go free."

"And The Destruction wouldn't have happened if I hadn't saved the life of a boy named Nate," Vi says, her voice thick with tears. "Or maybe it would have. Maybe someone else would have caused it, just as some other guardian-hater who was locked in Zell's dungeon might have come after us and Victoria." She pulls me closer and presses her tear-stained cheek against mine. "We can't do this to ourselves. We can't look back and say 'what if.' It changes nothing. And yes, this still hurts more than anything I've ever endured, and I don't understand how it can ever *stop* hurting. But … I'm not alone. Ryn's here and you're here, and none of us is hurting alone. We hurt together because we love each other."

And just like that, the guilt-beast's existence is snuffed out like a flame in a breeze.

We move to the blanket then and I sit with the two of them for a while. Vi keeps hold of my hand, and we talk about the mountain and Chase's team and the investigation on Dad. We speak of where Ryn and Vi might go now and what they might do. We cry some more, and we even end up half-laughing when Ryn suggests he and Vi live in the human realm and start a circus as their new profession. Filigree hops over the grass as a rabbit and joins us. I scoop him up and snuggle against his soft white hair, whispering thank you over and over again. He's the reason I'm still here. He's the reason the curse was broken.

As the afternoon sun sinks toward the horizon and the mirror in my pocket lights up with a familiar mischievous face, I stand and say goodbye to Ryn and Vi.

"Come back later," Vi says, sniffing and wiping away yet more tears. "We can have dinner together. Bring Chase." Ryn looks at her with raised eyebrows. "What? I sense many family dinners together in our future. We should start getting used to it."

I nod, appreciating that she's making an effort when it would be so much easier for her to curl into a depressed ball and stay that way. "I think dinner time here lines up around about lunchtime at the mountain, so we can make that work."

I leave the lake house and head through the paths to the old Guild ruins. I step out to find Perry already there. "You called?" I say to him with a smile.

"Holy moly." He pushes away from a vine-encircled tree trunk. "That was one heck of a fight last night. I thought you were dead after that witch threw you down on the monument. Then I thought your brother was dead. Then Draven … well, thank goodness he's gone for real now."

"Yeah." I smile down at my feet, knowing I can't tell Perry the truth about that last bit. "I heard you teamed up with the gargoyles and helped my brother and his wife get away. She didn't know who you were, but when she explained what happened and what this mysterious young gargoyle rider looked like, I knew it was you."

"Yeah, people always tend to remember my good looks."

I smile and, since Gemma isn't here to do it, smack his arm. "Seriously, though," I add. "I'm very grateful, and so are they."

"Well, what else was I gonna do? Number one, I recognized him as your brother. Obviously. Since everyone knows Ryn Larkenwood. Number two, I don't think Griffin Gifted should be discriminated against. And number three … I guess I just have the special touch when it comes to gargoyles. They loved me."

I laugh. "Well, thank you. Were Gemma and Ned there?"

"Gemma wasn't. She's been avoiding me, so … I didn't tell her. And, you know …" He rolls his eyes. "Probably also for the same reasons you told me not to go: I didn't want her getting hurt. Ned was already at the Guild when I got there, so he heard what was happening and decided to come with. The Councilors already knew, actually, so you needn't have asked me to pass on the message. I'm glad you did, though. Just in case."

"Did Ned join you and the gargoyles?"

"Oh, no, he didn't want to go near 'those Unseelie

creatures.' Probably thought he'd wind up in trouble with the Guild. He's actually …" Perry scratches his head. "Yeah, he's not too pleased with me. Said I should have been catching Gifted faeries, not helping them get away. Told me I need to think about where my true loyalties lie."

"I'm sorry. That's tough."

"Yeah. Not tough figuring my loyalties out, of course. I know exactly what I believe to be right and what I believe to be wrong. It's just tough trying to have that kind of conversation with a friend who only sees in black and white and thinks the law is never wrong, you know? Anyway," he continues loudly before I can answer him, "how was that giant-ass tear in the sky last night?"

I give him a knowing smile. "You don't like it when the conversation takes a serious turn, do you?"

He shrugs, looking down at his shoes. "It's not my favorite conversation territory." Peeking up at me with a grin, he adds, "You know me well by now."

"I do," I say with a laugh. "But I'll happily go along with your change in subject. Tell me what's happening with the veil. Now that my brother's not welcome at the Guild, you're my only source." Gaius has his own Guild source, but it can sometimes take a while to hear back from him.

"Yeah, it's been a chaotic Sunday, I can tell you that." Perry leans against the tree and crosses his arms. "Not for me, obviously. I was just kinda hanging around listening to everything. So far, every attempt to seal the tear or pull the edges back together has been unsuccessful. Guardians are stationed there permanently, keeping a glamour in place and making sure no one touches the monument. Spells are being prepared to root the monument to the island and keep it from being moved. Right now, it looks like the only solution may be to guard that thing forever. Well, until someone intelligent enough comes up with a way to seal the gap."

"And the prison?"

"It's being repaired, but they're still figuring out what to do about it once the repairs are complete. All the escaped prisoners who survived have been rounded up, but no one wants to keep the world's most dangerous criminals right next to a gap into the human realm. I heard talk of them slicing right through the island, leaving the prison to move around as it did before and just a little piece of floating land for the monument to stand on."

"I suppose that could work," I say. "It's probably easier than building a new prison."

"And then there's the tower," Perry says with a long sigh.

"Ugh, it makes me sick every time I think of it," I say, covering my face with my hands. "All those people. All those lives, ended for *nothing*."

"Yeah. We're having a huge ceremony tomorrow for everyone who was killed. Probably the biggest ceremony since—"

"Since Draven's reign ended," I murmur.

"Yeah."

"And what about Angelica and the witch who survived?"

"Some are calling for the death sentence. They're saying none of this would have happened if Princess Angelica and every other close follower of Draven's had been sentenced to death ten years ago instead of life in prison. Oh, and a whole bunch of people are demanding that Head Councilor Bouchard resign. They want to know how he could ever have freed Princess Angelica from prison. He, of course, says the decision was purely the Queen's and that he had no choice. Oh, *and*," Perry adds, "everyone's now talking about the coronation of the new king, Princess Audra's son. Told you it was a chaotic Sunday."

"Yeah, I can imagine. And you were probably totally chilled in a corner somewhere absorbing all the information flying back and forth."

"Mostly, yes," Perry says with a grin. "But I also took advantage of the chaos and did some snooping around the Seer level. I discovered which senior Seers the visions are sent to. The Seers who decide which visions are urgent and which aren't. They send the not-so-urgent visions to Councilor Merrydale's office, and *that*—" Perry removes a rolled up wad of papers from his back pocket "—is where I found these." He hands the papers to me. "I had plenty of time to copy them while everyone else was hurrying about."

"This is brilliant, Perry," I say, shuffling through the papers. "I can't tell you how, but I can promise you that any non-expired visions here will be taken care of."

"Awesome," Perry says. "I don't need to know how. Like I said, I know what I believe to be right and wrong, and if giving you those 'surplus' visions is going to help people, then it's the right thing to do."

I nod. And then I almost ask if he knows about the drakoni club owner. Zed's friend. I almost ask if he knows whether the drakoni was questioned with truth potion, and if he revealed Zed's whereabouts. But I stop myself. I force the question out of my mind. I don't need to know that information. I don't need to go after Zed. I need to move on with my life, just as Ryn and Vi are attempting to do.

I open my mouth to thank Perry again, but I pause as a faerie paths doorway opens nearby. I conceal myself quickly, relishing the fact that I can do it without having to worry about any curse. It's Gemma who steps out of the paths and looks around. I'm about to pull my projection back, but she yells "What the hell, Perry?" and I decide it might be better to remain invisible.

Perry glances at the empty space where I was standing a moment ago, then back at Gemma. "Um …"

"Ned just visited," Gemma says as she stomps across the ruins toward Perry. "He told me all about last night. You two were *there*! And you didn't tell me it was happening or that you were going!"

"Well … it was dangerous."

"I KNOW!" she shouts as I take a few quiet steps backward. "That's my point. You could have died!"

"You know we're training to be guardians, right? The possibility of death is always—"

He doesn't get to finish his sentence because she closes the final distance between them and throws her arms around him, pressing her lips to his. Perry stands there frozen while I try to keep from clapping my hands in glee and crying out, *Finally!* Then Perry wakes up, slides his hands into her hair, and pulls her closer, deepening their kiss.

I roll up the papers and turn away with a smile. Something tells me Perry won't be surfacing to finish our conversation for a while.

* * *

Later, when it's almost evening at the lake house in the human realm, I sit on the grass beneath a tree and watch the reflection of the setting sun as I wait for Chase. He doesn't announce his arrival, but I hear quiet footsteps before he sits with his legs on either side of me and wraps both arms around me. I lean back against him, just about glowing with happiness that we can have simple moments like this without having to worry about the urgent, impending end of our world. Well, aside from the tear in the sky over Velazar Island, but it sounds like the Guild has that under control for now.

"I didn't think," Chase says quietly, "that I would ever feel at peace like this. I've always felt like I was playing catch-up, trying to do more good, save more people, but it was never enough to make up for all the wrong. It still isn't enough, and it never will be, but now that I know that, I can stop trying to reach the point where it suddenly *is* enough. I can protect and help people because it's something I want to do, not because I'm constantly trying to cancel out a debt." He kisses my neck. "Thank you for helping me realize that."

My laugh is small, quiet. "How on earth did I manage to do that if I couldn't see it when it was my turn? When I was the one who kept thinking I had to *do something* to get Ryn to forgive me."

"I suppose it's easier to see the truth when you're not the one weighed down by the burden of guilt."

"Yes. It is. And now neither one of us has to be weighed down any longer." My gaze moves to his arms wrapped around me. I trace part of the twisting vine tattooed on his left arm, raising a few unintentional sparks across his skin. "Why did you choose this pattern to permanently mark your skin?"

He rests his chin on my shoulder. "It's … a little silly, perhaps. I wanted something to represent who I was then and who I am now. The past with the present. Death with life. There are so many symbols I could have used, but in the end I chose this. The thorns are pain and death. A reminder of who I was and what I did. The vine is life. A reminder to keep doing good, to keep living this second-chance life the right way."

"I like it," I say, continuing to trace the pattern as he falls silent. "Mine have almost faded completely," I add, "except for the flower. I'll have to think of something else to try out next. Lace gloves going up my arms, perhaps. That would be pretty."

"Don't forget about the phoenix," he says, removing one arm from around me, then pulling my hair aside and tracing a finger up my spine.

A pleasant shiver spreads out across my skin. "Don't worry, I haven't forgotten." I tilt my head back as he moves to kiss the side of my neck. "Oh, look at the sky!" I exclaim, straightening and staring out in wonder at the colors streaked across the evening sky. Peach, pink and purple swirled together and melting into orange-gold and yellow. "Have you ever seen anything so beautiful?" I breathe.

Chase's arms tighten around me. "I'm glad you like it."

Something in the way he says those words makes me shift around to face him and ask, "Did *you* do that?"

He smiles. "Painted especially for you, Miss Goldilocks."

I lift one hand and trail my fingers across his cheek. "How many girls get to be with a guy who literally paints the sunset for them?"

"Hopefully just you, Calla," he says, and the way he looks at me, the way he says my name, ignites flames inside me and sends a shiver along my skin. I move closer to him, feeling my gaze drawn down to his lips before I let my eyes slide closed. I kiss him softly, slowly, knowing there's no whirlpool to interrupt us and we can take our time. Tentative, touching, tasting. His arms around me are firm but gentle, slowly lowering me to the ground as he leans over me. I sense sparkles zipping across my lips as our tongues touch. My hands slide around his waist, my fingers press into his back, and I yearn for him to be closer still. My pulse races dizzyingly. Our lips move more hungrily, more desperately, and beyond my closed eyelids, light explodes. My fingers fist in his T-shirt. He breathes my name in between kisses, and my blood rushes even faster. I don't know which way around the world is anymore, and it doesn't matter, because all I want is for this moment to last forever.

When eventually his lips slow against mine, I'm breathless. His words are hot against my mouth when he speaks. "Do you think—" he kisses my bottom lip "—it would be rude—" then my top lip "—to stay out here all night?"

I blink at the smoking leaves above us. The leaves we're probably responsible for setting fire to. I release a sigh as my eyes move back to Chase's warm gaze. "Sadly, yes. In fact … Ugh." I cover my burning face with my hands. "Do you think they can see us from the house?"

Chase sits up and looks across the grass toward the lake house. "Well, if they can, it's too late now." My laugh is half a groan as I sit up and lean against him. He puts an arm around me and kisses my temple. We watch the last rays of sunlight disappearing in the distance before he says, "I guess we should go inside."

"Yeah, we probably should." We get up and walk hand in hand toward the house.

"Is it silly that I'm nervous?" Chase asks. "This is almost as intimidating as having dinner with your parents. And it's been little more than a week since … since Vi and Ryn lost their daughter. They probably don't even want us around."

"They do," I tell him with a reassuring squeeze of his hand. "They need time to themselves, but they also don't want to be alone too much. Vi said she thinks the distraction of having other people around sometimes will help."

"Okay." Chase breathes out a long sigh and swings our hands between us. "Since we're not currently on the brink of a magical disaster, there are so many things I want to show you in my world. I want to show you where I grew up. I want to take you to a movie, and to art galleries, and to every romantic destination mankind ever came up with—"

"—and the bagel place," I add, remembering the bagels Gaius became obsessed with after Chase introduced him to them.

"And the bagel place," he says with a laugh. Without

warning, he grabs hold of me and swings me around. As a squeal escapes me, he places me on my feet, dips me down, and kisses me. Long and full and passionate. Then with one sweep, he swings me upright again. "Sorry," he says with a grin. "Just stealing one more kiss before we go inside."

"That's okay," I say, laughing and hanging onto him as the world spins around me. "You're forgiven."

CALLA'S STORY IS TOLD IN
A FAERIE'S SECRET,
A FAERIE'S REVENGE,
& A FAERIE'S CURSE

FIND MORE CREEPY HOLLOW
CONTENT ONLINE
www.creepyhollowbooks.com

Acknowledgements

Wow, this one really took it outta me! But God got me to the end again, as He always does. At its heart, Calla and Chase's story is one of forgiveness and redemption, and I can only truly write of such things because my Father first forgave me (and continues to, every day).

Thank you SO MUCH, Kimberly and Heather, for taking the time to give me valuable feedback on every part of this story. I'm grateful for your willingness to help me out, no matter how tight the deadline, and for your encouragement.

Thank you to my amazing team of early readers who waited so long for this one!

And to all the Creepy Hollow fans out there, your enthusiasm helped power me onward to finish Calla's story. Thank you!

And, as all my acknowledgements sections end ... Thank you, Kyle! Thank you for putting up with having 'no wife' while I worked waaaaay past my deadlines to get this one finished. Love you.

© Gavin van Haght

Rachel Morgan spent a good deal of her childhood living in a fantasy land of her own making, crafting endless stories of make-believe and occasionally writing some of them down. After completing a degree in genetics and discovering she still wasn't grown-up enough for a 'real' job, she decided to return to those story worlds still spinning around her imagination. These days she spends much of her time immersed in fantasy land once more, writing fiction for young adults and those young at heart.

Rachel lives in Cape Town with her husband and three miniature dachshunds. She is the author of the bestselling Creepy Hollow series and the sweet contemporary romance Trouble series.

www.rachel-morgan.com

CPSIA information can be obtained
at www.ICGtesting.com
Printed in the USA
LVOW08s1214300417
532745LV00003B/547/P